WORTH THE TEST

ETERNITY SERIES
BOOK FOUR

JENNIFER J WILLIAMS

Copyright © 2024 by JJW Productions, LLC

All rights reserved.

No part of this book may be reproduced in any form or by any electronic or mechanical means, including information storage and retrieval systems, without written permission from the author, except for the use of brief quotations in a book review.

This book is intended for audiences over the age of 18. It contains mature subject matter. If you do not like steamy sex scenes, adult content, and all the laughs, this book is not for you.

Cover designer: KB Barrett Designs

Photographer: CJC Photography

Model: Dominic C.

Editing: Brenda Bastien

For all the women who identify as a little less than a hot mess: please join me on the room temperature chaos train. I'll bring queso and wine.

A NOTE FROM JEN

Hello, my friends! While most of my books are cozy and fluffy, Worth the Test does cover some pretty intense topics that I feel you should know about before reading. As always, take care of your mental health first before tackling any fictional stories of mine.

Death of a spouse (off page)
DV from past relationship (off page)
Therapy (both hero and heroine)
Online bullying of a child

Play List

Listen to the PlayList on Spotify

Die With a Smile - Lady Gaga, Bruno Mars
Why Why Why - Shawn Mendes
That's So True - Gracie Abrams
i like the way you kiss me - Artemas
Good Luck, Babe! - Chappell Roan
Please Please Please - Sabrina Carpenter
Guess - Charli xcx, Billie Eilish
we can't be friends - Ariana Grande
Wildflower - Billie Eilish
Lose Control - Teddy Swims
Stargazing - Myles Smith
Beautiful Things - Benson Boone
Belong Together - Mark Amber

Chapter 1

Alex — June

It's a rare Friday night where I'm out with my two brothers and two brothers-in-law. Their wives are home with their children, and it's remarkably empty without all the chaos. My two kids are with my parents, as they usually are on the rare opportunity for me to go out.

"Thanks for coming with me, guys," Luca says after we all grab a beer from the bar. We're here, at a hole-in-the-wall pub on the southwestern side of Denver, to see a band.

"Remind me why we're here?" Stone asks as he takes a long swig of his beer. Stone has been my best friend since we were kids. It took me a bit to get on board with him and my baby sister, but looking back, I can see they were inevitable. Arianna shows him the joys of life, and he brings a peace to her that she craved.

"I played hockey with Declan growing up. He played in Dallas, and retired this year. He moved back to Denver and invited me to come watch his band. He plays the bass," Luca explains, pointing to a tall guitarist. My brother recently retired from the Denver Wolves NHL team, and has since accepted a coaching position with the Eternity Springs High School hockey program, home of the fighting Eagles.

I've already received five texts from my daughter, Abbie, for various reasons. She's twelve going on twenty, and her mood swings rival those pirate ship rides at a carnival, where we just don't know if it's going to flip all the way over or not.

Tonight's infractions? Her nine-year-old brother, Ben, looked at her wrong, whatever that means. Her bestie from school, Heather, apparently gossiped about Abbie's hairstyle today, and now Abbie hates Heather. Nani, the nickname all the grandkids have for my mom, had the audacity to only make spaghetti for dinner, when Abbie expected Nani's homemade lasagna.

The horror.

"You still getting texts from Abbie?" Dom asks, peering over my shoulder.

I sigh and nod. "She's doing my head in."

"Sienna is too. I didn't think hormones and puberty would be an issue this early." Sienna is a year younger than Abbie, and Dominic's oldest. She's struggled over the years since her mom decided to leave, but fortunately Dom asked Kate to nanny his kids, and then fell in love with her. I've never seen my brother smile so much, and it's been incredible watching his three children blossom. It wasn't just the addition of Kate that made them grow. It was the way Kate helped Dom to be present in every experience, and to show everyone in his life how important they are to him.

"Apparently we're the lucky ones to experience it early," I murmur. Dom doesn't respond, but I can feel what he almost said. He'd undoubtedly talk about how Kate is helping, how it's so great she's in their lives now to give a female perspective. I wish I had that, honestly. Because six years ago, our world stopped turning when my wife, Sara, was killed in a car accident. I was on assignment overseas and didn't find out for a week. Abbie was six, and Ben was only three. While Abbie was old enough to have a few fleeting memories of Sara, Ben barely remembers his mother.

I honestly don't know how I functioned that first year. Sara knew me like no one else. She was my other half, the only person I've ever met that could calm me down. Whenever I had a bad day, she'd demand a dance party in our kitchen. It never failed to raise my spirits.

I haven't danced like that since she died, and I don't know if I ever will.

"You okay, man?" Stone asks, his eyes studying me. I don't bother hiding my pain.

"No, not really. But I'll be fine. I always am."

"Can I ask you a personal question?" Stone inquires.

I can't help but chuckle. Even if I say no, he'll still ask. "Yeah, go ahead."

"When's the last time you got laid? You're pretty tightly wound."

I wrack my brain. "Fuck, man. I don't even know. It's been at least a year. Probably closer to two."

"Is there a reason why you aren't at least pursuing some one-night-only situations?" he asks.

I shrug. "I don't know. I haven't wanted to deal with dating. I'm too old for that shit."

"You do know you can fuck without dating, right?" Stone laughs.

"Yeah, but there's still conversation and flirting. That's what I don't want to deal with. My hand doesn't expect dinner and chemistry."

"Jesus," Luca says from behind me. "I had no idea you were this depressing, Lexy. I'm glad I got us some shots. Let's loosen you up."

"Great," I mutter, as I take the shot glass with an unknown clear liquid inside. It's probably tequila. If anyone were to do tequila shots, it's definitely Luca.

We all *cheers*, then toss back the shot. My eyes immediately water as the liquor burns my throat. Fucking tequila is disgusting. Travis watches with an amused grin as Dom slaps me on the shoulder, placing another shot in front of me. "You need another one, Lexy."

"Why must you always bring out that nickname when we're out?" I groan.

"Because we know how much you hate it," Luca snickers. "Bottoms up."

"I drove, asshole. Not about to get a DUI," I retort. I'm a fucking police officer. Kinda frowned upon in our ranks.

"I'll get all of us home safely. I promise," Dominic answers, a weird glint in his eye. "Come on, Alex. You deserve a night to let loose. We'll make sure you have fun, but also that you get home in one piece. Unless you end up going home with someone."

"That will not be happening," I tell him, completely horrified at the thought. I'm thirty-eight, and I've only had a couple of one-night stands in my life. It's not my preference. Plus, I met Sara when I was twenty-three. Since her death, I've barely looked at another woman with thoughts of a relationship. Sure, I've had sex a handful of times in the last five years, but it's been more to scratch an itch and less to make a connection. I have no desire to connect with anyone.

"You deserve to have some fun," Luca says quietly. "Even if you just hang with us. Take the shot, we'll play some darts, and we can all relax."

I sigh, a sound full of resignation and frustration. I know my brothers are right. They aren't pushing me toward anyone. They just want me to enjoy myself. I've focused so much on providing for my kids that I've ignored what kind of social life I could have. Other than Stone, I barely have contact with any friends from high school. Sara's funeral brought tons of people out of the woodwork, but I was in no place to interact with them. My heart and soul were crushed. I barely had a moment to grieve before I was thrust into single parenthood, and it wasn't long before I deployed again. I'm thankful my parents could take Abbie and Ben in, giving them at least a tiny bit of normalcy in a world that was violently shaken up. But it's been nonstop ever since.

So, yeah, I could probably stand to use some time to relax and unwind. Which is why I don't say no to the third shot.

I'm in no way drunk. I have a pretty high tolerance for alcohol. I kinda had to, considering military life isn't for the faint of heart. I learned to love beer quickly, and I figured out the best tricks for not getting hangovers that lasted all day. Three shots tonight has me feeling relaxed, enough that I'm actually enjoying the evening.

After excusing myself to hit the men's room, I'm in a back hallway with crappy lighting where the floors are undoubtedly sticky no matter the time of day, and I overhear a couple arguing. The woman's voice sounds somewhat familiar, but I can't place where I've heard it.

"It was one time," the guy says, exasperation evident in his tone.

"It wasn't one time. This is the fifth," she replies. Damn. Fifth time for what? Cheating?

"So? It's your fucking fault anyway. If you did things like I tell you to do them, none of that would ever happen. I run this fucking show, little girl. You'll do as I say."

"I broke up with you, Rob. That isn't how any of this works," the woman says with a noticeable tremor to her voice. When I finally find the couple in question, they're shrouded in darkness. All I can see are two silhouettes, the male towering over the female.

"I say if this relationship ends, not you."

"No, I —" she stammers, and he takes a threatening step closer, grabbing her arm and yanking her toward him harshly.

"I will shut you up any way I fucking please."

Oh, fuck that.

"Woah, woah, woah!" I shout, sliding in between them and pushing the guy back.

"The fuck you think you're doing?" he snarls.

"You don't treat a lady like that, asshole." I stare the guy down — what was his name? Rob? He looks like a Rob. We're about the same height, but I've got him beat in weight. One look at his scrawny arms tells me I've got him beat in strength too. Looking quickly over my shoulder, I see the hint of a black eye on the woman. Her green eyes widen when I catch her gaze. I know her. I swear I do.

"You better back the fuck up," Rob growls, he shoves me hard, then bitch-slaps me across the face. I find joy in that movement. Because now my response is considered self-defense.

"Mistakes were made, Robbie," I tell him cockily as I crack my knuckles.

"The fuck does that mean, assh —" Thwack! My fist crashes into his face, the sound of his nose breaking like music to my ears. It's been a while since I've had any need for hand-to-hand combat. With each passing year in the Air National Guard, I had more managerial responsibilities and fewer fun and physical activities. But it seems my taekwondo training from decades ago is ingrained in my muscle memory, because I quickly take a stance to protect the woman behind me.

As soon as Rob staggers back toward me, he throws up a fist, ready to fight back, but I'm quickly surrounded.

"I'd like to fucking see you try to win this one," Luca says deeply, his arms crossed as he glares at Rob. My brother, though retired from the NHL, is still a massive brick wall of a man. Stone and Dominic stand off to the side of Luca, ready to get involved if needed. I have no idea where they came from, but I'm glad they're here.

Turning, I say to the woman, "Are you okay?"

I take in her gorgeous features. Beautiful chocolate brown locks of hair cascading down her back, smooth alabaster skin, and eyes such a unique shade of green, they remind me of a clear mountain lake.

"Alex," she breathes, her voice soft and hesitant as she stares up at me. She knows me. Knows my name. And I realize why her voice sounded so familiar. But before I can say anything, she throws her arms around my neck, and kisses me.

I'm being kissed. It takes me a moment to respond, and I know I will shove her away. In a second. Maybe a minute.

I'm not sure how my hands find her ass, or how my tongue circles hers perfectly. Or how I feel her moan into my mouth, and the sound goes straight to my cock.

I forgot how much I love kissing, and this is one hell of a good kiss. Great kiss, even.

But I certainly never thought I'd be kissing her.

My sister's best friend.

Chapter 2

Alex — July

I can say with absolute certainty that none of my siblings saw their significant others for the first time and knew their lives were changing for the better.

I knew the moment I saw Sara Taft that I would marry her one day. After our first date, I could picture our wedding. Within a month, I envisioned our children. I knew exactly how I was going to propose, and how she'd respond. I'd never felt so peaceful in my life. Sara was comfort and home.

After attending a football game on the College of Colorado campus in Boulder with my younger brother Dominic, a full-time student there, I took the long way back to my car, walking past so many large dorms and apartment-style buildings for students. I had a momentary twinge of jealousy over what they might experience there, but I shook it off. I knew a long time ago that college wasn't for me. It's why I joined the military. I wanted out of Colorado. I wanted to see different places of the world, one where I wasn't "one of the Santo kids," and featured on the small-town gossip website every couple of days.

Staring up at the large dormitories, I wondered what it would have been like for me if I'd chosen to attend. Dom was in his glory at college. Learning had always been a passion of his, and he was determined to take over running Everlasting Hotel and Spa one day. I loved that for him, but not for me. Don't get me wrong: I love the hotel my family has owned and operated for generations in my hometown of Eternity Springs, Colorado. But I didn't want to work there.

What kind of degree would I have gotten at CCB? Something business related, like Dom? Or something I was interested in, like physical therapy, or sports management? Maybe kinesiology. Something that involved my entire body, working in a field that I had a genuine interest in. I thought about poly-sci briefly, until I realized how sedentary that job would be, and I felt like puking. I can't stand to sit still.

My job in the National Guard technically fell under security forces, which is the military's nice way of saying I was a police officer. When I was here, in Colorado, it was boring as fuck. We'd patrol our tiny base, and check ID's at the gate. Most excitement I'd seen was when a drunk guy mistook the gas for the brake, and rammed into, ironically, the anti-ramming vehicle barriers that servicemen manning the gates can deploy. Another time, a troop exited his car to check on a gap in perimeter fencing, and a pronghorn took the opportunity to get in the security forces vehicle. Pronghorns aren't that big. They're just the size of a small antelope, but it still managed to do thousands of dollars' worth of damage to the car.

In any case, my military job stateside was pretty boring. When we'd get the opportunity to go overseas, that's when it would get exciting. That's when I'd feel my best. When I'd be busy and constantly on the go. I missed my family every time I deployed, but I didn't have anything I felt that I was truly leaving.

Until Sara.

Walking to my car after that random football game, the voice of an angel asked for my help. "Quick! Grab those papers!"

As I turned, I only saw a flash of blonde hair before a flurry of white blew around me. I grabbed as many as I could while listening to this tiny woman mutter to herself.

"Are you okay?" I asked with a chuckle.

"Stupid anatomy class," she snapped. As I handed her the papers, she turned, and I felt like my world tilted on its axis. Porcelain skin, eyes the shade of a Colorado blue sky, and the plumpest pink lips I'd ever seen. I saw her lips

moving, but couldn't make out any sound, until she waved a hand in front of my face. "Are you okay?"

"Yeah, uh, sorry. What is all this?"

"My stupid anatomy and physiology class assignment where we had to color all of these nerves and muscles, and honestly, if I wanted to major in art, I would have done that instead of nursing, because this is ludicrous!" she said, her voice getting louder and louder as a lock of pale blonde hair fell across her forehead. I had to resist the urge to move it out of the way so I could see her eyes better. When she huffed, the puff of air blowing the hair away, I couldn't help but grin.

I was meeting my wife. I knew it deep in my soul.

"I'm Alex," I remember saying as I thrust my hand into her space. "What's your name, and can I take you to dinner?"

"I'm Sara," she laughed. "And yes."

I never looked back from that moment. She was my future.

When her hand hit mine, I didn't get a crazy zing that some people talk about. Like lightning coursing up their arm. Instead, a sense of peace overtook me. Warmth flowed slowly across my skin, like sliding into the hot springs at my family's hotel. That was a great way of expressing our entire relationship. Warm and homey. We rarely argued, instead having almost all of our morals and values lined up perfectly. On the rare occasion we disagreed, a calm discussion took place.

I proposed after two years of dating, and we were married only a few short months later, on our joint birthday. That's right, we shared a birthday. What better way to celebrate than tying our anniversary to our birth date? So, when Sara turned twenty-three and I turned twenty-five, we pledged to love one another until death parted us.

I just didn't think it would end up being as early as it was.

And today, as I sit by her grave, I hate how I can't hear her voice. Get her advice. See her with our kids. I want more Sara.

"God, I miss you," I sigh, leaning my side against the large gravestone and absentmindedly tracing the letters of her name with my forefinger. Sara Taft Santo. I hadn't seen a reason to put her maiden name on there, but her parents demanded it. Since they bought the rather ostentatious gravestone, I didn't have much say in the matter. Bad enough that my wife was buried in their family plot, with no room for me. Never occurred to me that *she* should have updated *her* will with specifics about her death, but again, I assumed if either of us would die, it would be me. Maybe I could have voiced an opinion, but frankly, I was so inconsolable I could barely function.

Sara was killed in a head-on collision with a drunk driver. Our kids were with my parents, thankfully, but I was deployed. Out in the desert, with no communication, it took almost a week for news to reach me. By that point, Sara's parents had already planned everything. Even immediately leaving Afghanistan, it took me two days to get home. I walked into our house to find Sara's parents and my parents fighting.

"You can't take them!" My mother shouted.

"It's what our daughter would have wanted," Sara's mother, Nancy, insisted.

"What would she want?" I asked.

"Daddy!" Ben sobbed, running into my arms. He shook as he cried, and I'll never forget that feeling. My poor child, at only three years old, had lost his mother.

"What would Sara want?" I asked again.

Jim, Sara's dad, squared his shoulders as he turned to me. "We want to take the kids back to our home. They can't continue to live here with your schedule. They need to be in a home with two parents."

I stared at them incredulously. "Are you fucking kidding me?"

Nancy gasped. "Language!"

"I don't fucking care, Nancy!" I shouted, jarring Ben. My dad grabbed him out of my arms so I could address my in-laws. "How dare you come in here and try to take them away. You're doing this right now because you wanted to get them before I came home. Would you have even let me see them?"

"Of course we would – we will. We've already spoken to an attorney, Alex. We're suing for custody," Nancy cried, her voice hysterical with grief.

"You go ahead. Waste your money. Just know that Sara and I both have wills, and our instructions for our children are incredibly specific." I knew there was a section of her will, mine too, that stated the children would not be taken away from either of us in the instance a spouse passes away.

"What does that mean?" Jim boomed. My father-in-law always tended to puff out his chest when he was trying to appear more foreboding and authoritative. To me, he always just looked like a fat baboon.

"It means that your daughter specifically stated in her will that the two of you," I pointed to both of them, maintaining eye contact to ensure they were paying attention, "were allowed visitation, and nothing more. I actually think she has a stipulation in there that you are not allowed to gain guardianship or custody of the kids, no matter the circumstances."

"She wouldn't!" Nancy whispered. "What kind of monster are you? You brainwashed our daughter! We'll fight this!"

"No, you won't," I sighed. "You're hurting and upset right now, but you know this is for the best. My entire family is here. The support system my kids have is unmatched. You live two hours away. You'd be ripping them away from the family, their friends, and the schools and daycares they know."

Nancy's lower lip trembled as she studied me. "They're all we have left of her."

"They're all I have left of her, too," I whispered, closing my eyes as hot tears built. I had yet to cry. I couldn't cry in front of my unit, or on the five flights it took me to get home. But at that moment, in our home, where I could still smell the comforting notes of Sara's perfume, I knew I was in danger of collapsing into an emotional heap.

"Please — please don't take them away from us. They're a part of Sara, and it would kill us if you didn't let us see them," Jim said brokenly, his eyes covered with a sheen of tears.

"I would never do that," I told them. "You're their grandparents. They love you. But you can't take them away from me. I'm their father. This is the only home they've ever known. I'll change my schedule as much as I can to be home more. We can schedule dinners with you every week if necessary. But if you take them away from me ... I won't survive losing my entire family."

"Oh, Alex," Nancy breathed, putting her arms around me. "We didn't think — we just reacted. We're so sorry. We lost our baby girl, and now we don't know how to move forward."

"Neither do I," I confess quietly. Neither do I.

It took an hour of talking to Sara's parents, calming them down and assuring them that I'd keep them in their grandchildren's lives, before they finally left to drive home. Halfway between Denver and Colorado Springs, Jim *and Nancy Taft owned a beautiful upper-class home in a sought-after neighborhood in Castle Rock, Colorado. Sara grew up with everything she could ever need, yet somehow never expected anything. She was the most selfless person I knew.*

Was. I've never hated a verb tense more.

Looking at the picture Jim and Nancy had etched onto the gravestone, I don't notice the tears that trace down my cheeks. "I hate my life, Sar. Fucking hate it. I'm miserable without you. I hate my job. I've been doing it for a year and I know I can't do this for twenty years. I'm so alone, and I have no one to talk to."

Date.

I scoff. "I'm not dating anyone. No one could replace you. You know that."

Date anyway.

"No."

Love someone else.

"Absolutely not. I'll never love anyone like I love you. How can you even ask me to do that?"

It's okay.

"No, it's not. I could never love someone else. My heart will always belong to you. You. No way could I do that to you." Pretty sure I'm shouting.

You can love another woman. I want you to be happy.

"No," I say adamantly. How can she ask this of me? How am I supposed to move on like she wasn't the love of my life?

You have to let go.

"No." I look down in my hands, gripping my keys tightly, where just the keychain sits against my hand. Sara made it years ago. On one side is a picture of us in front of Everlasting, and on the other is a picture of us with our kids. It's one of my most prized-possessions, and I took it with me on each deployment. I considered it to be my lucky charm.

The number of times she talked about how she couldn't wait until our kids were older and she'd introduce them to her love of crafting … and then she died before either of our children really enjoyed it. Since

I don't have one ounce of creativity, I certainly haven't attempted to continue her ideas.

I'm doing such a shit job as their only parent.

Rubbing both palms across my face, I finally say the thing I've thought a million times. "It should have been me."

A gust of wind whips around me, unsettling loose leaves that only recently fell from the Aspen trees. Aspens were Sara's favorite, and we made countless trips into the mountains each autumn to see the leaves change. It was a huge production each year: scouting out the location, planning stops, and what to bring for lunch. It wasn't an hour trip. No, we were gone the entire day. Sometimes overnight. My wife loved everything about Colorado in autumn.

I haven't taken the kids once.

"I'm failing them, Sar," I whisper brokenly. "I can't do this without you."

Yes, you can. You will.

"I need you," I rasp.

I know. But she needs you too.

"Abbie?"

No.

"Who?"

You'll see.

Chapter 3

Natalie — Mid-August

I've always prided myself on my independence. Got my first job at fifteen. Worked all through college, sometimes carrying a full course load and a full-time work schedule, because I was determined to graduate with zero debt. Thanks to a handful of scholarships and grants, I was pretty close to meeting my goal, and my parents were incredibly relieved that they didn't have to worry about paying for anything. Yeah, those four years I basically lived in my car, and I didn't have a social life at all. But it was worth it.

Which is why I'm still not sure how I ended up here.

Living with a man who has gotten more and more abusive the longer we've been together. Hating the school I teach at, in a well-off area of a Denver suburb, where the parents run the school. I spend way too much time trying to defend my own decisions in my classroom, and the district superintendent, a man who hasn't spent a day in an elementary school classroom and makes at least double my salary, makes all the big decisions for me. Many of the districts in Colorado have adopted a school calendar that closely resembles a year-round schedule, and I've already been back in the classroom for a couple of weeks now. It's only the second week of August.

I hate this.

I hate my life, and I don't know how I got here.

But worst of all, I don't know how to change any of it.

Rob and I have been dating for two years. When my lease was up about a year ago, he convinced me to move in with him. I brought up all the usual concerns, of course. Would I be added to his lease? How would we split rent and utilities? If we break up, how will we handle that diplomatically? Rob blew all of it off, assuring me we were end-game, so all of my questions were moot. Besides, he said, we wouldn't be in his apartment forever. I'll be on the mortgage of our future house, once I share his last name.

I giddily moved in with him, thinking I'd found my forever, and ignored every damn red flag right in front of my face.

"Are you even listening to me?" Rob asks. My eyes whip to his, and I immediately notice the tense jaw.

"I'm sorry," I blurt out. I've found it's easier to apologize as soon as I see he's getting angry. It's not that he's always violent. He's not. But there are so many mind games at play, and he gaslights like a pro.

"I don't know why I bother," he snaps. "I deserve someone who pays attention to me, Natalie."

I don't respond. I want to agree with him, but I don't want another woman to put up with this. Other women aren't strong enough to deal with Rob. I hate this, but I've mastered the art of dissociation when it comes to this man.

When we began dating, Rob was an absolute joy to be around. No, he didn't wine-and-dine me. I've never wanted, or needed, that kind of attention. I felt like Rob saw me. He recognized what I needed, and he was all too happy to give it. Once he realized I just wanted someone to spend time with me, he gave that to me in droves.

About six months ago, things began to change. Text exchanges grew shorter. His patience became razor-thin. Our arguments were louder, and longer. Everything was my fault. I only recently took stock of our relationship and realized how often he gaslit me, and the number of times I was all too keen to take blame over things that were not my fault.

It certainly wasn't my fault when he got a parking ticket after 'surprising' me at a dinner with my girlfriends, nor was it my fault when he shoved me into the car door.

A month later, he slapped me, but seemed so apologetic and

remorseful that I forgave him. Besides, it was only because I didn't have dinner ready when he got home that night. But things escalated.

Last night, he punched me.

The obvious black eye he gave me wasn't something I could cover with makeup, and I took a very rare sick day from teaching today. Considering it wasn't the first black eye he gave me, I knew this one wouldn't be believable. A person can only run into a doorknob so many times. So, once Rob leaves for work, I make the two calls I know I have to make before I can get a plan in place to get out of here.

I call one of my best friends, Arianna Santo Dixon, and I call my brother, Shawn.

My hot-shot brother plays for the NHL, living his dream each and every day. He's in his final year of a lengthy contract, and he's mentioned in passing that he's thinking about retiring. Growing up with him, I know how rough he's always been on his body. As a defenseman in the league, he's the first one to post up on the ice to defend his teammates. I have no doubt his body is wearing down.

"Hey, little bit," he answers. For the record, I'm not little. He's just a giant.

"Without setting off too many warning lights in your brain, can I borrow some money?" I blurt out.

"What happened?" he immediately asks.

"I don't want to go into details just yet, but I need to borrow some money."

"I need a little more information, Nat. You need a new car, or to buy something for mom and dad? Sure. You're planning on taking your fifth graders on a bender at a dispensary as a field trip? No." I chuckle at the thought of a field trip to a marijuana dispensary. I mean, it's Colorado. Stranger things have probably happened here.

"Do you promise not to ask many questions, not to tell mom and dad, and to let me handle things?"

"Yeah," he murmurs.

I sigh, deciding to rip the Band-Aid off. He's one thousand miles away, and the season is getting ready to start. He's not going to show up here to take care of me. "I am looking to relocate, and my bank account is currently missing the zeroes it needs for getting a new lease and moving expenses."

I hold my breath as I wait for the inevitable Shawn explosion. I'm not disappointed. "What did that motherfucker do?"

"Jesus, Shawn," I hiss as I pull the phone away from my ear. "Pretty sure my neighbors just heard you."

"Answer the question, Natalie. I know he makes good money, so if you're needing it, to relocate, as you vaguely said, it means something happened. And *that* means the fucker did something, and that means I'm about to introduce the back of his fucking throat to my fist." With every word, Shawn gets louder and more staccato.

"It doesn't matter what he did," I'd argue. "It matters that I'm getting a plan in place to get out of here."

"Fuck, sis," he swears. "Did he hit you? He had to have. You're the strongest fucking person I know. You'd have no problem telling him what upset you, and demanding he change. He had to have hit you for you to want out."

I don't respond. I knew calling Shawn was a risk. Other than my besties, Shawn knows me better than anyone. He'd read right through my brave act and get to the nitty-gritty immediately. And I'm not surprised when he's dropped ten thousand into my account before our conversation ends. I doubt I'll need that much, but I felt immediate relief at having a little bit of padding.

Next, I call Arianna.

We met because our brothers were playing in the same hockey league growing up. When there aren't many girls at the rinks, you bond with the ones that are. It turned out that Arianna, our other best friend, Claire, and I all had a lot of similarities. I'm a few years older than Ari, with Claire in the middle, but we bonded over our love of the shows *Pretty Little Liars* and *Switched at Birth*, our hatred for most sports, and the joy of being the sister to a star athlete. While Ari was a few years younger than her brother, Luca, I was only a year younger than Shawn. Still, hanging with Arianna and Claire made the hockey practices and games almost enjoyable.

I don't beat around the bush when she answers. "You think you can reach out to your contact at the elementary school and see if they still have that open position?"

"Why? What happened?" she yells.

"It's nothing. I just need out of here."

"Don't do that, Nat. Tell me what happened."

"It doesn't matter. I'm trying to get all my ducks in a row."

Arianna sighs. "I'll see what I can find out."

"Just —" I break off in hesitation. "Don't text it back. Okay? I can't have Rob finding out until it's already settled and I'm out of here."

"Jesus, Natalie, what did he do?" she whispers.

"I'm not saying anything because I think you'll tell Stone, and he'll end up over here, and I refuse to be a reason why you have to visit your husband in jail."

Arianna is silent for a moment before she speaks again. "If the position is open, I'll text and ask if you want to grab lunch tomorrow. If you don't hear from me, it's not open. But I'm spending the rest of the day going through every contact I know, and finding you a job elsewhere. Do you need an apartment, too? Where do you want to go?"

"I don't care," I whisper brokenly. "As far away from here as I can get."

"I got you, boo. We can get you cleared out of there this weekend."

"I don't think that will happen. I need to let my school know, and I'll have to do things slowly, Ari. Rob is getting more volatile, and I don't want to anger him right now."

"I'm calling my brother. He has to have some contacts with the Denver police that can advise you."

"No!" I shout. "No. I don't want the police involved yet. I'm not doing anything without another job and a new place lined up."

"Alright," she murmurs. "But we're getting you out of there."

I feel overcome with emotion. Rob isn't awful. Well, most of the time. But I can see where it might go. I don't want to become someone I barely recognize, and I can't let myself live in fear every day. This version of Rob is not someone I want to be around. Could he change? Maybe. But I've given him too many chances. How I ever let it get this far is mind-boggling.

And I can't let Arianna call her brother.

She still doesn't know he kissed me.

Wait. I kissed him. He definitely didn't expect that. And for one glorious moment, he kissed me back. I felt his hand grip my hip, then slide down to my ass, as his lips suctioned against mine, and it was phenomenal.

Then Rob groaned, which spooked Alex, and he bolted. I won't forget the look of regret and despair he cast my way as he stalked back down the hallway.

The night I saw Alex was the second night I was determined to leave Rob. He'd slapped me the previous afternoon, hitting enough of my nose to give me a black eye that I'd had to cover it with makeup. I'd avoided Rob the entire day after texting him that we needed to part ways. I was ready to catch up with a friend from high school, only to have Rob track me down. I think he could tell I was having thoughts of ending the relationship, and attempted to love bomb me into staying. I shouldn't have stayed, but that self-doubt infiltrated my mind. We had a good couple of weeks, and then old behaviors began to creep into his actions again. His violence yesterday was the final straw.

How am I supposed to explain all of this to Arianna, the one person who knows me better than anyone else?

"The position is open, and the principal wants to interview you," Arianna says suddenly, jarring me back into the present.

"What? How did you get that set up so fast?" I ask incredulously.

"Girl, if you have to ask how I'm this awesome, clearly you don't know me that well," she jokes.

"I don't know how I'll be able to interview. I wouldn't be surprised if he's got the apartment bugged," I admit. "I probably shouldn't even be on the phone with you like this."

"Do you want to text me instead?" Arianna whispers, making me laugh.

"I don't think he'd be able to hear you through the phone, Ari."

"Why don't you come over for lunch tomorrow? I'll see if the principal is okay with doing a FaceTime interview. That way you're here, which means Rob can't think it's anything out of the ordinary. You're here all the time. He still works weekends, right?"

"Yeah. I just ... look, you need to know that I've got a black eye. Okay? And tell Stone to be prepared. It looks worse than it feels, but I don't need either one of you going vigilante or something and trying to defend my honor."

"Oh, Nat," Arianna gasps, before sniffing repeatedly. "I'm so sorry. I just feel awful."

"It's not your fault. I thought I could judge character pretty well. I guess I was wrong."

"No, that's not it at all. You're always one who can see past the bullshit to get to the root of things. Rob had us all fooled." Maybe everyone except Claire. She was apprehensive about him from the beginning, but I chalked it up to her being reserved and mistrusting of everyone except those in her inner circle.

"Well, it doesn't matter now," I sigh.

"Will you do me a favor?" Arianna asks quietly.

"Sure."

"Bring over a bag of your stuff. Think of it like a go-bag. If something happens and you need to get out of there quickly, you can come here and at least have some of your things."

That's actually pretty smart. "I can do that. I'm going to go through my closet and get rid of a bunch of things. Do you know if the women's shelter near you needs donations? There aren't any close by me that won't charge for the clothing, and I'd rather they go to an organization that actually helps women get back on their feet."

"I bet they're accepting stuff. My mom always donates things, and they never turn her away."

"I always think I'll sell some of the things I don't want, but it just takes too much time and effort," I chuckle.

"I'm that way with kids clothes! So many consignment sales, but I'm too busy to deal with getting all of my things organized for that."

"They have consignment sales strictly for kids clothes?" I ask, intrigued. I'm secretly relieved for the change in topic. I hate feeling inferior, and admitting to anyone that I need help.

"Oh, yeah! There's a huge one that has toys, furniture, and even maternity clothing. It's a week long. Stone yelled at me last time because I spent a couple hundred bucks," Arianna giggles.

"On what?" I exclaim.

"Clothes, mostly. But I found a bunch of super cute books for toddlers too. I know Bianca is only one, but we both love reading to her. It's become my favorite part of the day as we put her to bed," Arianna confesses.

"Okay, that's seriously cute."

"It really is," she giggles. "We all cuddle on the floor while she brings us her favorites."

"She has more than one favorite book?"

"Oh, absolutely. Right now one of the cutest ones is called *That's Not My Monster*. It's a touch-and-feel book, and Stone makes all kinds of growling noises to go with each monster. Bianca won't let us turn the page until he makes up a sound."

"I'm going to need a video of this in order to believe it, because I just can't see Stone growling to appease his daughter," I joke.

"I'll see what I can do, but he's pretty private about his monster noises," she teases.

"Oh, come on. Just take a video of him and send it to me."

"A video of who?"

I shriek, jumping in my chair, completely unaware that Rob silently crept into the apartment. His face appears passive, but it's hard to tell if he's masking anger. "Jesus, you scared me. Did you forget something?"

"Obviously. What man are you wanting a video of?" he asks again, and the subtle clenching of his jaw is all that I need to know. He's pissed, and I have about ten seconds to explain myself before he starts yelling.

"I'm talking to Arianna. She was telling me about reading to Bianca, and how Stone makes all kinds of noises to go along with the books they're reading before she goes to bed."

"Who is Bianca?" Rob asks.

"Oh, I really hate him now," Arianna hisses.

"Uh, their daughter? You met her a couple months ago at her birthday party?"

"Oh. That's the twerp who cried and then puked on her cake, right?"

I hear Arianna gasp, and I instantly try to diffuse the situation. "Bianca isn't a twerp, Rob."

He shrugs. "You just say that because she's your friend. All kids are twerps."

"I will end him," Arianna growls.

Rob watches me, then slowly ambles over to bend down, his hands perched on his knees. "You don't want kids, right? Cuz I'll be damned if I'm saddled with some little bastard. Hell, your ass is already thick. Can't imagine how fat you'll get after pregnancy."

My mouth falls open as I stare at him in shock, watching as he ambles back to the bedroom.

"Did he seriously just call you fat?" Arianna whispers.

"I think so," I stammer. I glance down at my body. I'm definitely overweight. As a size sixteen-eighteen, I know I'm technically plus size. While I know I could exercise more, I'm by no means lazy or sedentary. But now that I think about it, Rob has made some offhand statements about my size over the past six months or so, and they've been increasing in frequency. That might actually piss me off more than any other nasty comment he's made recently, because I fucking love my body. I know I turn heads. Could I lose some weight? Yes. But I rock my curves, and you'll never find me thinking otherwise.

"Don't you dare let him get in your head, Nat. You are gorgeous. Guys check you out all the time," Arianna tells me passionately. "If I didn't love you so much, I'd hate you. Shit, that didn't come out right. You get what I'm saying, don't you?"

"Sure," I murmur, but even I can tell there's no heat behind my statement. I slide a hand along my waistline, gripping the inch or two roll that pops out beyond my lounge pants, and I feel the inevitable wave of hot tears burning behind my eyes. I can't believe how quickly Rob diminished me with two sentences. "I need to go get the crockpot started for dinner, Ari. I'll see you tomorrow, okay?"

"Don't forget to bring some things," she whispers. After saying goodbye, I quietly walk into the kitchen. It only takes me a few minutes to decide on a meal, but my mind is elsewhere.

I don't know how I got here. How I let a man slowly and systematically break my spirit. I've let him destroy the parts of me that were most important to me. Now I'm debating on which meat to use for our dinner based on whether or not one might make him mad.

I don't want to be like this anymore.

Chapter 4

Natalie — Mid-to-late August

It's amazing how quickly a bunch of people can empty out an apartment when you're trying to avoid an abusive ex-boyfriend.

The principal couldn't do a FaceTime interview, but we scheduled an in-person interview in town for the following weekend. As a domestic violence survivor herself, Mrs. King was more than willing to meet me in Denver for the interview. In a surprising move, she offered me the job on the spot. I asked if that was legal, since most hirings go through a school district, and not the individual schools, but she shrugged it off. The teacher they had hired quit with no notice, and they were desperate to fill the position.

Arianna met me immediately afterward to take another bag of my belongings back to Eternity Springs, and then decided to follow me back to Rob's apartment to grab more. Her being at the apartment wasn't unusual, but typically she had Bianca with her. It wasn't lost on me that her daughter was not on this trip. Ari managed to sneak out a lot of my extra skincare and makeup, a handful of books clogging my bookshelf, and a photo album from my childhood that she feared Rob would destroy out of spite.

Rob didn't take too kindly to my final decision to end our relationship. He begged, cried, and promised me the world if I'd reconsider. I asked for time, just hoping he'd leave me alone so I could get more things ironed out. Arianna had a lead on a studio apartment in Eternity Springs, and I gobbled it up sight unseen. Afraid Rob was potentially monitoring my laptop, I had another dinner with Ari, and filled out all the paperwork at her house. It gave me an opportunity to love on her daughter a little more, and I'll never say no to that. I, of course, took a large bag of clothes with me, just to get some things out of Rob's grasp.

We devised a plan. Arianna and Stone would be with me when I told Rob it was over permanently, then I'd take just a small portion of belongings with me. I'd come back for the furniture that was mine, along with anything else I hadn't moved yet.

I hadn't planned on two things: that Rob would willingly let me go, and that a handful of guys from the NHL team, the Denver Wolves, would show up to assist with emptying the apartment that very same night.

"I don't understand —" I stammered.

"Oh, your brother called Luca. He wanted to help, and asked if any of the guys on the team could give up an hour or two. Luca already spoke to a couple of the guys, and intended to call Shawn anyway. He didn't want Shawn to hear about a bunch of Wolves players helping you out through the grapevine."

The apartment I'd called home for way longer than I should have was emptied of my things in record time. I removed the key from my keyring, and placed it on the kitchen counter.

"Nat," Rob whispered. As I looked at him, I saw a glimpse of the man I fell for. "I know this is my fault. I'm sorry. I really am."

"Get help, Rob. Don't do this to another woman." He nodded at me, and I walked out with my head held high.

Now, a few days later, I'm blissfully going through a haul of houseware items I got from a thrift store on the western edge of Denver. It's a set of mismatched patterns, a hodgepodge of glasses, and way more forks than spoons, but I'm tickled that they're mine. Nearly everything in Rob's apartment was his, or something we bought together. These things are *mine*. Floral small plates, bold plaid bowls, a mishmash of patterns and designs on larger plates, and I feel like they actually represent my style pretty well. I'm generally louder than most, but have the patience of a saint when it comes to kids. I'm whimsical and bohemian when it comes to some styles, but also love an all-black ensemble. I've been told on more than one occasion that I need to make sure my face doesn't show my thoughts, but what can I say? I've got one hell of a resting bitch face going on. As I place each item carefully next to my sink, my phone pings with a text. Checking the notification, I see it's from my BFF group chat, and I'm already smiling as I open it up. Someone is guaranteed to make me laugh at least once a day in our group text. Kate is married to Dominic, Hannah to Luca, and Arianna to Stone. Claire is the only singleton besides me in this chaotic group chat.

> Kate: A couple years ago, I believe I threatened in this very chat to try not to harm someone's brother, and I'd like to bring that up again.
>
> Arianna: For the love. My brother worships the ground you walk on. What the hell could you be complaining about now?
>
> Hannah: Too much sex?
>
> Claire: Too much life altering sex?
>
> Me: Too much oral sex?
>
> Me: For you, not him. I mean, we don't really care if he gets his, do we?
>
> Arianna: I like giving head. Stone will do whatever I tell him to do afterward.
>
> Claire: Are you suggesting he wouldn't do something in the bedroom before?
>
> Arianna: No, I mean outside of the bedroom. I could ask him to paint the shingles turquoise, and he'd totally start looking up the cost of supplies.
>
> Hannah: Please don't ask him to do that. Your home value would plummet.

Me: I kinda want to see him try, tbh.

Arianna: Listen. I love a husband challenge as much as the next woman, but even I have boundaries I refuse to cross. Having all of the neighbors hate me more than they already do is the deal breaker.

Hannah: Your neighbors hate you?

Arianna: Well, I assume they do. We're the youngest, and the only ones with a toddler. There may have been an ... incident last week that makes me think they really do hate me.

Me: Oh, please do tell.

Arianna: Sigh. Fine.

Arianna: ...

Claire: The suspense is killing me.

Kate: Just wait.

Me: You already know? No fair! Besties don't share secrets until we can all make fun of you together at the same time!

Kate: In her defense, Stone told Dominic, and he told me. There's probably some lost-in-translation details that they both fucked up, but I got the gist of it. And it's amazing.

Arianna: Okay. So a couple weeks ago Stone and I started spending some time together every evening after we put Bianca to bed. It started out innocently enough, but it shouldn't come as a surprise to anyone that we got a little handsy with each other. Then every night after that, it became a pattern of sorts where we tried to outdo the previous night's activities. Thus began a string of sexcapades all throughout our backyard. We were thinking it's dark, who the hell could see?

Hannah: This is why I'm glad I live where I live.

Claire: Apartments are no fun.

Me: Surprisingly, I've never had outdoor sex. The thought of getting bitten by something down there keeps my panties exactly where they're supposed to be, thank you.

Kate: That's actually pretty shocking. I would have thought you'd done it in the middle of that roundabout near the park.

Me: Sorry to burst your bubble. Does it count that I flashed my boobs at a passing car from a roundabout?

Arianna: ANYWAY

Arianna: Last week, I took all of my delicates onto the back porch to air dry in the sun. I figured we had a six-foot privacy fence, so the neighbors wouldn't be able to see anything. And if they did, it's just bras. What's the big deal? That's when I noticed Mr. Green, the old guy who always walks around with a stick, glaring at me from his deck. I never realized that his house is a few feet higher than ours, and he needed a deck instead of a patio out his back door. So, he can look directly into our yard if he wants to.

Me: Oh no. I see where this is going.

Kate: Trust me. You don't.

Arianna: So I waved to him, and he pointed at me with his stick. Weird, right? But then he pointed toward the back fence, and then again at his gutters above his back door. Y'all, he has CAMERAS ALL OVER THE PLACE! But it gets worse.

Hannah: How on earth could this get worse?

Arianna: He goes into his house and comes out with a bag, then yeets the damn thing into our yard. He flips me the bird, and honestly I'm surprised he even knew how to do that, since he's older than our country and all

Hannah: He's like seventy, but go ahead.

Arianna: You let me tell my story however I want to tell it!

Me: Focus, Ari. What was in the bag?

Arianna: Four of my thongs, two bras, and two pairs of Stone's boxer briefs.

Me: What the fuck???

Arianna: But wait, it gets worse!

Kate: This is like an infomercial. But wait, there's more!

Arianna: There was a USB drive in there. I thought about contacting Alex or Leo to see about scanning it for viruses, but I know Alex is pretty busy, and Leo has been pretty tight-lipped about his situation lately. And honestly, I'm glad I didn't, because on the drive were hours of footage of Stone and I getting it on all over our yard. HOURS.

Claire: That's awful, I'm so sorry, but also, kudos to Stone. Old man has stamina.

Arianna: That he does. Hashtag blessed

Me: Lowkey hating you right now, Ari. But where do the clothes fit in? Was he sneaking into your yard and stealing them somehow?

Arianna: Nope.

Arianna: MASON WAS STEALING THEM AND DEPOSITING THEM ON DOORSTEPS ALL AROUND OUR NEIGHBORHOOD.

Hannah: Oh. My. God.

Arianna: Never at our house! Oh, no. That fucking marmot could have left his little prezzies on our doorbell camera. That's not fun enough! Let's leave them at every old fart's house we can.

Kate: Wait. Dominic only told me your neighbor had some of your lingerie. How do you know Mason didn't leave them all at Mr. Green's house? And how did he know they were yours?

Arianna: Because he so kindly shared all the videos from everyone else's house too. The porches are different. Mason deposited my thongs at four different houses. The only house that got more than one item was Mr. Green's house. And that stupid fucking marmot waved on one of the videos. I knew they were mine because Stone has a certain style he likes, so I buy a bunch at once. I'm also the youngest on our street, by a couple of decades, so I just assume none of the other women wear thongs.

Hannah: Oh my word.

Arianna: I'm telling ya, I used to be pro-Mason. I found his shenanigans endearing. No more! It is ON SIGHT the next time I see that miscreant.

Me: So only Mr. Green had the videos of you going all Animal Planet in your yard, but everyone else got clothing on the doorbell cameras. But he has videos??

Arianna: Yeah, and he shared the videos with all of the neighbors.

> Me: Are you fucking kidding me? Arianna, that's illegal! He has videos of you and Stone, without your permission, and he shared them, again without your permission? You wanna talk about it being on sight with that stupid marmot! I'd be way more pissed with your neighbor!

> Arianna: Well, I mean, we were the ones out in the open.

> Kate: You were on your property in the dark. If he has videos that clearly show what you're doing, that means he has them facing your yard. And sharing that kind of video is a crime. I agree with Nat, and I think you should go to the police. Fuck what your neighbors think.

> Arianna: You understand if I go to the police, it means I have to talk to my brother, right? My brother who barely smiles and probably hasn't had sex in a half dozen years.

I hate that I still haven't told Arianna about kissing Alex. And I hate that I still feel my stomach flip, just talking about him. She doesn't even know I crushed on him when we were kids. He never looked twice at me, and once he met his wife, he barely noticed anyone around him. I doubt he'd even notice me now.

> Claire: Wait. Not trying to derail this titillating conversation, but weren't we originally talking about Kate's problem with something Dom did?

> Kate: Oh no. We're not even worrying about any of that now. Keep on, Ari.

> Arianna: Does everyone agree that I should speak to the police?

> Me: Absolutely.

> Kate: Yep.

Hannah: Yes.

Claire: Yup.

Arianna: Dammit. Do you think if I barter babysitting, Alex won't tell my family about all the sex shenanigans and clothing going missing?

Hannah: Babe, I hate to break it to you, but this is Eternity Springs. They probably already know. You're lucky it isn't on the gossip site yet.

Arianna: Fuck.

Claire: Just so you know, I'm never moving there. You will have to tear my urban Denver from my cold and dead hands.

Me: Don't hold your breath. I said the same thing.

Arianna: Nat, since you haven't started your new job yet, will you come watch Bianca while I go talk to Stone about this convo?

Me: Of course! You know I love time with my bestie.

Kate: You totally mean Bianca, don't you?

Me: Yep. She doesn't talk back as much as her mother does.

Arianna: I'm removing you as godmother.

Me: No, you're not.

Arianna: Sigh. No, I'm not.

Chuckling, I turn off my phone and throw it into my bag. Popping on the closest pair of shoes, I grab my bag and head out the door. I'm all too excited to see Bianca. It seems like every day she's learning new things, and I love watching her mind work. It's part of the reason why

I became a teacher. Seeing children learn, how their confidence grows? It's so unbelievably rewarding.

I'm pulling into Ari's driveway five minutes later. I can't complain about the commute between our houses now, although weekends and in the height of summer, the traffic is much worse due to tourists. On this late August weekday, it's easy to travel the one mile that separates our places.

"Hi! Thank you so much, Stone is just about to start another client, so I need to go talk to him beforehand. I'll be back in a half hour or so," Arianna rambles as she frantically pulls on shoes.

"It's fine. Where is little miss?" I ask.

"She's in her room. Hannah brought over this plastic tea set that her daughter didn't enjoy, but B is obsessed with it. She'll expect you to sit down for some tea. Bye!" she shouts as she runs into the garage.

"Mama! Mama? Mama!" I hear heavy footsteps as Bianca toddles down the hallway, her thick shoes slapping against the hard floor. When she reaches the doorway, her eyes zero in on me. "Ah! Mama?"

I'm not sure if she's calling me "Ah", but I'll take it. "Mama had to go bye-bye, sweet pea! I came to play with you."

Bianca's lower lip pops out, quivering, and I can tell she's about to cry. Quickly walking to her, I scoop her up. "Mama said you have a new tea set from Aunt Hannah! I love tea. Will you show me?"

Her mother forgotten, Bianca gives me a gummy grin. "E! E!"

I'm assuming that means "tea."

Walking back to her room, I take in the beautiful setup Stone and Arianna have created. It's not overdone in a feminine and girly way. No pink walls or tons of florals. A few roses are painted on one wall in varying shades of pink, and a throw rug in the center of the room is a quick burst of color. Everything else is in muted colors, showcasing the roses.

After a few moments of my favorite toddler aggressively shoving various portions of the tea set directly into my mouth, the doorbell rings. Unsure of what to do, I grab Bianca and tiptoe down the hallway to peer through the glass. When I see it's Alex, I freeze.

I haven't seen him since I kissed him at the bar in Denver. In fact, I haven't seen any of the Santo family members, other than Arianna, since that night. I don't think any of the other guys saw me kiss him, but I'd rather be safe than sorry, so I've avoided any potential run-ins.

As I'm about to sneak back down the hallway, Bianca chooses that moment to scream bloody murder. "Les! Les, Les, LES!"

Dammit.

"Bianca? Where's your mom? Get mama, sweetheart," Alex says through the door. Ari and Stone have a tint on the glass so it's incredibly difficult for people to see inside the house. Yet somehow, when Alex looks in, I know he sees me. His brow furrows, then his eyes narrow to slits. "Open the door, Natalie."

Holy crap, he did see me! I need to tell Ari that this shit doesn't work. Letting out a frustrated huff, I unlock the door. As I open it, Bianca lets out an excited squeal as she launches from my arms and into Alex's. "Hi, sweet pea. Where's your mama?"

"She ran to go talk to Stone about something. I said I'd watch Bianca," I answer nervously. Without Bianca in my arms, I'm fidgeting. Chewing on the inside of my cheek, I tap my nails against my thigh. God, I'm wearing plaid pajama pants. Why did I come over here like this?

"Why are you even here? It's the middle of the week. Don't you have a day job?" he sneers. That condescending tone gets my hackles up, and my spine straightens. He doesn't get to demean me.

"For your information, I took a new job and I start Monday. It just so happens that I was available when Ari needed someone to watch Bianca."

"And you came in your pajamas?" Alex asks.

"Yeah, so? It's my bestie's house. I don't think Miss B here judges me for my clothing. Who the heck am I trying to impress?" You, you big grumpy piece of man candy. I'd try to impress you.

"You know what? I don't care. When is my sister supposed to be back?" he asks, and that's when I notice the tension that seems to be emanating from him in waves.

"Are you — are you okay?" I inquire softly. His eyes whip to mine, and I feel like I could get lost in them. Sometimes they're super dark brown, but other times they almost take on a caramel color. I think I'd do just about anything he asked me to do if he growled at me all sexily and stared at me with those eyes. Shit. I'm not listening.

"... Needs a woman's perspective, and as much as I love my mom, she's too old for this, and doesn't understand what kids go through these days," Alex finishes.

"Abbie?" I ask, surprised I remember her name.

Alex nods.

"How old is she?"

"Twelve."

"Oh, middle school. It's brutal for tweens at that age." Alex snorts his agreement, absentmindedly dragging a finger down Bianca's cheek as she stares at him adoringly. "I could talk to Abbie. If you want. I mean, I don't want to step on anyone's toes, but she doesn't know me, so she might be willing to open up more to me than she would to Ari. She might assume Ari will report back to you."

"So would you," he retorts, as Bianca starts to get restless in his arms. Alex puts her down and she toddles over to a shelf of toys, immediately planting herself next to a tiny toy piano and beating on it with all her little might.

"If Abbie asked me not to, no, I wouldn't," I answer. Alex growls, and my eyes widen as the sound goes directly to my clit. Good lord. Does he know how hot he is? He can't know that I just about came.

"Let's get something crystal clear here, Sunflower," he says menacingly, as he takes a step in my direction. I hastily step backward, running into a buffet table against the wall, and Alex crowds me against it. My hands are up defensively, against his chest, and I feel his heartbeat against my palm. His words are growly, but his heart beats calmly. I don't feel scared by him, and I'm not sure how to process that. "If I let you near my daughter, you will tell me everything she says. Every. Thing. You understand?"

As Alex spits out his words, he places his hands on each side of my hips, caging me in. Trying to keep control of my breathing, I cast my eyes downward, only to have Alex's hand slide up my arm to my neck as his thumb forces my chin up. His nose almost touches mine, and our hot breaths mingle. When he moves his hand to cup my cheek tenderly, reverently even, I let out an involuntary moan. His eyes widen, and I see the moment his thoughts come back into focus. He lunges backward, scrubbing a hand over his face.

"I have to go," he says abruptly, turning toward the door. "I'll have Ari work out the details for talking to Abigail *if* I decide to let you."

"Alex," I call out, my voice clearly shaking. He stops, but doesn't turn to face me. "I'm more than happy to help. But if she asks me to respect her privacy, I won't tell you anything. You're going to have to trust me. And did you just call me Sunflower?"

With a shake of his head, Alex trudges out of the door.

Chapter 5

Alex — Late August

"I can't believe you said no before you even let me explain why I want it," Abbie whines.

"I said no because you're twelve. I don't care why you want it, Abigail."

"It's just a nose ring! It's not a big deal."

"It is a big deal. Again, you're twelve. I'm pretty sure the middle school rules even state you can't have anything other than ear piercings, but that's beside the point. I said no. When you're older, we can discuss it again."

"Like … next year?" she asks hopefully. "Like … maybe for my thirteenth birthday?"

"Like … no. Maybe for your sixteenth birthday."

"God, Dad! You're such a jerk, and I hate you!" With her hair hitting me in the face as she whirls around, I watch my daughter's retreating form stomping from the room. I sigh as I slump back in my chair, already exhausted from a long day, and arguing with Abbie doesn't help the headache that's been threatening to explode since lunch.

"You weren't kidding about the attitude, man," my brother, Dominic, says as he steps in the kitchen.

"What are you doing here?" I ask as I rub my temples.

"Mom asked me if I'd be okay taking the kids instead of her this evening. I guess Dad fell again, so she's got him at Urgent Care to see if he needs to go to the emergency room."

"Shit," I say under my breath. "That's like the third time this year he's fallen."

"Well, he refuses to acknowledge the fact that he's getting older, and he won't go to the optometrist to get his eyes checked. My guess is he needs glasses, or he has cataracts, neither of which will solve themselves."

"I'll stop by their house on my next off day and see if I can talk some sense into him," I murmur. Our father, Nick Santo, has always been a stoic guy, but I get along with him better than my siblings. It's possibly due to me being the oldest, or it could be that our personalities are somewhat similar. Whatever the case, he needs to slow down before he ends up sending our mother to an early grave from incessant worrying.

"Why'd you need a sitter tonight anyway? I thought you worked the day shift," Dominic says.

"I do. Town open house tonight," I tell him. Once a quarter, our small touristy town of Eternity Springs, nestled into the mountains to the west of Denver, Colorado, holds an open house for all new residents. A representative from police, fire, utilities, and town council delivers a few words and introductions, then passes out materials for the residents to take. I drew the short straw this quarter.

"One of the best decisions I ever made was delegating that task from my desk onto Hannah's," Dominic muses. Hannah, our brother Luca's wife, is in charge of special events for our family hotel.

"I'd delegate if I could, but I figured my time was coming. They let me avoid it for this long. Not sure what I'm going to say to these people though."

"Just say how you're proud to serve them, the crime rate is low, and the most newsworthy topics in Eternity are related to that stupid marmot stealing shit. Actually, tell them to keep their doors locked. I found a diary of Mrs. Michaelson's in the trees at the top of the property last week, and some of the pages were chewed on. She claimed she didn't fully close her front door a couple weeks ago, and Mason got in there."

"I fucking hate that marmot." Some towns have dogs as their mayors, or bears that wave as you drive by. I'm not quite sure why we were gifted a critter that should live above tree-line, but instead wreaks havoc on our small town by stealing things from residents, then posing with his treasures in doorbell camera lenses at different houses. Half the people love him, and half despise his existence. I'm not even sure who named him Mason, if there is more than one Mason, or if Mason is even a boy. Did someone catch and release him? Who knows.

"I hate him too. Seems like all the men in this town understand he's a terror, and the women think he's adorable and quirky."

"What does Kate think? Sara thought he was cute," I tell Dom.

He smiles widely, a smile I now recognize as the one reserved for his wife. "Katharine is the exception. She thinks he's adorable, but hates the trouble he causes. He absconded with one of her bras a few weeks ago. Minor compared to what happened with Ari, though."

"How the hell did he manage that one? And do I want to know what happened with Ari?"

Dom chuckles. "She forgot to grab it from the night before. We, uh, were in our backyard, and, uh …"

"Nope. That's enough. No more," I tell him, making a big show of plugging my ears with my fingers. "How did you figure out Mason took it? Wait. I don't care about that either."

"Good call. So you haven't heard what happened to Arianna?"

"No," I respond.

"Shit. I thought she would have gone to you first. You need to talk to her about it."

"If it's going to involve a story like yours with Kate, I don't know if I want to hear anything," I tell him.

"Whatever, asshole. Tell your kids to get going. Katharine's making dinner, and I need to get your two back so we can feed them all before hanger takes over."

"Ben!" I shout, then jump when my shoulder is tapped from behind. "Jesus, Ben. How long have you been standing there?"

"Around three and a half minutes, I think," he answers matter-of-factly.

I run through the conversation with Dom, checking to see if anything was inappropriate for Ben, and decide nothing was said that would scar him too badly. "You're going to Uncle Dom's for dinner."

"Oh, thank goodness," Ben says with a relieved exhale, his shoulders sinking as he settles into the chair next to me. "Nani keeps making lasagna because of Abbie, and I don't want to eat it again."

"Why? You've asked for it a hundred times."

He shrugs. "Now I don't want it anymore."

"Alright. I'll try to remember to tell Nani that. Where's your sister?"

"Screaming along to a Sabrina Carpenter song in her room. Do we have any noise-canceling headphones? I'd like to keep them in my room. We share a wall, and Abbie could work on her tone and presentation. She's off-key more than she's on, Dad."

For fuck's sake. Getting up, I walk toward the stairs as I say, "I'll look for the headphones when I get back after this meeting."

Taking the stairs two at a time, the sound of screeching reaches me before I get to the door. I knock twice, and when my daughter doesn't answer, I try the knob. It's locked. Shaking my head, I reach for the top of the door trim, where I keep a key to get into the room. When I don't find it, I know somehow Abbie has gotten it and hidden it from me. No worries, because I have spares. Heading into my room, I reach into the top drawer of my dresser, pulling out the small key. I'm unlocking Abbie's door a moment later.

"Dad!" Abbie screams.

"What?" I answer calmly.

"You can't just enter my room whenever you want! I thought I had —" she breaks off, her eyes widening as she realizes she's admitted to taking the key.

"First of all, we had a rule, young lady. And you broke it when you locked the door, and stole the key. Secondly, I did knock. Your music is so loud that you couldn't hear me."

Crossing her arms across her chest, the defiance emanates in waves from my firstborn. "Well I don't like you coming in here."

"Well, I don't like you locking the door. If you do it again, we'll discuss consequences."

"I don't understand why I can't lock the door," she whines. "Ben just comes in here and rummages through my stuff."

"I'll deal with Ben." Sighing, I cross to her and pull her into a hug. Her arms hesitantly slide around my waist. "I want to respect your space, Abs, but as a parent, I also need to watch what you're doing. Online bullying is awful, which is why I haven't let either of you have a computer in your room, and why I've limited some of the social media apps you've asked to download."

"I'm like the only kid in my grade that doesn't have those," she whispers grumpily.

I smile as I rest my head on top of hers. "You aren't missing much excitement, sweetheart. After your thirteenth birthday, I'm willing to discuss allowing one app as long as you give me the login information, and you allow me to check your account regularly to make sure everything is as it should be. There are adults who will make fake accounts, hoping to prey on teenagers. I want you to be safe."

"I know," she says quietly. "Can I pick which app?"

"Yes, but I'm allowed to veto the choice."

"Veto?"

"It means overrule."

"Oh. I'm sorry for yelling at you. I don't hate you."

I give her a squeeze as I kiss her temple. "I know you don't. Teenage emotions are hard. Hormones are even worse."

"Thanks, Dad," she whispers as she steps away from me.

"Love you, munchkin."

"Love you, too."

After getting my kids out the door, I sit heavily on the couch, staring at the empty space above the television. At one point, I intended to fill the entire wall with family pictures. We'd had family pictures taken every year since Abbie was born, the last set being shortly before I deployed over five years ago. I thought about hanging them when I was home for Sara's funeral, but couldn't bring myself to do it. They've been sitting in an unopened box since then, and we haven't had any pictures taken of the three of us either.

I hate that I've become this way. That I can't — or subconsciously don't want to — move on. In some ways, I've buried every piece of Sara so I don't get reminders everywhere. But in others, I wallow in the memories.

Sighing, I reluctantly stand up. Running a hand through my hair, I can tell bits are standing in places, but I don't care. I couldn't give two fucks about these people finding me attractive. As long as I answer their calls in a timely manner, it doesn't matter what I look like. It's not as if I'm going to be hitting anyone up for a date. Only action I've gotten recently, other than my own damn hand, was with … her.

She who must not be named.

She who *should* not be named.

Bad enough I kissed her back, but even worse that I've thought about it since then. And now I'm thinking about that kiss, and her, again. Then she goes and offers to help Abbie, and I don't want her to be a nice person. I want to hate her.

"Dammit," I mutter. At least I can avoid her most of the time. She's rarely in Eternity Springs, and the last I heard, Arianna says she went back to the boyfriend anyway. But that was a while ago. After that night.

Shaking my head in disgust, I trudge out to my truck. There's a crispness to the air that tells me winter, and snow, aren't too far away. Great, I think to myself. When all of my "they're playing music too loudly" calls will turn into "I forgot how to drive in snow and need assistance" calls. I never thought I'd hate being a police officer, since I loved it so much in the Guard. But I do.

As I start my truck, I notice the time on the dash. The open house has already started. Eternity is pretty damn small, so I'll get to the elementary school where it's being held in about five minutes, but I know it looks really bad for me to be late.

A few minutes later, I'm jogging into the elementary school. Not much has changed at Eternity Springs Elementary since I went there a few decades ago. Sure, they've updated a good chunk of the interior, but the bones of the building are still the same faded red brick that I remember. I pass by my fourth-grade teacher's room; Mrs. Stinson. I was part of her first group of fourth graders. She mellowed quite a bit since she'd had me, but some mannerisms stayed the same. She always made this heinous disapproving 'hmm' sound that reminded me of the way Marge Simpson's sisters sounded on The Simpsons. Ben thought she was weird, and seemed relieved he wouldn't have her as his teacher. I should probably do a better job of encouraging a different opinion of her. She retired last year, and a new teacher was hired to replace her. That new teacher quit almost immediately, and since then, the class has been split amongst the remaining classes.

As I round the corner leading toward the cafeteria, a woman exits the bathroom beside me, and I crash into her. She lets out a startled shriek as she begins to fall to the ground, but I grab a hold of her arm and pull her against me.

Two things happen simultaneously. First, I recognize the woman, and secondly, she throws up her other arm to block her face in a defensive stance.

"What the fuck?" I blurt out.

Natalie lowers her arm to stare at me. "Alex?"

"Why are you in my elementary school?"

"Yours?" she asks.

"Yes, mine."

"Are you a student here?" I don't miss the subtle teasing lilt to her voice, and that pisses me off even more.

"My son is, Natalie. Answer the fucking question," I snap. "And it is still my school, because I went here as a kid, and I patrol this neighborhood."

Natalie takes a hesitant step backward. "What was your question again?"

"Why are you here?"

"Well, for a couple of things. I guess you haven't talked to your sister lately," she stammers.

"Not in a week or so, I guess."

"Hmm. Well, I took a job here, and I'm still getting my room all set up the way I want it."

"Your room?" I ask, confused.

Natalie cocks her head slightly as she studies me. I try not to focus on her eyes, still the most extraordinary color of green I've ever seen, and instead zero in on the bridge of her nose.

"Uh, did you not know that I'm a teacher?"

I stare at her in shock, unblinking as I let the words sink in. "You're teaching? At my son's school? Did you do this to get close to me?"

Natalie's eyes open comically wide, before they narrow to slits. "Are you being serious right now? No, I did not do this for you. A position opened up and I interviewed for it. You were the last thing on my mind."

It's relatively rare that I let emotion cloud my judgment enough that I don't filter my thoughts, and I immediately recognize I owe Natalie an apology. As I'm about to sheepishly tell her I'm sorry, she whirls around and stalks toward the cafeteria. I trail behind her, yelling out, "Wait! That meeting is for new residents only."

Natalie turns around, fire in her eyes. "I'm well aware of that, *Officer* Santo. I am a new resident."

"Thought you lived in Denver," I comment.

"I did. Now I don't."

"You still with the douche?" I ask, internally wincing at my own slip up. Even I'm embarrassed at the question.

"No." Turning again, she opens the door only enough for her to slip through, before it closes in front of me. I growl under my breath as I watch her walk toward the tables, only noticing after she sits down that my gaze never left her ass, and that I'm still standing in the hallway.

"Now we're opening up the floor for any new questions for any of our panelists," the mayor says, motioning wildly toward those of us unlucky enough to be tasked to be here. Representatives from each school, the parks and recreation department, the streets department, utilities, fire, and police are all here to welcome new residents. After doing a quick introduction, the mayor droned on for a half hour about his current campaign to become re-elected. I saw just about everyone yawn more than once, except for Natalie. Not that I was looking at her. And clearly I wouldn't know that she never looked at me the entire time I've been sitting here, facing her.

When my phone buzzes in my pocket, I discreetly remove it to make sure it isn't an issue with my kids. Seeing it's the group text I have with my siblings, I turn off the screen and shove it into my jacket right as I hear my name being called. Popping my head up, I see a frazzled mother carrying an infant, and holding onto the shirt collar of a toddler.

"What are the speed limits on all secondary residential streets?" she asks.

"Uh, twenty-five in most cases, but around the schools, it is twenty."

"We moved over onto Whistle Dance Road, and there's a group of teenagers that race up and down the street all the time. I've got four kids, Officer. I don't even feel comfortable letting them into the front yard when these teens are being so reckless. Can we slam a speed bump in there or something?"

I stifle the chuckle that threatens to break through my lips. "Uh, no, ma'am, we aren't allowed to add speed bumps everywhere. I will make a note of that street, and I'll see if we can start a rotation with the department to patrol more often. If they are in fact minors, it usually only takes a teenager getting one ticket for the parents to take away car keys."

"But what if it doesn't stop?" she asks, and I can hear the emotion in her voice.

Standing, I approach her. "Here's my card. If in a week you haven't seen any improvement, give me a call. We'll figure it out."

The woman nods, her eyes glazing over with tears. "Thank you. It's just — it's that my husband is overseas with the military, and I moved us here alone two months ago. I'm trying to do it all, but I can only do so much."

I wish I'd handled it better, but the moment she said her husband was overseas, I jolted. Jumping backwards, I stammered something about calling me, and then bolted out of the cafeteria.

Did Sara ever feel that way? Did she cry in a meeting because I was overseas? What if this woman dies? How will her kids be? How will her husband find out?

I barely make it to the bathroom before I'm retching into a trash can.

God, I'm so fucked up.

When I know I'm done, I quietly wash my hands, before cupping them to fill my mouth. Swishing, I'm unprepared when I hear Natalie's sweet voice at the doorway. "Alex? Are you okay?"

I let my head drop against my chest. Am I okay? No. Never. But I won't tell anyone that. "Yeah, I'm fine. Just sick."

When she doesn't answer, I assume she's gone. I wait a few more minutes before making my way back to the cafeteria, only to find Natalie waiting for me.

"Everyone left," she whispers, her gaze zeroed in on me. "And you're not fine."

"I said I'm sick," I lie.

"No," Natalie says softly. "You're not sick. What happened back there? Was it her comment about her husband being deployed?"

How the fuck did Natalie recognize it that quickly? I'm about to deny, tell her again that I got sick, claim it was food poisoning, but instead, I say, "Yeah. Yeah it was."

"Your wife," I hear her murmur, more to herself than me, her gaze breaking from mine. I don't respond. I can't. I don't know how to explain what I'm feeling.

"Why did you move here?" I ask, determined to change the subject. "And don't lie to me."

"I wasn't lying earlier. Arianna told me about the position. I interviewed. Gave notice at my job, and moved out that same weekend."

"Why, Natalie? *Why* did you move?"

She sighs, pain etched in her features, before adjusting her shoulders and meeting my eyes. "Because he hit me for the last time."

Fuck.

Chapter 6

Natalie — Late-August

The look that comes over Alex's face is so similar to how my brother reacted when I told him about Rob, that I almost laugh. I guess I understand. I'm his sister's best friend. Well, at least one of them. And it probably means I'm family by association. I'm a pseudo-sister.

Even I'm surprised when a steel look of resolve, plus a healthy dose of malicious intent cover his face a moment later. "Give me his fucking name and address right the fuck now, Sunflower."

"What's with the nickname?" I breathe, finding it ridiculously hot how he seems to be ready to go fight for my honor.

"Natalie," he growls.

"I'm not giving you his name or address, Alex. You know what? If you're going to call me Sunflower, then I'm going to call you Alexander."

"That's not my fucking name."

"Well, what is your name?"

"I'm not telling," he says, crossing his arms over his chest.

Raising a brow at him, I give him a challenging look. "Oh? Cool."

Whipping out my phone, I pull up my favorites and call Arianna.

"Hey, can I call you back? I'm in the middle of something," she says breathlessly. I hear Stone in the background growl something, and I roll my eyes. Those two have more sex than anyone I know.

"This will literally take five seconds. I ran into Alex at that open house thing, and he's being an asshole. What's his actual first name? I'd like to irritate him with it."

"Oh, I love this for him!" Ari gushes gleefully. "It's Alessio. Bye!"

I give him a victorious grin as I place the phone back in my pocket. "Your move, Alessio."

"Jesus Christ," he mutters. "No one calls me that, Natalie."

"Great!" I say cheerfully as I walk past him. "I like knowing that I'm the only one."

"I hate my name. Why do you think I've always gone by Alex?"

"Why not Lex?" I wonder aloud.

He snorts. "Because I'm not that big of a jackass."

"Eh." I pantomime weighing two items. "You say potato, I say jackass."

I turn down a hallway and hear Alex pause behind me. "Where are you going?"

"To my room. I have to grab my things. Night!" I call out, glad to be away from him for a moment. Once in my classroom, I putz around for a handful of minutes, admiring my handiwork as I've put my personal touches on the space. Come Monday, I'm hopeful my kiddos will find joy in the room. They've been separated amongst the other fourth-grade classes, and I know it's going to be difficult to transition again.

Closing the door to my room, I scream when a voice speaks directly behind me. Whirling around, I find a bemused Alex. "You about gave me a heart attack!"

"Did you really think I'd leave you to walk alone to your car in the dark?" he asks.

"Please. Nothing ever happens here unless it's a varmint wreaking havoc," I scoff. It's not that far off from the truth. Eternity Springs is quaint, and it's certainly eclectic with all the cute shop names and family-friendly events, but for a single girl in her thirties, it's boring as fuck.

"It only takes one crime to change that, and I'll be damned if it's on my watch," he says as we walk out the main entrance. "Where are you living now?"

"Arianna hooked me up with a studio apartment on Fifth Street," I answer.

"A studio?"

"It's actually a great space, and I'm really comfortable. I'm just me. I don't need much," I shrug. Rob and I lived in a more upscale apartment complex, with all the bells and whistles. Other than the gym, we didn't use any of it, but our rent was three grand a month for a one-bedroom. My little studio in Eternity Springs is under fifteen hundred, with water and trash removal included. I'm able to save money for the first time in recent memory.

"I don't live far from you," Alex comments.

"Oh yeah?"

"Mmm-hmm. A couple of blocks away."

As Alex continues to walk next to me, a wave of awkwardness overcomes me. Do I thank him for walking me to my car? Should I offer a handshake, or a weird side hug? A high five, or a wave? Maybe I should just start sprinting to my car now, and hope it confuses Alex just enough that I make it to my car before him. As that option begins to show merit, I notice only two cars are left in the entire parking lot. Of course he would be parked next to me.

"You drive a Dodge Challenger?" he asks incredulously.

"Yes, why?"

He shakes his head in disbelief. "I guess I never considered that. I assumed you'd either have some cutesy car that had sentimental value, or a safe SUV that you bought after reading every article on Consumer Reports."

He's not that far off from the truth. "I read the reports on the Challenger, if that makes you feel better. I almost got a Subaru, but didn't want to be *that* Coloradan."

He snickers, and the sound is like a melody, lifting my confidence greatly. I've never made Alex laugh before. I'm damn proud of myself.

"My mom is the only one in my family who owns a Subaru," he confesses, prompting me to throw back my head in a shout of laughter.

"Mine too!"

As we approach our cars, I realize we've both slowed down drastically. I turn to Alex, ready to thank him for walking with me, but he's already speaking. "Thanks for checking on me. After the open house, I mean. You could have just left, but you didn't. And that means a lot."

I give him a shy smile as I nod. He waves briefly before walking to his truck.

Parked in front of my building, the thought of going inside to my apartment, knowing I have nothing to eat, makes me walk a couple of blocks to my favorite hole-in-the-wall diner that serves breakfast all day. I've eaten here a few times with Arianna over the years, since she knows my love of breakfast food, and I've already gotten on a first-name basis with the owners. A perk — but also a hindrance — of small-town living is knowing everyone by name, and I find that to be pretty neat.

Growing up, my mom routinely served us breakfast for dinner, and now as an adult, I can see the appeal. I spent ten hours working on my classroom, filling out paperwork, and doing some new teacher induction things for the tiny school district. Since I lost track of time and had to go straight to the community open house, I haven't eaten since lunch, and I'm well past starving at this point. While I try to curb my attitude in front of others, there's a very thin line between hungry and hangry for me. I should not be held liable for decisions I make when I just need protein and water.

The interior of Dixie's Diner is all classic fifties and sixties style. Elvis Presley, Marilyn Monroe, and James Dean posters dot the walls. Old records are stapled haphazardly on the ceiling, and a jukebox stands in the back corner of the space. I take a seat at the bar, grab the menu, and begin perusing it to see what strikes my fancy. I love trying new foods, as long as they're within my budget. My move to Eternity Springs has been expensive, even with the loan from my brother. I didn't feel comfortable taking *any* money from him, and definitely not as much as he deposited into my account. Once I get a gauge on my bills for an accurate budget, I plan on giving most of it back to him. I know he has more money than he knows what to do with, but I firmly believe that family and money should not go hand-in-hand.

After ordering a spin on eggs benedict that includes asparagus, I pull out my phone and scroll through Instagram. I'm only vaguely aware of someone sitting next to me, until I hear a scoff that I only heard a short time ago. Looking up, I stare into the glaring eyes of Alex Santo.

"Seriously, are you following me?" he demands.

"I got here first!" I blurt out.

He appears nonplussed. "This is all a little too coincidental, Sunflower. The bar, my sister's, the school, and now here? Did you know this is my favorite diner?"

"How the hell would I know that? Contrary to your misguided belief, my world does not revolve around you. And stop calling me Sunflower, unless you're going to tell me why you are doing it."

"Nope," he says. "Now that I know it irritates you, I think I'm gonna do it more."

"I never actually said it irritated me. I just want to know why," I tell him. It totally irritates me, in an 'it's making me hot and I don't want to be' way. Well, that's somewhat of a lie. I'd very much like to be in a too hot situation with Alex. But considering he's still glaring at me, with one eyebrow cocked in such a way that he's even sexier, I hate that I want him like this.

At a couple inches over six feet, with dark tousled waves and penetrating brown eyes, Alex exudes masculinity and power. I feel a pull toward him, like an invisible tether, drawing me into his orbit. But the way he's looking at me right now makes me think he'd rather I be anywhere but here.

"Hey, Alex. You want your usual?" the server asks, a woman who looks to be about my mom's age. She smiles warmly at Alex, and he nods in return. "You two eating together? I'll bring your food out at the same time then."

"Oh, no, we're not —" I stop when she walks away, having already decided we're together. "Great."

"Hope you aren't concerned with gossip," Alex says nonchalantly.

"Huh?"

"I'll bet you the price of your meal that the site has a picture of us sitting next to each other within the next thirty minutes, and an article stating we're on a date."

"The site? What's the name of it again?"

"*The Eagle Has Landed*. Stupid fucking website. It has never been used for its actual purpose."

"What purpose was that?"

"As an actual news and community website. A place for tourists to learn about the town, community events to be announced, and whatnot. Instead, it's all gossip and bullshit they make up half the time."

I screw up my face in distaste. "Could I get in trouble with the school if I'm seen on that?"

"Doubt it. My family is on it all the time. They dragged Dom and Kate often during the start of their relationship. Even suggested Kate and I had a thing going on."

I choke a little on a large gulp of water. "Did you ever have a thing with her? I mean, I didn't think so. I thought she had the hots for Dom the first time I met her. She was always watching him out of the corner of her eye."

Alex's lips pull up in a half smile, the closest I think I've ever seen him give me a real smile. "Yeah, he did the same thing. They probably could have gotten married a good year before they did, but they're both stubborn asses."

I chuckle. Knowing what I know about Kate, it's true. They butt heads quite a bit, but the support and love they have for one another is remarkable.

"To answer your first question, no. I never had anything with Kate."

"Oh," I whisper. This conversation turned awkward quite suddenly.

"Besides, I don't think that is a concern for me anymore. A relationship, I mean. And Kate has always been a relationship kind of girl."

"Why don't you think you'll ever have a relationship?" I ask quietly.

He shrugs, looking down at his hands, his fingers intertwined together tightly. "I had my shot. Lightning doesn't strike the same place twice."

"That's actually not true." When he looks up, anger evident on his face, I throw up a hand in mock surrender. "I mean about lightning. It literally can strike the same place twice. My friend Becca is a meteorologist in Denver, and she's taught me all kinds of weird weather facts."

"Alright. What's the weirdest weather fact she's told you?"

"Dammit, you're not supposed to put me on the spot," I mutter. "Hold on. I can look back through our texts. She's a nerd, and always gets so excited about weird weather."

"Ben loves weather. He's convinced he either wants to be a storm chaser or go into the Air Force when he grows up," Alex comments as I scroll through my texts.

"Really? How do you feel about that?"

He shrugs again. "I don't know. I guess if he gets a degree in meteorology, and chases storms on his off days, I'm fine with that. But if he wants to just go out there and live off gas station food while he can't make ends meet elsewhere, I'm not okay with that. I want him to enjoy a career, whatever that may be. But he needs to be self-sufficient however he does it."

"What if he's like that crazy dude who always points at storms in his selfies? He's got a website, and he sells his videos to news channels."

"I guess," he says slowly. "I'm not too stressed about it now. He's got quite a few years before we can start arguing about careers."

"And you're cool if he follows in your military footsteps?"

Alex lifts one shoulder. "If it makes him happy. I just don't want him to do it because he thinks I want him to."

"What if he doesn't want to go to college?"

"Oh, I don't care about that. I didn't go to college. If he wants a job that is more of a trade, I'm cool with that. Those guys make bank. And if he's happy, I'm happy."

"That's actually pretty decent of you, Alessio," I tell him with a wicked grin.

Alex rolls his eyes as he chuckles. "I'd hoped you forgot about that, honestly."

"Nope."

"Did you find any weird weather facts?" he asks, changing the subject suddenly.

"Hmm. Oh! Here's one. Did you know you can tell the temperature by counting a cricket's chirps?"

"Really?"

"Yeah. And if it's a mild autumn, spiders will be larger when found in your home."

"How the hell did someone figure that out?" he asks incredulously.

"I don't know. Becca doesn't explain the weird facts unless I specifically ask."

"And you didn't ask about the spider one, obviously."

"Hell, no," I say with an exaggerated shudder. "I'm the president of the arachnophobia club of Denver."

"That's — that's not a real thing, is it? I'm just really not sure what to trust when it comes to you," he says with a chuckle.

"Unfortunately, it's not a real thing. Although if it were, I'd definitely be involved. I'm not a fan of spiders."

"Have you ever been down to southern Colorado to see the tarantula migration?"

Pretty sure my heart stops in my chest. "Excuse me, the what now?"

"The tarantula migration. Male tarantulas come out in the late summer, traveling around to find a mate."

"Oh, good God. I think I would completely pass out if I saw a tarantula."

Alex's eyes narrow as he stares at me. "Noted."

"I swear to God, Alessio, if you ever come at me with a tarantula, I will have no problem cutting off any of your appendages, so make your decisions wisely."

Alex laughs, but quiets when he notices I'm not joking. "You're serious."

"As a heart attack. Ask your sister if I ever joke about arachnids."

We're quiet for a few moments, lost in our thoughts, before plates are dropped in front of us. Identical plates.

"I can see why y'all are eating together, seeing as how you like the same things," the server says with a wink.

"Thanks, Nancy," Alex says as he grabs a napkin and places it in his lap. "I don't even know what to think about you ordering that."

"I swear, I didn't know," I stammer.

"This is a lot of coincidences," he murmurs. I don't answer. There's no way he thinks this is coincidence. I'm beginning to wonder if something else is at play here.

We eat quietly for some time before Alex clears his throat. "I've never spent a lot of time with you, but you seem like the kind of woman who is a ballbuster. A girl who won't take any shit from anyone. And that's why I really don't understand how you got in a relationship where someone was hurting you."

I sigh as I think of how to respond. "He wasn't that way for a while. It was a great relationship for so long. I think he lulled me into a false sense of security. Looking back, I can tell when his personality changed, and he began to gaslight me. I'd never get better than him. I couldn't live without him because Colorado is such an expensive place to live. No one would ever accept me because I'm fat. All the stupid things. He fed into every insecurity I had. Once he realized he had me, line, hook, and sinker, that's when the arguments started to escalate. That's when he'd get so mad about stupid things. I started walking on eggshells around him, convinced if I could just keep him happy, then I'd still have a boyfriend, and everything would be fine."

"What changed for you?" he asks softly.

"Seeing how happy Arianna and Kate are. And especially seeing how Dom and Stone are with their kids. I couldn't have a man like Rob in my kids' lives, you know? If he hits me, would he hit our daughter? Would our son think it's okay to hit? I can't be responsible for encouraging another generation to abuse women," I confess. When

Alex doesn't respond, I look quickly out of the corner of my eye to find him studying me. "I'm guessing that isn't what you thought I'd say."

"Uh, no. Not at all. I figured your brother or dad saw a bruise and raised hell. That's probably what I would have done," he answers truthfully.

"I hid it from them. My brother only knows now because I borrowed some money to put the deposit down on my apartment here, and I paid a fee to get my name off Rob's apartment in Denver. I'm a teacher. I'm barely making ends meet as it is. I was stuck."

"What did Shawn say?" Alex asks. My eyes whip to his in shock, making him laugh. "I know your brother, Sunflower. Not only because I'm a hockey fan, but because he's friends with my brother. I might be older than everyone, but I can still hang on occasion."

"I didn't mean anything like that. I had no idea you knew him, that's all."

"I've been to a lot of those summer league games too, you know. Probably talked to you and that other girl who Arianna is friends with. Not that I remember," he says with a chuckle. Oh, we barely talked. I never spoke to him. I was all gangly knees, braces, and thick thighs even then. Alex seemed larger than life to me, and I couldn't speak when he was around. I think I cried for a week the first time he brought his wife to one of Luca and Shawn's games. Honestly, the fact that I'm sitting next to him, holding a civilized conversation where I'm not a bumbling mess, is pretty damn surprising. Only Claire knew of my crush on Alex. I certainly couldn't tell Arianna.

As we both finish our meals, I watch as Alex carefully pulls out his phone. "Damn."

"What?" I ask.

"My kids fell asleep at Dom's house. It's been a long time since that happened. His kids must have run mine ragged."

"Kate says she's never gotten better sleep than she has on the days she has them nonstop. Well, that was before Dom. I mean, before they were married and having all the back-breaking sex. I think. I mean, I know they're having sex. And she goes into detail, which I could do without, and honestly, I'm surprised that he has the stamina he has at his age. Don't you guys lose that at some point?" Jesus. Someone muzzle me.

"Uh, I'm not sure I can comment on my brother's stamina," Alex murmurs, staring straight ahead. When I'm about to say goodbye so I can go scream into my pillow in humiliation, Alex turns to me. "But I assure you, Sunflower, we old guys don't all lose our stamina."

Holy hell.

"Do you want to go back to my place for sex?" I say loudly, then gasp, covering my face with my hands. "Oh my God. I can't believe I just said that. It's just, well, it's been a while since I've had a good C in the V, because Rob certainly wasn't packing a punch. To proposition my best friend's brother in the middle of a restaurant is a new low for me, if I'm being honest."

"If you say things like this sober, what the hell do you say when you're blitzed?" Alex asks. Peeking through my fingers, I find a bewildered look on his face.

"I think it's best if I don't discuss what I say when I'm drunk," I whisper.

He leans toward me. "State secrets? Connections to a Mexican cartel? Let me guess, you actually know who is hiding JFK."

I gasp. "How did you know? Except for the JFK thing. He died ten years ago."

The grin that covers Alex's face is so beautiful, I'm momentarily stunned. It's a smile I haven't seen in years. Straight white teeth, except for a hint of a snaggle tooth on one side, that somehow makes him even more attractive, and perfect lips that I'd really like to experience again. His beard covers a chiseled jawline that I want to feel between my fingers ... and my thighs.

"Natalie."

"Hmm?"

"I said, are you ready?"

"Oh," I say, embarrassment covering my face, "I just need to pay my bill."

"We need to work on your situational awareness, Sunflower. I already paid it."

I stare at him in confusion. "Huh?"

Alex shakes his head at me. "It's paid for. Come on. I'll walk you to your car."

He motions for me to walk in front of him, and I'm acutely aware of the possibility he might be staring at my ass. Casting a quick look over my shoulder, I'm pleased when I find his eyes cast downward. Once outside, I turn to him. "I, uh, parked by my apartment, so I'm walking home."

"It's dark out, Natalie. I'll walk you to your door. My mom would kill me if I didn't."

"Your mom wouldn't know," I mumble.

"You haven't lived here long enough to understand this, so just trust me. My mom knows everything, or knows someone who will tell her everything. She'll find out." From what Ari has told me, I don't doubt it.

Arriving at my apartment building entrance, I again turn to Alex. "Okay, you did the gentlemanly thing. You can live another day without any mom-on-son violence."

He absentmindedly scratches at the hair on his chin. "Well, you know someone probably told her that you propositioned me at the diner, right?"

The blood drains from my face. "So I need to move again, right? I can't ever see your parents again. Oh, your Nonna will hate me forever —"

My words die out when Alex's mouth covers mine.

Chapter 7

Alex — Late-August

Am I going to regret this? Absolutely.

But at this moment, I'm finding it hard to care.

It's been so long since I've felt, well, anything good. Maybe I've let myself wallow in misery for too long. Or stopped myself from connecting to anything. And while this interaction with Natalie can't — won't — go anywhere after tonight, I need it. And from the way she just melted against me, I'd say she does too.

"Ask me inside," I demand against her mouth, catching the fullness of her bottom lip between my teeth. When she doesn't answer, I take the keys from her hand and unlock the door. "Which apartment is yours?"

Natalie only points up the stairs, and I'm secretly relieved she isn't on the ground floor. Eternity Springs is a safe town, but stupid criminals are everywhere. I don't want to worry about her.

Fuck.

I will not worry about her. This is just a one-night stand. That's it.

Let her in.

No.

I will not be having conversations with my dead wife right now. Christ. I'm losing the plot.

After Natalie unlocks her apartment door, I'm pleasantly surprised at how homey the space is. Her bed clearly also serves as a couch, but stacks of pillows make it appear comfortable and inviting. There must be a dozen potted plants in various places, and a cart with what appears to be an intricate coffee machine sits beside a small dining table. I see brightly colored coffee mugs next to the machine, and I wonder what her coffee tastes are.

"Alex," she whispers, drawing my attention back to her. With only moonlight coming in through the two large windows along one wall, her eyes appear to be clear. "Are you sure about this?"

I can hear the hesitancy in her voice. There's a slight tremor in her hand, and I realize she's as out of her depth here as I am. I haven't had a relationship in years, and she hasn't had a one-night stand. Different, yet somehow the same.

"I can only do one night," I tell her quietly. "I'm not — I'm not made for anything longer. I won't lead you on. But if that makes you uncomfortable, I can leave right now."

Her eyes dance between mine as she contemplates my words. I find myself carefully taking her throat in my hand, unsure why I need to touch her so badly. I feel her pulse under my thumb, beating wildly, and I wonder if my own is as fast. Pupils blown, Natalie watches me as I slightly squeeze her neck, and her breath catches when my tongue sneaks out to lick my lips. I feel the whimper before she makes a sound, and I know her decision before she says a word.

Natalie reaches for me while I pull her into my arms, our lips meeting in a dazzling kiss. Her taste explodes on my tongue, the hint of cinnamon from her chai tea latte at the diner still evident. I turn her and push her against the door, snaking a hand down to grab the back of her thigh, hoisting it up to wrap around my waist. I let go of her neck to grab her other thigh, picking her up so my groin hits perfectly between her legs. Natalie lets out a nervous squeal, but it immediately turns into a deep moan when my hard length hits her core. Even through all our clothing, I can feel the heat emanating from her, and I'm desperate to experience it firsthand.

"Doesn't this hurt?" Natalie asks when she breaks off the kiss.

"What?" I drag my tongue down the side of her neck, letting it dance over the pulse point I felt beneath my thumb.

"I'm too heavy," she protests.

My head pops up as I stare at her incredulously. "The fuck?"

Natalie's gaze darts everywhere except my face. "I know I'm heavy, Alex. You don't need to pretend."

"Is that what that motherfucker told you? Baby, you aren't fat. Your curves are perfection," I tell her, holding her ass as I step away from the door. Did I just call her baby? I haven't called anyone that since … since. "Any man who talks about your weight as if he has any right to do so needs to have a fucking reality check. I don't want a beanpole wrapped around me. I want a soft woman that has something I can grab onto while I'm fucking her."

To prove my point, I squat down as far as my knees will let me. Military life wasn't too kind to my knees, which has nothing to do with Natalie's weight. I don't have to say a word, because she immediately tries to put her feet down.

"Nope," I grunt, clamping my arms down on the outside of her thighs. "You're not going anywhere. Bet your ex couldn't do this, could he?"

She shakes her head slowly.

"Exactly. You don't see me getting all worried that I might be too big for you."

She laughs sardonically as she motions up and down my body. "That's because you look like this!"

"Everyone has insecurities, Sunflower. I'll have you know, I don't have a six-pack. But your asshat ex might. However, I also know I have a tongue like you've never experienced before. You think I'm gonna focus on my lack of abs, or on how many orgasms I think I can give you before you pass out?"

"Holy hell," she whispers, her eyes wide. "Plural?"

"Have you never had multiple orgasms before?"

Natalie shakes her head. "I figured it wasn't gonna happen for me. Ari and Kate talked about it, even Claire, but I thought it wasn't something I'd experience."

"We're going to ignore you talking about my sister and orgasms for a sec —" Natalie giggles, making me smile in return, "— and address the elephant in the room. Do you want to have multiples?"

"Yes, please," she whispers solemnly.

"Are you cool if I am the one to give them to you?" I tease, surprised at my own lighthearted banter. This is so unlike me.

Natalie lets out a breathy laugh as she nods. "It sounds as if you're the master, so by all means, teach me your ways."

Standing to my full height, I let her legs slip from around my waist. When she's standing once again, I notice how tall she is. She has to be only five or six inches shorter than my own six-three. "I like how tall you are."

Natalie seems surprised at my admission. "Most guys hate it."

I shrug. "Most guys have inferiority complexes. Fortunately for me, I'm tall."

She giggles, then shrieks as I push her backwards onto the bed. Before she's even made it onto her elbows, I'm on my knees, removing her socks and shoes. "Oh, you mean now? Like, right now? Multiples, now?"

"Did you have a better time in mind?" I ask dryly.

"Uh, maybe after I shower? Bathe? Do anything that involves a little hygiene?"

"Nah," I say as I grab a hold of the waistband of her leggings, peeling them down her legs. "I don't like the taste of soap."

White cotton panties with sprigs of lavender cover Natalie's pussy, and I waste no time in yanking them to the side and covering her with my tongue. I can't help the victorious grin that covers my face when she lets out the loudest, most guttural moan I think I've ever heard. One hand immediately grips my hair, holding me in place, as her other hand unconsciously grabs her breast. Moans of varying depths continue to come from her mouth, a phenomenal melody I hope I'll remember tomorrow. She's so fucking responsive. Hips already subtly moving, I slowly slip one finger inside her channel to find her completely soaked. This is going to be one hell of a one-night stand.

Am I going to be able to keep it to one night?

No.

Shhh.

I can't focus with another voice in my head.

Quickening my pace, I bring Natalie right to the brink. Feeling her walls begin to flutter around my digit, I back off, and she lets out a frustrated whimper. I chuckle against her, knowing it'll send her back up, this time sucking her clit harshly into my mouth. Her orgasm is immediate, soaking my face, and I'm no longer laughing. Her cum fills my mouth, a taste so perfect I know I could become addicted.

I'm ready to give her another orgasm when she moves a leg, bending it in such an angle that I realize she has to be incredibly flexible to manage, and uses her foot on my shoulder to shove me back. Moving with a burst of laughter, I stumble as she scampers to her knees, her face rosy with a fine sheen of sweat covering her forehead.

Damn, this girl is gorgeous.

Exactly my type, which is why I'll steer clear of her after tonight. Hell, I shouldn't even be doing this. But when Natalie beckons me with a slow crook of her finger, it's like an invisible rope is tethered to my body. I move forward, my cock clearly making the decisions, as Natalie yanks me onto the bed. Our lips meet in a deep kiss as I fall on top of her. I can't keep my hands still, running them along every bit of skin I can reach. Her sighs and quiet moans are making me as hard as steel, and I wonder how long I'll be able to last once I get inside her.

Do I still have a condom in my wallet?

Do condoms expire?

Shit. Focus.

Kissing down Natalie's neck, I find a spot below her ear, but not quite onto her collarbone, where goosebumps bloom, making her immediately shiver. I feel her fingernails dig into my shoulder blades before she starts dragging my shirt up. Sitting up, I reach up and over to rip my shirt off. I hear Natalie's quick intake of breath as she takes in my chest and abs. I wasn't kidding about the six-pack. I've never had the best abs, and it wasn't a big thing that was important for me to focus on. And now, at thirty-eight years old, I've got a layer of fat that has taken up residence along my waistline. But I've got killer arms, and I'd rather have biceps that are good for literally picking up a woman than a set of abs no one but me ever sees.

Let. Her. In.

"No."

"No?" Natalie parrots, her hands stopping on my shoulders. "Do you not want me to touch you?"

"Shit, no. That's not what I meant." Sara, get out of my head. Please. "Don't stop."

I can see Natalie is concerned — get in line, Sunflower, because clearly I'm going insane — so I lean down to take her lips in a deep and passionate kiss. That does the trick for both of us. Her lips are exquisite. Perfectly plump pillows that fit so well against mine. I love that she doesn't mind kissing me when she has to be tasting herself on my tongue. I love the little sounds she makes into my mouth. And I love how her body feels underneath me. I don't know how long it's been since I felt this alive.

I can't think about that. Stay in the moment, dumbass.

Breaking the kiss, I sit back on my haunches and motion toward Natalie. "Shirt. Off."

"Yes, sir," she says breathily, following it with a giggle.

I raise an eyebrow at her. "I could get on board with the sir thing."

She rolls her eyes in response. "Not happening. Your name is Alex, not Dom."

"Did you just make a sex joke that included my brother?" I ask, failing to hide a smirk.

"I did."

"At least you didn't call me Alessio."

"Well, damn. Missed opportunity," she says sassily, whipping her shirt over her head. As my gaze zeroes in on her red lace bra that barely contains what I can only assume are fucking phenomenal tits, I notice the front closure, and reach out to snap it open. When big and glorious breasts fill my vision, I push Natalie back so I can get a rose-colored nipple in my mouth. She lets out a loud moan as she throws her head back in bliss. "Oh, God. Yes. So sensitive, but suck harder."

Damn. I like that she tells me what she needs. That's incredibly sexy. Women seem to think men are mind readers. News flash: we aren't. Point us in the right direction.

I give both breasts equal attention, nibbling a little before laving away any pain with my tongue. Natalie grows restless, thrashing around beneath me on the bed. "Alex, I need you. Please."

Placing one kiss between her breasts, I stand beside the bed and pull out my wallet. Thankful I still have a condom in here, I throw it next to Natalie. "Take off your panties."

"How about I take yours off?" she says seductively, rising to stand in front of me. Her eyes meet mine as her hands find my belt buckle. I was thankful I didn't have to wear my uniform to the event tonight, but I still dressed professionally. Well, as professional as I can be. I prefer comfortable clothes, and this pair of khakis with a polo shirt isn't it.

When Natalie drops to her knees to help me out of my pants and dress shoes, I take a moment to admire how beautiful she looks, visualizing how it might look, and feel, to bury myself into the back of her throat. But when I feel my cock leak, I scrap the idea and pull Natalie off the floor.

"I wanted to —" she starts, but I interrupt her.

"I know what you want to do, Sunflower. And while I have no doubt I'd enjoy it, I'd rather get you on my cock right now. Okay?" I tell her, sliding a hand up to bracket her throat again. I'm not sure why I keep doing that. I've never been a proper dominant, and I certainly don't get off on BDSM. But there's something inherently sexy about collaring this woman.

I grab the condom off the bed, handing it to Natalie. "Put it on me."

"Oh," she says, her eyes widening when she looks down to see my bulge. Natalie doesn't move, her hands still halfway between her body and mine, as she stares at my boxer briefs. "That — that's not going to fit, Alex."

I can't help the amused chuckle that bursts from my lips, nor how pleased I am at the blush covering Natalie's cheeks. "I guarantee it'll fit."

"Can you guarantee I won't need a wheelchair at school on Monday?" she asks.

"A wheelchair?"

"Yes, because I won't be able to walk!"

I throw my head back in raucous laughter. Arms crossed over her ribs, the move brings her breasts up perfectly, like she's bestowing a present to me. Her lower lip sticking out in an exaggerated pout, Natalie is a goddamn vision. "You won't need a wheelchair."

"Promise?"

"Uh, I promise I'll go slow. But how about we have you on top. That way you control the speed and depth." After pushing down my underwear, I sit on the edge of the bed, patting my lap for Natalie. She looks even more terrified than a moment ago. "What's going on in that head of yours, Sunflower?"

"It's just ..." she trails off in hesitation.

"Go on," I encourage.

Natalie sighs. "I'm not comfortable on top. I'd rather be on the bottom."

Ah. I know what's bugging her now. "Natalie, I promise you, I find you insanely attractive. I want to taste every fucking inch of your skin. I'd like you to try it, and if you don't like it, we'll switch positions."

"Promise?" she whispers again, and I see the vulnerability in her eyes. She's trusting me with more than just an orgasm. She's trusting me with her confidence.

"I promise." I take the condom from her hands, noticing how delicate her fingers are. Quickly donning the rubber, I look back at Natalie. She tentatively places her hands on my shoulders, moving closer to me, but her eyes are trained on my dick. "Eyes on mine, Sunflower. Watch me."

She puts her knees on the bed, hovering over me, and I wrap one arm around her waist. Using my other hand, I drag the tip of my cock through her wetness, groaning at the feeling. Even with the condom on, I can feel how hot she is. Notching my dick at her entrance, I encourage her to lower herself onto me. As soon as Natalie covers the tip, she sighs softly, and rests her forehead against mine.

I didn't think this through.

This is intimate. A connection. It isn't just sex like this. When

Natalie drops her head to my shoulder, I'm relieved. Now I can close my eyes and focus.

Get her off, get off, and get the hell out of here.

But I already know I'm going to want her again.

And again and again. When was the last time I felt this insatiable? I haven't even fully fucked her yet, and I can tell it won't be enough.

My mind taking over, I don't register Natalie has fully seated herself in my lap. It isn't until she shouts, "Alessio!" that I even realize where I am.

"Sorry," I grunt, squeezing her ass with both hands. The move brings her closer to me, and the base of my dick rubs against her clit. She lets out a cry of pleasure, and I rotate her against my body again.

Grabbing a hold of her waist, I pick Natalie up until my cock is almost fully out of her, then slowly, painstakingly, lower her again. She grips my shoulders as we get into a rhythm, and before long, I'm feeling the tingling sensation of an impending orgasm at the base of my spine. Pulling out, I turn and put her on the bed. "Hands and knees."

Natalie scrambles to do as she's told, casting a quick glance over her shoulder as she flips her hair around. Oh, that won't do. Once I slide back into her channel, I gather her hair into a makeshift ponytail, wrapping it around my fist twice. Pulling it, Natalie moans, and I begin drilling into her.

"Told you it would fit," I grunt.

"Alex ... so good," she mutters.

"Are you close?" I grit out.

"Almost, I think?"

Shit. "Baby, touch yourself. You gotta get yourself there."

I know the moment she touches her clit, because her walls clamp down on me like nothing I've ever felt before. I couldn't stop this orgasm if I tried. Spots dot my vision as white-hot pleasure barrels toward me at breakneck speed, and as I spurt stream after stream inside Natalie, I feel her walls flutter as she has her second orgasm. I could have done better. But I was too eager to get inside her.

I'm unprepared when Natalie's arms buckle and she falls forward, and since I'm still buried inside her, I go down too. I manage to roll to the side as we hit the bed, exhaustion overtaking me.

"Holy hell," Natalie mutters.

"Yeah," I answer.

She lets out a big yawn. "I know you said one night, but can we at least do that one more time before you go?"

I smile sleepily, removing the condom and dropping it onto the floor. I'll grab it later. "Uh-huh."

Jarred awake when something hits me in the chest, I bolt upright. I'm momentarily confused until I remember the evening. Looking to my left, I find Natalie curled up against me, her arm splayed across my ribs. The clock on the stove tells me it's two in the morning. I have to be to work at seven, and I haven't talked to Dom about getting my kids, but they're usually up fairly early, so I need to get out of here. I grab a blanket on the edge of the bed, and cover her up so she doesn't get cold. Carefully extricating myself from Natalie's bed, I quietly get dressed, pick up the condom with a tissue, and put it in my pocket. Then I grab my shoes, and silently exit her apartment.

At home, I turn on the shower in my bathroom. As I wait for it to warm up, I remove the tissue from my pocket, and notice a clear rip down the side. Assuming it ripped while I jammed it into my pants — and not while I jammed it into Natalie — I toss it into the wastebasket.

Chapter 8

Natalie — Early September

I wasn't surprised that Alex was gone when I woke up. Disappointed, but not shocked. I know he fell asleep for a little while, because he snored a bit. I'm a pretty light sleeper, so his snores jarred me awake a few times. But that also tells me that Alex snuck out, and I wonder if it was due to regret, or if he was worried about how awkward our interactions might be in the morning.

I knew it was difficult for him that night. I could tell when his mind would drift, and I assume he was comparing me to his wife. It's not like I could ask him not to do that. I compared him to Rob, who unfortunately took up the last couple years of my sexual experience card spots. God, can you just imagine if we all had to carry around a card, like the old school library cards in the front of the books, with the stamped dates? Natalie Jackson, age thirty-two. Sexual partners, ten and rising. Most recent partner, a jackass named Rob who thought rutting into me as quickly as possible was a stellar move. Time of partnership: sixteen months. How long should the partnership have been? One month, maybe two.

If you ask my friends, I'm the girl who is ready to burn down the world for them. Which is why I really don't get how afraid I am to confront a significant other. Yeah, things became pretty dicey with Rob when he got angrier and angrier, but even I don't understand why I stayed as long as I did.

I'd really love to talk to them about my night with Alex and how likely it is to blow up in my face, but obviously I can't do that. Arianna is his sister. Kate is married to one brother, and Hannah is married to another. While Claire isn't connected to the Santo family in any way, she's so sweet, hates gossip, and would undoubtedly announce in the group text about my shenanigans. I love my friends, but I don't want to tell them about Alex yet. Maybe ever.

Rolling over, I bury my face in the pillow, taking in a big whiff of Alex's cologne. I wonder if I take the pillowcase off, and go to a department store, if I could find it?

Lord. Even when I think I've reached the bottom of the pitiful barrel, I sink to a new low. I lunge off the bed, stripping the sheets, and pile them next to the door. The only place I'm going right now is the laundromat.

I'm a bundle of nervous energy Monday morning, my first day as a fourth-grade teacher at Eternity Springs Elementary School. Usually the kids match my energy level, but this is a unique situation. When the previous teacher quit with no notice, the class was separated and absorbed into other classrooms. It's been a month, and now they're to be reassigned to me. I worry that they'll have difficulty acclimating to all of the changes. I try to remind myself that kids are resilient.

By mid-morning, I've got a handle on which kids I know will need a little more attention to stay on task. Right before lunch, the principal stops in to tell me they've made a last-minute change, switching out two kids. As I take the paperwork she hands me, I look down and see a familiar last name.

Santo. Benjamin Santo.

And when I look up, I'm met with the exact same eyes that I haven't been able to get out of my mind, albeit in a smaller package. Benjamin is the spitting image of his father. I'm two seconds away from calling the principal back and explaining a quick conflict of interest, but Benjamin speaks before I can.

"Hello, I'm Ben Santo. I want to be a pilot in the Air Force when I

WORTH THE TEST

grow up, and I'll need as much math and science experience as I can get. If you can't give that to me, we'll need to go our separate ways," he states seriously.

Holy crap. The serious and stoic apple doesn't fall far from that tree, and I think I fall a little bit in love with the littlest Santo on the spot. I guess Alex was right about potential Air Force aspirations, too. "Hello, Benjamin. Would you prefer I call you Ben?"

"Yes. Now, about the math and science stuff?"

"Are you asking if we'll be covering both subjects this year, or would you like me to prepare extra work for you to complete at home?"

"Extra work, please," he says with an emphatic nod.

"Alright, I can do that. I'll need to take some base testing to determine your level, and then we'll go from there."

"Oh, no need. I'm the smartest in this whole school."

A small voice pipes up from behind me. "He really is, Ms. Jackson. He's not lying."

"Hmm. Okay. Let's all get ready for lunch, and I'll handle getting Ben some extra work."

"Just not reading fictional stories, please. I refuse to live in a make-believe world." His expression is steadfast, resolute even, but his eyes tell a different story. How a beautiful little boy indeed found out that fairy tales and make believe aren't real, when he lost his mother so early on in his life.

"Let's take it one day at a time, Ben. Caitlin, you're the line leader for this week. Take us down to the cafeteria, but stop at the end of each hallway," I tell the class as they line up quietly.

Ben waits until the last child leaves before turning to me. "Ms. Jackson?"

"Yes?"

"Can you not tell my dad about the extra homework? He thinks I spend too much time on school work, but if he thinks it's assigned, he can't tell me not to do it." He gives me a head nod as he joins his peers in the hallway, and I'm left standing in the classroom with a gobsmacked expression covering my face.

This is going to end so badly.

By the end of my first week, I feel like I'm settling in nicely to Eternity Springs, both the elementary school and the town. I love the quaint small-town living aspect, and how quiet it is every evening once all the tourists and day travelers have left. I feel incredibly fortunate to have a great group of fourth graders, and can already see their personalities coming out as we get more comfortable with each other.

I've always had the standard practice of spending one hour on Friday afternoons setting up my classroom for the following week. As much as I'd like to immediately leave to go lounge around in my apartment, I know it'll make Monday morning that much easier for me. I've got all my copies completed, new books circulated around the room, and the individual whiteboards the kids use cleaned. The only thing left to complete is the daily schedule on the large whiteboard.

I'm incredibly unprepared when the door to my classroom is flung open, smashing against the wall, and I scream as I whirl around. I'm startled to find a fuming Alex staring at me with malice in his eyes.

"You! You're the one behind this? Are you trying to kill me, woman?" he growls, advancing toward me in such an aggressive fashion that I reflexively step back.

"What are you talking about?" I stammer.

He flings a handful of papers at me, which slowly drop to the floor. "This. What is wrong with you? Can't kids just be kids? They're nine! Is this some bullshit way to get back at me for leaving the other morning? How are you even his teacher anyway? Shouldn't that have been the first thing you discussed with the administration team?"

I feel myself sinking into the wall I've been backed into. Alex's eyes are like coal, but with a fire behind them, and I'm trying not to find him attractive in this moment. But I also notice that I'm not recoiling from him like I always did Rob, and that makes me stand taller. "First of all, this has nothing to do with you, and I'm disappointed you would think that. Secondly, I did explain our, uh, situation to the administration team after Ben was placed with me, and they didn't feel it warranted another change. He wasn't originally in my class, but there was another situation that required a change for a separate student."

"What was that situation?" he asks bluntly.

"I'm not at liberty to say, Mr. Santo. It is not your child, so you don't get that information," I reply hotly.

"Fine. But stop sending this bullshit home with them. It's too much." Alex stands to his full six-foot three height, and I wish I had worn anything with heels today. Anything to stand a little taller.

"What I choose to send home to my students is my decision, Mr. Santo. It is based on ability level and desire for work. If you wish to discuss this further, please reach out via the front office, and we can schedule a meeting with the principal present." Yeah, how do you like that, asshole? I'm not fucking cowering anymore.

"You've got a lot of nerve, Natalie —"

"No," I interrupt him. "It's Ms. Jackson. You don't have the privilege of calling me by my first name. You can see yourself out, Mr. Santo."

Turning away from him, I'm unprepared when his hand latches onto my elbow, whirling me around, as his other hand brackets my throat. Alex's lips are on mine before I can voice a sound of protest.

Against my better judgment, I moan, and Alex swallows the sound. The hand on my throat squeezes subtly as his tongue circles mine. God dammit. I hate how good this feels. How excellently he kisses.

This is my classroom.

I am his son's teacher.

This is so unbelievably wrong. Unprofessional. Disrespectful.

As I force my hands between our bodies to push him away, Alex jumps backward. His eyes meet mine for only a moment before he stalks out of the room.

I am in so much trouble.

I hit the liquor store on my way home from school, and treat myself to a good bottle of merlot. Well, a mid-grade bottle. Since I'm on a very strict budget right now as I attempt to pay my brother back, I'm not allowed many extra items. Tonight, however, this one is needed.

As I'm pouring myself a rather large glass to go with my super fancy frozen lasagna, I get a text from Kate.

> Kate: I was thinking about you today. For some reason, I had this feeling you needed to talk.

Shit. I feel tears start to form as I try to think of how to respond.

Fuck it. I need advice, and she's the only one who I can talk to right now.

> Me: You are correct.

> Kate: Want me to come over? Dominic took the kids to his parents' place tonight, then he's meeting his brothers for a beer.

> Me: Yes, please. I'm eating a crappy dinner right now, so come over whenever you want.

> Kate: That's good, because I'm in the parking lot.

> Kate: Now I'm at the front door. Buzz me up.

She really has no idea how much I need her advice right now.

Buzzing her in, she's at my door in less than a minute. After welcoming her inside, she takes a long look around my space. "Boy, you weren't kidding when you said it's a studio apartment."

"I don't mind it. Less for me to clean," I tell her, motioning for her to sit down at my tiny two chair table. "I have some merlot if you'd like it, but honestly, I plan to polish off this entire bottle by myself."

"Do you, boo. I'm cool with water. Plus I have to drive home. Can't have Officer Santo pulling me over. The whole family would never let me live it down, even if I'm sober." Kate must notice an expression or reaction of some kind, because she cocks her head to the side and studies me. "You have something to tell me about Officer Santo, Ms. Jackson?"

I sigh loudly, resting my head against the wall.

"Oh, yes. I love this for you," she says giddily, clapping her hands. "You had a crush on him as a kid, right?"

"I did," I answer. "But he never even saw me. Once I was an adult, he was with his wife, and then he *really* never saw me."

"Okay, so what happened?"

I recap the time he helped me out with Rob at the bar, and how I kissed him afterward. "I can't believe I've never heard about this. Weren't all the guys there?"

"Yup," I say. "I think they were focused on Rob, though. And Luca was pretty drunk."

"Dominic came home completely shit-faced," she laughs. "He'd told me he would be DD, then ended up calling a ride share to take everyone home. I took great joy in blasting show tunes the following morning as I drove everyone back to their cars. I'm not sure which one had the worst hangover."

"So it could be that they saw me kiss Alex, but they don't really remember it."

"Possibly. So is that it? Cuz I feel like that's not it," she says slyly.

I sigh again. "No, that's not it. We ran into each other at that community open house event —"

"Oh, I completely forgot about that! You went as a new resident, and it was his turn to be the officer there!"

"And we had a little bit of an argument, but then something was said to him, and I think it triggered him about his wife. He ran out of there, and I followed him to check on him. We ended up sort of having a civilized conversation."

"That's not it," Kate states, her grin wide and infectious.

"We ended up at the same restaurant for dinner, and there may have been some flirting. He volunteered to walk me home, and one thing led to another, and ..."

"Oh my God, you fucked Alex Santo!" she shouts gleefully.

I grimace. "A little louder, girl. I don't think he heard you, wherever he is."

"Well, good for you! I mean, it was good for you, right?"

"Oh, God, yes, it was so good," I admit.

"So? What's the problem?" she asks.

"Alex was very clear that it was a one-time thing. He left at some point in the middle of the night, and I hadn't heard from him since. Well, until today …"

"I fucking love this story," she murmurs.

"You're not going to love this, I don't think. Ben got placed with me."

"Ben? Ben Santo? His son?" Kate's face drops. "Oh shit. You're a fourth-grade teacher. I never even thought about that."

"Yeah, me neither. I knew Alex had kids, but I didn't know their ages. I guess I thought they were older."

"His daughter is. She's twelve. But Ben is nine, almost ten. That late birthday would have held him back a year though," Kate explains.

"Ben's incredibly smart. Possibly gifted," I comment.

"Yeah," Kate says fondly. "When he gets with Carter, I wonder if they could formulate a plan to take over the world." She lets out a vindictive cackle, making my brows raise in question.

"What was that for?"

"Taking over the world? Pinky and the Brain?" When I continue to stare at her in confusion, she rolls her eyes. "You missed out on some excellent nineties cartoons, my friend. Look that shit up online."

"I'll, uh, get right on that. Anyway, Ben asked me to send him home with extra work, but not to tell Alex about it. He said Alex would get mad, because he wants kids to be kids. But if Alex thinks the whole class gets the work, then he can't be mad."

"And I take it Alex got mad?"

"Yup. Showed up in my classroom after school today, ranting about the extra work, and why can't nine-year-olds just be nine. Then asked if I'd disclosed our relationship to the administration team at the school, because clearly, I shouldn't be Ben's teacher."

"God, he can be such an ass when he wants to be," she comments. "Must be a Santo thing, because Dominic is the same way."

"I actually did speak to the principal. Explained that Alex and I had a very brief history before I knew Ben would be my student. But she had already spoken to Ben, checking on him while at recess to see if he was okay with switching classes. She spoke with me today at lunch, telling me he saw her this morning and he spoke highly of me again. He gushed about how he could tell I would be an excellent teacher, and he couldn't wait to see what extra assignments I came up with. He told her that he knew I was going to challenge him better than any of the other teachers in the school. The school, Kate!"

"And Alex doesn't know any of that, does he?" she asks quietly.

I shake my head. "I can't break my promise to Ben."

"So what did you say to Alex?"

"That how I choose to assign work is based on ability level and interest."

"How very diplomatic of you."

"Then he called me Natalie, I told him he needed to call me Ms. Jackson, asked him to leave the room, and he backed me up against the wall and kissed the hell out of me."

Kate's mouth dropped open. "That's — that's not how I thought the story would end."

"Me neither."

"I really hope you two didn't get it on in your classroom," she blurts out. "Even I have a limit for voyeur experiences."

I choke on a mouthful of wine. "No! I pushed him away, he looked horrified, and basically ran out of the room."

"Ah. That's more like Alex. I always figured he had no game with the ladies."

"Really?" I ask. "That's not at all how I've viewed him. He was ... very convincing. Quite dominant. He kept doing that thing with my neck. What's it called? A hand necklace?"

"No fucking way!" Kate shouts. "Oh, I love reading about that. It seems so hot. Dominic does it occasionally, but he's pretty gentle about it."

"Alex was not gentle, I don't think," I admit. "It was hot as hell."

"Damn. I have to admit, I wondered if he lost his confidence after his wife died. Dominic says he's never dated since then, and rarely even has sex."

"You know you can't tell him any of this, right? I have to be professional with Alex now. I have to put Ben first. One night with Alex — and one kiss afterward — isn't a big deal. Besides, I don't want a relationship, or whatever the hell it might be with him. He's clearly not over his grief yet."

"I don't think it's grief," Kate says softly. "I think it's guilt. I think Alex convinced himself that Sara wouldn't have died if he hadn't been deployed. And he hasn't been able to move on from that stage since."

If I were in his shoes, I'm not sure I'd be able to either.

Chapter 9

Alex — Mid-October

I hate when I know I'm wrong, but I can't bring myself to apologize. It's not that I can't ever admit I'm wrong. I'm stubborn, but not *that* stubborn. No, in this instance, it's *to whom* I owe an apology.

The day Ben came home and told me he was moved to the new teacher, I immediately knew it was Natalie. I wanted to call the school and demand he be moved again, but Ben was so excited about the "vibe" he got from Natalie. His word, not mine. He claimed he knew Natalie was going to challenge him better than any other teacher, and he could barely wait until the next day. I tried to remain optimistic, that is, until the first packet of extra work came home. Ben worked for two hours, and only finished a few pages. When I looked at the work, it was well above a fourth-grade level. Granted, Ben is smart, but it seemed intense, and over the top. How are all the kids handling this?

As soon as Natalie said she assigned work based on interest and ability level, I knew Ben was behind it all. Don't get me wrong, I want my son to be happy. But I also want him to enjoy his childhood by just being a kid. Nine-year-olds shouldn't already be mapping out college preparatory classes, and which extracurricular activities will look better on their applications. I love that he has big goals and dreams, but I don't want that to be the only thing that drives him.

Needless to say, Ben has been thriving under Natalie's tutelage. I think he finally has someone who recognizes how he thinks, and understands ways to tap into it. Our pediatrician called it higher order thinking. It isn't just being smart enough to memorize something. Ben can see the problem. I'll watch him look off in the distance, his mouth moving as he works through a complicated math problem that I definitely wouldn't be able to solve without a calculator, and then his eyes will light up when he finds the solution.

I hate that Natalie is the one behind all of this, but I love that my son is being both challenged and supported.

And now I have to tuck tail between my legs, eat crow, or whatever other ridiculous saying can be said here. I have to go into the parent-teacher conference with Natalie and tell her that I think she's doing a great job with Ben.

Usually I bring my kids with me to conferences, but this time I chose to drop them off at my mom and dad's house. It's totally a strategic move, in case our conversation diverges into anything but Ben's education. I'm also hoping I don't lose my cool and kiss her again.

I can't do that again.

So when I roll into Natalie's classroom, I should be relieved when I find her vomiting into a trash can. Instead, I put my foot in my mouth — again, because I can't seem to hold my tongue around her — and blurt out, "Did you come to school with a stomach bug?"

Rightfully so, Natalie glares at me. "Do you ever think before speaking, or do I just bring out the best in you?"

Wiping her face with a handful of tissues, she takes a deep breath. I notice her hand shaking subtly as she carefully removes the lined bag within her trash can, and ties a knot in the top. "Um, I'll be right back. I need a moment."

"Sure. Yeah, okay. That's fine," I murmur. Head down, Natalie quickly walks past me, and I turn away. I usually have an iron stomach, but I'm not the best with vomit. I'd rather not add to her misery by requiring my own walk of shame with a barf bag.

I slowly meander around the room, noticing how bright and colorful it is. When we did the back-to-school night with Ben's original teacher, it was stark and boring compared to this. In just a few short weeks, Natalie has livened up the place. Artwork lines one wall, and large posters chronicling important world events cover another. What appears to be a class library with cozy pillows sits in the corner, and I notice a stack of handmade books on top of one shelf entitled "My Family."

Rifling through, I find Ben's, and immediately whip it open. There are pictures of my parents, his cousins, all his aunts and uncles, and a whole page devoted to his sister. What I don't see is anything about me, or Sara.

"What the fuck?" I mumble.

"I assume you're wondering why neither you, nor his mother, are featured in there," Natalie says suddenly, jarring me from my focus. Turning, I see her standing awkwardly in the doorway. Her face is quite pale, but not as sickly as a few minutes ago. "I asked Ben about that. He said he always talks about you, so he wanted to feature other people in your family."

"That's an interesting explanation," I murmur, staring down at the photos in his book. "How did he get these pictures? He never told me about this project."

"I believe your mom was assisting. Ben said he goes to her house fairly often after school, due to your work schedule."

Oh. That makes sense.

"I guess I'm surprised. Ben usually loves to tell everyone about me being a cop, and about his mom ..." I trail off. How do you tell someone that your kid enjoys talking about his dead mother?

"That's something I wanted to talk to you about, actually. Can we sit down?" Natalie asks, gesturing for me to take a seat at a table shaped like a semi-circle. Once seated, she places her hands over a folder, and I notice she's gripping her fingers together tightly. "First of all, let me just say that Ben is an absolute delight. He has the most unique imagination I've ever experienced, and I love watching him work through problems. He is excellent at helping his peers, and he is usually quite good at finding things to do when he finishes his work early ... which is pretty much every day."

I chuckle. "That sounds like Ben. Alright, hit me with the negatives."

Natalie cocks her head to the side as she studies me. "Excuse me?"

"The shit he does wrong. I know how this works. You're doing the whole positive-negative-positive thing. You've told me a bunch of good things, then you'll tell me where he's not doing well. You'll finish up with positives again. This isn't my first conference, Natalie."

Her lips purse as her eyes narrow. "I believe we discussed that we would not be on a first-name basis in this capacity, Mr. Santo."

I sigh, rubbing the bridge of my nose. "Fine. Tell me what he needs to work on, Ms. Jackson."

"I'm just going to rip off the Band-Aid, okay?" When I nod, she continues. "All the notes from previous years talked about how Ben brought up his mom all the time. He hasn't talked about her once this year. A couple of times I've tried to broach the subject, and he's either shut down and refused to talk at all, or he's had a meltdown. I'd like for him to begin seeing our school psychologist."

I stare at her incredulously. "How the fuck does his dead mother equate into a parent-teacher conference? And where the hell do you get off thinking you have any right to talk about this? We fucked once, Natalie. Get the fuck over yourself."

"There are children in the building, Mr. Santo. I suggest you be more respectful, or I'll let the principal know that you need to be barred from the school," she responds with a glare. Those beautiful green eyes that I've spent way too many nights thinking about seem to have an eerie glow, casting a wicked aura to her stance.

"Fine," I hiss. "But you're out of line."

"No, I'm not," she responds. "I will not apologize for looking at my students from every angle. I've spoken to his second and third-grade teachers. They both agree that his behavior is different this year. I'm not saying anything is wrong with him, Alex. I just want to give him an opportunity to talk to an adult if he needs one. Now, if I suggest you should speak to a therapist, then I'm crossing a line."

"Is that what you're saying now? You think I need to see a therapist?" I explode, standing up so quickly I tip over the tiny kids chair. I grab one leg, standing it upright, and slamming it down against the floor. In contrast, Natalie calmly rises before crossing both arms under her breasts. Not that I noticed them. Really.

"You know what? Yes. I am saying that. Because this reaction isn't okay. It's not normal. Knowing the little I know about you, I can tell you're ready to bite my head off because you think I'm emasculating you. But that's not it at all. I can't even begin to comprehend what you and your kids went through. It's completely unfair that they're growing up without their mother, and you're living without your wife. It's okay to allow others to help. You have no problem asking your parents or siblings for help, whether it be picking Ben up from school, or attending an event when you're working. How is it different to ask someone for help with your heart?"

The fight swooshes out of me in one exhale. What the hell am I doing? I have no reason to be taking any of this out on Natalie. I fall back into the tiny chair, stretching my legs out in front of me, and my foot rests on some kind of blue stool. "I'm sorry. You didn't deserve any of that. I don't even know why I reacted that way."

Natalie slowly sits, leaning toward me. Only then do I notice her hand trembling, and I realize I must have frightened her. God. I'm such a fuck-up. She clears her throat, before quietly stating, "I can't answer that for you. I can say, however, that if I were in your shoes, I'd probably assume the woman had ulterior motives. I can see where you'd automatically think that about me. But I promised you that I would keep things professional here. This is about Ben. Nothing more, nothing less."

"Except the part where you said I needed a therapist," I comment wryly, lifting an eyebrow at her. One corner of her lips tip up in a smile.

"Okay, so maybe that was a teeny bit unprofessional of me. I'm a big advocate of mental health, and I will always suggest seeking out the assistance of a therapist. They may just help you continue through the grief process, or uncover some trauma you don't know you've buried. Or they'll help you find closure — wait, let me finish," Natalie puts up a hand when I open my mouth to interrupt her, "because closure isn't necessarily moving on to another relationship. Closure can be just closing that chapter of your book. It doesn't mean your story is over. Every chapter can be whatever you want it to be."

"Wow," I blurt out, making Natalie giggle. It's a melodious sound that hits me right in my core, a sensation I haven't experienced in so long. "I'm sorry. I've never thought about it like that. When Sara died I felt like my life was over. Honestly, I've been going through the motions."

"I really think therapy might help, Alex. It's definitely helping me," Natalie says softly, her cheeks showing a hint of embarrassment as she looks at her lap.

"You're in therapy?" I ask.

She nods. "My last relationship did a number on me. I knew I needed some help before I could possibly trust another man again."

"That's why you were okay with it being one night," I comment, the sudden realization hitting me square in the chest.

"I'm not saying my trauma is worse than yours."

I nod. "I know. Trauma is trauma. Grief is grief. I guess we're all suffering on some kind of fucked up spectrum."

She giggles again, and I feel weirdly proud of eliciting that sound from her lungs. "The grief spectrum. It's probably a real thing."

When Natalie casts a glance at the wall, I follow her gaze and see we've gone twice the length of my allotted parent-teacher conference time. "Shit, I'm sorry. Do you have anyone waiting?"

"No, you're the last for the day. I'm pretty sure I would have stopped the conversation from getting so off track if I'd had another parent coming in."

"You're only pretty sure?"

"Well, you were on a roll. You're lucky you apologized," she says with a vindictive gleam in her eyes.

"You sound like you're oddly disappointed at that fact."

She shrugs. "Ask your sister if I forgive and forget."

"What the hell does that mean?"

"Oh. Well," she says, scratching the side of her face with a peculiar expression covering her face, "I'm not sure what I should tell you. It may make me look bad as your child's teacher. Suffice it to say I have no problem committing a misdemeanor to support my friends."

"Did you really just tell a police officer you've committed some crimes?" Just when I think I understand Natalie, she throws me a curveball.

"Technically I said I didn't have a problem with it. I never said I had already committed a crime. And hypothetically, any crime would be out of your jurisdiction, since I've only lived here for a couple of months." Natalie looks at me triumphantly, assuming she's bested me.

"That's cute you think I don't have contacts all across the Denver metro who would help me out. You got any warrants, Nat? Should I do a quick search for you or my sister?"

Her eyes narrow slightly. "You wouldn't dare turn your sister in."

"Depends on what the crime was." I totally wouldn't go searching for Arianna's name, mostly because I'm scared of what I might find. My baby sister was a terror when she hit adulthood. I'm lucky Stone was around to keep an eye on her when I wasn't. I certainly didn't know he was fighting his feelings for her at the time, but considering they're married with a toddler now, it all ended well.

And now that I know she was running around with Natalie, and their other friend Claire, I wonder what trouble they got into.

"I'll admit, I'm intrigued by what my sister might tell me about you, but I like knowing you've always had her back," I admit.

Natalie's face softens. "She's like a sister to me. I can't imagine not supporting her."

"I hope my kids are like that one day. I can't see it happening anytime soon. Abbie hates everyone right now."

"My brother and I were like that growing up, too. Now he's one of my best friends. Give her some time, Alex. Puberty and hormones are awful. I can still talk to her if you want someone who isn't a family member," Natalie says quietly.

I take a moment to think about her offer. Abbie bit my head off this morning because I took longer than a second to respond to a question about her hair. Then she burst into tears and refused to eat breakfast. Her question referenced some person I've never heard of, and a YouTube tutorial for a special type of braid. She's lucky I can handle a simple ponytail.

But the thought of letting Natalie into my home, into my family, is scarier than any teen hairstyle I'd have to learn a billion times. "Thanks, but I'm sure we'll be fine."

A flash of something akin to hurt crosses Natalie's face, but she schools her expression quickly. "Let me know if you change your mind."

I nod, tapping twice on the table before awkwardly rising to my feet. "Is there anything else you need from me? For Ben, that is."

"No. He's doing a great job. You should be really proud of him, Alex. You're raising a great kid," she says warmly. After standing, she gestures to me to walk toward the door.

"And, uh," I stammer as I turn to face her, "I appreciate your thoughts on the help. The therapy. The therapy help?"

"I get what you mean," Natalie says, giggling. The sound again makes my heart skip a beat, and I'm incredibly weirded out by the sensation. Avoiding her gaze, I look back where we were sitting, and again notice the odd blue stool.

"What is that thing?" I ask, pointing to it.

"The blue stool?" When I nod, she continues. "It's a chair. Technically it's called a wobble chair. It's designed to help children focus, but also allows some constant movement. It's really great for kids who struggle with ADHD, but everyone can benefit from it."

"That's pretty cool," I comment. "Why do you only have one?"

"Because they aren't cheap, unfortunately," she sighs. "As much as I'd love to buy them, I use my classroom budget for other things that I need more."

"Like what?" I ask. "Doesn't the school give you a budget?"

"A small one, yes. But it's nowhere near enough for what I'd love to have in my classroom. Take Ben, for example. He loves all kinds of building toys, and anything that requires him to creatively manipulate variables to build new items. I'd buy all the kits I could find to have on hand for him, because he also enjoys showing his peers how he's built things. But extending my classroom library takes precedence. And when I need to get more dry erase markers, or colored pencils, or loose-leaf paper, I need some budget left for those things. I still end up paying out of pocket for a lot, though."

"Seriously?"

"Unfortunately, yes. Education isn't a lucrative field, and the schools aren't raking in the dough."

"That's fucked up."

Natalie laughs sardonically. "Trust me, I know. I'm not in it for the money. I've always wanted to be a teacher, and I love it. But the politics at play drive me bonkers."

"You should send home a list of things you'd love to have for your classroom. A wish list. I bet parents would buy stuff, or even give you gift cards," I offer.

She shrugs. "Maybe. But I'm new here, and I don't want to ruffle any feathers."

"Think about it, Nat. You shouldn't be spending your own money on classroom supplies."

"I'll think about it," she replies. Before I can respond, a shrill sound comes from a different table in the room. Casting a quick glance, I see a phone on top of a stack of folders, the screen lit up with an incoming call. I recognize the sound, and immediately know who is calling Natalie.

"You seriously have the ESPN NHL theme song as your brother's ringtone?" I tease, my face breaking into a wide grin. Her mouth drops open.

"I can't believe you recognize that tune!"

"I played as a kid, and my brother played with your brother growing up. And I'm a guy who loves hockey, so yeah. I recognized it."

"I need to answer or he'll assume I'm dead in a ditch somewhere," Natalie says with a laugh. I didn't know Shawn all that well, but I know how I react to things with my sisters. I'm sure she's not too far off on what her brother would think.

I nod quickly as she walks across the room to get her phone, then leave. It's only when I reach the car that I realize she never confirmed her brother was the one calling. I'm even more irritated when it dawns on me how much that fact bothers me.

Chapter 10

Natalie — Mid-October

I've done some pretty embarrassing things in my life.

Dance barefoot on a dirty bar in New Orleans? Yup.

Gotten in a car with a guy I didn't know? Guilty.

Basically stalked a boy I liked in college who literally didn't know I existed, and then got caught outside his fraternity with binoculars? Possibly.

So I'm not too surprised that I'm adding a new item to my list: barf into a trash can in front of your best friend's brother, who also happens to be your only sex in the past few months.

And an even worse detail is that I'm pretty sure I'm puking because said best friend's brother knocked me up.

My period is two weeks late. Actually, I'm not sure how late it is. My period has as big of a personality as me, and has never been very regular. But if I didn't know it was late, I'd be concerned with the other symptoms: my boobs are sore as hell and a half-cup size bigger than normal, I cried watching a TikTok video this morning while eating breakfast, and I snapped at my principal as I ran from the teacher's lounge when I caught a whiff of the catered lunch and thought I was going to hurl all over the floor.

Today quite literally blows.

Since this is a small town, and gossip here runs rampant, I ordered pregnancy tests online. I hate that I had to stoop to that, but I've barely wrapped my own head around this predicament, and I certainly don't want others to be chatting about it. If I am pregnant, I need time to figure out how to tell everyone. Especially Alex. I know he's going to hate me, and I don't know how to start off a co-parenting relationship with that attitude.

Knowing the tests have arrived at my apartment, I'm anxious to get home. But I'm also insanely nervous about taking a test, and I wish I could tell any of my friends about it. But again, Alex needs to be the first to know, and I'm not sure the girls wouldn't tell their husbands.

As I'm debating on texting Claire to see if she'd like to chat, my phone rings. Lo and behold, it's Claire. Answering the call, I say, "Were your ears ringing? I was just thinking about calling you."

"Huh," she says. "It's odd, because I got this weird premonition that I needed to call you."

"Really?" I ask as I climb into my car.

"Yeah. You okay?"

"I'm not sure," I admit. "Can I call you when I get home? Conferences just ended for the day."

"I'm actually in Eternity. Have you eaten dinner? I can grab something."

My stomach revolts at the thought of food, and I swallow harshly. "I'm not hungry. It was a long day, and all I really want to eat is cereal."

"I have days like that too," she laughs. "I survive off cereal and microwavable meals in March and April." Claire is an accountant, and due to the tax deadline of April fifteenth, she's incredibly busy and stressed for the weeks leading up to it.

"I'll be home in a couple minutes," I tell her.

"I'm here already. Should I be concerned that there's a three-pack of pregnancy tests with your name on them by the building door?"

I feel the blood drain from my face. A couple years ago, Colorado did away with plastic bags, and clearly in my barfing stupor, I forgot about that. "They didn't come in a box? Fucking Instacart! I didn't think about the bag thing here. Oh my God! Anyone could have seen them!"

"At least now I know why I felt the need to call you," she says quietly. "I didn't realize you were seeing someone. Unless it's Rob's?"

"It is definitely not Rob's, and I'm not seeing someone," I state miserably. "It was a one-time thing."

Claire hums noncommittally as I drive home. We're quiet for a few moments before I pull in next to the small building where my apartment is. I see she's holding the boxes, carefully covering as much surface as possible, but I can tell they appear to be shrink-wrapped together, as if it was a set of three from the back of a store that hadn't been processed yet. We don't speak as she follows me upstairs to my apartment.

"Where do you think your shopper got these? You'd think they'd just charge you the ten cents for a bag. Must have been a male shopper. They wouldn't think about that kind of thing," Claire whispers when I unlock the door. "How long have they been out here?"

"A couple hours, I think. I didn't check what time I got the delivery notification." Throwing my keys on a shelf by the door, I toe off my shoes and quickly stuff my feet in my fluffy slippers. My studio apartment is tiny, and I mostly sit on my bed, but I've always loved wearing slippers. They make me happy, even in this minuscule room.

"Alright. Spill. Who's the guy?" Claire asks as she pulls off her coat, folding it perfectly, and places it on the back of a chair.

I sigh as I think of how to answer her. "I hate to put you in this position, but I have to ask you not to tell anyone what I'm about to tell you. No one, Claire."

"No one?" she whispers, her eyes wide. "Not even the girls?"

"Especially not the girls." I sit heavily on the bed, staring down at my slippers. "Do you remember me telling you about the night when Rob followed me to that hole-in-the-wall bar, and how someone saved me?"

Claire nods. "You never told us who. Just a guy."

"That's because it was Alex that saved me."

"Alex?" Claire inquires. "Alex Santo?"

I nod. "I never told anyone."

"Why?"

"Because I kissed him that night. And he kissed me back," I confess.

"Okay," Claire drawls out. "Listen, I know it's been a hot minute since you had sex, but you do know kissing doesn't get you pregnant, right?"

I roll my eyes. "I know that, dork. But I ran into Alex again a month or so ago. We were both at the Eternity Springs community night, then ended up having dinner at the same diner. One thing led to another, and —"

"Holy shit!" Claire shouts. "You're knocked up by Alex Santo!"

"A little louder, Claire. I don't think the residents of Denver heard you," I remark dryly. Claire is almost always soft spoken. She carries herself with grace and dignity. It's always a shock when she gets loud and rambunctious.

"No wonder you don't want to tell anyone else. This will get back to Alex so freaking fast."

"I'm not even sure if I'm pregnant."

"You're totally knocked up, Nat. Your boobs are enormous. Well, they're bigger than I've ever seen. I've always been jealous of yours, since I'm basically a minus A cup."

"Thanks, I guess?" I laugh. "And yours aren't minus. Last time I checked, you weren't concave."

"Just speaking the truth. Now go pee on the stick so we can plan a course of action." Claire rips open the shrink wrap, grabs a box, and tosses it to me.

In the bathroom, I painstakingly read the directions, as if I've never taken a pregnancy test before. I've definitely had scares. But this feels different, and I find myself dragging my feet to take the test, knowing my world is most likely going to change dramatically in the next few minutes.

Once done, I slip the test back into the box, wash my hands, and return to my bed. I don't speak, choosing instead to numbly stare at a spot on the wall across from where Claire sits.

"We've never talked about our views on pregnancy before," Claire comments. "Are you pro-life, or pro-choice?"

"I believe every woman should be allowed to choose what happens to their own bodies. As for me personally, I'm pro-life. I know I couldn't abort my baby."

Claire nods in agreement. "That's how I feel, too. I'd hate to be forced into something by someone who has no reason to be interfering in my medical care."

When I don't respond, she continues.

"Furthermore, no man should make decisions about a woman's body unless we can make decisions about him. Why aren't all men given a vasectomy when they hit puberty? Those suckers are reversible, so when he's in a committed relationship and wants to try to conceive, it's an easy fix. A woman can't get pregnant if the man is shooting blanks."

"That's a very interesting theory," I respond, my lips twitching up in amusement. "I have no doubt our government, run mostly by close-minded geriatric males, will totally be on board with your suggestion."

She shrugs as her watch makes a sound. "It kept your mind off waiting for the test, so it's all good. It's been three minutes."

I stare at the box in my hands, suddenly feeling like it's a ticking bomb. "I don't think I can look at it."

Claire stands, coming to sit next to me on the bed. Placing an arm gently around my shoulders, she squeezes reassuringly. "One step at a time, Nat. If it's positive, we'll figure out a plan. You're not alone, okay?"

I nod as my eyes fill with tears. "I — I think I want it to be positive. Not because I want to trap Alex. I figured kids wouldn't be in the cards for me, and now that it might be, I'm afraid of seeing a negative test result."

"Why do you think it wouldn't be in the cards for you?"

I shrug, sniffing as I wipe a lone tear from my cheek. "Rob really wasn't interested in kids, and I think he might have convinced me to be the same way. At the beginning of our relationship, I was happy with him, and I figured I have my students, and they'd be enough. But then watching Hannah and Arianna both have babies made me start thinking about it. I know the older a woman is, the harder it is to get pregnant, so I guess I thought I might be running out of time."

"Look at the test, Nat. Rip off the Band-Aid."

I shakily pull out the test, screen side down, and flip it over, but my eyes are on Claire. "You tell me what it says. I can't look."

I watch as Claire inhales a gasp, and her eyes glaze over. "You're gonna be a momma, Nat. You're gonna be the best momma."

I whip my eyes down to see the word "pregnant" on the digital test, and immediately begin to cry. "Oh my God."

"Who are you telling first? Alex or Arianna?"

I let out a shaky laugh. "Alex, obviously. Plus I'm scared to tell Ari."

"I would be too."

I'm going to be a mom. Cradling my soft stomach, I'm suddenly overcome with maternal protectiveness. I'll make sure this little nugget is happy, even if his or her father isn't involved.

Chapter 11

Natalie — Early-November

Claire spent the rest of that evening with me, mapping out a plan for how I'd tell Alex, my parents, and my brother, but I chickened out on all of them.

It didn't help that I was more exhausted than I'd ever felt in my life, and whenever I was awake, I was nauseous or vomiting. It was a feat in itself how I'd manage to hold in my retching until I could take a break at school. It's frowned upon to leave a class of students alone, obviously.

Knowing the exact date we had sex helped me to determine how far along I was in the pregnancy, which was helpful since I couldn't get in to see an obstetrician until I'm almost twelve weeks along.

My appointment is next week, and I assured Claire I'd tell Alex before that so he could attend if he so desired. I'd already decided to tell Alex he didn't have to be involved, and I expect nothing from him. Knowing him, however, I assume he'll want to attend as many appointments as possible, and provide anything he can for the baby. I've caught myself referring to the baby as a tater tot, and I don't know why.

As the days inch closer to my appointment, I'm still nowhere near ready to tell Alex. I also haven't seen the man once around town, and I don't have his phone number. As Ben's teacher, I absolutely could access the school records to get it, but I didn't feel comfortable doing that for a personal call. Plus, I think this is something that needs to be done in person. I *could* ask Arianna, but that conversation wouldn't go well. "Hey, bestie. Your brother knocked me up a couple months ago. Whoopsie. Can I have his digits to let him know?"

Yeah.

Arianna would blow a gasket.

Which is partially why I have a minor stroke the day before my appointment, cyber stalk Alex, somehow find his home address, and show up at his door a couple hours after dinnertime. It's been a month since our parent-teacher conference, and I've run out of time. Clearly I'm not making good decisions at this stage.

Smart? No. Pregnancy hormones are pushing me to make horrible life choices. I bought a pair of leopard print leggings the other day. Leopard. I also brought in a massive bag of discounted Halloween candy for my students, then sent them all home sugared up and completely wired. Honestly, I was surprised Alex didn't contact me to complain about that one. A hyped-up Ben is a very loud and talkative Ben.

So now I stand on his front stoop, admiring the cute, but somewhat plain, white house at the end of a road, when the door opens. Expecting Alex, I'm surprised when a young girl answers. "Can I help you?"

"Uh, hi. Abbie, right? I'm Natalie Jackson. I'm Ben's teacher," I blurt out, figuring this is my quickest way to get in the house. Jesus. It sounds like I'm trying to case the joint and need entry to do so.

"Oh, hi. Did you come here for Ben?" she asks, her eyes dipping to study my tee shirt and jeans. I automatically look down, noticing a huge stain on the hem. It's brown, so I'm sure Abbie assumes the worst.

"It's chocolate," I announce, rubbing viciously at the stain with my fingernail. "My dinner tonight was chocolate chunk ice cream, and I knew I dropped a piece, but then I got sidetracked and forgot to check again."

"You had ice cream for dinner?" Abbie says with disdain. "That's incredibly unhealthy."

Oh, now I see the attitude Alex is talking about. "Everyone is entitled to a cheat meal here or there, Abbie. It's not like I eat ice cream every night for dinner. Last night I had grilled chicken and roasted potatoes."

I totally didn't. Last night I threw up four times.

"Abs, who's at the door?" I hear called from another room, and my breath catches in my throat. Fuck. Even knowing what I have to do, I don't want to do it.

"Um, it's Ben's teacher? Nancy Johnson?" Abbie shouts.

"Natalie Jackson," I mutter. "But sure, we'll go with Nancy Johnson."

"Nancy Johnson?" Alex asks. "He doesn't have a teacher named Nancy."

Abbie shrugs one shoulder. "Who cares what her name is, Dad. She says she's Ben's teacher. God, just come to the door."

I hear shuffling as Alex rounds a corner, stopping dead when he sees me. "Nancy Johnson?"

"I told her my name," I say defensively. "Not my fault if she has teenage ears that don't work right."

Abbie glares at me. "Rude."

"Oh, you can judge me, but I can't judge you? That's rude."

"I wasn't judging you, I was making a comment about your unhealthy eating habits. That's not judgmental."

"No, you judged me when you stared at the mark on my shirt, and you rolled your eyes when I explained my reasoning for a cheat meal. That's the judgment I'm talking about."

"What the hell is going on here?" Alex mutters before turning to Abbie. "Go see if your brother is done with his homework. Natalie, I mean Ms. Jackson, what can I help you with?"

"Uh, I need to talk to you for a sec," I say as I watch Abbie walk away, seeing her head is cocked just slightly to the side as she eavesdrops. Rude.

"Do you want to come in?" he asks, his intense eyes watching me.

"Actually, can you step outside for a moment? I'd rather talk in private, and your girl there is very much listening." It's mid-November, but it isn't freezing, so I call this a win. I hear Abbie scoff from around the corner, telling me my girl intuition was right on the money about her eavesdropping.

"Abbie!" Alex shouts. "We've talked about this!"

"God!" Abbie whines. "Why won't you let me do anything?"

Alex steps out the door, shutting it behind him.

"You weren't kidding about the sass," I comment.

"I may take you up on your offer to deal with her. I'm losing my mind," he says, rubbing his eyes. "Is something going on with Ben? How did you find out where we live?"

"Nothing is going on with Ben, and I did a simple internet search. You should probably try to lock down the info available online. It was way too easy to find your address," I stammer, trying to force my heart rate to slow down.

"Home sales are public. Anyone can find my address. Why are you here, Natalie? Are you in trouble?"

"Yes," I blurt out. Alex's eyes narrow.

"Is it your ex? Is he stalking you or something?"

"No, it's nothing like that. Alex, I don't know how to say this. Shit," I mutter. My chin drops to my chest.

"Rip off the Band-Aid," he murmurs. Lifting my head, my eyes meet his. He's looking at me with a hint of a smile on his gorgeous face, a couple days of stubble covering his jawline. He doesn't motion for me to get to the point, or roll his eyes impatiently. He just waits me out.

"I'm pregnant," I blurt out, watching his eyes widen. "Shit. I'm sorry. You said rip the Band-Aid off, but I could have been a little more tactful. But yeah, I'm preggers. With child. Knocked up. And, uh, I know this is last minute, but my first appointment is tomorrow, so I thought you should know, in case you wanted to go. But you don't have to. I don't expect anything. I can do this alone, if that's what you'd rather do. No expectations here."

As I rambled, Alex's face drains of all its color. Shock evident, he stares at me without speaking. I handled this so poorly. "Fuck, Alex. I'm doing a really shitty job. Um, I should go."

"You're pregnant," he states.

"Yes," I nod.

His eyes don't leave mine, barely blinking as he seems to digest the information. "And you're sure it's mine? You just got out of a relationship, Natalie. How can you be sure it's mine?"

I take a couple of deep breaths, willing myself not to snap at him like I want to. "I'd had my cycle a couple weeks before we were together. And I hadn't been with Rob in quite some time."

Alex continues to stare at me, saying nothing.

"So anyway, my appointment tomorrow is at a clinic in western Denver, if you want to go," I say with hesitancy clear in my voice.

"I have to work. Why Denver?" Alex asks, crushing my spirit slightly.

"Small town. Didn't want to get the vultures into an uproar until absolutely necessary. And if you don't want anything to do with the baby, then I'll move somewhere else anyway."

"Why?"

I stare at him incredulously. "Seriously? Why would I stay here? I doubt you'd want to see a constant reminder of our night, and I certainly won't want to see you and know you don't want to be in his or her life."

"I never said that," he says suddenly.

I sigh, realizing we're getting nowhere. "Well, now you know. You can take some time to think it over. I'm, um, I'm having the baby, in case that wasn't obvious. So the ball is in your court, I guess."

"What is your end game here, Natalie?" Alex asks angrily, as he reaches out to grip my wrist.

"I don't have an end game, Alex. I'll honor your wishes, whatever they are. Unless you tell me to get rid of the baby. That I'm not doing."

"I'd never tell you that. Christ, Natalie. I'd never say that," Alex responds passionately, then drags one hand through his hair. "I can't — this is my fault."

"It's no one's fault," I say gently. "It happened. It doesn't matter how things transpired. I'm a glass-half-full kind of girl, and I try to find the positives in everything. I'm not going to point fingers at you."

"Well, my glass is fucking empty, so there's that," he says bitterly. "This isn't how this should happen. I can't — I can't fucking believe this. I'm not equipped to deal with this."

I struggle to maintain my composure as I watch Alex fall apart in front of me. I know what he's thinking. It shouldn't happen because I'm not his wife. He should only have children with her. I get it. Really, I do. But it still hurts my heart. I didn't ask for any of this either. I certainly never thought I'd conceive a child with a man who is still desperately in love with his dead wife.

Knowing I'm only a few moments away from breaking into sobs, I shakily pull a ripped piece of paper from my pocket and push it toward Alex. "Here's the address for my appointment tomorrow. If you don't want to go, I understand. Please believe me, okay? I'm not forcing you to do anything. At the bottom is my phone number. If you want to talk or anything. I'm gonna go now."

Alex reluctantly takes the paper from my outstretched fingers, barely holding it between his thumb and forefinger, as if it's tainted. I turn away as the first tear falls, quickly walking to my car. I keep my head bowed so Alex can't see the tears streaming down my cheeks as I slide into my car. I cast a quick glance toward his house, finding him sitting on the stoop, head in his hands, his shoulders shaking. He's crying, and I hate that I'm partially responsible for his anguish.

Driving away, I try to reconcile the feeling that I'll be attending my appointment alone, and I wonder if Alex will even want to be part of this baby's life. I thought he'd surely want to take part, but now I don't know.

Chapter 12

Alex — Mid-November

Pregnant.

I'm going to be a dad again.

I should feel happy. Or at least content. Something.

Instead, I feel devastated.

I'm sitting alone on my back patio, bundled up against the cold November air, trying to find something good out of Natalie's news. All I can feel is pain.

Somehow, I feel like I'm losing Sara all over again. I can't have a baby with another woman. That would mean I'm moving on from Sara. I can't do that to her.

Yes, you can.

God dammit. Not this again.

Don't think-talk to me like that.

"Come on," I groan aloud. Does every widower have conversations with their dead wives, or is it just me?

It's not just you. A bunch of us up here do it. You're the only one who talks back, though.

"This isn't funny, Sara," I whisper. "I can't do this with her. I can't have a baby that isn't part of you."

I gave the best parts of me to you in Abbie and Ben. But you still have more to give.

"No, I don't."

Yes, you do.

"You never argued this much when you were alive," I grumble.

I was safe. She isn't.

Holy fuck. Natalie isn't safe. I never thought about that before. She scares the hell out of me. Natalie and Sara are at opposite ends of the spectrum. Sara was cooperative and peaceful. Natalie is somehow a juxtaposition between patience and chaos. She's colorful and happy, but in a way that feels like she'd jumble up everything into disarray, and still make it look like she planned it that way.

You need her.

"No, I don't."

I feel the moment Sara leaves my thoughts. Like she stated her final opinion, and she knows I need time to come to terms with it.

I need to talk to someone, but I don't know who to call. I should have asked Natalie if any of the girls, especially my sister Arianna, know yet. If they know, their husbands know. And that would mean my parents probably also know.

Picking up my phone, I call Arianna's husband, Stone. He's been my best friend longer than he's been her husband, so I'm hoping he'll keep what I have to say between us for now.

"Hey, man," he says when he picks up.

"Hey. You busy?" I ask, immediately noticing how off my voice sounds.

"I don't have to be," he answers warily. "What's going on?"

"Is my sister right there?"

"She's putting Bianca to bed. Why?"

"Has she told you anything about me today?" I inquire.

"That's random," he laughs. "No, you haven't come up in conversation."

"Huh. I guess that's good, then. I had to have been the first to know," I muse.

"Know what?"

"That I got her friend Natalie pregnant."

A long pause.

"I'll be at your house in two minutes."

Five minutes later, Stone sits beside me on the patio, both of us drinking from long-neck bottles of beer.

"What did you tell Ari?" I finally ask.

"That you needed help with something. So we better come up with a suitable story before I go home," Stone laughs.

"There's no way Arianna knows. She'd have busted in here immediately, and I doubt she'd have kept it from you."

"I agree. I can't decide if she should hear it from you, or Natalie, though. She's going to be hurt either way."

"Take this with a grain of salt, Stone, but your wife can fuck right off with that selfish thinking. This isn't about her. This was definitely not planned. It happened once, and until tonight, I hadn't seen Natalie again. Well, that's not exactly true. But it definitely only happened once. Hell, she had to look up my address on the internet because we never exchanged phone numbers."

"I don't think she'll be hurt in the way you think. She'll know how hard this will be for you, and how much Natalie has struggled. She'll be heartbroken for both of you to be in this predicament. She's keeping the baby, I assume?"

I nod. "I'd never tell her to get rid of it, but she was pretty clear that she was keeping it."

We're silent for a few minutes as we nurse our beers.

"You okay?" Stone finally murmurs, his voice quiet.

I pause before finally saying, "No."

"I figured."

"I feel like I cheated on Sara," I admit.

"You didn't. Sara would say the same thing."

"I know. I hear things in my head in Sara's voice sometimes. It's like she's talking to me. She's been saying 'she needs you' for a few months," I say, with air quotes, "and it took me until today to realize she wasn't talking about Abbie. She was talking about Natalie, as if she knew Natalie was a foregone conclusion."

"Maybe she did. I'm not a very spiritual guy, but I do believe there's a higher being. I won't even begin to think about how things go in the afterlife. Maybe Sara is talking to you. Maybe she knows what's going to happen, and she's asking you to trust the process."

"If the roles were reversed, I highly doubt I'd be welcoming a man into Sara's life," I say with a bitter chuckle. "I'd be haunting that son of a bitch."

Stone laughs. "You say that now. But maybe Sara has watched you suffer for so long that she sent you someone to help you move on."

"I'm not moving on with Natalie," I snap.

"I never said you were moving on with her, man. I said moving on. You're stuck in your grief process. You ever thought about talking to a therapist?"

"Funny you should mention that. Natalie brought it up at Ben's parent-teacher conference."

"Fuck," Stone breathes. "She's his teacher, too? Damn."

"Yeah. That's where I've seen her. Since that night, anyway."

"How the hell did therapy come up in conversation at a conference?" he wonders.

"She mentioned that Ben used to talk about Sara in previous grades, and Sara would be featured in class projects. But this year, Ben has clammed up. Won't acknowledge his mom at all. Natalie suggested Ben might benefit from a children's therapist, and I, of course, snapped at her. Then things snowballed, and she told me the same thing you just said. I'm stuck in grief and I need help to move forward."

"She's a smart one, that's for sure. Borderline psychotic on occasion, but so fucking smart."

"She also insinuated she may have committed some crimes, but that I'd never turn her in, because then I'd have to turn in Arianna, too."

Stone throws his head back in a bark of laughter. "Why does that not surprise me at all? Seriously, you're lucky you were deployed so often when they just hit legal drinking age. Natalie, Arianna, and Claire were such fucking trouble out at bars and clubs in Denver. I could barely keep track of all three of them."

"Arianna told me about one event that you followed them to," I confess. When Stone's head whips to stare at me, I chuckle. "Maybe her twentieth birthday? I don't think she was legal yet. Someone had to be giving her drinks though, because she said you were pissed and basically threw her over your shoulder to bring her home. She was so fucking excited that she had made you mad."

"For fuck's sake," he mutters. "That right there is the epitome of our entire relationship."

"Then," I correct. "It was your relationship then. Anyone within a fifty-mile radius can see how much you adore her. And she'd cut someone off at the knees if they upset you in any way."

Stone smiles. "And she's the calmer one of that bunch."

"Isn't Claire the quiet one?" I ask, taking another pull of my beer.

"Mostly. But when she gets going and really lets loose, there's no telling what might happen. One night last year, the three girls met for dinner and drinks. She told Nat and Ari that she was going home, but then texted them the following day from Alaska."

"Alaska! What the fuck!"

"She's never been fully open about the details of that night. Every now and again, Arianna tries to drag it out of Claire."

"Jesus. I guess Natalie could be worse," I murmur.

"Listen. Natalie is wild a lot of the time, but not in the sense that you think. She's incredibly passionate about her friends and family. She will hunt someone down if they made Arianna cry. She was ready to go to the state board of obstetrics for how an obstetrician treated Kate a few years ago. She fights for the ones she loves. And she's excellent with Bianca. There are worse people for you to knock up. She's one of the good ones."

"I guess it's good that she's a teacher," I comment. "Although she snapped back at Abbie today. I was a little surprised."

"Your daughter needs that. Everyone walks around her like she's breakable. Abbie needs someone to stand up to her, but to also teach her how to stand on her own two feet." Stone's phone buzzes, and he immediately stands. "Shit. Arianna's asking questions. What do you want me to tell her?"

I think for a moment, wondering what she'll believe. "Tell her I'm struggling and needed someone to talk to. That I needed a man's perspective. She can't get mad at that."

Stone lifts a brow. "You clearly underestimate your sister."

I laugh. "Maybe so. Once I know if Natalie wants to tell her personally, I'll feel comfortable letting the cat out of the bag. I don't want to step on anyone's toes."

"This is your baby too, you know," Stone says, then laughs. "God, I can't believe you knocked up Ari's best friend! Now all we need to do is hook Claire up with Leo, and everyone would be linked in some fucked up Santo circle."

"Nah," I say with a chuckle. "Leo's still got a thing for this chick he dated back in the day. He won't say anything about it, though. But I know he does."

"How's he doing?" Stone asks quietly.

"Who knows," I sigh. Leo was injured in a military event overseas. He's always been very hush-hush about his deployments, which I obviously understand. We didn't find out he was injured until a few weeks afterward, and even now, a year later, we aren't exactly sure what he's doing. After multiple surgeries at a military base in Germany, he was moved to a rehabilitation facility in the States. He's either still there, or he returned to active-duty service. Phone calls with Leo are few and far between, and he rarely returns text messages. Even with our common military experiences, he won't open up.

"I should hold off on sharing the baby daddy info with Arianna, right?" Stone asks.

"Yeah. Let me confirm with Natalie what's going on before anyone else finds out. I just needed to talk to — someone. I'm struggling with how to handle this."

"Well, the good news is pregnancy is nine months. So you have time to figure it all out," Stone says quietly, slapping me on the shoulder before walking through my house and out to his car.

I don't sleep a wink that night. My mind whirls at warp speed. How will Ben and Abbie react to a new sibling? What will my parents say? What will Sara's parents say? It's all too much.

A selfish part of me wants to tell Natalie I don't want to be involved. I feel like I'll see Sara every time I'm around Natalie. But I know my own moral compass won't let me. I can't have a part of me walking around, not knowing who I am. Regardless of how this pregnancy is making me feel disconnected to the life I miss, it's a child. A new baby. I get to have a new baby to love.

I'm fairly subdued as I get my children ready for school in the morning, and I notice Abbie studying me more than once. When I ask if anything is wrong, she shakes her head, but continues to watch me.

After dropping Ben off at the elementary school, Abbie finally turns to me.

"Why was Ben's teacher at our house last night?" she asks bluntly.

"Just had to discuss some things with me."

"Then why did Uncle Stone show up a couple hours later?" she asks.

I fail at hiding the smile that threatens to peek out. It's only been a few months that Abbie has been calling him that, but Ben transitioned immediately upon knowing Stone and Arianna were together and expecting a baby. Like in many things, my daughter took her sweet time acclimating to the new normal, which is why I decide to do something very out of character for me.

Pulling over the car onto a side street, I pop it into park and turn to her.

"Dad, what are you doing?" she asks nervously.

"You want to know why Ben's teacher was there, and then why Uncle Stone was there?"

Abbie nods, chewing on the inside of her cheek. Hands gripped tightly together in her lap, I know she's struggling to keep a nonchalant expression on her face. Abbie internalizes a lot, much like me, and it's rare that she shows her emotions. Well, emotions other than snark, and teenage angst.

I take a deep breath and begin to tell Abbie the news that is going to rock her world. "Ben's teacher is a friend of Aunt Arianna. Did you know that?"

She shrugs. "I mean, I guess she looked a little familiar."

"She hasn't been to many family events, but she's definitely been around us because her brother played hockey with Uncle Luca in high school. That's how she met Aunt Arianna."

"Okay?"

"I've run into Natalie a few times over the last few months. She was in a bad relationship with a man who hit her."

Abbie's face noticeably pales. "How long did she stay in it?"

"You know, I'm not exactly sure. I think a couple years."

Abbie scoffs before rolling her eyes. "I don't get why women do that. Why would they stay? The first time a man hits me, I'm outta there."

"I think that's easy for you to say, but when you're in the situation, it's different. I handle domestic disturbances often, Abigail. Men don't suddenly hit a woman. They systematically destroy a woman's self-confidence first, until she thinks she *can't* leave."

"I still don't understand why she was at our house last night, Dad."

"I'm getting to it," I mutter. I try to remember the terminology I used when I gave Abbie the birds and the bees talk a couple years ago. The only thing more awkward than that conversation would be trying to explain what a tampon is, and how to insert one. I haven't had to do that yet, but seeing as I don't have the same bits and pieces as a woman, I plan on asking one of my sisters to step in to assist when the time comes.

"I'm waiting," Abbie huffs, crossing her arms in annoyance. God, the sass from this child of mine.

Rip off the Band-Aid.

"Ben's teacher and I spent a night together," I say hurriedly. "And she came over last night to tell me she's pregnant."

Closing my eyes, I steel my spine as I prepare for Abbie's inevitable explosive reaction, but she shocks me. "Seriously? You got Ben's teacher pregnant?"

"I did," I sigh.

"Wow."

"Yeah."

We sit for a few minutes in silence, lost in our own thoughts. Finally, Abbie breaks the quiet. "How does this work now?"

"What do you mean?" I ask.

"Well, you aren't with Ben's teacher, right?" I shake my head. "So when the baby is born, does it stay with her, or with us? Is it going to have our last name? Who am I allowed to tell? Is that why Uncle Stone came over last night? What did he say? Does Aunt Arianna know yet? Do Nani and Papa know?"

"Only Stone knows. No one else, especially Nani and Papa." My parents will be split in their reactions. My mother will be ecstatic, thrilled to be adding another grandchild to the mix. My father will undoubtedly be disappointed I knocked up a girl out of wedlock.

"How are you feeling about this, Dad? You kinda look like you might hurl, and I swear if you puke on me, I'm not responsible for how I react," Abbie threatens ominously.

I can't help but chuckle. "I'm feeling pretty freaked out, Abs. I never thought I'd have another child, and I certainly didn't think it would be with someone I barely know."

"Well, Aunt Arianna knows her, and we all know she wouldn't allow someone into her inner circle unless they were a good person. Aunt Arianna won't put up with bullshit," Abbie says proudly. It's honestly true, and I'm not surprised that my baby sister has bestowed that little nugget of wisdom onto my daughter.

"That is true," I murmur. Looking over at Abbie, I see her head tilted as she watches me. She looks so much like Sara right now, my chest aches. Reaching up, I cup her cheek. "This is a lot for a twelve year old. But I wanted to be honest with you, and give you enough time to wrap your head around everything."

"I'm stronger than you think, Dad."

"I never said you weren't strong, sweet pea. But you have always needed extra time to adjust when there are major changes to your life. This qualifies as a major change."

"When are you going to tell Ben?" Abbie asks quietly.

I hesitate. "I'm not sure. We'll need to make sure there aren't any district policies about Natalie being Ben's teacher. I need to tell all your grandparents as well."

"Why do you need to tell Grandma and Grandpa? It won't be their grandchild," Abbie comments. My heart squeezes.

"It's still a big part of my life. Of our lives. When they come to see you on your birthdays, there will be another baby there. They deserve to learn about it beforehand."

"They'll probably tell you to have the new one call them Grandma and Grandpa too. They love kids when they're little," Abbie says wistfully. I detect a minor bite to her tone that wasn't there a moment ago, and I'm not sure what it's about. Has she gotten the impression her grandparents don't care about her since she's older? I make a mental note to ask Sara's parents if they've noticed anything when they had Abbie and Ben for the weekend a few months ago.

I vowed after Sara died to make sure I kept Jim and Nancy involved in the kids' lives, and I've stuck to that vow. At first, it helped me to be close to them. It was another piece of Sara that I latched onto with both hands. But over time, I've felt more and more awkward when they've asked about my social life. Nancy point-blank asked me a year ago if I was dating anyone, and I inhaled so quickly that I choked on my food.

Sara was their only child, and I don't know how they'll react to the news of me having another kid. Hell, I don't know how my own damn family will react.

"I'm not worried about anyone else right now, Abs. I'm only worried about you, and what you're thinking. It's okay to be upset, too."

"I'm not upset. I guess it's weird, cuz I'll be so much older than it. And I don't like knowing you had sex," she says with an exaggerated shudder. I've never sugar-coated things with Abbie, and I won't with Ben either. Our birds and the bees talk allowed her to ask me blunt questions, and I've answered her with honesty and truthfulness.

"You'll be almost thirteen years apart," I muse. "I never thought about that."

"Listen, Dad, I'm cool with this whole conversation, but can we get a move on? I don't want to get a tardy."

Effectively put in my place by my twelve-year-old, I chuckle. "As long as you're sure you're okay. You promise to come to me with any questions?"

"I promise, as long as you promise I don't have to change any poopy diapers."

"I'll do my best, but I make no guarantees. If he or she poops while you have them, it's on you."

Abbie lets out a horrified gasp. "Like, *on me*, on me?"

I laugh heartily. "Not literally on you, Abs. That only happens rarely."

Abbie pauses as she digests my words. "Do they really poop on you?"

"Like I said, not very often. But little boys sure do pee on you a lot."

She shudders. "Guess I'm praying for a sister then."

I'm not sure I can take another run at a teenage girl, but I do appreciate this conversation going easier than I thought it would.

Chapter 13

Natalie — Mid-November

"The doctor will be in to see you soon," the nurse says warmly as she hands me a sheet. "Everything off from the waist down. You can keep your socks on if you'd like."

Yes, I'd like. It's about fifty degrees in here, and I'm literally shivering. That could be due to nerves, though.

I never heard from Alex. Not that I expected to, necessarily, but I had hoped he'd let me know if he planned on attending today. I'm sure if I had asked, my mom would have come. But they live over an hour away, and I didn't want to stress her out. Meteorologists are calling for snow today, and she hates driving in winter weather. But more importantly, since she doesn't know about the pregnancy yet, dropping it out of the blue yesterday would have been too much for her.

But I need to tell people. No one at school knows because I'm terrified of it getting back to Alex's family before he can tell them. I think Gail, the principal, suspects something, because she's caught me vomiting in the staff bathroom twice over the past two weeks. The nonstop nausea has been crippling, but the vomiting is the worst. I can't stand puking.

I'm debating on calling Claire for moral support when there's a knock at the door.

"Hi, Natalie. I'm Doctor Morales," a woman says warmly as she steps into the stark white clinical room. The waiting room is warm and inviting, with rows upon rows of baby pictures adorning the walls. But this room is painfully stale and cold. "Will dad be joining us today?"

"Uh, I'm not sure. We aren't together, but I told him about the appointment. I guess he decided not to come," I whisper, suddenly overcome with emotion that I didn't expect. "This is stupid. Why am I crying? It was a one-time thing, and he doesn't owe me anything."

Doctor Morales sits on her stool, wheeling it over to me, and places her hand on my arm. "It's not stupid. You're pregnant and hormonal, and from my records, I see this is your first baby. You're anxious and nervous about all the unknowns. You're completely valid in your reaction, okay?"

I nod as I wipe away an errant tear on my cheek. "Okay."

"Since you haven't had an ultrasound before, I'm first going to do a vaginal ultrasound. If you're far enough along, I'll switch to the external one for your stomach."

"Why do you do an internal one?" I wonder aloud.

"It's easier to see a tiny embryo when the probe is right up against the uterus, and doesn't have to scan through layers of fat or organs. Once the fetus is large enough, abdominal ultrasounds are the better option. Scoot down for me, and put your feet in the stirrups."

I scoot down, then scoot some more, until my ass is hanging completely off the table.

"Okay, I'm going to insert the scope, and you'll feel my fingers. Can you pull the sheet up slightly toward your head?"

"Oh, sure," I say, then immediately yank the sheet so hard it pulls completely off my legs. A perfect opportunity for the door to open, and Alex to walk in, his gaze immediately drawn to my wide open bottom half.

"Oh, shit," he blurts out, turning toward the door as he throws a hand to cover his eyes. "I'm so sorry. I should have knocked. I know how these things go and I didn't fucking knock."

"Dad, I presume?" Doctor Morales says dryly.

"Yeah. Um, should I leave?" he asks bashfully.

"No!" I shout. I'm two seconds away from having a nervous breakdown, and he's the only one here, so he needs to hold my hand and calm me down. "Just get up here so you're not watching the whole show."

I hear him snicker as he carefully sidesteps the small rolling tray holding the probe, then gives me a curt smile. "I'm sorry I'm late. Had to respond to an accident and it took much longer to clear than I anticipated."

I give him a shaky smile in return. "I figured you weren't coming. You didn't text, so I assumed —"

"I know," he interrupts. "I should have texted. Or called. Or showed up at your apartment. Something. I'll be as involved as you want, Nat. As involved as you'll let me."

"Alright, let's get this party started," Doctor Morales says as she holds up the probe, which mostly just looks like a giant wizard's wand with an electrical cord. Definitely not what I expected. I take a relieved exhale as I'm able to focus on her, instead of focusing on Alex. It's what I wanted to hear from him, but instead of feeling peace or happiness, I'm overcome with emotion as tears cloud my vision.

I don't speak as she begins to insert the probe. It's a tiny bit more uncomfortable than a regular gynecological exam, but when Doctor Morales hits a button on the ultrasound machine, a quick beating heart sound fills the room, and I cease breathing.

There is a baby in me. *In* me.

Holy fucking shit.

"Wow," Alex breathes. "Nat, look."

I follow his pointed hand to see the screen on the machine, where I can clearly make out the shape of a kidney bean with limbs. I don't realize I've reached out to grab Alex's hand until he squeezes it.

I'm completely speechless. I'm growing a human. One that will be a mixture of me and Alex. A baby that will depend on me for everything. It's daunting, but exhilarating at the same time.

"From my measurements, I'm putting you at just shy of twelve weeks along. That will put your due date at May twenty-eighth of next year," Doctor Morales states.

"That's good. You can finish out the year," Alex comments.

"Oh?" she asks.

When I don't respond, my eyes unable to move from the image of my baby, Alex supplies the answer. "Natalie teaches fourth grade."

"Ah. As long as you watch signs your body isn't being pushed too much, and sit as often as needed, you should be fine to work well into May."

When Doctor Morales excuses herself to allow me to get dressed, Alex clears his throat. "I'll, uh, meet you in the waiting room."

"Why? Not like you haven't seen it all before," I respond.

"Just trying to be respectful here, Nat. I'm not sure of expectations in this situation."

"Neither am I. But please, just stay. I don't want to be alone," I blurt out. I take a quick glance at Alex to find him staring at me incredulously, both eyebrows raised. "Did I stun you into silence?"

"Maybe a little," he admits with a low laugh. Scratching at the scruff on his chin, he grabs onto his bullet proof vest, holding onto the neckline that sits snugly against his collarbone. My eyes automatically dance down his body, admiring how handsome he looks in his uniform.

"I've never seen you up close in your uniform before."

"I'm not surprised. We work similar hours for the most part, and I'm never at the elementary school."

I stare unabashedly, somehow finding it incredibly hot to see his holstered gun. But my eyes bug out when I notice the gleaming handcuffs, and my mind immediately takes me to a dark place where all of my fantasies go to die.

"Eyes are up here, Nat," Alex says with a laugh.

"Huh?"

"You're staring at my crotch."

"That is incorrect. Technically I was staring at your belt, which is on your waist."

"Care to enlighten me as to what on my belt had you so riveted?"

"No. And since you got quite the view as you came into the room, I think it's only fair that I do as well."

He laughs again, a sound that fills me with joy. For as long as

I've known Alex, he's always been introverted. He exudes power, but he's quiet and focused. Alex doesn't give out his laughs willy-nilly, and I feel like I need to memorize them when they're focused on me.

"Alright. Get dressed. I have to go back to work," he says finally, but a newfound twinkle in his eye stops my movement again. This is new. Very unlike the stoic Alex Santo that I've known. "What? You're looking at me weird."

"Nothing," I say hurriedly. "Just feel bad you have to go back to work."

"How'd you get out of teaching this afternoon?" he asks, turning so I can get dressed in privacy.

"Just told them I had a medical appointment, and I couldn't find any times that worked better. I think my principal is on to me, though. She's caught me barfing a couple times."

"You've been throwing up?"

"Yeah. At least once a day. I just wish it helped with the nausea. Basically I feel like shit all the time." I quickly slip on my underwear and leggings before sitting to slip my feet into boots.

"Sara threw up every morning as soon as she woke up, and then she'd be nauseated until dinnertime. The doctors were worried about her weight because she was so skinny."

"Well, that won't be a problem for me," I mutter. I'm surprised Doctor Morales didn't talk about my weight during the appointment. Not only am I creeping up on 'advanced maternal age,' but I'm also obese. Most doctors latch onto that with all their claws. Casting a quick glance at Alex, I assume I'll find a pained and anguished expression on his face as he reflects on memories of Sara, but instead, I find him staring at the ultrasound picture in his hand. He looks almost pleased. Peaceful. Borderline happy. But his head whips up to stare at me.

"What do you mean it won't be a problem for you?" he asks.

I shrug as I feel my face warm, looking down at my boots. "Obviously I won't have to worry about being too skinny. I could stand to lose a few pounds."

Bending down to scoop my purse off the floor, I move to scoot past Alex, but his hand on my forearm stops me.

"What?" I ask quietly.

"I don't ever want to hear that kind of talk come out of your mouth." His voice is so low, dangerously low, that I refuse to make eye contact. I'm afraid of what I might find, and I don't need another reason to find him attractive. Just hearing him speak right now is making me horribly wet.

"I'm not saying anything out of the ordinary," I say defensively. "I'm fat. I get it. It is what it is. I like my body. I own it. But I know I'm fat."

"You are not fat."

"But I am. Clinically obese. I wear size eighteen clothes, Alex. That isn't a normal size. I'm fat. It's fine. You don't need to be the prince who strides in and says all the right words to save the day."

I try to get past him, but he puts a hand on the door, ensuring it stays closed. "Your body is fucking spectacular, Sunflower. Your curves are what men dream of. I remember every inch of you, and I know how toned you are. You aren't fat. You're voluptuous and breathtaking. They can take their stupid BMI tests and shove it up their asses, because they're wrong about you."

I'm in complete shock as my eyes meet his. Alex stares back intensely, as the air around us crackles with electricity. His touch on my arm is like burning embers, setting me on fire in a way that I've thought about too much since our night together.

As quickly as the moment came, it's broken when Alex steps away, quickly opening the door. "I'm sorry, I have to go."

Before he can lurch out of the room. I call out for him. "I want to tell Arianna. Or at least I want her to know. Do you think it should be you who tells her?"

Alex scratches his chin thoughtfully, but I notice he avoids eye contact. "Honestly, I think it would be better coming from you. I'm her brother, but you're her best friend."

"I think you don't want her to hurt you," I tease.

He chuckles and nods. "She's always packed one hell of a punch, and I know she won't hit you." He gives me a subtle smile, taps the door twice, then strides down the hall.

I decide to stop by Arianna's on the way home from my OB appointment. I don't want to hide this from anyone, and she needs to be the first to know.

Ignoring my churning stomach, I slowly walk up to Arianna's front door, feeling like I'm walking up to a firing squad. When Stone answers the door, he chuckles. "You ready for this?"

My mouth drops open in shock. "You know, and you haven't told her?"

"Told me what?" Arianna asks as she rounds the corner with Bianca toddling behind her.

"I'll leave you to it. Come on in, Natalie," Stone says warmly, then grunts as Bianca barrels into his knees. "At some point, she's going to learn how to give soft hugs, right?"

"Dada wub do," Bianca says as she wipes her nose on Stone's sweatpants. I notice her cheeks are fairly pink, and she looks pretty miserable.

"What did she say?" I ask.

"Wub do is love you in Bianca language. She can mostly say it correctly, but the congestion and fever have made it pretty difficult for her to speak coherently," Arianna explains.

"Well, wub do is pretty adorable."

Stone shuts the door behind me. "I'll take her for a bath, see if the warm water and steam can loosen up some of the gunk in her lungs."

"Good idea," Arianna agrees. "Let's have a glass of wine, Nat. I feel like I haven't seen you in forever."

Shit.

"Uh, no wine. Not drinking."

She raises an eyebrow as she studies me, pulling down one wine glass from a hanging rack next to her kitchen. "Who knocked you up?"

"Um," I stammer nervously. "Well, that's actually why I'm here."

"What?" she shrieks. "That was a joke! Are you really pregnant?"

I nod. "Can we sit down?"

"Oh my God, yes. Shit. I won't drink either, then. Camaraderie. No preggo left behind. Wait. I'm not pregnant, so that didn't make any sense. But you understand what I'm saying. Shit, Nat! I can't believe you're pregnant!" Pushing me into their great room, I marvel at how much the home has changed since Arianna moved in with Stone. Stark white walls have been replaced with a soft blue paint. Framed photos are haphazardly strewn throughout the room, some on the walls, and some on tables. I can't help but smile when I see one of me, Arianna, and Claire when we were teenagers, then another picture only a few years ago including Hannah and Kate. I've created quite the little found family here, and I'm petrified my news is going to shake up our dynamic.

Sitting down, Arianna shakes with excitement. "How are you feeling? Do you know how far along you are? Have you puked a ton? Do you have a baby bump yet? Wait. You can't be that far along. I'd have known already. Do you need the name of an OB? I really like the one in town. Hannah and I have both used her."

I take a deep breath. "I'm around twelve weeks, I think. Actually eleven. Yes, I puke constantly, and the nausea never goes away. I don't have a bump, and I used an OB in Denver."

"Why did you go to Denver for an OB? Why didn't you ask me for a recommendation?" she asks, her expression puzzled.

"Because I didn't want the rumor mill to get wind of it just yet. Not until I told everyone, especially you," I say quietly.

"Why?" she whispers, her face draining of color.

My eyes well with tears. "Because I'm scared you're going to hate me, and then I'll lose my best friend in the whole world, and then everyone will turn on me and I'll have no support whatsoever, and my family is too far away to do anything, so I'll be a miserable single mom with no one."

Arianna's eyes dance between mine as she processes the information. "The only way you could possibly think I'd hate you is if you got pregnant by one of my married brothers."

"Oh, no. I didn't get pregnant by one of your married brothers. But I did get pregnant by Alex."

Her eyes bug out comically wide, and she snorts. "Alex? My oldest brother, who can barely stomach being in the same room with the opposite sex without waxing poetic about his dead wife? The same Alex who barely says two words to anyone when he's in public? That Alex?"

I nod, but find myself defending him. "He's not always like that. At least that's not what I experienced. And you don't know the half of what he's done for me. Remember me telling you that Rob followed me to a bar, and that a guy stepped in to separate the two of us?"

"Oh my God," Arianna breathes. "That was Alex?"

"Yeah, but I didn't tell you, or anyone for that matter, that I kissed him that night. And he kissed me back. Well, for a couple of seconds. Then he freaked out and bolted."

"That's the Alex I know," Arianna jokes painfully.

"Then we ran into each other at that community night for new residents, and we ended up at the same restaurant for dinner. One thing led to another, and I was inviting him back to my apartment. I didn't think he'd actually say yes, but he did. We agreed it was a one-time thing, but here we are." I sniffle, thinking back to waking up that morning, and being disappointed Alex was gone. I knew it was only a one-night situation, but I guess I'd hoped to say goodbye. Or get a morning dicking before he left.

"Does Alex know about the pregnancy?" she whispers.

I nod. "I told him last night."

"How long have you known?"

I wince, embarrassed at how long I held onto this information. "About a month. I kept thinking I'd talk to him when I saw him, and ask to meet up. But I haven't seen the guy at all! So I finally had to do some cyberstalking to find his address, and I showed up at his house last night. Your niece is a piece of work, by the way."

"Oh, yeah. The sass on that one is strong. How did Alex react?"

I close my eyes as tears fall. I'll never forget the look on his face, or seeing him cry. "Not well. But he showed up at my appointment today, which is good. I'd expected to go it alone."

"He'd never do that," she says resolutely. "My brother can be a complete jackass, but his moral compass is borderline perfect. He'd never expect you to go through any of it alone. Jesus, Nat. I can't believe you're pregnant!"

"I know," I say, with a chuckle, as I wipe my eyes. "Are you okay with this? I can't lose you, Ari. You're the sister I never had."

"Of course you won't lose me!" she cries, wiping her own cheeks. "Is it going to be awkward with Alex? What have you guys discussed moving forward? Co-parenting? Oh! You should move in with him! Then it would be easier for both of you to be with the baby."

"We haven't gotten that far, girl. Like I said, I'm only eleven weeks. I literally just told him yesterday."

"Oh God, Thanksgiving dinner is going to be epic," she says with a snort. "You going home to your parents? You should come to our family event. It's always chaotic, but it's fun."

"I don't think that's wise," I say hurriedly. "I don't think Alex has told anyone other than Stone."

"That MOTHERFUCKER!" Arianna bellows. "I knew something was up when Stone went over there last night, but he acted all nonchalant. 'Oh, Alex just needed some help.' That's bullshit! Do our marriage vows mean nothing to him?"

"In sickness and in health does not mean I gossip about your brother's news, Princess," Stone drawls from the hallway. "It was their story to tell, not mine."

"God dammit," she mutters. "I hate when he's right, and he's all nice about it, not rubbing it in. Sanctimonious jerk."

"I heard that," Stone calls.

"Whatever." Arianna glares in the direction of her husband.

"Stop glaring at me."

"I wasn't—"

"Yeah, you were. Don't lie."

Arianna growls next to me, and I let out a loud guffaw of laughter. "It's almost scary how well he knows you."

"Then he should already know he's sleeping on the couch ton — God dammit!" she shouts, as Stone rounds the corner with a blanket and pillow in his hands.

"Precautionary. We both know you'll let me back in the bed by midnight," he says huskily as he drops the items next to Arianna, bends down to apply a quick kiss on top of her head, winks at me, and heads back through the hallway.

"I'm angry with him right now, but he's absolutely correct," she says sheepishly, shaking her head as we both laugh.

Someday, I hope to have a love like they do.

Chapter 14

Alex — Late-November

My parents were much more accommodating about Natalie's pregnancy than I thought they'd be, surprisingly enough. I assumed my mom would be excited, but Dad is excited too. He's gotten much more go-with-the-flow since he fully handed over the hotel reins to Dom, and it's good to see him be relaxed for a change. As for my brother, having Kate in his life has only made things better for him, and he's finally figured out how to delegate.

It's been ten days since Natalie's first OB appointment, and I haven't spoken to her. I know, it's a bullshit move. But I misplaced the paper with her number on it, and I'm too scared to ask Arianna for it. That expression 'she is tiny, but fierce' was very much made with Arianna in mind. She would have no problem cutting off any of my appendages, and I'm kinda partial to all of them. Including the one that got me in this predicament in the first place.

Tonight I'm telling Jim and Nancy about the baby, and I'm more nervous about telling them than I was with my own parents. I've always brought the kids to their house for an early Thanksgiving dinner the Sunday before Thanksgiving, because my entire family has a massive meal on Thanksgiving proper. Jim suggested it first, knowing that my kids would enjoy spending time with their cousins on Thanksgiving.

What I didn't expect, however, was the fact that Jim and Nancy would take it upon themselves to invite a single woman to their dinner.

"Who's this?" Abbie bluntly asks as we hand our coats to Jim.

"Abigail, this is Bethany," Nancy explains. "When we found out she would be alone for Thanksgiving, we had to invite her for dinner."

"It's not Thanksgiving," Abbie deadpans. Brows low on her face, she glares at Nancy and Bethany. "Pretty sure you know how to read a calendar, Grandma."

"Oh," Nancy says with a light laugh. "This is our Thanksgiving though. Your grandfather and I don't celebrate it on Thursday. Bethany was understanding. We thought she might like to meet the three of you."

"You thought wrong." Damn. Abbie is pissed. I can feel the animosity coming off of her in waves of teenage hormones and rage.

"Now, Abigail," Nancy starts, but Abbie interrupts her.

"No. This is awful, Grandma. Dad is perfectly capable of meeting someone himself. You shouldn't insert yourself in his business."

"Oh, well, I guess that's true," Nancy murmurs.

Bethany makes no effort to hide her thoughts as her eyes slowly drag down and up my body. I get a lot of looks like that when I'm in my police uniform, but getting it while dressed in slacks and a sweater is new, and I'm not sure that I like it.

You'd like it from Natalie.

"Not now, Sara," I hiss.

"What?" Bethany asks.

"Nothing." I motion for Bethany to walk in front of me, then turn to Nancy, lowering my voice. "Please tell me this is all a coincidence, and you didn't bring a woman here for me."

Nancy gives me a pat on the arm. "We just want you to be happy, Alex. It's been five years, and we don't see you moving on."

"If I wanted to move on, I would have already done it," I say through gritted teeth. "This is insanity. I loved Sara. I can't just move on from that."

"Dad, I told Grandpa about the new baby!" Ben shouts from the hallway.

Nancy's eyebrows raise. "What baby?"

"I don't think Dad was ready for that, Benny," Abbie says with a wicked grin. Leave it to her to find joy in my suffering.

"Shit," I mutter. "Not how I wanted this to come out. And sorry, Brittney, but whatever Nancy convinced you may happen, it won't be. Ben and Abbie will be getting a brother or sister next spring. No, I'm not with the mother. We're going to make it work as co-parents," I pause, realizing I've never spoken to Natalie about, well, anything, "I think."

"Jim," Nancy bellows, her eyes never leaving mine, "bring out the good bourbon."

"Already did, hon," he hollers back.

"Um, so," Bethany says as she points back and forth between us, "no chance of anything?"

"Yeah, that's a no. My plate is a little full," I tell her honestly.

She turns to Nancy. "I'm gonna go. Nancy has my number if you change your mind."

It's an awkward goodbye in the entryway as Bethany finally scoots past all of us, but not before she settles a hand against my abs and drags her hand around my waist.

"What the fuck?" I mutter, grabbing her wrist and tossing it to the side.

"Oh, I'm sorry. It's tight to fit in here."

"You had more than enough room. You groped me in front of my daughter. Rest assured, Barbie, I won't be calling you."

"It's Bethany," she says, irritation evident in her tone.

"I really don't care," I say, turning away from her. Grabbing Abbie's hand, I move us down the hallway and into the dining room. Jim gives me a look as he hands me a tumbler of bourbon. "Thanks."

"You're gonna need it, son. Nancy will have questions."

Two hours later, on my third glass of bourbon, I'm feeling incredibly relaxed. I rarely drink, and their 'good' bourbon is indeed quite good.

Nancy has already offered up her guest room, and since the kids are off all week for Thanksgiving break, I'm taking her up on the offer. Abbie and Ben share a room here for the time being, but I can see Abbie wanting her own space as she gets older. Right now, she tolerates Ben.

"So, tell us about the girl," Nancy finally prods. I look around the room to find Ben immersed in a game on his iPad, headphones in place, and I know he won't hear a thing. Abbie went upstairs right after dinner, after rolling her eyes in disgust at the dessert selection. I asked if she wanted anything, she started to cry, then ran upstairs and slammed the door. I have no idea what set her off.

"Hmm?" I mumble, eyes closed as I lounge on the couch. Nancy is an excellent cook, bringing out all the traditional Thanksgiving dishes. She also made a pumpkin pie from scratch. Not canned pumpkin. From scratch.

"The girl. The one having your baby," Nancy says gleefully.

"I can't believe you're happy about this," I respond.

"Why wouldn't I be?"

"Because it's not Sara's. You don't even know Natalie. She could be an ax murderer. A serial killer. A Republican." Jim and Nancy make no qualms about sharing their political views, but they also don't argue about them.

"We wouldn't care if she's a Republican, and we know she couldn't possibly be either of the other options."

"How do you know?"

"Because we trust you, and we know your family. You said she's been a friend of your sister's for years. Your family wouldn't allow a bad seed to infiltrate their circle."

I think back to my brother Dom's first wife, Savannah, and what a bad seed she turned out to be, but I don't bring it up to Sara's parents. They rarely interacted with Savannah, and I don't want to talk about it.

"Abbie says Natalie is Ben's teacher," Jim pipes up.

I groan. "Damn narc."

"Is that allowed? I'm not accusing anything. I'm wondering what the rules are for schools these days."

"I'm not sure. I haven't talked to her in a couple weeks."

Nancy gasps. "Alex! Why on earth not? You should be checking in with her every day!"

"I didn't want to make her feel uncomfortable. Well, that's not true," I admit. "I didn't want to feel uncomfortable. I don't know how to talk to her now. Everything is a mess, and I hate it."

"You've never dealt well with big changes," Jim comments. When I look up at him, he throws his hands up. "What? I might be quiet, but I pay attention. Never could understand how you could deploy with no issues, but then have difficulty with getting used to a new car."

I chuckle. He's not wrong. "There are a lot of unknowns in deployments, but it's still a job, and I knew it well. I hated being away from Sara and the kids, though. I put on a brave face for them, but I'd have at least one night of crying once I got over to the sandbox."

"They'd put on a brave face for you too, you know," Nancy says quietly. "Sara would bring the kids here, usually the weekend after you left, and she admitted it was tough being home without you. She was so proud of you, though. So proud."

"I miss her so much," I whisper, scrunching my eyes closed as I feel the sting of tears forming behind my eyelids. "So fucking much. If I hadn't been gone …"

"Then you might have been in the car with her, Alex," Jim says. "Or all four of you. I can't imagine the grief you must feel, and I know we exacerbated that by our own grief when we tried to take the kids. But you are not responsible for Sara's death. You hear me?"

I don't fight the tears that roll down my cheeks. "I am responsible. I am! She wouldn't have been on the road at that time. The kids wouldn't have been at my parents. I'd have been there. I didn't get to say goodbye. I'll never forgive myself for that."

"No one got to say goodbye," Nancy says tearfully. I hear a sniff, and look up to see her dabbing a tissue on her cheeks. "I take great relief in knowing she was killed instantly, Alex. That she had no fear, no pain. And while her life was short, she was so unbelievably happy. She got to be a wife and mother, thanks to you."

"Why don't you hate me more?" I wonder aloud. "If she'd never met me, she may have married a different guy. Lived down the street from you. She might still be alive."

"Or she could have died in a car accident years before she did. You can't play the 'what if' game here, Alex. We have no idea what might have happened if she never met you that day after the football game. All I can tell you is I know my daughter, and if I could ask her right now if she regretted marrying you or having those two kids, she'd say absolutely not."

She's right.

I can't help but chuckle.

"I don't think anything I said was funny," Nancy says, her tone snappy.

"It's nothing you said. The last few months, I swear Sara talks to me. She said you're right about her not regretting marrying me, by the way," I confess.

Jim smiles widely. "She talks to me when I'm working in the garage."

Nancy nods. "When I'm in the garden."

"Isn't it weird? I feel like I'm losing my mind sometimes."

Nancy shrugs. "Maybe it's all in our heads, or maybe she really is talking to us. I won't sit here and claim to understand how death and the afterlife work. All I know is thinking about Sara, and hearing her voice, makes me happy."

"It makes me miss her even more," I say quietly. "I need to hold her and tell her all the things I should have said thousands of times. I want to feel her hand in mine, and smell her grapefruit scented shampoo. And every time I argue with Abbie, I want to point at Sara and remind her that her mini-me is a hormonal teenager, and that Sara should deal with her now."

"We've never brought this up before, but I think now is as good a time as any. Son, you need to speak with a professional. Someone who deals with death and grief." Jim looks intensely at me, waiting to see my reaction.

"I don't see how me dredging up the past is going to help anything. I can't bring her back," I snap.

"You're stuck in the anger phase of grief, Alex. And that's not good for anyone in your family. Now that you're going to be bringing a new baby into the world, you need to think about the future. It's like you're in this big lake, and your head is barely above water. You're not moving, you're just waiting to drown," Nancy says softly.

I look around the room, still adorned with pictures of my wife. Our wedding day, pics with the kids, and even her college graduation photos. I find myself rubbing my fist around my chest, hoping to quell the ache inside my heart.

"You know we love you, and we've always loved you. You're like a son to us," Jim says, clearing his throat. "But if coming here is too painful for you, we understand. We've moved past our grief, and it's clear you're not there yet. For the sake of your children, Alex, you need to speak with someone."

I'm quiet as I help get the kids ready for bed. Quiet as I strip down to my boxers in the guest room, and quiet as I think about everything Jim and Nancy said. They aren't wrong. I'm barely keeping my head above water. Sara was my partner. She was who brought me happiness. There was a comfort there, a level of contentment, that I'd never experienced before. I don't think that is something I can replicate with anyone.

But they're right. I can't keep living like this, with my feet firmly in the past. My children deserve more from me. Tomorrow, I'm calling around for a therapist. I fall asleep quickly, but wake abruptly when I dream of holding her.

Not Sara.

I dream of holding Natalie.

Three incredibly busy days meant I didn't try to find a therapist. In fact, I barely thought about it again. I certainly didn't dream about Natalie every night either.

That last one definitely didn't happen.

More than once each night.

Thanksgiving arrives, a cold, blustery, and snowy one that brings an eerie sense of quiet and calmness to Eternity Springs. Up until last year, we had our Santo family Thanksgiving at my parents' house, but we're quickly outgrowing that. This year, my parents decided to save one of the banquet rooms at Everlasting for our dinner. Some of my siblings choose to stay at the hotel for the night. I like my own bed too much, so I intend to drive home. After spending too many holidays on crappy cots, or even hard floors, I refuse to sleep anywhere that might be uncomfortable. I'm getting too old for that.

A decade ago, Dom began a new tradition of blacking out large portions of rooms on Thanksgiving or Christmas. He flip-flops every other year, using it as an opportunity to whittle down the staff needed to work the holiday. Yes, my family takes a hit on income, but we've always valued employee contentment highly, and our retention every year shows that.

Commandeering the hotel kitchen for the day has made my mom entirely too giddy. Nothing makes her happier than cooking for her family, especially when almost all of us are home. She plans to make double this year so the few hotel guests we have will still get a traditional Thanksgiving meal, and many of my siblings are flitting in and out of the kitchen as we take orders from our mom.

We all received a quick 'Happy Thanksgiving' text from Leo, but none of us have spoken to him. But now, as Mom happily traipses around the kitchen, enjoying the use of all the professional appliances, I sit on one of the covered patios on the back of the hotel, enjoying a cigar with Dom. It's not something I do very often, but it's nice to relax and shoot the shit with my brother.

"How was dinner at Sara's parents' house?" Dom asks.

I shrug, taking a slow puff on the cigar before blowing a ring of smoke into the crisp air. "It was fine. They tried to set me up. Had a girl there and everything."

"No fucking way," he laughs.

"Yeah. Abbie was pissed."

"What doesn't piss Abbie off these days?"

"Not much. But she was more mad because of other things."

"What?" Dom asks, sitting up to put his elbows on his knees. Watching me, he waits for me to explain.

I sigh. "Gonna rip the Band-Aid off here, Dom. I had a one-night stand a few months ago. She's pregnant."

"Holy shit," he breathes, sitting back into his chair with a loud slam. "That is not at all what I thought you were going to say."

"It kinda gets worse," I stammer.

"Fucking hell," Dom mutters. "How the hell could a one-night stand getting pregnant have something worse?"

"It's one of Arianna's friends," I blurt out.

"Oh shit. Yep, that's worse."

I nod in agreement. We're silent for a few minutes, the only sounds from puffing on cigars and light snow landing on the ground in front of us. It's a beautiful scene, one that never gets old to me. While many of our hot spring areas are closed in the winter months, we have half of the springs and pools open. Today, however, the entire spa and hot springs area is closed, and it's so peaceful and quiet.

"Which friend?" Dom finally asks.

"Natalie Jackson." I turn to see our grandmother staring at me with a victorious expression on her face, as if she's stolen a handful of cookies from the cookie jar.

"That name sounds really familiar," Dom murmurs, before snapping his fingers. "She teaches at the elementary school. Shit, she's Ben's teacher, isn't she?"

"It doesn't surprise me that you'd be interested in her. Here, give me a puff," Nonna says, sitting beside me on the lounger. I'm too shocked to respond as she plucks the cigar out of my mouth, taking a couple drags on it, then hands it back to me.

"What the hell, Nonna?" Dom says incredulously. "Since when do you smoke cigars?"

Nonna raises one eyebrow as she stares back at Dom. "Once upon a time, gentlemen, I was the life of the party. I could tell you amazing stories from Woodstock. Well, the parts I remember."

I turn to my brother. "Wouldn't Dad have been born by then?"

"Yes, he was. He went, too."

"You had a kid at Woodstock?" Dom asks.

"There were tons of children there. It wasn't all drugs and parties." Nonna turns to me. "So. You're having another baby."

"Yes." No reason beating around the bush. Nonna is like a bloodhound sometimes. She'll sniff out the details, regardless of whether I participate in the conversation.

"Well, are you marrying her?" she asks.

"What? No! Why would I marry her?"

"Because you'd be doing the right thing. Supporting her and the baby. It's fine if you don't want to, but I'm honestly surprised your moral compass is allowing you to do that."

I rub the bridge of my nose in annoyance. "I don't like how everyone assumes I'm perfect and never think about doing bad things."

"It's not that exactly. Everyone thinks bad things. That's human nature. We just know you won't allow yourself to do anything bad." Dom gives me a look, almost daring me to argue.

"Clearly I had a one-night stand, so your argument is invalid."

"It doesn't matter, Alessio, because you're going to fall for her, and then your family will be complete again," Nonna says matter-of-factly.

Before I can respond, Kate pops her head outside. "Sorry to disturb the brotherly bonding, but Alex, Natalie is here? And she says she's looking for you?"

"What the hell?" I murmur.

"She came here looking for you? That's creepy," Dom says quietly.

"She doesn't have my phone number," I admit.

"Jesus Christ, man. She has no way to contact you? That's incredibly fucked up."

"I know." I won't try to deny it. I cannot compartmentalize Natalie, and I don't know how to move forward.

As I walk quickly to the front of the room, I see Arianna glaring at me. I clearly see her mouth, "motherfucking jackass" and I don't disagree. I'm absolutely a jackass right now. When I approach Natalie, I immediately realize something is wrong.

"I'm sorry for just showing up. Arianna invited me, but I was going to go to my parents' house in Greeley. Then it started to snow, and I decided to stay home."

"It's fine, we always have extra food —" I start, but Natalie interrupts me.

"No, Alex, you don't understand. I'm bleeding a little, and I'm freaking out, and I don't know where to go. Or what to do. Everyone is here, except for Claire, but she's way out in Denver, so I just figured I'd come here and maybe get Ari or Kate. But they're with their families, and I have no one, and …" she trails off as she hiccups, then sobs a little as she looks around. "They're all staring at me. Do they know?"

"No, not everyone," I murmur absentmindedly.

"*Angiolo*? Is everything okay?" Mom says as she steps next to us.

"I shouldn't have come here. I'm sorry. I interrupted your dinner," Natalie says hastily, trying to wipe an errant tear away.

"We haven't eaten yet, Natalie. You're welcome to stay," Mom answers. "How are you feeling?"

Natalie's mouth drops open, as her eyes whip to mine. "Okay, so *she* obviously knows. Mom, Nat said she's bleeding a little."

The smile gets wiped from my mom's face immediately as she ushers us out of the room. Calling back to my dad, she says, "Get Travis."

"Travis?" Natalie whispers.

"Giana's husband. He's a paramedic," I respond.

Mom brings us to couches beside the massive stone fireplace that adorns the wall looking west. As I sit beside Natalie, I notice she's shaking. "Are you cold?"

"A little, but it's fine," she says hastily.

I'm wearing a sweater over a long-sleeve shirt, and I immediately yank off my sweater. "Arms up."

When she doesn't move, I push the sweater over her head. "Alex!"

"Well, I gave you a chance to follow directions, Sunflower."

"You still haven't told me why you call me that," she murmurs, her voice muffled as we work together to get the sweater on.

"Yeah, and I won't be telling you today either."

"Fine," she huffs. "At least tell me what your mom called you back there."

"*Angiolo*? It's angel in Italian."

"Of course she calls you all that," Natalie mutters.

"No, just me."

"Seriously?"

"She has different nicknames for all of us."

"Just when I think your family is the cutest it can be, you up the ante," she says with a hint of a smile adorning her face. No longer white as a sheet, I can see a pinkish hue dotting her cheeks, and the glow of the fire makes her green eyes appear iridescent. Holy fuck does she look spectacular right now.

"Hey, what's up?" Travis says as he walks up to us, jarring me from my thoughts.

"Uh, hi, I'm Natalie. I'm not sure we've ever met? I'm Arianna's friend —" her eyes whip to mine before glancing back at Travis, "— and I'm about thirteen weeks pregnant. I'm bleeding a little, and I freaked out. I didn't have anywhere else to go, and Arianna invited me here tonight anyway, so ..."

Travis's gaze hits mine, with both eyebrows up to his hairline. He deduces quickly what the situation is. "Okay. A little bleeding can be normal. You have two options here. One is you can go home and wait to see if anything else happens, or you can go to the hospital for tests and an ultrasound. I do not have the equipment to help, or I'd do it. I know how nervous you must be. If it were my wife, I'd tell her to go to the hospital."

"It's Thanksgiving —" Natalie starts, but I interrupt her.

"Will it give you some peace of mind to go?" I ask, and she nods. "Then we're going."

"Wait, I didn't mean you'd have to go. Your whole family is here."

"So?" I respond, standing extending my hand to her. "Our current situation makes you family too, Natalie."

I hear her quick intake of breath, and a very quiet "good boy" from my mother, who is clearly eavesdropping from ten feet away. Natalie hesitates before placing her hand in mine, and I don't miss the shock that reverberates up my arm at the contact. This is how it's been each time I've been in close proximity to Natalie, and I don't know how to interpret that.

When I see my kids staring nervously at us from across the room, I beckon them over with a quick flip of my wrist. Ben immediately bolts toward us, running past me and into Natalie's open arms. She stoops down so she can talk quietly to Ben. Abbie walks hesitantly as she watches her brother.

"Why was Uncle Travis talking to you? Is everything okay?" Abbie asks. I pull her in for a hug, feeling her tremble. My sweet girl puts on a strong and dramatic front, but she's just as concerned about her future sibling as I am.

"Well, —"

Natalie interrupts me. "I just needed your dad's help with something."

Shit. "Nat, they know."

Her eyes whip to mine. "They know?"

"Yes."

She sighs as she turns toward Abbie. "I'm not going to lie to you. Okay?"

Both kids nod, Ben stepping out of Natalie's arms so he can be next to his sister.

"I'm bleeding a little. Uncle Travis says it's probably nothing, but I wanted to tell your dad just in case. We're going to go to the hospital to get the baby checked out, just to be safe."

"Could it be something bad?" Abbie asks quietly.

"It could be, but ..." Natalie trails off, her voice breaking. I crouch next to her, wanting to provide comfort. I put my arm around her shoulders, and when she turns her head to look at me, I see all the emotion swimming in her eyes. I hate that she was alone when this happened, unsure of what to do, with no way to contact me.

"But we're optimistic it's nothing. You stay with Nani, and I'll update all of you as soon as I can." Abbie nods as I finish, but Ben continues to look frightened. "You okay, bud?"

"I don't want anything to happen to you," he blurts out, staring at Natalie. "You're the best teacher I've ever had, and you're the healer. I know it."

"The healer?" Natalie asks.

"Yeah. You're like a cardiologist, but you just do it by being yourself. You're healing our hearts."

Holy shit. My son even thinks Natalie is here to heal our family.

She needs you.

Dammit. Not now.

But they need her more.

Fuck me.

Chapter 15

Natalie — Late-November

I don't speak as Alex carefully walks me out to his truck, refusing to acknowledge how he's handling me like precious cargo. He's worried, that much I know. But I can't tell much more. He wears a mask much of the time, choosing what he wants those around him to see. The only time I've seen him drop his façade was in my apartment. Other than that, he's closed off, or pissed at me.

Our drive to the hospital takes twice as long due to snow-packed roads, and I'm secretly relieved I crashed the Santo family Thanksgiving, because I hate driving in the snow. I've never been a fan of it, but ever since Arianna and Stone were involved in a horrific crash around Christmas a few years ago, I'm even more paranoid. Eternity Springs doesn't have a full twenty-four-hour hospital, and we have to head closer to Denver to get to one. I can see how tightly Alex grips the steering wheel, and I turn my head to cast a quick glance at him. His jaw is clenched, lips pursed, and his entire body is tense. Every few seconds his body slightly twitches, and I wonder what is going on.

"Are you okay?" I whisper.

"I should be asking you that," he responds wryly.

"Well, I keep seeing you twitch."

He sighs. "My phone keeps buzzing in my pocket. I know it's my entire family asking questions."

"Do you think they all know now?" I ask quietly.

"I'm assuming so. I'll admit, I told Dom right before you got there.

Obviously my parents knew, and now Travis knows. The Santo family gossip mill probably took care of the rest."

When my phone buzzes in my pocket, I pull it out to see a text from Arianna, along with an attachment.

> Arianna: Brace yourself. No clue how, but the gossip website in town already got the scoop about your bundle in the oven.

> Me: You have got to be kidding!

> Arianna: Sorry, girl. Dom is pissed. Now he knows it's someone associated with the hotel, and he's ready to lay down the law. Kate had to convince him not to fire everyone on the spot.

> Me: Shit, Ari. I hadn't told my boss yet. My parents don't know. This is bad.

> Arianna: Honestly, I'm surprised they waited this long for the article. They've been sitting on a picture of you and Alex together on a sidewalk. I'm guessing the night he walked you home?

> Me: Hold on. I need to read this.

"Alex," I murmur as I open the attachment, "That stupid gossip website here posted an article about us."

"Fuck," he mutters. "Read it aloud, please."

Another one bites the dust!

When Eternity Springs Elementary School hired seasoned teacher Natalie Jackson, a best friend of Arianna Santo Dixon, we knew it was only a matter of time before Ms. Jackson snagged herself an eligible bachelor from Eternity Springs. But even we're shocked that she's roped in Alex Santo. Our favorite military hero (tied with his brother Leo, of course) had been pining in grief for his lovely wife, Sara, who perished in a deadly car accident five years ago, and we assumed Mr. Santo would never date again. Imagine our surprise to find out Ms. Jackson scored herself a hottie by getting knocked up! That's right, Eaglets, Ms. Jackson is pregnant with Alex's third child. Sources tell us she's already in her second trimester. The same sources say this is strictly a co-parenting relationship, but we're taking bets on how long it'll be before Alex slaps a ring on her to mark his territory. Any takers?

"Fucking hate that website," Alex hisses.

"Who runs the damn thing? Can we force them to take it down?" I ask.

"We don't know who runs it. Every time we've told them to take down an article or blind item, they've just posted more."

"Arianna said Dom is pissed. To get the news up there that fast means it came from inside Everlasting."

"Shit," Alex swears. "I didn't think of that."

"I hadn't told my boss yet," I confess.

"What?" Alex asks incredulously. "Why not?"

"I don't really know. My focus was on telling you, and then I was focused on telling my parents this weekend. But now I'm stuck here, and I can't exactly tell them over the phone, so I don't know what I'm going to do."

"Snow's supposed to end after midnight. I'm sure you can get home tomorrow or Saturday. Greeley, right?"

"Yeah. I think I was secretly relieved to have more time before I had to tell them. They aren't exactly monks, but they're pretty conservative. Me getting pregnant from a one-night stand may not sit well with them."

"Let's worry about one thing at a time, okay? Make sure everything is okay with you, and then we can figure something out with your parents," Alex says as he pulls into the hospital entrance.

Once inside the emergency room, we're whisked back to a triage room quickly. I guess a possible miscarriage pops me to the front of the line. I should feel bad about skipping ahead of the people waiting impatiently, but I won't allow myself. I'm already so attached to this baby, and I don't know what I'll do if I've already lost my tater tot.

After getting all the normal vitals out of the way, I'm asked a handful of questions, mostly about normal life.

"How far along are you, ma'am?" the nurse asks.

"About thirteen or fourteen weeks, I think."

"I'll call and get someone from OB down to check you shortly." With a tap of the pen, the short and to-the-point nurse steps out of my curtained area. Alex stands awkwardly next to the bed, his hands shoved deeply into his jeans pockets. Neither one of us speaks.

"If you want to leave, you can," I finally whisper.

"Do you want me to leave?"

"You can if you want."

"That's not what I asked, Sunflower." He steps toward the curtain leading out to the desks, and I'm momentarily stunned into silence. When he comes back with a chair, I let out the breath I didn't realize I was holding. "Now then. Why do you want me to leave?

"I never said I wanted you to leave."

"Am I making you uncomfortable?"

"Not really." I pause. "Okay, maybe a little."

Alex arches a brow as he watches me. "I'm going to need an explanation."

I exhale a loud sigh, closing my eyes and resting my head against the thin piece of fabric this hospital calls a pillow. With my eyes closed, I can speak a little more freely. "I don't know how to act around you. We were together once, and you bolted. I saw you crying when I told you about the baby, and I hate that I made you upset. I hate that this has thrown a wrench in your life. I hate that I'm going to be a single mother. I hate that this is making you miserable, and I wish you'd just take the out I gave you because it'll break my heart if you see pain every time you see our baby."

Alex is quiet, obviously thinking about my words, but I remain as still as can be. That is, until I feel a hand under my chin. "Open your eyes and look at me, Sunflower."

I open my eyes, feeling his hand slide from my chin to cup my cheek. He pulls my face toward his, and when our eyes meet, I see emotion swimming in his. "I will never see pain when I look at our baby, Nat. I promise. I will love our baby just like I love my other two children. It doesn't matter how we made him or her, okay? And don't refer to our kid as a wrench."

I let out a sniffly laugh as a tear slides down my cheek, and Alex tenderly wipes it away. "You know what I mean."

"I'd say it's more of a curveball," he says with a quiet chuckle. "I won't lie and tell you I didn't cry that night when you left. I was completely overcome with emotion. I never thought I'd have another — that I'd have the *opportunity* to have another child, and it hit me harder than I ever thought possible."

As I'm about to pepper him with a barrage of questions, someone says, "knock, knock. I'm Doctor Vogel, I'm with obstetrics."

"Come in," Alex says, sitting up straight in his chair. I feel the cool air hit my face as he slides his hand from my cheek, and I'm only disappointed for a moment before he takes my hand in his, intertwining our fingers together.

Curtain pulled back, a very young doctor steps into the room. A very young male doctor.

"Woah, Doogie, what the hell?" Alex spurts out.

"Excuse me?" Dr. Vogel says, brows furrowed in confusion.

"Yeah, what's Doogie?" I ask.

"Jesus. *Doogie Howser*? I'm not that much older than you, Nat. You've never heard of that show? Teenager becoming a doctor?"

I giggle as I look at Dr. Vogel. He is young. Alex isn't off the mark here.

"I'm not a teenager, but I can say that's the first time anyone has ever referenced a television show," Dr. Vogel says with a chuckle.

"Look it up. But I'm gonna need to know your age before you lay a hand on her," Alex says tensely, a clear warning edging his voice ominously.

"I assure you, I'm of age, completed medical school just fine, and my mom even let me drive all by myself to work today," Dr. Vogel snaps.

"Funny," Alex quips. "Age."

"Thirty-four."

"How long have you been practicing medicine?"

"Including my internship and residency?"

"Did you work on patients during that time?"

"Yes."

"Then yeah."

"I completed my undergraduate degree in three years. Medical school in four years, then I began my internship and residency program. I began my internship when I was twenty-five, so I've been practicing for nine years. I've been fully licensed for four years, and have worked with this hospital for the entirety of that time."

Alex sighs. "Alright, I guess."

"Did I pass the inspection?"

"Am I even here?" I shout. "While it was rather captivating watching you two volley back and forth, I'm actually the patient."

Dr. Vogel gives me a smile. "That you are. Tell me, Mrs. Jackson — oh. It's Ms. Jackson."

I hear Alex growl, and the doctor's smile grows. "What do you need to know from me?"

"When did the bleeding start?" he asks.

"This afternoon around three."

"Was it full bleeding, or spotting?"

"Uh, spotting, I guess."

"Any clots?"

"No."

"That's good. Any stomach cramps or pains?" he asks.

"No."

"Good. Let's do an ultrasound to check." Dr. Vogel pops his head outside the curtain, murmuring to someone. He's followed back into the room by the no-nonsense nurse from earlier, who is wheeling a portable ultrasound machine. "Usually I'd prefer to do a transvaginal ultrasound, but we don't have one at our disposal. Let's see if we can get some good images on your abdomen. If not, I'll hunt down a machine for us to use."

Alex's hand tightens on mine as I push down my leggings. I'm embarrassed to have him so close to my stomach. These bright hospital lights aren't doing me or my stretch marks any favors. As Dr. Vogel turns his back to us as he tinkers with the machine, Alex shocks the hell out of me by leaning forward and placing the gentlest of kisses against my stomach. He rests his forehead against my skin for a brief moment, then kisses my hand. Looking at me, he whispers, "It's gonna be okay, Sunflower."

"Alright. The gel will be cold, just a warning," Dr. Vogel says as he turns around and squeezes a tube onto my skin. I hiss as it hits my skin. "I know. Our permanent machine upstairs has a warmer for the gel. There's no possibility for me to warm it up in this situation."

I close my eyes as he presses the wand into my stomach, hoping and praying to hear that rapid heartbeat again.

"Nat, look," Alex whispers, squeezing my hand. I open my eyes, and Alex points toward the screen.

"This baby is doing gymnastics right now," Dr. Vogel comments. "Are you feeling any kicks or movements yet?"

"A little flutter here and there, I think," I murmur absentmindedly, utterly captivated by the images on the screen. "Is anything wrong? Is he or she okay?"

The sound I had been waiting for fills the space. "Heartbeat is right where it should be, and from the looks of it, your kiddo is doing just fine in there."

"Really?" I ask, my voice cracking as my eyes heat with tears.

"What about the bleeding?" Alex inquires.

"We can't know for sure. Take it easy for the next few days. No exercise or heavy lifting. If you need a doctor's note, I can provide that."

"I'm a teacher. I stand all day, but I'm off until Monday," I tell him.

Dr. Vogel frowns. "I'd like you to take a few more days off as a precautionary measure. I'm confident your baby is fine, but better safe than sorry. I'll get a note for you to take to your superior."

The nurse hands me a towel to wipe off the ultrasound gel, and they leave immediately, pulling the machine with them.

"What do you need from your apartment?" Alex says, turning my attention to him.

"What?"

"You're staying with me until you go back to work. What do you need? I can send Ari to get stuff."

"No, that's — I — she —" I sputter.

Alex gives me a rare smile. "She can get into your apartment, right? I assumed she had a key. She can get you some clothes and whatever toiletries you need."

"I don't need to stay with you," I protest.

"Baby doc said to take it easy."

"So? My apartment is like two hundred square feet, Alex. I doubt I'll get winded on the six steps between my bed and the fridge."

"But what if you do? What if you don't have your phone, and you can't call me?" he asks pointedly.

Dammit. "Baby Doc did not say I had to have a sitter."

His grin grows wider. "Baby doc said to take it easy, which means the same damn thing. Accept this, Sunflower. You're coming home with me."

"I will only if you tell me why you call me Sunflower."

"You're coming home with me because I drove, and I refuse to take you back to your car or your apartment."

"But your kids!"

"They'll be fine with it. Neither one seemed upset about the baby."

"How were they when you told them?"

"I told Abbie the day after you told me. Told Ben this past weekend. They have questions about things, but they aren't upset about the baby."

"Holy …" I trail off as my mind goes in a million different directions. "The kids seemed fine with the baby. Seriously?"

"Ben didn't really care. He'd like a brother, by the way. He just doesn't want to share a room. Abbie was pretty cool about it."

"Seriously?"

"Yeah. When I told my in-laws —"

"You told them?" I screech.

"Technically, I didn't tell them. Ben did. Or maybe it was Abbie? I can't remember. Abbie was really pissed that my in-laws tried to set me up by having a girl at our Thanksgiving dinner last weekend, and I think she was the one who blurted it out."

"How did they take it?" I whisper.

"Really good, actually. They want to meet you."

"Hard pass," I blurt out.

His eyebrows raise. "Why not?"

"That would make me incredibly uncomfortable. Why would they want to meet me? To confirm I'm not taking their daughter's place? Or to make sure that I don't measure up to her? Whatever the reason, I want no part in it." I cross my arms over my chest, anger seeping into my veins. I don't want to be reminded of Alex's wife. It's bad enough that I have to think about her every time I think about Alex, and how I know he wishes this pregnancy was with her. I don't want to get that reminder from her parents as well.

"Alright," he finally says. "If that's how you feel. I don't think they'd be comparing you, though."

"Yes," I laugh bitterly, "because I'm so far beneath everyone it would be evident immediately."

Alex cocks his head to the side as he studies me. He takes a long moment before speaking. "I don't think I realized how much Rob broke you. Your confidence. He really did a number on you."

Too stunned to speak, I shake my head.

"You are not worthless, Natalie. Whatever Rob said to make you think that? Get it out of your head."

The no nonsense nurse pops her head in. "Sir? Can you come give us some information? Doctor Vogel would like to check on Ms. Jackson in a few days, and we need some contact info."

"Oh, I'm sure he does want to check on her," Alex mutters, letting go of my hand and standing up. He hesitates before leaning over me and brushing his lips against my forehead. "I admire what you're doing, Nat. How you're handling things. You're worthy of being loved by someone who sees how phenomenal you are."

As Alex walks out of the room, I realize that I'm in deep trouble, because I really want that someone to be him.

Chapter 16

Alex — Late-November

As we left the hospital, I received a text from my mom saying she was at my house with the kids. They wanted to sleep in their own beds, and I don't blame them. So much of their time over the last five years was spent at my parents' house, due to my deployments. Honestly, looking back, I should have requested a discharge right after Sara was killed. I should have been here for them. But some part of my mind thought that a 'new normal' meant going back to my job.

"Arianna dropped a bag of my things off at your house," Natalie says quietly.

"Good."

"Are you sure this is okay? I don't want to upset your kids."

"We'll explain what happened when we get home." I'm taken aback at how normal it sounds to refer to my house as Natalie's home, but I shake off the feeling. I'm too tired to process that.

"How honest are you with them? Do you want to sugarcoat anything?" she asks.

"No. I try not to be extremely blunt, but I also don't skirt around issues. Life is hard. They're going to be challenged often. Bad things happen. I want them to be ready when lightning strikes instead of frozen with shock."

"Well, if either of them wants to discuss how the baby got in me, I'm telling them to ask you."

"What, you don't want to tell them you needed the old C in the V?" I ask dryly.

Natalie groans, covering her face with her hands. "Oh God. I forgot that's what I said. Any chance you can erase that from your memory?"

"Not a chance, Sunflower."

I hear a very feminine growl emanate from the passenger seat, and I fail to hide my snicker. "At least tell me why you insist on calling me that."

"Nope." I'm not completely sure why I do, honestly. Just that she's this bright spot that seems to stand above the crowd, no matter how much I try to ignore her. I'm pulled to Natalie, whether I want to be or not.

Once home, Natalie awkwardly waits for me to walk inside. My mom sits at my kitchen table, reading a book. When she looks up, she smiles warmly, then stands to give Natalie a hug. "How are you feeling, *girasole*?"

Woah. Now my mom is calling her sunflower?

"What does that mean?" Natalie asks, her brow furrowing in confusion.

"Nothing," I blurt out. "I'll walk you out, Mom. Wait here, Nat, and I'll show you to your room."

I grab Mom's arm, pulling her toward the garage. I hear her chuckling behind me. "Slow down, *angiolo*!"

"I need to get you outta here before you get into more trouble," I mutter.

"What? I think *girasole* fits her perfectly."

"You know that's what I call her, Mom."

She stops abruptly. "You call her *girasole*?"

"No, I call her Sunflower. Which you knew."

Mom adamantly shakes her head. "No, I promise you, I didn't know. Natalie has always seemed like a sunflower. Larger than life. She makes me smile when I see her. I think she makes a great opposite for you, the whole yin and yang thing."

"She's not anything for me, Mom," I say defensively. "There's nothing going on with her."

"I know, I know. Let me rephrase. I think she'll be an excellent woman to raise a child with, regardless of the circumstances. She'll be a good role model for Abigail."

"Abbie doesn't need a role model." Mom's eyes darken when the irritation is obvious in my tone. A light snow has started again, snowflakes dancing around us as she ducks into her car to start it.

"She needs someone who isn't related to us, *angiolo*. A woman she can objectively ask questions to. The teenage years are incredibly challenging, and I'm sure she assumes anything she talks about with me or your sisters will end up getting back to you. We aren't objective at all."

"Why? If Sara were still alive, she wouldn't be objective."

"It's very different when it's your own mother, Alessio."

I sigh, reaching up to grip the back of my neck. When my mother uses my full name, I know she's about to get crabby. "I don't want to talk about this, Mom."

"At some point, you need to address your feelings. You've refused to talk to me and your father, and you've only opened up to Dominic a few times. We're worried about you, Alex. I feel like you're digging a hole to bury yourself in, and I don't know how to pull you out of it."

I tip my head up, watching the snowflakes slowly scatter across my face. "I don't know how I got here, Mom. This isn't how I thought life would end up."

Her hand softly grabs my forearm, squeezing it gently. "I know some of this is about Sara, but are other things bothering you? I think this is the unhappiest I've ever seen you."

I struggle to maintain my composure as I think about what I want to say. How I hate the police job. How I don't have a clue what I want to do if I quit. How I'm worried I'm going to be a shit parent for this new baby because I was gone so much when Ben and Abbie were little. How I'm finding myself feeling lonely, but then I'm overtaken by a wave of guilt so severe that I want to crumble to the ground. Suffice it to say, I'm fucking miserable.

"Alex," Mom whispers. Opening my eyes, I look down at her. With a kind expression on her face, she says, "Have lunch with me next week, and we'll talk. Just you and me. We'll figure out little ways to give you some happiness."

I give her a chagrined nod, thinking there's no way I can bounce out of this life I've settled into, when her hand finds mine. I feel her slide something against my palm. "Don't look at it now, but just think about it. He comes highly recommended."

As I watch Mom's tail lights disappear into the snow, I look at what she gave me. I can't help the chuckle.

It's a therapist's business card.

Seeing an email at the bottom, I decide to email the guy immediately. What's the worst that can happen? I fire off a quick message asking him to let me know if he's accepting new patients, then head back inside, assuming I'll find Natalie standing in the kitchen, undoubtedly too self-conscious to explore my home.

I definitely don't expect to find Abbie and Natalie talking on the couch, their heads tilted toward one another as Abbie peppers Natalie with questions.

"What was my dad like as a kid?"

"I rarely interacted with him. By the time I was brave enough to say hello, he was already with your mom."

Did you —" Abbie starts, then clears her throat before continuing. "Did you like my dad back then?"

"I think I had a teenage crush on him. But even then, it was obvious he only had eyes for your mom."

"I wish we had more time with her," Abbie says wistfully. "Not that I'm trying to push you out of the picture or anything."

"I know what you mean. You miss your mom. You miss your life as it was then. I can't even begin to imagine how hard this must all be for you."

"It's weird, you know? My grandmother and aunts want me to confide in them, but it feels off. Like they're trying to take my mom's place. I know they aren't, but I don't want to talk to them. Makes me feel like I'm cheating on my mom somehow."

"How do you think your mom would feel? Would she hope you'd

confide in your aunts?" Natalie asks, her voice even and controlled. What an odd conversation to have, yet she's handling it like a pro.

Abbie sighs in her normal tween angsty sounds. "She'd want me to have someone. She'd probably yell at me for not talking to my aunts. She'd understand me not wanting to talk to Nani. Nani's like old, you know? She won't get what is going on in my life."

"Which aunt do you think you have the closest relationship with? Who understands you the best?" Natalie inquires.

"Hmm," Abbie murmurs. "I guess Aunt Ari. Although Aunt Hannah is cool. She taught me how to hold a spoon on my nose."

"A very admirable trait that is bound to come in handy one day," Natalie teases.

"It was fun. But the questions I have ..." Abbie trails off.

"What?"

"Well, it's stuff I'd ask my mom. And it's just weird asking them."

"Wanna try a question out on me? Then we can see how awkward it is, and maybe pick which aunt will understand the best. I do happen to know all of your aunts."

"Oh yeah! I forgot about that. Okay. So, like, what is the main difference between a tampon and a pad? Tampons scare me, and my friend Paige gave me one of hers last week when I got my first period, but I didn't know what I was supposed to do."

Holy shit.

She got her first period?

What the fuck do I do?

Should I go in there? Tell her she's a beautiful growing woman, and I'm so proud of her? Ignore it and move on? Go to the store tomorrow morning and buy every fucking option of tampons and pads out there?

Why didn't she tell me?

"You got your first period?" Natalie finally asks.

"Yeah."

"What did your dad say?"

Abbie gasps. "I didn't tell him. He's my *dad*! What would he know?"

She's right, but that still hurts. I massage a point over my heart where I imagine the invisible knife just slashed through to my insides.

"Abbie, just because he's a guy, doesn't mean he won't want to know about big and monumental parts of your life. Getting your first period is a big deal, girl. I bet your dad would have immediately run out and grabbed every available product on the market. I wouldn't put it past him not to watch YouTube videos on ways to help you from a single dad perspective. He'd never want to make you uncomfortable."

"I guess."

"Do you want to know what my dad did when my mom told him?" Natalie asks with a giggle.

"What?"

"He showed up at school to pick me up, and in front of all my friends, he said, 'I hear my little girl is a woman now.' I was completely humiliated."

"Oh my God! I'd have to change schools," Abbie says, laughing.

"I asked. My mom said no. She didn't want to drive me to a different school. I have a brother, and since he plays hockey, our mom was already driving too much. She refused to allow me to move based on her carpool restrictions. I will say, though, that my first period happened twenty years ago, and social media wasn't a thing back then. If it happened today, a video of my dad showing up would have been plastered all over the place. Then I would have died of embarrassment."

"Someone took a picture of my butt," Abbie blurts out.

"What?" Natalie breathes. "When? Who? Did you report it? Was this in the bathroom? That is complete bullshit! Do you want me to go to the school? I will burn that damn building down ..."

Natalie's voice grows louder as Abbie stares at her in shock. "Oh, I mean, I was wearing pants. But the blood went through? That's what they took a picture of. And it got posted on Snapchat, I guess. I only heard about it. Dad won't let me have Snapchat."

"Oh, sweetie," Natalie says, her voice quiet again. Jesus, that was intense. Her entire demeanor changed. "I'm so sorry. That's awful. I used to wear a pad and a tampon at school, just in case. But sometimes it just happens. I hate that someone didn't have any empathy with you."

"Do you think —" Abbie breaks off. "Never mind."

"Go ahead. Ask away."

"Do you think you could show me how to use a tampon? Or maybe find a video that explains it? I tried, but it hurt, and so I stopped."

"I can absolutely explain how to do it. It takes some getting used to, but it should never hurt. I'll help you out anytime you need, okay?" Natalie says quietly.

"Thanks, Natalie." Abbie stands up, then turns toward the couch. "I know it's weird, you having a baby with my dad and all, but I'm glad you're here."

As Abbie skips away, I watch as Natalie leans her head back against the couch.

"I know you're there, Alex."

I chuckle as I walk around the couch, choosing to sit on a chair across from Natalie. Watching her interact with Abbie has thrown me for a loop. That, on top of the conversation with my mom, has my mind whirling.

"How much did you hear?" she whispers.

"Quite a bit, I'm guessing. You having a crush on me, and me only having eyes for Sara. Hannah and the spoon. Her first period, a picture of a butt, and you wanting to burn a building down. We'll ignore the part about the tampon, because frankly that was too much for me, and double-back to the burning of the building."

"Shit," she hisses. Closing her eyes, she covers her face with her hands, just like in the car. "I had hoped you didn't hear that. I'm not sure what came over me, but the thought of someone taking advantage of Abbie in such a delicate state? I was furious! Who the hell does that, Alex? Who thinks it's okay to take such an inappropriate picture of a twelve-year-old girl and put it on the internet?"

"That's why I won't let her have Snapchat. But do you normally threaten to burn down buildings without knowing the whole story, or is this pregnancy hormones?"

"Hormones." She pauses. "Actually that's really a toss-up. Arianna's ex-fiancé never told her that his car got towed right after the Children's Hospital ball, when he introduced her to his actual fiancée. Also signed him up for every inappropriate magazine I could find, and sent them to his parents' address. Honestly, that was money well spent."

"I'm both impressed and scared of you right now, Nat."

"As you should be," she says with a yawn.

"Come on, killer. I'll show you to your room." Arianna already texted that Natalie's things were in my guest room, so I motion for her to follow me upstairs. "It's not much, but it has an attached bathroom, so you'll have some privacy."

"It's wonderful. Honestly, this is more than enough, Alex. God, what a day." She sits on the bed with a long exhale, exhaustion evident on her face as she rifles through her bag. "Crap. Arianna sent me stuff that's too small now. My stomach kinda popped this week."

"Here, I'll grab you one of my shirts." I jog across the hall to my room, finding it odd how pleased I am that she'll be sleeping in my clothes. Heading back into the guest room, I hand it to Natalie, who quickly changes in the bathroom.

"I thought the worst when I saw the blood. I'm so attached to this tater tot. I don't know what I would do if I lost it," she says as she steps back into the room. It's an old Air Force t-shirt, and I'm surprised at the visceral reaction I have to seeing her wearing it. It hugs her curves perfectly, outlining her tiny baby bump, and her nipples pucker against the fabric as I unabashedly stare. Shit. I need to rein this in. *Get it together, dick.*

I cross the room to check the window blinds, behind thick blackout curtains. "Let's not think negatively, okay?"

"I've been feeling this flutter, and I think maybe it's him. I've been calling it a him more and more," she says bashfully as she sits on the edge of the bed.

"Do you think I could feel?" I ask, immediately embarrassed. Natalie's eyes widen. "I'm sorry, that was out of line. Ignore me."

"No, it's totally okay. I'm not sure if you can feel the flutter, but you can try." She moves to stretch out, resting her head on the pillows. I cautiously sit next to her, then extend to lay alongside. Resting my head in one hand, I extend another hand toward her. I hesitate, suddenly unsure of where I can touch her. Where am I allowed?

Natalie laughs as she takes my hand and pushes it into her abdomen. "Everything I've felt has been right here. It's like little bubbles."

"Can I just sit here? With my hand on your belly? If that's okay, I mean. I've been a shitty baby daddy, but this is the closest I've been to him —" I break off abruptly, then laugh. "Now you've got me calling it a him, too."

Natalie gives me a brilliant smile. "I bet Ben would be so thrilled to have a brother."

I laugh, unaware that I've begun slowly stroking Natalie's stomach through her shirt. "He'd be stoked, that's for sure. He said he's fine with a sister as long as she doesn't go near his Legos."

"Smart kid," Natalie says, her eyes slowly drifting closed.

We don't talk anymore, as Natalie falls asleep with my hand on her belly. I can't seem to force myself to leave, feeling this connection to my unborn child, and to its mother, as a tethering lifeline I didn't know I needed.

At some point I fall asleep. I wake with Natalie snuggled against me, and I try to force myself to go to my own room. But I can't. Just another hour or two. I pull a throw blanket from the foot of the bed, covering us both. Burying my head in her hair, I fall back asleep, and it's the best sleep I've gotten in months, possibly years.

Chapter 17

Natalie — Late-November

I wake up with Alex wrapped around me, his morning wood fitting perfectly between the globes of my ass, and only the slightest shifting of my thighs gives me a zing of pleasure so strong it knocks the wind right out of me. I'd read in a pregnancy book that some women experience an increase in their sex drive, and I wondered if I'd be part of that group. I've always embraced my sexuality, but I've never considered myself to be a nympho. Right now, however, I feel this out-of-character urge to roll over and mount Alex, demanding that he get me off, whether he likes it or not.

As if he knows my inner thoughts, Alex tightens his arms around me, sliding one hand up to grab my breast. Pregnancy has made my nipples remarkably sensitive, and I struggle to withhold the moan that wants to come out. I shift again, and with a slight push back against him, Alex's cock hits my clit perfectly. God, this feels so good. It's bad, though, right? I was in the emergency room last night for light bleeding, would a quick orgasm possibly cause an issue?

Alex shifts, causing his cock to slide against my core, and I'm helpless to stop the orgasm wave as it crests over me. The last time I came like this was my night with Alex. Holy hell. This is the fastest I've ever come, and it steals the breath from my lungs. I didn't realize how much I needed that, and I don't have a second to feel embarrassed before the rug is ripped out from under me.

"Fuck, Sara. That was hot," Alex mutters behind me, squeezing my nipple, and it's as if I've been doused with a bucket of ice water. I stiffen, my back ramrod straight, as his words repeat in my mind. Sara. Sara. Sara. It'll always be her.

"Get off me," I whisper, tears filling my eyes.

"Hmm?"

"Get. Off. Me," I repeat, a sob breaking through.

"What's wrong?" he asks. "Is the baby okay?"

Once Alex lets go, I quickly rise from the bed. Striding to the attached bathroom, I grab my phone from the nightstand as I go. "My name is Natalie."

As I turn, I see Alex's eyes go wide and the color drains from his face. "Shit. Fuck. I'm sorry, uhh …"

"Natalie," I growl. I cross my arms tightly, as if the motion can somehow protect me from the pain he's causing. I know it isn't intentional, but that doesn't mean it's painless.

Alex stands, his hands in front of him in a defensive stance, approaching me slowly. "I'm really sorry. That wasn't intentional."

"I know. Can you take me home, please? Or should I call a rideshare?" I tip my chin to stare up at Alex defiantly. I'll be damned if this man gets one more ounce of my emotions.

"I'd rather you stay here," he says hesitantly.

"No."

His eyes narrow as he watches me. "Why not?"

"Because I don't want to be around you."

"It was a mistake, Natalie. An accident."

"A mistake is giving someone the wrong gift. An accident is stepping on someone's toe. Calling someone by your dead wife's name while in bed? Neither of those," I hiss, suddenly aware the bedroom door is open, and the kids could be listening.

Mirroring my stance, Alex crosses his arms and studies me. "I'm not taking you home."

Jackass. "Fine."

"Fine."

I step into the bathroom, closing the door. Listening carefully, I wait until I hear Alex shuffle out of the room, then pull up the rideshare app. I refuse to stay here for one more second.

Dramatic? Maybe. I'm a crazy, hormonal bitch, and he only got me off because he thought I was his dead wife. I can't process that, and I don't want to.

After peeing and washing my hands, I notice Arianna stocked the bathroom with my toiletries. While incredibly thoughtful, I'm ticked at having to waste time packing it all back up. There aren't many things I splurge on, choosing most extra funds to go toward what I need in the classroom. The one major thing I never give up is good skincare, and I'll be damned if I'm leaving it here.

Exiting the bathroom, I breathe a sigh of relief when Alex isn't loitering in the hallway. Grabbing the bag of clothes Arianna brought over, I quickly tiptoe down the stairs. My phone vibrates with a text that my ride is here right as I unlock the front door, and that's when all hell breaks loose.

"Ms. Jackson?" Ben's sleepy and sweet voice asks from the kitchen, as he rounds the corner, stopping to wave at me. I wave back as I'm opening the door, then shriek when the loudest damn alarm screams throughout the house.

Of course he'd have an alarm system. Looking up, I see Alex tear down the stairs, his eyes on me, and I freak out. Bolting out the door, I run through the yard, assuming I'll have better traction in the snowy grass than on his driveway, which looks to be snow-packed and covered in icy spots.

"Natalie!" Alex sprints after me, barefoot, and he reaches me as I open the door to my ride. He grabs a hold of my arm while simultaneously closing the door. "What the fuck?"

"Let me go, Alex."

"You shouldn't be alone right now. What if something happens?"

"Nothing is going to happen. I've been fine all night. Go back inside before you get frostbite."

He thrusts a hand through his hair, all mussed and gorgeous, as he studies me. I steel my spine as I stare back at him. "I'd feel more comfortable if you were here."

Before I can think twice, I blurt out, "I'd feel more comfortable if I didn't feel like I was competing with a ghost. We don't always get what we want."

Alex takes a step back, stunned, his mouth open in shock. I take the opportunity to open the car door, darting inside.

"You okay, ma'am?" The young male driver studies me in the rearview mirror, his eyes wide. "Should I go?"

"Yes, please go." I refuse to take another glance at Alex, but I know he's still standing there. I can *feel* the jerk now.

"Not cool referencing his wife, you know," the guy mutters, and I growl. Stupid small towns and their stupid gossip. I don't respond, because I know whatever I say will end up on *The Eagle Has Landed*. This entire exchange is probably already on its way to whoever writes the articles.

I'll apologize to Alex. I will. Not about me leaving, or getting upset about him calling me Sara. But I'll apologize for saying I'm competing with a ghost. He deserves that much. But right now, I want to sit and stew in my anger. My sadness. This isn't how I thought my life would turn out. I always imagined I'd meet a man, fall in love, get married, then welcome a couple of kiddos and maybe a dog or two. Instead, I have a one-night stand, and get knocked up by my best friend's brother, a man who is pining desperately for his dead wife, and I'm barely making ends meet in a studio apartment the size of a matchbox.

When am I gonna catch a break?

I last in my apartment for less than thirty minutes before I pack a bag, catch another ride to Everlasting to retrieve my car, and I get on the Interstate. On a normal day, the drive from my apartment to my parents' house in Greeley takes about ninety minutes. But today, with roads less than ideal and tons of Black Friday shoppers out and about, it takes well over two hours. I'm relieved to pull into my parents' driveway, because I can't wait to get a much needed hug from my mom, but also because I forgot to pee before I left my apartment. I figured the need to pee a million times a day would start much later in the pregnancy.

"What a nice surprise!" My mom, Judy, says, opening her arms wide. My dad, Mark, looks on with love, and it's all it takes for me to break down in earnest. "What's this? Why is my beautiful daughter crying?"

Dad sighs as he pulls me from my mom's arms. "Come on, munchkin. Mom will put on a pot of coffee."

As he directs me toward the back of the house, I let out a sniffle and respond. "It'll have to be decaf."

"Oh? Why?" Dad asks, as Mom simultaneously says, "Oh, shit."

"What? I don't understand. Did you decide to give up caffeine? You love everything caffeinated!" Oh, my sweet but clueless father.

"I am giving it up, but not by choice," I whine as we reach the family room.

"Well, this will be good. Sister." I look up to find my brother, Shawn, staring at me with a wide smile.

"What are you doing here? I thought you didn't have any time off this week!" I sob. God, these hormones are going to be the death of me.

Shawn reaches for me, yanking me into his arms. Shawn is at least eight inches taller than me, even taller than Alex, and my head fits snug under his chin. He leans down to whisper, "Please tell me the caffeine thing isn't what I think it means."

"I guess I'll just be silent, then," I whisper back.

"Fuck. Who's the guy? I'll call up Santo again. He'll have no problem laying down the law for me," Shawn teases.

"Probably won't work this time," I murmur.

"Why?"

I pull away from him, looking up to see his green eyes watching me carefully. "Because the guy is his brother."

"Jesus Christ, Nat. Seriously? Which brother? Aren't they all married by now?"

"It's Alex. The oldest. Technically he's not married, I guess?" I comment, scratching my chin. I'm sure Alex thinks he's still married, but I didn't do anything wrong.

"There is no technicality here. He's either married or he's not." My parents watch the two of us volley back and forth, my dad still blissfully ignorant to the topic at hand, while our mom massages her temples.

"There is an odd technicality here, Shawn. His wife is dead, okay? He's a widower. But he's still hopelessly in love with her, and I'll never measure up, and it was a one-time thing, but then he got me off this morning while saying her name, and what the hell am I supposed to do with that?" I ramble, then break into a new current of tears. "How can I raise a kid with him, knowing he'll undoubtedly compare everything I do to her? She'll be the better mom in every sense, no matter what I do. I can't compete."

"Raise a kid? What … oh. Oooh," Dad says, finally catching on. "Oh, munchkin. You're pregnant?"

I nod. "I'm sorry, Dad."

He scoffs. "Why are you apologizing? You're a grown woman. I highly doubt you set out on a quest to get pregnant."

"I'm just thrilled the father isn't Rob," Mom blurts out.

Shawn nods. "He's left you alone, right?"

"Yes, why?" I ask uncertainly. When Shawn shrugs, I poke his chest. "What did you do?"

"Nothing major. Just helped him understand that he's not to fuck with you again, or I'd make his life a living hell."

"I don't even want to know how you'd do that, but thanks, I guess?" I may not wholeheartedly approve of his display of chauvinistic masculinity, but I appreciate the heart behind it. Even from one thousand miles away, my brother is always looking out for me.

"I think we're going to need a bit more information, Natalie," Mom says, right as the oven timer goes off. "Excellent timing. The breakfast quiche is ready. Everyone to the table so Natalie can tell us what's been going on in her life. Evidently, it's more than we knew."

After sitting down at the same table my parents have had my entire life, I fill my family in. How Rob followed me to the bar, and Alex saved me. Running into Alex at the town community night, then having dinner together. Being Ben's teacher, and how Alex is clearly still grieving his wife. After my outburst with Shawn, I don't regale my family about this morning, just saying that Alex called me by his dead wife's name, and I'm really struggling with where I fit in.

"Are you interested in more with Alex?" Mom asks quietly, her keen eyes already knowing the answer. My mother has always been able to tell me how I'm feeling before I can verbalize it myself.

"It doesn't matter," I answer sullenly. "That's not something he wants."

"I didn't ask what he wanted, or how he feels. I'm asking about you, sweetheart. We can't control how anyone else thinks, feels, or acts. We can only control ourselves. I want to talk about you, and give you strategies for interacting with him in the future. Regardless of your feelings, you and Alex will have to co-parent for eighteen years. That's a lot of birthday parties, little league games, ballet recitals, and holidays," she says pointedly.

"I don't know how I feel," I sigh. "I had a crush on him when I was a kid, but he was already in love with his wife. He never looked twice at me."

"I'm sure the fact that you were jailbait probably didn't help," Shawn jokes.

"Exactly how much older is this man?" Dad asks, frowning.

"He's thirty eight, Dad. Shawn is acting like he's fifty or something. I crushed on him when I was around sixteen, though."

"That's still almost six years difference, Natalie. That's a lot of life he's lived in those years. And he's a veteran?" Dad inquires.

I nod. "He's retired now. He completed twenty years with the National Guard. He was deployed when his wife died in a car accident, and I think he struggles with a tremendous amount of guilt."

"Does he have any other children besides Ben?" Mom asks.

"A daughter, Abbie. She's twelve. You'd really like her, Mom. She's full of sass and attitude."

She fails to hide her smile. "Sounds like someone else I know."

"I'm surprised Alex didn't bite my head off when I met Abbie. She got snotty with me, and I just dished it right back at her. He walks on eggshells around her, but I wasn't having it. She gets away with a lot, I think, just because he feels guilty."

"It's easy to assume that's the dynamic at play, munchkin, but you don't really know. She's also struggling. I can't imagine how she must feel, dealing with middle school and the looming teen years, all those hormones, and no mom to go to. It's bound to feel incredibly difficult."

I nod. "I had to stay at their house last night, and she cornered me. Poor girl started her period last week, and didn't feel comfortable telling Alex."

"Why did you stay there? You said you 'had' to stay there. Why?" Shawn presses, using air quotes.

Shit.

"Oh. Uh, it's fine now, but I had a little bit of bleeding. Alex took me to the emergency room, and they did an ultrasound. Everything looked fine, but Alex asked if I'd stay at his house in case anything else happened."

"Oh, honey," Mom murmurs, reaching over to grab my hand. "On Thanksgiving? You poor thing."

I look down at my empty plate, not sure how quickly I ate the quiche as I talked so much. That must have been ridiculously unattractive of me to inhale the food like that, but I'm finally over the nonstop nausea.

"It's fine. I'm lucky I knew where he was so I could go to him and ask for help."

"You weren't with him?" Dammit. "I thought you said you were having dinner with Arianna's family. Alex would have been there."

I sigh, wincing at my slip-up. "I told you that so you wouldn't worry about me. Arianna did invite me, but I chose not to go because of Alex. I knew where they were, though."

"So you were home alone? On Thanksgiving? Honey." Mom looks like she's close to tears.

"Seriously, Mom, it's fine. It's just a holiday. It's no big deal."

"Did you at least get some of your favorite foods to eat?" she asks, sniffling.

"Well, um, no? I mean, I've had a crazy amount of nausea and vomiting, so I just planned on eating whatever didn't look bad in my apartment." I won't tell her that ended up being buttered popcorn dipped in strawberry ice cream.

The doorbell rings, jarring the conversation. "Who could that be? Jack, are you expecting any packages?"

"No, I don't think so. My two favorite packages both surprised us this morning."

"So you were a surprise, too?" I ask Shawn, and he nods.

"Coach decided to give us the day off. He hinted we'd still have afternoon skate today, but changed his mind late yesterday. I got a flight at six this morning, and ... what the fuck?"

"Natalie," Mom calls, "does this belong to you?"

Turning around in my chair, my mouth drops open when I find Alex staring expectantly at me.

Chapter 18

Alex — Late-November

I'm usually a calculated man. I weigh the pros and cons of a decision before I make it. I look at all angles of a situation before determining the best outcome. All my life, I've known what I wanted to achieve, and how I wanted to achieve it. Hell, I knew the moment I laid eyes on Sara that I'd marry her, and had a plan in place after only a few dates on how to make that a reality.

But Natalie? Fucking hell. This woman has me off kilter every moment of the damn day. I'm pissed off, turned on, and aggravated at the same time. I want to take her over my knee for disrupting my life, kiss the hell out of her, and then see if I can fuck my feelings away.

I never know what she's going to say, how she's going to act, or what I might do in return. And yet, when I see her in one piece, sitting at her parents' table, I'm shocked at the thing I feel the most: relief.

She's alive.

She's okay.

I spiraled on the drive up to Greeley, thinking about every worst-case scenario I could think of. I studied every set of tire tracks on the road, worried I'd find her Challenger stuck in a ditch. Clearly I have some PTSD about car accidents I need to deal with.

Natalie's eyes are red-rimmed and puffy, and her brother is glaring at me from the chair beside her, but she's here. I take a deep exhaling breath, one I didn't know I'd been holding since she tore out of my house hours ago.

It took me a few minutes to realize I needed to go after Natalie, and I had to get my kids situated before I could head out. By the time I arrived at her apartment, she'd already left. I quickly texted Arianna, who assured me she tracked Natalie's location as a safety precaution, and told me Natalie was on the interstate heading toward Denver. We accurately assumed she was coming to Greeley to see her parents, although I didn't expect to find her brother here as well.

"Sorry for interrupting," I stammer, suddenly aware they're all staring at me.

Natalie sighs, a sound full of resignation, and she turns away from me as she gestures to her family. "It's fine. Mom, Dad, this is Alex, the baby daddy. Shawn, you clearly remember him."

"What's up, motherfucker," Shawn says, a glint of evil shining in his eyes. Jesus. They're the same shade as Natalie's eyes, and that may take some getting used to.

"Shawn! Ignore my son. I'm Mark Jackson. You've met my wife, Judy," Mr. Jackson says, standing to offer me a handshake. "Please, come sit down."

"Actually, I was hoping to speak with Natalie, if that's okay," I say. I see her spine straighten as she looks to her brother. They appear to have an unspoken conversation, and it reminds me of my twin siblings, Gia and Leo. When I see Shawn nod, Natalie lets out another loud sigh before pushing back from the table.

"Why don't you take him upstairs to your room, sweetheart?" Mrs. Jackson says cheerfully. She pats me on the shoulder as she scoots past Natalie to sit beside her husband.

"Come on, let's get this over with," Natalie mutters sullenly. I smother the chuckle that's threatening to burst from my mouth as I follow her up the staircase and into her bedroom.

"Holy …" I look around the room as Natalie takes a seat on the bed. A four-poster bed, complete with a lacy canopy. A kaleidoscope of colors covers each wall. A record player sits in the corner, and vintage album sleeves are adhered to the wall in two columns. Looking across her bed, I see a dresser and mirror, with post-its taped to the mirror. Some are inspirational sayings, but others are all about body image and weight loss. Fuck. I hate that. Fucking hate that even then, Natalie thought of herself as less than.

"What?" she whispers.

"Oh. I don't think a room could exist that describes you better than this."

"How?"

I think about how to respond. "Chaotically comfortable."

She frowns for a split second before a snort escapes. "Chaotic comfort."

"Yeah. There's a lot going on in here, but that's you. I'd never describe you as bland or beige. You're colorful. Outgoing and full of pizzazz. But you're empathetic and loving. You wear your heart on your sleeve, even when you know it's going to hurt you. You're comfortable in your personality."

"I don't know about that," she mutters. "Say what you want to say, and then you can leave. You could have just called, you know."

"Oh, sure. Not that you would have answered."

"I might have."

"Don't lie."

"Well, I would have listened to the voicemail," she snaps.

"I don't even believe that."

"Alex, just get on with it, okay? I don't see a reason to be in each other's company any longer than needed. You don't need to rub it in any further." I notice the gleam in her eyes even before she realizes she's crying, and I resist the urge to wipe away her tears.

"Rub what in any further?" I ask.

"That I'm not … her. That I'm not up to par. I get it, okay? Nothing will ever match up with what you had. Just say whatever it is that had you thinking it was worth it to drive all the way up here." Crossing her arms, Natalie looks miserable. Her full lower lip, a lip that I've thought about too much, sticks out in an adorable pout. She's still wearing my shirt.

She's still wearing my shirt.

"Alex? Are you okay?"

I shake my head as I stare at her. She's wearing a bra now, which means she consciously chose to put my shirt back on. What the hell does that mean?

"You're kinda freaking me out here," she whispers. Dammit. I'm losing my mind.

"You're the opposite of her. Sara, I mean. You're the exact opposite," I blurt out.

Natalie frowns. "Duh."

"Shit. I didn't mean that as a bad thing. It's just —" I stop, ripping a hand through my hair in frustration. I don't know how to explain a goddamned thing. "Sara was quiet. Peaceful. Easy. We vibed immediately. We never fought."

"I'm aware of all of this, Alex. Really. You didn't need to drive up here to tell me I don't measure up."

"Fuck," I mutter, dropping to my knees at her feet. "It was easy with her, Nat. And yeah, you aren't easy. You challenge me. You make me question things. One second I think you need to be tied to a damn chair so that you'll listen, and the next moment, I want to tie you to my fucking bed so I can have my way with you. And I don't know how to deal with that difference. I spent a decade loving a woman who was simple, quiet, and kind. I don't know how to categorize how I feel about you."

Eyes wide as she stares at me incredulously, Natalie doesn't make a sound, so I continue. "This morning? I knew it was you. I did. Not only because of how you felt in my arms, but your hair smells like vanilla, and I think about that all the damn time. Sara used grapefruit shampoo. Or maybe it wasn't grapefruit. Maybe it was just citrus. I never thought about her shampoo, but I sure as fuck think about yours. The sounds you make are different too. When you came, I was thinking how right it felt, having you in my arms, and how different it was from Sara. Somehow my dumbass brain spouted out her name. But I swear, Natalie, I knew it was you. I'll apologize over and over again until you believe me."

"That's not at all what I thought you were going to say," she finally responds, her voice so quiet I almost don't hear her. I smile softly as I place my hands next to hers on the bed, still unsure of things. I feel like I want to touch her, to kiss her, but I'm incredibly confused.

"I don't know what I'm doing," I confess, closing my eyes as my head falls until my chin touches my chest. "When Sara died, I thought my life was over. I knew I'd never want to be with anyone else. No one would compare, right? But then you basically came into my life like a wrecking ball, and you don't compare. It's like bananas and onions. Completely different categories. And I'm having difficulty coming to terms with that."

I don't realize Natalie has leaned forward until her forehead rests against me. "I believe you. And I'm sorry for what I said about competing with a ghost. That was completely out of line. I was hurt and I lashed out."

Her hair is like a blanket around us, the very vanilla scent I love giving me a feeling of peace. "Did you think you were competing? I didn't understand that."

"I don't want to compete with her, Alex. She's your wife. I get that she's in a league of her own. But I feel like when we take one step forward, whether that be as friends, co-parents, or … more, then we take five steps back. It's exhausting not knowing where you're at, and I'm so anxious about upsetting you that I don't know how to act anymore. Can I ask about Sara? Do you expect me to raise our child the same way you raised yours with her? Should I have any relationship with Abbie and Ben outside of school, or is our child completely separate? Do you want to have specific parameters for our interactions? What if I want more with you? When the baby comes, how are we handling this? So many unknowns, and sometimes it's too much."

"Do you — do you want more with me?" I ask, my heart beating so wildly I wonder if Natalie can hear it. I realize, right at this moment, that I want her to say yes, and that scares the shit out of me.

"I think I do, but I don't think you're ready for that," she says, and my bubble bursts.

"Oh," I respond, oddly hurt.

"I want us to be friends. No matter what may happen, we're in each other's lives for the next eighteen plus years. I want to know I can count on you, and that we'll support one another through everything. I'd like to get to know you better."

"Why are you still wearing my shirt?" I blurt out.

Natalie's gaze looks slightly terrorized before she schools her expression. "I didn't change before I came up here."

"You're wearing a bra," I point out.

Pink creeps up her face, and I can't resist reaching out to trace a finger down her jawline. Natalie involuntarily shivers, but she doesn't make a move. I'm spellbound, powerless to move, taking in the facets of her face as my hand slides back into her hair. Gripping it tightly, Natalie gasps as I tilt her head to expose the length of her neck. "I think you chose to put my shirt back on because you wanted me wrapped around you."

I watch as a silent war rages in her gaze. She wants me, but also doesn't want to admit it. God, I really admire her spirit and tenacity, even when it's mostly directed at me.

"It's not you," she finally says, lying straight through her teeth. A grin spreads across my face as she continues. "Do you have any idea what these fucking hormones are doing to me? I'm finally not puking all the time, and all I want is sex. All the damn time. It's not fair, you know? My toys don't seem to work for me like they used to. Plus the stupid apartment walls are crazy thin, and my neighbor commented on hearing me only talking a couple days ago, so now I feel like I'm this building pariah that everyone hates. I know I get loud when I come, so I should try to dial it down now, and it's nowhere near as good as it could be, and especially not as good as it was with you — you're really good at sex, by the way — but what am I supposed to do? It's like a nonstop itch on the middle of my back that I can't reach, except it's my vagina and *I just need to get off all the fucking time.*"

"Woah," I breathe, throwing my head back into raucous laughter. "That's definitely not what I thought you'd say, either."

"This is all your fault, you know." Natalie crosses her arms in her lap, bottom lip sticking out again in a perfect pout, and I resist the urge to lean forward and bite it.

"I know."

"How the hell did this even happen? I was on the pill, and you used a condom."

Oh shit. "About that. I forgot to tell you that the condom ripped."

"Seriously?" she shouts, grabbing a pillow and hitting me on the head. It's such an unexpected move that I lose my balance, toppling over onto the floor. "You're telling me this now? Three months after the fact? Don't you think you should have told me immediately, or maybe the next day?"

"In my defense, I didn't realize it until I got home, and then I honestly forgot about it. Since I hadn't heard from you, I figured we were in the clear."

"Obviously not," Natalie growls, picking up another pillow and chucking it at me. "Stupid men and their stupid choices. What the fuck, Alex?"

Another pillow whooshes past my head. "How many pillows do you have up there? That one almost hit me — damn, are there bricks in this one? That fucking hurt, Sunflower."

"I swear to God, you better tell me why you call me that, or I'm gonna …"

I grab her wrist before she pelts me again. Raising an eyebrow, I ask, "Or what?"

Natalie's eyes narrow, her lips purse into a straight line, and one hell of a growl emanates from her body as she launches at me. Not expecting such a sudden movement, she catches me completely off guard, and I go down hard, slamming my elbow and head onto the floor. I can't even react to the pain searing up my arm, because Natalie sticks her hand between my thighs and digs her fingers into the spot about three inches above my knee. That spot just so happens to be the most ticklish spot on my body, and only a few people know about it. "I'm going to kill my sister!"

"Not if you can't get up," Natalie says cheerfully, swiveling to get the other thigh. Two can play at this game. I dig my thumbs into her waist, and she immediately shrieks, stiffens, and falls to the side. I push out an arm to cushion her fall, ensuring her stomach doesn't hit, and then silence. At the same time, our heads turn toward each other, and we burst into laughter. It's the kind of laughter that wracks my entire body, and I can't remember the last time I laughed this hard. As our laughter trails off, Natalie winces as she grabs at her foot. "Somehow my shoe came off and my foot hit the bed frame. Ow."

"Here." I motion for her to give me her foot, and when I dig my fingers into the arch, Natalie lets out a loud moan. Reaching over, I slap a hand over her mouth. "Maybe dial down the porn moans, babe. I'd rather your parents not think I'm fucking the anger out of you in your childhood bedroom."

"Don't promise something you can't deliver on, Alessio." The wicked glint is back in her eyes as she gazes at me. This Natalie I know. The one who takes it as well as she dishes it out. The broken and crushed Natalie from before is thankfully long gone. I don't think she's called me Alessio since our night together, which makes my dick take notice. Before I can process that, Natalie jumps to her feet. "Come on. I bet you haven't had breakfast yet, and my mom's quiche is definitely worth the drive."

"I may not be able to enjoy it if your brother kills me first," I mutter as I rise to stand next to her. Damn, my elbow is throbbing where I hit the floor.

"Eh. He's all bark. My mother will chop off your balls and feed them to the chickens next door if you hurt me, though."

I stiffen as I study Natalie, trying to gauge how serious she is. When she smiles sweetly at me, I chuckle. "Apple doesn't fall far from that violent tree, huh."

"Nope."

Chapter 19

Natalie — Late-December

Before I know it, winter break is upon us. The month of December is sheer bedlam in the classroom. Lots of days with indoor recess, coupled with excitement for Christmas, and tons of extra activities in school and at home mean the kids are sugared up, sleep deprived, and running on empty. The final day before our two week break has me lying on the floor in the middle of my classroom, utterly exhausted and unable to pack up and go home. That's where Alex finds me.

"What the hell, Nat? Did you fall?" he shouts as he rushes to me.

My entire body jolts as he scares me. "Jesus, you scared the crap out of me! I'm fine, Alex. Just tired. I needed a minute to sit here."

"Fuck," he mutters. "I think you just sheared at least a couple years off my life."

It's then that I notice he's in his uniform, and holy hell does he fill that thing out well. I rarely see him when he's working. Actually, since Thanksgiving, I've only seen him once. He asked me to have dinner with him and his kids at the beginning of December. Alex has made a conscious effort to get to know me better, which I've appreciated. We've chatted on the phone a few times, and he checks in via text fairly often. It's nice.

I am a little surprised he hasn't suggested anything physical, after I admitted how sexually frustrated I've been lately. Thank goodness for online shopping, because I'm now in possession of way too many adult toys. They've taken the edge off, but they're nothing like the real thing. And I happen to know Alex Santo delivers one hell of an orgasm.

"What are you doing here?" I ask as I roll over and slowly get to my feet.

"Arianna said you went to the doctor today."

"What? How the hell did she know that?" I yawn, rubbing my eyes. I need to sleep for a few days at least. The second trimester is supposed to be the best one, but I'm too tired to enjoy it.

"Small town, Nat. It was on the website."

"For the love. I hate that website," I murmur.

"You and me both. Keep up. Why did you go to the doctor? Is something wrong?" Alex asks, doing that super-hot cop thing where he hangs onto his bullet proof vest. Am I drooling? Yeah, I'm definitely drooling. "Natalie."

"Hmm?" I respond, my eyes taking a leisurely stroll down his trim body. God, what I wouldn't do to take a ride on him again.

"Focus," he snaps.

I reluctantly drag my gaze back to his. I expect to find a smirk, as if he knows exactly where my mind went, but instead, he's glaring at me. "It was just a normal checkup, Alex. Nothing wrong. I go back in four weeks."

His mouth opens slightly, and his expression is one of shock and disbelief. I'm slightly uncomfortable, so I make my way around him and to my desk.

"You had an appointment today? A standard monthly appointment?" he asks, his voice deceptively calm.

"Yeah?" I turn off my computer and collect my things I'll need at home during the break. Putting my coat on, I walk back to where Alex still stands.

"Why didn't I know about this appointment?"

"You had to work," I respond, confusion evident in my tone.

"So did you, yet you were there."

"Well, kinda hard to have a baby appointment without the one cooking it there," I joke awkwardly. I'm not surprised when Alex doesn't laugh. In fact, he looks even angrier.

"I told you I wanted to be as involved as possible, Sunflower. I meant that. Why aren't you letting me?" he says exasperatedly.

"I don't see why it's a big deal." I walk toward the door and stop to turn off the lights. Alex follows me, stepping into the hallway, and I close the classroom door. "There wasn't even an ultrasound. The OB asked some questions and listened to the heartbeat."

Alex wordlessly follows me downstairs and out into the parking lot, not speaking until we're out of earshot. "The point is I should have been told about the appointment. You didn't even give me the opportunity to go, Natalie. You took the decision away from me."

"You had to work," I say again, approaching my car. "I didn't think you could go, and I didn't think you'd want to go. It's not that big of a deal."

"Stop saying that," he snaps. "I'll decide what's a big deal for my own fucking life. You don't get to unilaterally make these decisions. If I say I want to be told about every appointment, I mean every fucking appointment. I don't care if it's to a podiatrist to get a hangnail removed. As long as *my* baby is in *your* belly, you tell me everything."

I've never seen Alex so angry, and my hackles go up. "Your baby? Not mine? How positively prehistoric of you, Alessio. Will you also be telling me how my birth plan will go? As the man, I assume that's your right, yes? Heaven forbid I make my own decisions. I'm just a silly little woman."

Fire dances in his eyes as he steps toward me. "That's not the same thing, and you fucking know it. I would *never* tell you what you need to do to your body. But that baby is as much mine as it is yours. You disrespected me, and now you're trying to make it my fault."

"Oh my God. I'm not having this conversation right now. I'm tired, and I want to go home. Have a lovely Christmas, Alex." I open my door with a flourish, then slide into the driver's seat. Alex steps out of the way as I slam the door shut. Starting the car, I peel out of the parking lot. Good riddance, asshole.

I'm removing my shoes ten minutes later when someone pounds on my door. Assuming it's the landlord, I open it, unprepared for an angry Alex to push inside. He slams the door behind him and crowds me against the wall. "I am so fucking angry with you, Natalie. So fucking angry. Don't take these moments away from me. Don't assume that I can't do something, or won't want to be there. I missed out on so much with Abbie and Ben because I was deployed. Don't take this away from me."

I feel the blood drain from my face as I stare at him. His eyes, typically a lighter brown, are alive with hurt, anger, and pain, the darkest I've ever seen them. I never thought he'd respond this way. I *did* assume. I figured it was a routine checkup, and he'd been through countless ones before. "Shit, Alex, I'm so sorry. I never thought —"

The words die on my lips when he thrusts both hands into my hair, holding my head in place. His nose touches mine, and hot breath courses over my skin like fire. "That's right. You didn't think. You lumped me into the same category as your dick-for-brains ex, not even allowing me to change your mind."

Holy shit. He's right. I did put him in the same category as Rob, and as every other ex I've had. I just assumed he wouldn't be interested, or be pissed about asking him to take time off.

Alex tightens his fingers in my hair, his nails lightly scratching my scalp, and I let out a reflexive moan. I find my hands bunched against his chest, noting he's removed his bullet proof vest and belt. I don't even know when that happened. "Why are you here, Alex?"

He steps forward a handful of inches until his body lines up with mine. "Because."

"Because why?" I whisper as he drags his nose up and down the length of mine, my eyes slowly closing as one hand slides down from my hair to bracket my neck. I whimper when his thumb finds my pulse point, my heartbeat wild in my chest.

"Because I don't think I can fight this anymore," he finally says, crashing his lips against mine. I can't help the gasp that flows from my mouth into his as he skirts his tongue along mine. It's been months since I experienced an Alex kiss, but his taste bursts forward like a favorite memory that I'd only briefly forgotten. His hand moves around to the back of my neck, and I feel centered. Treasured. Safe.

How can one simple move strike me to my core so completely?

I take one hand and slide it up his spine, feeling a subtle tremble as I thrust my fingers into his hair. Most of the time, Alex keeps his hair in a military-grade cut. I've noticed recently that he's been keeping it longer on top, allowing for a tousled look that looks perfect on him. Alex is always composed and organized. Even while briefly in his home, I noticed that everything had a place, and I'd bet even his socks and boxers were meticulously folded in his drawers. But I know how Alex is at night, when he lets loose. How he allows his senses to take over. Grabbing onto his luscious locks, I pull tightly, just as he did to me only moments ago, and the subsequent groan Alex unleashes tells me I'm on to something.

Alex breaks off the kiss, and before I can voice my displeasure, he nips at my jawline, then moves to my neck. Grabbing one thigh, he hoists my leg around his hips, and I rise to my tiptoes, seeking the friction I crave. I feel Alex chuckle against my skin as he grabs the other thigh, picking me up and holding me against the wall.

"I want to fuck you right here," he whispers, peppering kisses along my exposed collarbone. "Want to feel you break apart on my cock with your back against the wall, with me controlling you. When you move. How you come. What you feel."

"God, yes, please," I moan, moving to get down so I can remove my pants. He can have me anywhere. *Anywhere.* I just want this never-ending itch to be satisfied, because I'm certainly not scratching it enough by myself.

"Another time," he murmurs as he drags his tongue up to my earlobe, sucking on it gently. Hands under my ass, he steps away from the wall, and I gasp.

"Put me down before you hurt your back," I protest.

"What?" he asks incredulously. "We've been over this, Sunflower."

"I mean, I know I'm not tiny, but my weight isn't the whole reason. You're in your late thirties, and you're a cop! I know it's a physical job, and I can't be the reason why you might struggle with normal cop duties."

"Trust me, Sunflower, the majority of my job is answering calls about the goddamned marmot, and doing paperwork. Eternity isn't a hotbed for criminal activity. Besides," he says, as he drops me onto my bed, "it's about five feet from your door to the bed. I think I can handle that. Now take off your fucking pants."

Because I'm nothing if not an aggravation to Alex, I pop a foot up and place it on his chest. "If you want them off so badly, you do it."

His eyes darken as he grins wickedly at me. "Twice now, I've told you I've thought about tying you down to make you listen. You want to know what happens if I have to tell you again?"

Alex leans down, bracketing me against the bed, and waits for my answer. Neither one of us is surprised when I answer honestly, "Yes."

I am, however, shocked when I'm unceremoniously turned over, my pants and underwear yanked down to my ankles, and a thwack sound reverberates around the room before the pain registers. "Did you just spank me?"

Thwack. "You asked for it."

Thwack-thwack. "I didn't exactly ask —" thwack, and oh God, I'm positively dripping now, "— fuck, Alex. Why does that feel so good?"

He smooths a hand over my ass as he admires his work. "Because you're my dirty girl, aren't you? Fucking knew you'd like this."

"Then why suggest it as a punishment?" I moan.

"Never said it was a punishment, baby." I feel his lips on my skin, kissing away the sting, before he grabs my hips and pulls so my stomach and thighs are in the air. With where my pants still hang around my ankles, and Alex's knees on either side of my feet, I'm in a precarious position, with my pussy on full display.

But I'm too focused on how he called me baby, and I'm not sure if Alex even realizes he said it. He's done it before. Secretly, I love it. There's something so comforting, and yet electrifying, about Alex calling me baby. It's like I'm his. As I'm thinking about the term of endearment, he spreads my cheeks, admiring my core.

"This has got to be the prettiest cunt I've ever seen," he murmurs, lightly stroking one finger up and down, before sliding it to my back hole. "Should have spent more time here. Bet the men you've been with have never treated this ass to pleasure."

He'd be right. I've always been intrigued with anal, and only finally got the courage to ask Rob about it when we'd been together almost a year. He bit my head off, telling me that if a man enjoys anal, he must be gay. It never really made sense to me, but I didn't bring it up again, and — oh my fucking God, is Alex rimming me with his tongue? The guttural moan that bursts from my lungs is loud enough to wake hibernating bears. Holy hell, the pleasure coursing through my veins is unlike anything I've ever experienced. Starbursts of color explode behind my eyelids, and every synapse beneath my skin hums with endorphins. I feel a fingertip press against my clit as what seems like two fingers slide into my channel, finding my G-spot immediately. Alex is playing me like a violin, hitting every perfect spot to make me sing.

And, yeah. I sing.

The orgasm that overtakes me steals my breath. It goes on for what seems like minutes, and Alex patiently strokes me through it. When my body finally stops shuddering, he gently lays me on my side. Panting, I wait for my breathing to regulate before I peel open my eyes, only to find the room empty. Did he leave? Again?

I hear the sink in the bathroom turn on, and I take a relieved exhale. It's possible I have a little bit of trauma from our one night, because I can't believe how quickly I jumped to that conclusion. When Alex returns, he gives me a sheepish smile. "I hope you don't mind, but I used some of your mouthwash."

"Why?" I ask, befuddled. "Your breath is fine."

"Uh," he says, reaching behind his head to scratch at the back of his neck, "I want to kiss you again. And I don't feel comfortable after doing ... what I did."

I stare at him in shock. "You just licked my asshole, but you can't say the words out loud?"

He throws back his head with a bark of laughter, but I notice the slight pink hue that creeps onto his neck. "I guess not."

Kicking off my pants and underwear, I beckon him to come closer. "Come here, then. I need a kiss."

When his brow furrows, a little wrinkle appearing between them, I'm confused. "We, uh, have to switch positions, Sunflower."

"Why?"

He points to my belly once, then again, before making eye contact. "The baby. You have to be on top. Can't crush the baby."

Lord. I'm so focused on orgasms that I can't even think straight. "I guess it's good that one of us is being level headed and thinking clearly."

"One of us is currently cum-drunk, so the other is paying attention," Alex says with a teasing smile. I can't help but stare. Alex is incredibly handsome no matter the time, but smiling Alex, carefree and happy Alex, takes my breath away. "You're staring, Sunflower."

"I just …" I trail off, clearing my throat. I want to tell him how lovely it is to see him smile without sounding like a complete lovestruck dummy. "I like when you tease me."

Alex smiles softly as he grabs my hands and pulls me to standing. "Gotta admit, I like teasing you."

He sits on the edge of the bed, patting his lap. Straddling him, I sink into his lap as I wrap my arms around his shoulders. When he reaches up to push my hair behind both ears, I'm suddenly overcome with insecurity. In the quiet of my apartment, sitting half naked in Alex's lap, I'm struck by how different this interaction is, even from our night together. Worried that I'm the only one feeling the connection, I try to duck my head and put it on his shoulder, but he intercepts the movement with one hand on my chin. "What's going on in that head of yours?"

As his brown eyes study me, I struggle with finding a suitable answer, as my own version of word vomit churns up my throat. "This is odd. Right? I'm not wearing pants, and you're still completely clothed, and you licked my ass, Alex. You could barely be in the same room with me weeks ago, yet now we're here, and what the hell is this? Are you going to sneak out again? Will it be weeks before I hear from you? This is just so weird, and I think I need some parameters so I know what to expect."

I watch as the shutters close on his eyes, as Alex builds up the walls again. I knew I should have stifled my voice. I always struggle with lacking a filter, but this pregnancy has made me doubt everything, and I thought maybe I could express myself with tact and respect. Instead, I played the 'what is this' card while sitting in his lap, when I know he wants nothing from me.

"Alex, I'm sorry. That was so out of line, and please just ignore everything I said. Please," I say quietly, humiliation dotting every one of my words.

Alex clears his throat before responding. "I'm struggling, Sunflower. I think I have feelings for you, and I'm working through it. I've never felt like this. I'm so fucking attracted to you, and I don't know how to process that. I know I've done a shitty job of supporting you, and I promise I'll do better. But I don't know what all I'm prepared to offer right now. I don't know how to move forward."

"Oh," I mumble. "It seems like you hate me most of the time, so I guess it's confusing when you suddenly seem to ... not hate me."

"You think I hate you?"

"Well, yeah," I shrug. "You didn't want anything with me, and now you're forced to have a kid with me. We've argued almost every time we've talked."

"That's not — that's not because I hated you. It's because I *wanted* you."

Chapter 20

Alex — Mid-to-late December

I don't hate Natalie. It's so fucking far from the truth. I hate that I want her. That I crave her. How the moment I kissed her tonight felt like coming home, and how guilty I feel about that.

"I'm sorry, I ruined everything," Natalie whispers, tightening her arms around my neck. I slide my hands against her back and pull her closer to me. She subconsciously snuggles against me, and I feel the heat of her core soaking right through my uniform pants onto my stiff as a board cock. When she shimmies, I let out a groan.

"You didn't ruin anything. And unless you want to feel me come in my pants like a teenager, stop moving," I rasp, my voice husky as the little vixen immediately stops, then starts again. "Fucking hell, Sunflower. That spanking taught you nothing."

"It totally didn't," she pants, finding a rhythm against me. "But this feels too good to care."

I debate on letting her finish, then sitting her next to me so we can continue the conversation. So I can be clear with my expectations. Maybe we scratch this itch. Maybe I help her scratch the itch every now and again. How can I tell her that I don't know what to name this — whatever this is — without sounding like I'm just using her to hook up?

I'm about to tell her to stop so I can pull out my cock, but Natalie senses what I'm about to say and reaches between us to undo my pants. Her little hand wraps around me, and I let out a harsh swear as that tingling at the base of my spine hits. "Hurry up, baby, or else I'm coming on your stomach."

Pushing my pants and boxers out of the way, we let out simultaneous moans when Natalie slides down onto me, her tight heat engulfing me perfectly. It's been so many years since I went without a condom that I have to grit my teeth and start chanting some of the cadences I learned in basic training in an attempt to get my dick to behave. I'm ready to blow, and the vision before me isn't helping matters when she throws her head back in bliss, her long hair dragging along my thighs.

Grabbing both of Natalie's arms, I thrust them into the air so I can remove her sweater, then groan in delight. Her ample breasts explode out of a black lace bra, and I salivate with sheer need as I yank her bra straps down and immediately suck a tip into my mouth. Natalie cries out, clutching my head against her chest, and I feel her pussy clamp down on me. Her tits have gone up at least a cup size in pregnancy, and she was already well endowed. I'm a boob man, and I'm all too happy with this new playground. As I switch to the other breast, Natalie mumbles, "I didn't think they'd be this sensitive."

"Yeah?"

"Alex, you're gonna make me come again if you keep going."

I know if she comes, I'll follow her right over the cliff. I'm barely hanging on as it is, and as much as I'd love to experience her orgasm just from playing with her breasts, I want to bring her there with my cock. Letting her nipple out of my mouth with a resounding pop, I grip Natalie's waist as I raise her until just the tip of my cock remains inside her core. Eyes closed, she waits for me to move her, but when I don't, her eyes open. When they connect with mine, I state clearly, "Keep those eyes on me."

Her gaze doesn't waver as I begin slowly thrusting into her from below. I know I'm not lasting long. Her pussy feels exquisite, gripping me so tightly. She mumbles to herself, "So fucking good."

Indeed.

Best I've ever —

No. Shaking my head to remove that thought, I refocus. Sticking my tongue out, I touch the tip to her nipple, and her pussy flutters around me. Jesus, they really are sensitive. "You gonna come on my cock like a good girl, Natalie? Milk me, baby. Make me come."

I lean forward and wrap my teeth lightly around her nipple, biting softly, and Natalie seizes up in my arms as she comes violently. She struggles to keep her eyes open, but I'm too far gone to care. The wave of pleasure starts at my toes, sweeping over my body as I thrust harshly into her. Spurt after spurt releases as I grunt through my own intense orgasm.

Natalie collapses against me, her head lolling on my shoulder as we both regain our senses. Moments later, when she's still quiet, I assume she's fallen asleep. Suddenly lifting her head, she looks me directly in the eye and says, "Promise me something."

"Okay?" I respond hesitantly.

"If this is just a one-night thing, promise me we can do that again before you go home. We have to do that again."

I chuckle as she gives me a coy smile. "I think I can make that happen."

We don't have sex again. What occurs instead is one of the most confusing nights of my life.

After ensuring my kids will be fine at Dom's house for dinner and a sleepover, Natalie orders food for delivery. Hours later, after discovering a shared love of home improvement shows, we discuss all the ways we'd rebuild and decorate her apartment and my house. Our tastes are night and day. Natalie is big colors, cozy furniture, and loads of personality. I'm clean lines, minimal accessories, and organization in every area.

Yet as we discussed our ideas, they were cohesive. We could share a space and showcase both of our personalities. After having a decade long relationship with someone so similar to me, it throws me off kilter to recognize meeting a woman in the middle and not feeling like I'd given up so much.

I told her various stories about growing up with six siblings, and she regaled me with tales of her brother's antics. Natalie's ability to tell a story is on par with my grandmother. Her eyes light up with mirth and mischief, hands thrown about as she tells me tale after tale where Shawn got into trouble. It seems my Sunflower comes by her cantankerous personality genetically.

My Sunflower.

Natalie falls asleep with her head on my shoulder, and after turning off the television, I pick her up and place her under the covers.

"Don't leave," she mumbles, half awake. "You promised more sex."

"Not really into somnophilia, Sunflower," I murmur.

"Some no what?"

"Nothing. Go back to sleep."

When her breathing deepens, I move to sit on a chair, my elbows on my knees as I watch her sleep. It would be so easy to climb behind her, wrap my arms around her and fall asleep with her amazing vanilla scent comforting me, but I won't. I can't.

You can.

"God dammit, Sara, not now," I hiss quietly.

She needs you.

Fucking hell. I hate this. Hate that I feel like I'm having an affair. Hate that I can't seem to move on, and Sara's been dead for over five years.

The wind seems to whoosh right out of my sails as I hear the words in my mind.

Sara is dead.

The only woman I've ever loved died while I was thousands of miles away.

I think up until this point, I'd referred to her as being gone or passed away. Somehow using the word 'dead' makes it more final and blunt.

Natalie sighs as she tucks a hand under her face, her other hand reaching as if she's trying to touch me. I have to get out of here. I can't handle this right now.

I get dressed silently, aware that I'm going to hurt Natalie again, but powerless to stop what I'm about to do.

You're an idiot.

I violently shake my head to remove Sara's thoughts, then grab my shoes as I quietly creep out of the apartment.

As I close the door, I see Natalie's eyes are open, watching me, but I don't stop. Even when I hear her shout, "You're a coward, Alex!"

I know.

It should be pretty emasculating to admit that I get home, immediately get in the shower, and then begin to sob. Once those flood gates opened, it becomes a raging river of grief, anger, and general sadness.

I cry for the life I thought I'd have, and what my kids are missing out on because Sara isn't here. I cry because I never really let myself break down when she died, thinking I had to be strong and steadfast for Abbie and Ben. I've always thought of their feelings before my own, and now I realize what a detriment that was to my own mental health.

Once out of the shower, I open up my email app to find the response I got from the therapist my mom suggested weeks ago. Pete Ducey responded almost immediately that day, but then I got cold feet and never answered his initial questions. I can't keep living like this. Regardless of any future romantic relationships, I have to take care of *me* for the sake of my children.

I feel somewhat lighter after the shower sob fest, and I wonder if I had been holding on to all that emotion for years. My thoughts seem remarkably clearer, and I recognize how poorly I've treated Natalie. She didn't ask for any of this, and I'm determined to figure out a way for us to co-exist as we move forward.

After a fitful few hours of sleep, I make my way to Dominic's early Saturday morning. A fresh dusting of snow blankets Eternity Springs, and I lovingly look around my hometown, noting all the beauty as the town wakes up. Isabella's bakery is already bustling, and I'm sure she's been slogging away over her ovens, completing normal daily items as well as special orders for Christmas cookies and cakes.

I find myself automatically turning to go down Natalie's street, and I'm surprised to find her outside, shoveling the sidewalk. Furious, I skid to a halt, throw the car in park, and storm across the street. "What the fuck are you doing, Nat?"

Her eyes meet mine, and I see the swirling of emotions. "What does it look like I'm doing, asshole? I'm shoveling the fucking sidewalk."

I attempt to take the shovel from her, but she scoots away. "Seriously, give me the damn shovel. I'll do it."

"No."

"Yes."

"No! I don't need your help with anything, Alex. Any. Thing. I'm sick and tired of your mood swings where you lull me into a false sense of security, then rip the rug right out from under me. So how about you leave me the hell alone, alright?"

"You shouldn't shovel while pregnant," I say gently. "I don't remember a lot from when Sara was pregnant, but I remember that one."

"Well, all of my neighbors are older than me, and the city never does this part of the sidewalk. It's safer for me to shovel than it is for me to fall on my stomach."

"Please let me finish. I can't sit here and let you do this."

"You can if I don't give up the shovel," she states defiantly, popping the shovel loudly on the ground as she stares at me, one hand on her hip. "I don't want you here, Alex. Do you understand me? I. Don't. Want. You. Here."

Each word grates on my heart, and I look at the ground. I notice she's wearing two different boots, then leggings under a long nightgown that she definitely didn't have on last night. A puffer jacket covers the nightgown, and a cute owl hat with a large pompom on top sits on her head. Nothing is the same color, her hair is in disarray, but

I honestly feel like the breath is stolen from my lungs as my eyes meet hers.

I'm taken aback at the intensity in her eyes, though. Natalie has never looked at me with such disdain and hatred evident in her gaze, and I wonder if I've finally managed to push her away.

"Okay, I'll go," I say hesitantly, pushing my hands up in surrender. I make a mental note to find a teenager that I can hire to shovel the rest of the block every time it snows the remainder of winter. When I look back at Natalie as she blows an errant piece of hair out of her eyes, I think how she's never looked more beautiful.

"Do you ever sleep in?" Still clad in pajamas with his hair sticking out in every direction, my younger brother rubs his eyes as he opens the door for me.

"No, and you didn't used to sleep in either," I point out.

"I have a hot wife warming my bed. I kept her up late last night," Dom says proudly.

"I assumed my kids would be up if you weren't," I explain as I remove my thick winter coat.

"Hi Dad," Ben calls from the kitchen.

Dom winces, then leans toward me to whisper, "I love your kid, but when he gets up before us, he ransacks the kitchen. Help me clean it up before Katharine comes down. He got into some kind of special coffee once, and she's never forgotten."

Great. I don't really want my sister-in-law to hate me, so I trudge after Dom to see what mess my son has made.

"Ben, what's on the ceiling?" Dom asks, and I stop in my tracks as I witness the destruction before me.

"It was a science experiment. Toilet paper and water. It didn't work as I anticipated."

"How did you think it would go?" Dom pries.

"Well, I thought gravity would allow the wad to fall down fairly quickly. But I didn't consider the viscosity of the wad, and that the wetness of it became like a glue," Ben says matter-of-factly.

"So you're saying you basically glued toilet paper to my ceiling?"

"Yes."

Dom continues to study the ceiling, tilting his head to the side. "It would appear there's some cereal stuck inside the wad of goo."

Ben giggles, then covers his mouth with his hands. "I attempted to weigh down the wad."

"Ben, how long have you been up?" I ask, rubbing my neck as I attempt to keep a straight face.

"Quite a few hours, Dad. I woke up because Aunt Kate kept shouting something, but I couldn't tell what she said. Then I heard Uncle Dom tell her to take it, so I figured she was going downstairs. I must have missed her, though, because no one was down here. I started watching my favorite YouTube channel about science experiments, so I was fine."

"Jesus Christ," Dom mutters.

"Take it?" I ask.

"I'm not going to clarify that, but I'm sure you can use your imagination."

"Lovely. You're lucky he didn't barge in there to check on Kate, man. Better watch it when my kids are here."

"Locked door and a chair under the doorknob. Got three kids of my own. I'm not taking any chances. Now hurry up and help me clean this up before Katharine has a heart attack."

The kitchen is cleaned in a half hour, and Ben is sleeping soundly on the couch when Kate meanders down a little bit later. None the wiser, we choose to keep Ben's science experiments — and what he heard after he went to bed — to ourselves. As long as Kate doesn't look at the ceiling, where a wet spot still resides on the paint, then she'll never know.

"How's the baby momma doing, Alex?" Kate teases.

I sigh, frustration emanating from me in waves. "Pissed at me for a variety of reasons."

"What did you do?" Dom asks. When I raise an eyebrow at him, he rolls his eyes. "Come on. I love you, but you're a fucking disaster. She's pregnant, hormonal, and has no one here. I'm on her side."

I quickly explain the last twenty four hours, leaving out the more personal details, but insinuate we slept together again. How I promised her I wouldn't sneak out, but then did anyway, and how she yelled at me when I found her shoveling this morning. I feel awful saying that I tried to help, and it only seemed to make Natalie even angrier. I explain how I've felt a pull to Natalie over the past month, and how I'm struggling with the vows I made to Sara.

"Was she angry about your help, about you leaving in the middle of the night, or about the ups and downs with you entirely?" Kate asks.

"All of the above, I think." I scratch my chin absentmindedly. "I don't mean to swing from one way to the other. I'm really struggling."

"Well, you never went to therapy after Sara died, and then spent half a decade pining for her. Honestly I'm not surprised you're having difficulty now," Dom says. Kate gasps and slaps him on the chest. "What?"

"Read the room, Dominic. That was incredibly uncouth," Kate chastises.

Dom shrugs. "He gave me shit about you. This is how brothers are. I'm not going to sugarcoat it. I've watched our entire family tiptoe around you, man, and it needs to stop. Mom said she gave you the name of my therapist. Have you made an appointment yet?"

"I — that was from you?" I stammer.

Dom nods. "I've been seeing him for a few years."

"But why? You're the most put together person I know."

Dom sighs, then looks to Kate, who squeezes his hand reassuringly. "I suffer from some pretty intense anxiety. Somewhere along the line, I became convinced that I had to control everything, and perfection was the only option. It was only when I married Kate that things began to come together, but I still see Pete once a month to touch base."

"I had no idea," I murmur.

Dom gives me a half smile. "I did a hell of a job hiding it. Mom only found out a couple years ago. I really think you should speak to Pete. He's helped me so much."

"But what should I do about Natalie?" I ask.

"You shouldn't do anything about it today," Kate says quietly. When I look up at her, she's smiling at me kindly. "Your mental health is what's paramount right now. You cannot have any relationship with her, whether that be romantic, or as co-parents, until you take care of what's going on in your head. You're struggling, and deep down, I know Natalie understands that. She might have been angry today, but give her time."

"I don't want any of this," I confess. "I don't want to want her. I don't want to have this fucking trauma hanging over me, and I don't want to have to talk to a shrink about it."

"We don't really get to pick our trauma," Dom says dryly. "I certainly didn't think things would turn out the way they did with Savannah. When she showed up at our renewal ceremony, our kids were traumatized. All five of us went to therapy. It helps to have an outsider objectively look at a situation."

"That's what Natalie said about Ben," I murmur.

Kate's eyes widen. "She suggested Ben needed therapy?"

I nod. "Teachers noticed some changes since last year, and Nat said Ben won't talk about Sara at all. I guess it never occurred to me that it might be helpful to allow the kids a place to vent. I figured we're men, and we suck it up with the emotional shit."

Dom smothers a laugh as Kate glares at him. He holds up his hands in surrender. "Direct that glare at him, Katharine. I've dealt with my emotional shit, and now it's his turn."

"You dealt with your anxiety shit, and I forced you to deal with your emotional shit," she points out.

"Semantics," he mutters. "Back to your original statement though. You said you don't want to want Natalie. So you do at least acknowledge a connection there?"

I sigh, closing my eyes as I rest my head against the back of the chair. "I don't know how to handle my thoughts about her. She couldn't be any more the opposite of Sara if she tried. Sara was comfortable and relaxed. Natalie challenges everything. Sara rarely raised her voice, and Natalie has shouted at me more than once already. Then I see her with Ben, and she's so fucking patient and kind. With Sara, it was making love. But with Natalie, it's —"

"Fucking," Dom says. "You never once thought you fucked Sara? Not once?"

"No," I admit. "I felt like our hearts were meeting. It was sexy and sensual. With Natalie, I want to rut her into the ground. I'm so fucking attracted to her that I can't see straight, and it's messing with my ability to make conscious decisions. It's primal. I feel like a damn animal when I'm around her, just trying to will my dick to stay calm."

"She had a crush on you growing up, did you know that?" Kate pipes up. When I nod my head, she continues. "She was super shy as a teen, apparently, and by the time she had gained some confidence, you were already with Sara. She said it was painful to watch the two of you together because she could see how much you loved each other."

"She told Abbie something similar. At least the part about seeing me with Sara. I don't think she told Abbie that it was painful to see me with Sara, though."

"Listen, Alex," Kate says, sitting up and placing her hand on mine, "I know you're struggling, but Natalie is too. This isn't how she thought her life would turn out either. Knowing both of you, I can say this with certainty: I really don't think Natalie will handle you breaking her heart very well. After what her jackass ex did to her, her confidence is nonexistent. So I want you to be very sure of what you want with her before you approach her about anything."

Dom nods, and I chuckle bitterly. "You agree with your wife?"

"I do. Natalie has the most to lose here, and she already has the past of wanting a connection with you. No offense, bro, but you deal with trauma and heartbreak by closing yourself off. You'll bounce back because you won't allow yourself any other option. Natalie will be stuck living here, with no family, and will see your miserable ass all over the place. If you don't know with certainty that you are going to end up with her, don't take that chance."

Chapter 21

Alex — January

Taking what Dom and Kate said to heart, I begin making a conscious effort to get to know Natalie more. Hell, we're going to be raising a child together. I should know more about my child's mother.

But, knowing how my body wants to get to know Natalie, I decide to begin with texts and phone calls.

Me: Hi.

Natalie: Uh, hi?

Me: How was your day?

Natalie: What is this, Alex?

Me: Just seeing how your day was.

Natalie: Fine. Long. Tiring.

Me: Ben told me you ran out of the room once. Is everything okay?

Natalie: Ah. Now I see why you're texting.

Me: I can be checking on you AND seeing how your day was, Nat.

Natalie: Fine. Your child kept kicking my bladder, and I had to run to the bathroom.

Me: MY kid, huh.

Natalie: Yup. Definitely your kid when he is being all troublesome.

Me: He? Do you know something I don't?

Natalie: Gut instinct. I don't know. I promise I won't keep you from another appointment.

Me: Thanks. I know things are weird between us, but I'll always support you in whatever you need.

Natalie: Right now I need to sleep for fifteen hours and eat my weight in ice cream. Well, maybe not my weight. Half of my weight.

Me: Noted. Other than needing sleep, how are you feeling?

Natalie: Okay. I guess I can't complain. Ari told me horror stories about pregnancy, and so far none of those have panned out, so I'm counting my blessings.

Me: Never believe anything my baby sister says. She embellishes heavily.

Natalie: Oh? So that story about you putting a live toad in her bed was embellished?

Me: Okay, so a lot of what she says is embellished. The toad story is true. I didn't think she'd be excited and decide to keep the damn thing as a pet, though.

Natalie: And that the toad got out of the room somehow, but you and Dom convinced her she had killed it in her sleep?

Me: In my defense, that was almost solely Dom. Although Luca put the little 'murderer' notes all over her room.

WORTH THE TEST

Natalie: Is sibling bullying a genetic trait? Should I worry about Abbie and Ben?

Me: I doubt it. Abbie is way too excited about having a baby to boss around, and Ben probably won't worry about that kind of thing.

Natalie: He'll be too invested in his own world of science experiments and hypotheses about the way everything works.

Me: Very true.

Natalie: I love that about him. I can see the cogs moving in his mind as he works out a problem.

Me: My mom said I was like that at his age, too.

Natalie: When I met Ben, he told me he wants to be a pilot in the Air Force when he grows up.

Me: Yeah. He's felt that way for a few years. He wants to go to the United States Air Force Academy after high school.

Natalie: And you're okay with that?

Me: Of course. Why wouldn't I be?

Natalie: It's a scary world, and I can only assume it must be nerve-racking to think about your son joining the military.

Me: It is. But I'd never hold back any of my kids from what they want to do based on MY worries. I'll support them as best I can.

Natalie: That's pretty awesome of you, Alex. There are quite a few parents who are the exact opposite.

Me: Not me. I'll support my kids. All of them, including ours.

Natalie: I like that.

Me: It's supposed to snow tonight. Do you need anything?

Natalie: No.

Natalie: Interesting that I've found a teenager shoveling the sidewalk when it snowed last week. Will the teenager be shoveling tomorrow as well?

Me: I don't know what you're talking about.

Me: But yes.

Natalie: Alex!

Me: You said you didn't want me to do it, but you never said I couldn't hire someone else to do it.

Natalie: It's not going to hurt me.

Me: Maybe, but maybe not. Did you know that people over a certain age aren't supposed to shovel snow, because if you're at a certain angle, the force could give you an instant heart attack?

Natalie: Really?

Me: Yep.

Natalie: For pregnant women? Or women in their thirties?

WORTH THE TEST

Me: Well, no, the info I saw was about people over the age of forty.

Natalie: So by asking you not to shovel, I was actually saving YOUR life.

Me: I'm not forty yet, Sunflower.

Natalie: I'm rounding up.

Me: Nice.

Natalie: There was more gray in your beard the last time I saw you. You get a walker yet?

Me: No, a cane looks better with my uniform.

Natalie: You should bedazzle it!

Me: What do you think I'm doing right now?

Natalie: I will give you everything in my bank account if you can send me a selfie right now.

Me: You know, my phone camera is acting up.

Natalie: Uh-huh.

Me: Next time, I'll definitely take a pic.

Natalie: You plan on bedazzling more canes soon?

Me: It's the talk of the entire department. Everyone wants a bedazzled police cane now.

Natalie: You'll be the talk of the entire state if that's true.

Me: Tourism is about to be booming!

Natalie: Good to know lol

Me: Ben told me you've started a unit on the human body, and now he wants to know specifics on how babies are made, as well as how they're born.

Natalie: I'm glad he asked you, because he brought it up in front of the class, and I will admit I choked. Told him to have you talk to him, then he could come back and report what he'd learned. I totally forgot to text you and warn you. Whoops.

Me: Whoops?

Natalie: In my defense, I came home and accidentally took a three-hour nap.

Me: Growing a baby is exhausting.

Natalie: You have no idea.

Me: How specific am I supposed to get? If he's reporting back to the class, obviously I can't tell him about the ole C in the V, right?

Natalie: Just when I think you've forgotten about that, we're here again.

Me: Never gonna forget, Sunflower. Honestly, I'm surprised that verbiage didn't end up on that gossip website.

Natalie: Well, it did. Very briefly. Then I threatened to sue, and the article mysteriously disappeared.

Me: Seriously?

Natalie: Yeah. Quoting private conversations? Not cool. I said it was illegal, but I'm honestly not sure if it is, but apparently that was enough, because they took my threat to heart and deleted the article. I figured they'd just remove the parts about our conversation, but they removed the entire article.

Me: How did I never know about this?

Natalie: I completely forgot. I started my job, and then started getting so exhausted that I'd pretty much eat dinner and fall asleep. I can't believe it took me as long as it did to realize I was pregnant.

Me: I assume when a woman is really busy, it's easy to ignore little symptoms.

Natalie: I guess. It's definitely not easy. Never realized how tired I'd be. Maybe if I was pregnant a decade ago, I'd have been better able to handle it.

Me: I don't know. I remember Sara telling me she was really tired with Abbie, but not with Ben.

Natalie: And you were deployed for both?

Me: For part of each. Fortunately I was home for both births. I had colleagues who were deployed for births, and I can't imagine how hard that must have been.

Natalie: I'm sure it was equally hard for you to be gone, no matter the time.

Me: Yeah, but it could be worse.

Natalie: It's not a competition for who has it worse, Alex. Your worst is still your worst, regardless of someone else's life. Don't undervalue what you experienced, and how you felt.

Me: That's true. Sara basically said the same thing. But I always felt guilty, like I was dropping the ball.

Natalie: It sounds like guilt is a four-letter word in your world.

> Me: Yeah, it is.

> Natalie: I need to tell you something.

> Me: What's wrong? Do you want to call me?

> Natalie: Nothings wrong with me or the baby. Well, at least the baby is fine. And I'd rather do this over text.

My mind whirls, thinking about what she could want to tell me. Immediately I think she's dating someone, and a wave of fury catapults over me so fast I forget to breathe. I have absolutely no right to be angry if she is dating anyone. I have no claim over her. And I honestly don't understand why that was my first thought, or why I reacted to it with such animosity.

Because you're falling for her.

"No I'm not."

Yes, you are.

"Stop it," I snap.

Not until you admit I'm right.

"You never argued with me like this before," I mutter.

Maybe I should have.

"Why didn't you?"

Because it was easier.

"Bullshit." Sara popping into my head right now is pissing me off.

Natalie: I yelled at Ben today. Like actually yelled at him. And I feel awful. He cried, which made me cry, and then I couldn't get a hold of myself, and the teacher across the hall had to call the admin team to come relieve me. Ben wouldn't talk to me for the rest of the day. I tried apologizing a dozen times, but he wouldn't listen. I don't know what to do. I've never felt so awful about treating a student like this.

Me: You yelled at him? About what?

Natalie: Our math unit is something Ben clearly knows very well, because he kept interrupting me to tell me how I wasn't teaching it correctly. I was trying to show the class there are different ways to estimate numbers, especially when fractions are involved. When he interrupted for the fifth or sixth time, I blew up at him.

Me: Define blew up.

Natalie: I sort of blacked out a little, so I'm not entirely sure of everything I said. But I know I told him since he's so smart, he should tell the principal that I need to be fired and he can take my place.

Me: Jesus, Natalie. That's a little extreme.

Natalie: I'm aware of that. I don't know what came over me! One minute I was patiently telling him to sit back down, and the next, I'm in his face.

Me: In his face?

Natalie: Not IN his face. I meant that I just yelled at him. I didn't get in his face. At least I don't think I did? But I feel awful. Should I come over and apologize?

Me: I don't think that's necessary. Ben needs to know that you're the teacher, and he has to respect your authority in the classroom.

Natalie: I assumed you'd be madder than this.

Me: I'm not happy about it, but I can see it from both sides.

Natalie: Well, I got reprimanded by admin, and it was reported to the school board. I guess the teacher across the hall also heard me yelling. They understand I'm pregnant and hormonal, but the fact that I'm connected to Ben in more ways than just his teacher makes it a murky area.

Me: I'm glad you were reprimanded.

Natalie: What?

Me: You can't just go around yelling at kids, Natalie. Pregnant or not. Teachers could have gotten away with it when we were in fourth grade, but not today.

Me: Honestly, you should be counting your lucky stars it was Ben you blew up on, because some parents in your classroom wouldn't stop until you were fired. You're lucky it's me you're dealing with.

Natalie: This is the Alex I assumed would show up tonight.

Me: What? The parent Alex? The voice of reason Alex? I'm not going to coddle you when you've made a mistake like this. I appreciate you reaching out to explain, and I'll talk to Ben about interrupting you. But if you blow up at my kid again, our history won't be a factor in how I respond.

Natalie: Noted.

"Dad?" A small voice asks quietly from behind where I'm sitting at the island in my kitchen. I turn to see Ben, a worried expression on his face.

"What's up, bud?" I ask, knowing full well he's going to talk to me about the situation with Natalie.

"Can we stop at the store on the way to school in the morning?" Ben inquires.

"For what?"

"Well, I made Ms. Jackson cry today. I didn't mean to, but I want to get her a flower and a card to apologize," he says solemnly. Red-rimmed eyes tell me he's been crying in his room, and I immediately pull him into my arms.

"We can, but I also know that she made you cry today," I tell him gruffly. "And that wasn't okay either."

"But if I had just listened to her, she wouldn't have yelled at me," Ben cries. "It's all my fault."

"You made a bad choice, son. You did. But Ms. Jackson didn't have to respond the way she did. You're both to blame."

"Can we still stop and get some flowers?" he mumbles against my shoulder, making me smile.

"How about you draw her a bouquet of flowers? Real flowers will die, but a picture can last forever. She'll cherish that so much more."

His head pops up. "Really? I could even make her a LEGO bouquet, that way it's a three dimensional object she can enjoy from all sides!"

I chuckle. "Let's start with the picture, then we'll move on, okay?"

"You'll help me?" he asks.

"Of course. I bet Abbie will help with the building part, too."

"Great idea. I'll go get her now. ABBIE!" he shouts, right beside my ear, and I wince.

"God, I'm right here," my sassy almost thirteen-year old says, and when I glance at her, I find her rolling her eyes.

"Dad said you'd help us build some flowers for my teacher."

Abbie's eyes light with fire. "I'm not helping you do a damn thing for that woman."

"Abigail!" I admonish. "Language!"

"Oh, please," she scoffs. "That was barely anything. It's not like I dropped an F-bomb. Besides, I heard what happened with Natalie. She's lucky I don't show up there and give her a piece of my mind."

"It was my fault," Ben says, defensively. "Well, mostly."

"You're a kid, and she's an adult. Even I know the difference —" Abbie stops talking when the doorbell rings. A malicious grin slowly spreads across her face. "I think I'm about to get my chance."

"Shit," I mutter. "Abbie, no. You keep your mouth shut."

"What?" she says innocently as she stalks toward the front door. "I'm just answering the door for our late night guest."

"It's not late night, it's late evening at best. And you don't say a word. In fact," courtesy of longer legs, I get in front of her, stepping between her and the door, "go sit on the couch. You don't need to answer it. What if it's not Natalie?"

"We both know it's her," Abbie hisses.

"We don't know that, so go sit on the damn couch."

"How come you get to say damn, but I don't?"

"Because I'm a damn adult, now go sit on the damn couch!"

"I can hear you, you know," Natalie calls from outside.

I point toward the back of the house. "Go. Now."

I hear her grumble something as she passes her brother, who stands with just his head peeking out from behind a wall. "Do you want to answer the door, or should I? I'm pretty sure she's here for you." Even though I fucking told her not to come over tonight, but am I really that surprised that the woman didn't listen to me?

"You answer it," Ben says timidly. I unlock the door, opening it with a steeled expression, ready to maintain my composure, but what stands in front of me steals my breath. Her face clear of makeup, hair in a floppy messy bun, Natalie wears a pair of black leggings, and a robe that covers my shirt. My shirt that she never gave back to me. It's now tighter around her midsection, but still has room to grow. She looks exquisite. Perfect. I fight the urge to pull her into my arms by gripping the doorknob with ridiculous strength.

You're falling for her.

Admit it.

No.

"Hi," Natalie says, her voice as quiet as I've ever heard it. "I know you said not to come, but I can't let Ben wait all night to hear me apologize. I know he'll probably be up all night worrying, thinking it's his fault. I know him, and he'll start to convince himself it's even worse than it is. I can't let him do that. I just can't."

Fuck me.

She described Ben so perfectly. So incredibly smart, gifted, and creative, but with anxiety that manifests itself in situations where he can take a tiny detail and add to it little by little until it's a massive ball hurtling toward his world at breakneck speed.

"But it is my fault, Ms. Jackson," Ben says quietly, stepping out from behind the wall. "If I had listened when you said to sit down, you wouldn't have yelled. Then I wouldn't have made you cry."

Natalie sighs, placing her palm against my chest and pushes me out of the way as she walks to Ben, and I close the door. Plopping onto her knees, she grabs Ben's hands in her own. "It's not your fault. It's mine. I'm the teacher. You're the fourth grader. I'm to blame, Ben. Not you. Okay? This was completely my fault."

"But I made you cry, and ..." he trails off as his lower lip trembles, tears filling his eyes. I hear a sniffle, and find Natalie crying as well.

"I made you cry first. And then that made me cry, because I am heartbroken over seeing you cry," Natalie says. "You were excited about what we're learning in math, and I should have been more patient with you. I promise I'll be better from now on."

"Did you get in trouble with the principal?" Ben asks, and Natalie nods.

"I did."

"I'm sorry," Ben whispers.

"It's my own fault. I have to accept responsibility for that."

"I can be sorry you're in trouble without feeling like it's my fault."

Natalie lets out a breathy laugh. "Yes, you can."

"I was gonna make you a bouquet of flowers. Well, Abbie and Dad were gonna help."

Abbie scoffs again. "Forced help."

"You were going to make me flowers?" Natalie asks, a beautiful smile stretching across her face. "How?"

"Well, at first I asked Dad if we could stop at the store tomorrow morning, but he reminded me that flowers die, and maybe I could draw you a picture."

Natalie looks up at me, her eyes softening as she nods. "Your dad is correct. A picture could be something I enjoy forever."

"Yes. Then I thought about making paper flowers, but I knew Dad wouldn't like the mess of that, so I didn't bring it up." He's not wrong. For as smart as he is, the child has no spatial awareness when it comes to glue.

"That would be pretty messy," Natalie snickers. I can tell she also knows about Ben's use of glue.

"Then I thought a three dimensional bouquet of LEGO flowers would be perfect, because you'd be able to see it from every angle of your desk. Abbie is the best builder in our house, which is why I wanted her to help," Ben says, casting a quick glance at his sister through his thick lashes.

Abbie looks stunned. "Really? I'm the best?"

"You are," I announce as I walk toward them. "Which is why you're going to help us build one now."

I extend a hand to Natalie, who looks equally as stunned. "What are you doing?"

"Helping you up, Sunflower. I thought that was pretty self-explanatory," I murmur, waiting for her to slip her hand into mine. When she does, a zing of electricity whips up my arm, followed by a lovely feeling of heat. I watch as Natalie's eyes dilate, and I slide my thumb to graze her wrist, feeling her pulse go wild. I pull her up, just close enough that her vanilla scent hits my nose. "You're going to stay and build with us."

"I am?" she says with a chuckle.

"Yes. Then we can both explain to Ben how babies are made."

"What?" she hisses. "You were supposed to do that already!"

"Well, I didn't," I murmur as I turn her toward the kitchen. Bending down so I can speak directly into her ear, I say quietly, "You want to spend the night? We can practice what we're going to say."

I'm not surprised when a speechless Natalie doesn't answer.

Chapter 22

Natalie — February

"Are you ready for your mantra?"

I sigh, grinding my molars as I glare at my therapist. "Violence isn't the answer. Relationships are a two-way street. I can't solve all the problems for everyone. Mostly."

Pete's eyebrows raise. "Mostly?"

"Well, I agree with two out of three. But can we modify one? What about the threat of violence? I've found people shape up when they think they're about to get clocked in the nuts."

Now it's Pete's turn to sigh. "Natalie. It's not okay to threaten violence either."

"I know," I grumble. "But I hate when friends are hurting and I can't do anything about it."

"You have a very compassionate heart. For the most part, you see the good in everyone. I'm sure people tell you often how bubbly and full of life you are," Pete says.

"Yeah, I get told often I'm the perfect school teacher."

"Which is why I really don't get where this violence comes from."

"I've never hit anyone." My eyes widen as I realize Pete must think I'm the same as Rob. "You know that, right? I'd never hit someone. And I don't think I've even ever threatened to hit someone. These damn pregnancy hormones are making me crazy, Pete. A year ago, I'd just use a little psychological warfare to fight. Sign someone up for a hundred different mailing lists. Put a very vague ad on an online marketplace with petty details about someone. But right now, I feel like I've got this rage under my skin that needs to come out. Is there a plate-throwing place near here? I need to break something."

"You need to break something?"

"Yes. I broke a plate last week, and the immediate relief I felt was amazing."

"Well," Pete pauses, tapping his lip with his pen as he stares up at the ceiling, "I think it's good that you're recognizing the feelings you're having, and that you've found a way to way to get relief. It's interesting that you speak of pregnancy hormones. How far along are you?"

I stare at him in disbelief. "Have I never mentioned pregnancy in our sessions?"

He looks back through his notes, flipping through a notebook. "No. We've had weekly sessions for around three months."

"Oh. I'm about twenty-two weeks, or a little over five months along."

Pete's eyes widen. "That's a big thing in your life to have forgotten to tell me about."

I shrug. "I didn't think that was part of the reason I came here. I wanted to get a little closure about an abusive ex-boyfriend — and now I understand why you're concerned about my weird violent streak — and didn't think the pregnancy factored into that. The baby isn't his, by the way. So that's good. Although the baby daddy, Alex, I have his son in my class. So there's a really weird gray area there. But these hormones are killing me. I yelled at Ben last week in class, made him cry, which then made me cry, and it's a mess."

Pete stares at me. "You're pregnant with Alex Santo's child?"

"Yeah. How do you know Alex?" Weird. We're in a neighboring town, but I guess the Santo family is well known all throughout the mountain towns. "Did you go to school with him or something?"

"Or something," he murmurs. "Listen, Natalie, I think we've made great progress with you over the past few months. You understand that you weren't at fault for Rob's abuse, and you've taken ownership over your own destiny at work. Unfortunately, I have a scheduling conflict that means I will be unable to continue your sessions. I have an excellent female therapist I'd like to refer you to. Is that okay?"

"Really?" I sigh, my lip popping out in a pout. Pete is definitely introverted and quiet, and it's not like we're close friends, but I don't want to start from scratch again. "I mean, I guess."

"Great. I'll pass along your file to her. You'll like her, I think. Her name is Grace. She's probably about your age as well," Pete tells me cheerfully. He jumps up from his seat, motioning for me to get up as well.

"Oh, I didn't think our session was over yet," I mutter as he pushes me toward his office door.

"No sense continuing when you'll be working with Grace from now on. Best of luck!" As soon as my shoes hit the hallway outside his office, the door is shut behind me.

"What the actual fuck," I mumble. I pull my phone out of my pocket, seeing that I now have an extra thirty minutes before I'm meeting Arianna for lunch. Something seems off with how Pete basically booted me from his office. And from his service. Maybe I can do without therapy. I think I'm doing okay. Except for the desire to break shit. That is a fairly new feeling.

Thirty minutes later, I'm seated at a booth in a small Greek restaurant on the outskirts of Denver. I had suggested Italian, because I've been craving lasagna like nobody's business, but Arianna turned up her nose at that. According to her, no one can beat her Nonna's cooking, so she's not going to bother trying to find a suitable alternative.

As I'm looking down at the menu, I hear the familiar baby babble of my favorite toddler, but I'm surprised to look up and find Arianna headed toward me with Bianca in her arms, and Nonna behind her. Now I also understand the reasoning behind the cuisine today.

"Hello, my little *girasole*," Nonna says as she pinches my cheek. Arianna busies herself getting Bianca settled in her high chair as I stare up at Nonna.

"What did you call me? I've heard it before."

"*Girasole.*"

"Oh, jeez," Arianna mutters. "This family and nicknames."

"What does *girasole* mean?" I ask, intrigued.

"It means sunflower. I thought you knew," Nonna says innocently, but I notice the way her eyes narrow ever so slightly as she watches my reaction.

"Obviously I didn't know that. I'm not sure how you knew Alex calls me that, though," I say hesitantly.

"Oh, sweet child. I know everything. Best if you remember that," she says, slapping my cheek gently before plopping into her seat.

"Hey!" I hear, and I swivel to find Arianna holding her cheek. "Gentle, Bianca!"

"Isn't it lovely that traits are passed down from generation to generation?" Nonna cackles. "Arianna was a big hitter as a kid. Her mother was, too."

"Mom is your daughter-in-law, Nonna, so I'm not sure how you're gonna claim that as something you passed on," Arianna says dryly.

"I take credit for everything." Nonna stares defiantly at Arianna, waiting for an argument. Arianna rolls her eyes and sits next to Bianca, directly across from me.

"So how was therapy today?" she asks.

"Weird. Halfway through the session, I sort of announced that I was pregnant, not realizing I'd never told my therapist. He suddenly got really skittish and told me he needed to switch me to a different therapist because of a scheduling conflict, then ushered me out of there immediately."

Both Nonna and Arianna stare at me before Nonna pipes up. "What's his name? I can have him disbarred by dinnertime."

"He's not a lawyer. You don't disbar therapists," Arianna retorts, but Nonna waves a hand at her.

"Whatever. What's his name?" Shoulders back with a serious expression on her face, Nonna looks like a serious competitor.

Loving how Nonna has become the new me, I gleefully tell her, "Pete. Pete Ducey."

I watch as the wind deflates her sales. "Oh. Damn. Never mind."

"What? Why?" I ask, crestfallen. Not that I really want him to be disbarred — or whatever it would be called for a therapist — but I liked that fact that someone was going to bat for me.

"I can't do anything to Pete. Dominic sees him, and I believe he's referred Alex to him as well. I won't mess with the mental health of my grandsons. I assume that's why your therapist ended your session, *girasole*. It's a conflict of interest because of Alex."

"But you'd mess with the mental health of the rest of his clientele?" Arianna asks, an amused lilt to her voice.

Nonna shrugs. "I'd help find them all suitable therapists."

"I'm pretty sure you getting a hold of his client list violates a gazillion different laws, Nonna," Arianna says, catching a cracker that Bianca throws in Nonna's direction.

"Eh. I could die tomorrow. They won't take me to trial. Besides, the county district attorney is scared of me."

"That doesn't surprise me at all. I'm sure the list of people scared of you is longer than the therapist's client list," Arianna remarks.

"I'm sure there's overlap. I've lived a long life. Lots of opportunities to make people scared of me," Nonna replies, a wicked gleam to her eyes as a grin spreads across her face.

"Did you say that Alex might have been referred to my therapist?" I ask quietly.

Nonna's smile falls, as she reaches over to pat my hand. "I believe so. He's trying, *girasole*. Give him time."

I wave my hand in the air, attempting nonchalance. "Whatever. It doesn't matter. I just want him to be happy, however that may be. For our child's sake."

"Uh-huh," Arianna remarks. "You're saying if Alex came to you today, telling you he wanted to date you, you'd say no?"

I think for a moment. "I think so, yes. I don't think he's ready for any kind of relationship. He needs to finish his own grief first. So I'm glad he's going to therapy. I suggested it to him months ago, for him and his kids. Clearly, it's taken him a while to recognize it himself."

"The Santos are a stubborn lot," Nonna says loudly. "Best recognize that if you're in it for the long haul."

"It's not a long haul. We're just co-parenting," I tell her.

She gives me a sarcastic smile. "Denial, thy name is Natalie. Keep telling yourself that."

Alex: I hear you had a run-in with my grandmother.

Me: I did. That woman either doesn't know what a boundary is, or just chooses to jump over them.

Alex: I like to think she has a motorized scooter and she breaks through anything in her way, running over people when needed.

Me: All in the name of awkward encounters.

Alex: It's a gift, honestly. We should be lucky she's in our orbit.

Me: Her boundaries also include wonderful stories from decades ago.

Alex: Fuck.

Me: A very interesting Easter parade.

Alex: I was five.

Me: You flashed a thousand people.

Alex: I. Was. FIVE.

Me: And a week later, you mooned your kindergarten class.

Alex: See above text.

Me: She said Ben also mooned his kindergarten class. Something about genetic traits being passed along. I wonder if our child will moon his or her class as well.

Alex: ...

Me: ...

Alex: For fuck's sake. She told you about the all-you-can-eat buffet, didn't she?

Me: She did.

Alex: In my defense, I was sixteen and a moron.

Me: What sixteen year old kid doesn't understand the rules of a buffet?

Alex: I was trying to impress a girl, and got carried away.

Me: By eating so much you had a pyrotechnic puking experience, and then slipped in your own barf and fell, breaking your arm.

Alex: Yup. Teenage boys are dumb.

Me: Clearly.

Alex: I know that's not all she told you.

Me: What? (She says innocently.)

Alex: I know where this is going. (He says sheepishly.)

Me: Honestly, it's pretty brilliant. I bet you never got too hot and heavy with a girl on her family's couch again. A walk of shame without pants? Diabolical.

Alex: You are correct, I never did it again. And I plan on creating that rule for Abbie and Ben.

Me: How would that work with Ben? He walks around the property line in his skivvies?

Alex: I haven't worked out all the details yet. But I'll never forget the wind whipping against my balls, and I doubt he will, either.

Me: Wait. You weren't wearing underwear?!?!

Alex: I'm not sure where I've gone wrong with you, Sunflower, that I have to explain how sex only works if clothes aren't in the way.

Me: I just figured you had them pulled DOWN. Not completely off.

Alex: Completely off. I was a teenager, and it was my first time. I thought I had to be naked for it to work right.

Me: It?

Alex: My dick.

Me: God, this just keeps getting better.

Alex: Do you have a grandmother I can call up, so I can get fun stories like this about you?

Me: Nowhere near as fun as Nonna, unfortunately.

Alex: That is a shame. Every family needs a Nonna.

Me: I can tell you my first time was in the back of a pickup truck, and we got caught by a deputy patrolling the farms a couple miles from my house.

Alex: I never understood car sex. There's not enough room to maneuver.

Me: The BACK of the truck, Alex. There's enough room back there for sixteen-year-olds.

Alex: OH. I thought you'd be inside in the back seat.

Me: Nope. I had this vision of sex under the stars. All I got was a bruise on my ass from the truck bed, a warning about indecent exposure, and being grounded for two months.

Alex: Damn. Did you at least get off?

Me: No. My high school boyfriend was incredibly sweet, but dumber than a box of rocks. He had no idea where the clit was. Ironically, he's now a deputy sheriff, and married with his fifth baby on the way.

Alex: Sounds like he figured out where the clit is.

Me: I'm not sure where I've gone wrong with you, Alessio, but you don't have to know where the clit is to get a girl pregnant.

Alex: I can do both, fortunately.

Me: That you can.

Chapter 23

Natalie — March

"Do you think we'll be able to tell the gender today?" I ask hopefully, my stomach a bundle of nerves as I watch the nurse take my vitals. At twenty-six weeks, my little bundle of joy isn't so little anymore, but he or she has been hiding the most important parts from us at the last two ultrasounds.

"Let's hope. You said you thought baby had turned into a head-down position?" the nurse asks.

"Yeah. I was really uncomfortable last week, and different parts were being kicked," I say with a giggle.

"Crossing my fingers for you, girl. Are you hoping for one or the other? And where's your man?"

"He's not my man. Just the baby daddy," I murmur, bitterness seeping through my tone. In the last eight weeks, we've had great texts, and then barely any interaction at my two monthly appointments. He's been stoic and closed-off, only asking if I need anything before leaving each appointment relatively quickly. He usually waits to walk me to my car, but rarely says anything before bidding me a good night and going to his own car. He didn't sign up for a winter parent-teacher conference, and I only know he's still alive because Ben mentions him occasionally, and then I get those wonderful texts. I thought we had gained ground after the night of flower building at his house, but our few in-person interactions have me confused. Then again, I'm hormonal and emotional, so it could completely be in my head.

"I'll check the waiting room once more before I go grab the OB," the nurse says. "You know the drill to get ready for the ultrasound."

I had ultrasounds at twenty and twenty-three weeks. Usually women have one around twenty weeks, called a diagnostic ultrasound, where all the organs are measured to determine the likelihood of any abnormalities or possible genetic conditions. Everything checked out fine, but the OB mentioned her concern that I hadn't gained any weight. Did I find it ridiculously ironic that a physician was telling me to gain weight? Absolutely. Since the baby appeared to be gaining fine, the doctor asked me to come back for another ultrasound today to confirm that trend continues.

Considering I barely make it home before I fall asleep, and a lot of foods still make me think I might puke, I'd say the little alien growing inside me is sucking the life right out of me, and I assume that's just how life is going to be for the next eighteen years.

"Knock, knock! You decent, because I found something that belongs to you!" Oh, this nurse has jokes.

"Uh, I don't belong to her," Alex says hastily, as if that's needed for clarification.

"She knows," I snap. "She's joking. She's been my nurse every fucking ultrasound, Alex, and we barely speak. The whole office knows where you stand on this whole debacle."

"Where exactly do you think I stand?" Alex asks quietly, holding a pair of gloves tightly in his hands. I hate that he comes to these appointments from work, and he looks delectable in his cop uniform. The man is too good looking, and it just generally pisses me off. And that's probably why I word vomit all over him.

"Where do you stand? Well, you'd rather be anywhere than here. You regret ever sleeping with me, and certainly the second time when you did the whole dine-and-dash on me even after I asked you not to. I don't even think you want this kid, so why the hell are you here? Put me out of my misery and take the fucking out I gave you months ago."

Eyes wide as he stares at me, I watch the blood drain from his face, but he doesn't have time to respond before there's a knock at the door. Doctor Morales steps in, giving us a warm smile as she takes a seat beside the ultrasound machine. I chose to continue with her even after word got out in town about the pregnancy, because I could just see some town cronies stealing the OB file to post my personal details in a gossip article. Plus it's nice to get out of Eternity every now and again. I love living there, don't get me wrong, but I feel like I'm constantly being watched and judged. The Santo family are basically Eternity royalty, and I've already heard more than one resident chatting about how I 'trapped' Alex.

"I'm determined to succeed today, Mom and Dad," Doctor Morales announces. "We're getting those images today. I can feel it."

As the gel is squirted onto my stomach, I cast a quick glance at Alex, and notice his crestfallen expression. Shit. My lack of filter was definitely lack of filtering today. Now I'm going to have to apologize to him, and while I don't necessarily hate apologizing, it's agony thinking about apologizing to him. I'm already so inferior to the entire Santo clan, and this just cements that.

"Do you both want to know the gender? Because I can tell you, or I can lock it away in my brain," Doctor Morales says nonchalantly.

"What?" I ask as Alex says, "Seriously?"

"Your kiddo is holding onto its ankles right now, see? The between the legs shot is pretty obvious."

I turn to Alex. "Do you want to know?"

"It's your decision."

"No, it's something we should decide together," I argue.

"After what you said before Doc walked in? No. This is all you. In fact, would you like me to leave? Since you've already made up your mind about me anyway."

"Maybe I should leave," Doctor Morales says hastily, but I grab the hand that's holding the ultrasound wand on my abdomen.

"No. No one is leaving. Doctor Morales, tell us the gender. I'm sorry for putting you in an awkward position. And Alex, I'm sorry for what I said. I'm emotional and hormonal, and I took it out on you. I apologize."

When he won't make eye contact with me, I turn toward the doctor. I try to hide the tremble in my voice, but fail. "Boy or girl?"

She gives me a pitying look as her eyes flip between Alex and me. "You're having a boy. Congratulations. Everything else looks good, Momma. I'll see you in four weeks."

A boy.

We're having a boy.

As the doctor leaves the room, I let out a little laugh. "I've got a penis growing inside me, Alex. Alex?"

I turn to where he was, only to find the room empty.

I can't help the tears that fill my eyes, but I don't allow myself to cry. This is my fault, and I absolutely earned his reaction.

I have no one to blame but myself.

Two weeks later, after an awful week of school where a vicious stomach bug slowly and systematically ransacked the entire building, I'm not surprised when I wake up vomiting. After a frantic call to the OB, I was assured that as long as I don't have any contractions, and continue to feel the baby move, I should be fine. Arianna dropped off a care package of Sprite, soda crackers, and every cleaning product under the sun, then texted me from the street to tell me she had been there. She wouldn't even knock on the door for fear of germs, and after spending a good chunk of the day wrapped around the toilet, I can't say that I blame her.

Around dinnertime, I'm ready to wave the white flag and convince someone to take me to the emergency room. I can't keep even the smallest sips of water down, and I'm worried about dehydration. Little man is happily bouncing around, though, so I hold off on calling in the cavalry.

When someone knocks on my door, I don't answer. They knock harder, and I muscle up all the energy I have to shout, "I'm sick, and I can't come to the door!"

I watch as the door unlocks, and I'm ready to shout at the landlord for entering when I see that it's Alex. "How did you — what are — what is go —"

"Excellent conversation, Sunflower. Please tell me you've moved from the bathroom floor at least once today," Alex comments as he sets a bag down on the table before coming to me. Crouching next to me, he takes stock of my setup. "You've got your phone plugged in, a Kindle, your pillow and two drinks. Were you planning on sleeping here?"

I nod sullenly. "Why move when I'll just end up back here in thirty minutes?"

"Did you speak to the OB?"

"Yeah. They said as long as he's still moving a bunch, I shouldn't worry."

"He's, uh," Alex clears his throat, "I guess he's moving a lot?"

"Yeah. He hasn't stopped all day, so I'm taking that as a good sign." I suddenly look up at him in horror. "You can't be here! You'll get sick!"

"I had it last week when Ben was sick. Kinda hoping there's an immunity thing going on here."

"I don't think that's how stomach bugs work."

He shrugs. "Well, I'm the only one who is willing to come within six feet of you, so I'm your best shot at being nursed back to health."

"Seriously how did you get in here?" I ask, noting Alex's eyes still haven't left my stomach.

"Arianna gave me a key," he murmurs absentmindedly. "Can I?"

"Can you what?"

He gestures at my stomach. "Can I feel? I haven't felt comfortable asking before, so …"

"You figure I'm more likely to say yes when I'm too sick to argue about it."

"Kind of, yeah," Alex chuckles. "Come on. Let's get you to bed and I promise I'll have everything set up perfectly for you."

"I haven't made it more than an hour without puking," I complain. "It's dumb to move from there when I'll just be right back."

"Sunflower, it's not even ten feet from your bed."

"Nine feet too many." I groan when he slides both arms under me, lifting me with ease. I hate that he picks me up so easily, as if I'm light as a feather.

"Thought we talked about this self-deprecating bullshit, Natalie. You are not fat. Your body is phenomenal."

"Did I say that out loud?" I wonder, my eyes wide as he gently deposits me on my bed. It's definitely leaps and bounds more comfortable than the bathroom floor, but I'm not telling Alex that. I might purposely try to barf on him if he starts walking around like he's God's gift. My brain and my body don't agree, and as I roll over, I let out a loud moan as I settle into the soft sheets and plush mattress.

"How long were you sick last week?" I ask as Alex rifles through his bag.

"About two days. Ben was over it within eighteen hours."

"Was there any overlap?"

"No. I had about twelve hours between when he stopped puking and I started."

"I guess that was nice of him," I joke.

Alex chuckles. "My whole family got sick when I was around twelve. Arianna was just a toddler, and she was the only one who didn't get it. Our poor parents were dealing with us hurling while they were trying not to do it beside us."

"Oh, God," I laugh. "Is that what parenthood really is? Just trying to keep kids safe and not puke on them? Sympathetic puking."

"There's a bit more to parenthood than that, but it's basically the gist. I'm not the best when it comes to vomit, but I can usually clean up after kids when they're sick. Abbie, for as smart as she is, can never gauge when she needs to make a run for it. She's the reason why the hallway upstairs is hard flooring."

"Really?"

"Really."

"It's a good thing you can handle vomit, because I can't. One of my students threw up all over her desk about a month ago, and I had to leave the room before I could pull the rest of the class out. I was so close to throwing up in a trash can."

Sitting beside me, perched on the edge of my bed, Alex lays a hand on my stomach. "I can't handle boogers."

"What?" I ask incredulously.

He grimaces and then shivers. "Seriously. Ben went through this booger-eating phase in kindergarten, and I literally threw up more than once when I saw him do it. Don't ask me to hold a tissue to a kid's nose, and they better not use my sleeve as a wipe. Just the thought of them is making me feel queasy."

"All kinds? Even when it's super clear and runny? Or just the big globs that kids never blow correctly?"

"Stop," he moans, "I can't. I won't even pick my own nose because everything in there just freaks me out. Sara used to tease me mercilessly."

I ignore the twinge of pain that flashes across my body at her name. "As she should. You're this big military man, and you're scared of snot. I have to say, Alex, this is disappointing. I had you up on a pedestal, but this definitely brings you down quite a bit."

He's about to say something, but the baby kicks hard, and we both see Alex's hand bounce. "Woah! That was him?"

"Yeah. He's been doing that all day, and that's how I know he's okay."

The baby kicks again, and the look on Alex's face is spellbound. "That is so fucking cool."

"I know. I think I'll miss it. Having that connection with him like this. No one else will ever know how his heart beats from inside someone but me."

Alex smiles peacefully. "I told the kids it's a boy. I guess I should have asked you first, to see if you wanted to be there when I told them."

"They're your kids, Alex. I don't have a say in what you choose to tell them."

He shrugs. "I just think maybe I should have had you there. You'd have enjoyed their reactions. They're both stoked. Well, Abbie is freaked about the baby peeing on her, because I told her little boys pee during diaper changes."

I gasp in horror. "Every time? Why? Are you sure that isn't a medical condition? Do all babies do it, or just boys? Should we ask the OB? Oh, we need to start vetting pediatricians. Kate said she really likes the one your brother uses. Wait. You're already a dad, so you already have a pediatrician. But do you really like him? We could change. I'd like to meet him though. Is that okay? Am I overstepping?"

"Sunflower," Alex says, throwing his head back in laughter. "Relax. We've got time for all of this. Let's worry about getting you through the night without any more puking."

I feel my face flush in embarrassment. I've been holding onto all of these questions for weeks, afraid to ask Alex anything. Our text conversations have been lovely, but I've held back so much, fearing he'd close up again. It's been nice just getting to know him. Right now, it's the most unguarded he's ever been, and my filterless ass decided to take my real vomit and turn it into word vomit. "Sorry. It's been ... odd with you, and I have all these thoughts and questions. But I didn't want to aggravate you anymore."

He exhales harshly. "That's my fault. It's been more of a struggle coming to terms with things than I thought it would."

"You struggle with having another baby?" I whisper.

"No." He pauses, looking up at the ceiling as he formulates a response. "I struggle with my feelings about you. I'm going to go grab the rest of your things from the bathroom. You should probably try to sleep."

With my heart in my throat, I close my eyes. Biting the inside of my cheek hard, I resist the urge to pepper him with more questions. Feelings? Good or bad? What does this mean? Does he like me? As in *like me*, like me? Or is he struggling with an aversion to me that makes him want to file for sole custody? I force myself to take a few calming breaths as I try to rein in my crazy. He's being super nice, coming to make sure I'm okay, and he's probably just wanting us to be on the same page for co-parenting. I cannot blurt out that I need all the answers right now.

Daring to sneak a peek at Alex, I see him returning from the bathroom with my necessities. I had high hopes to at least read a book while sick, but my eyes kept crossing and I couldn't remember how to increase the font size on my Kindle. Now I realize how foolish it was to take it into the bathroom with me, considering I also have the Kindle app on my phone. I've been too busy to read, and I'm three releases behind on what one of my favorite authors, J. Saman, just released. This is simply unacceptable, and I thought a good stomach bug was the perfect opportunity to catch up on some light reading. I didn't take into consideration how hard it is to focus on a Kindle screen when I'm having an out-of-body experience like I'm taking part in that barf scene from *The Exorcist*.

I must fall asleep for a moment, and when I come to, I find Alex setting a lined trash can next to my bed. "In case of emergency, Sunflower."

The next time I wake up, Alex is taking my temperature.

After that, I think he's cleaning. Is he seriously cleaning my apartment? This man is unreal.

I manage to make it to the bathroom twice more to retch, thus helping me keep the little dignity I have left, and finally fall into a deep sleep.

When I wake up the following morning, I notice immediately how much better I feel. Stretching my arms above my head, I feel a boob pop out of the maternity nightgown I'm wearing, and giggle to myself, thinking how good it is that Alex isn't here to see this. I know he probably snuck out at some point. He couldn't stay when we had sex, so I doubt he'd stay after caring for me when I'm sick.

"Don't cover up on my account," a voice rasps from the floor, and I shriek. My eyes pop open to find Alex stretched out a few feet from my bed, using one of my couch pillows and a throw blanket for comfort. When his gaze meets mine, I'm taken aback by the intensity in them, and it pisses me off.

"Stop looking at me like that," I snap. Covering my chest with my comforter, I glare at him.

"Like what?" he asks.

"Like you want to swallow me up."

"So?"

"I don't want to play this game anymore, Alex. I'm sick of the mixed signals."

"I know," he sighs. Getting on his feet, he scratches at his scalp, and I resist the urge to unabashedly stare. His hair sticks up in every possible direction, but it doesn't look chaotic. Everything on Alex looks tousled and sexy, no matter what he does. "You talked in your sleep."

"What? No."

"You did."

"What embarrassing thing are you never going to let me live down?" I mumble, covering my face in shame. I talked in my sleep a ton as a child, but I hadn't done it in quite some time. Rob certainly never mentioned it, so I assumed I'd gotten over it.

"You talked about how you worry you won't be a good mom, and that you wish you could provide a better life for our son," Alex says quietly. Grabbing his keys and wallet from the table, he walks to the door. "I think you're going to be an amazing mom, Natalie."

Alex turns to open the door, and I call out to him. "Thank you. For everything."

He tips his chin down at me. "Of course. Oh, one other thing."

"Hmm?"

"You told me I'm the best sex you ever had, and you wish you could call me up any time you need to get off."

Fucking hell.

"Sunflower."

"What?" I moan as I drag the comforter up to completely cover my face.

"You clearly don't remember that I told you I'll be waiting for your call."

I hear the door open and close, but I remain encased in my bedding. Did that really just happen? Not wanting to miss an opportunity, I bellow, "You're gonna have to earn that call, Mr. Santo!"

"I plan to!" he yells back.

Chapter 24

Alex — April

Knowing how stubborn Natalie is, I figured it would be at least two weeks before she bit the bullet and called me to scratch that itch. I'd be lying if I hadn't thought about our escapades all the damn time. I woke up every fucking morning, hard as a rock, having to jerk off in the shower to ease the lust coursing through my veins. I'd never felt like this, not even with Sara.

I want to try with Natalie, and show her that I'm making her a priority. Every morning, I text her hello. We typically text on-and-off throughout the day, and I end each day asking her for one good thing that happened that day. Usually she tells me something with her students, and I find it fun to hear her side of a story, when I've already heard about it from Ben.

It took a few days before Natalie began asking me what my favorite part of the day was, and the more I thought about it, the more I realized it was every interaction with her. I looked forward to our texts. I began checking my phone nonstop, hoping I'd missed a notification, even knowing she was teaching and not on her phone. I took a chance one night by calling her, and we talked for two hours. I laughed so loudly that Abbie asked me to quiet down. I felt like a new me, and even my therapist commented on it, too.

The therapist Dom recommended had me working through some pretty intense sessions to acknowledge and name my grief. He agreed with, well, everyone, that I was stuck, and I'd never made it fully through the stages. In all honesty, I absolutely hated the sessions. I realize that I wasn't stuck in anger or sadness. I was stuck in denial. I could talk all day about how much I missed Sara, but in every facet of my life, I denied she was dead. I rarely spoke about her to the kids, and I led a fairly celibate life, as if I was still married.

It took three weeks for Pete to break through that mental block I'd subconsciously set up, and another two for him to help me understand that Sara's death was not my fault. I'd never truly realized the guilt I held about being deployed, and I'd convinced myself she never would have been in that car had I been home.

"If I wasn't in the National Guard, she'd still be alive," I'd argued.

"Who's to say she wouldn't have died years earlier?" he pointed out. "We can't play the 'what if' game, Alex. We have no idea how one decision could change the trajectory of our lives. For every hypothetical situation you give me where Sara is alive, I could give you a different scenario where she may have died. Or worse, your kids may have been in the car too."

"I don't know how to move past the guilt," I'd admitted.

"Every time you feel that familiar wave of guilt, you say out loud that it's not your fault. It's not your fault, Alex. Sara's death is not your fault."

I hadn't felt the wave of guilt then, but rather a wave of emotion unlike anything I'd ever experienced. It wasn't my fault. I'd spent over five years blaming myself for something that happened when I wasn't even in the country. Thousands of car accidents happen every day, and who knows how many people die in them. It sounds callous to call Sara a statistic, but that black and white fact helped me begin to heal.

After that session, even Natalie could tell I was different. On our phone call that evening we talked about our families. How we were both raised. What we wanted for our son. I felt like, for the first time, Natalie and I were on the same page.

Over the last few weeks, I'd taken some big steps in my mental health. I talked to Abbie and Ben about my feelings, as well as seeing the therapist. I brought up how helpful it had been, and asked if either wanted to see a therapist. I was surprised when both said yes.

I'd also admitted to my entire immediate family that I'd been in therapy, and they were incredibly supportive. Our normally batshit crazy group text was a little more subdued, but still a bit nuts.

Which is why today, I'm laughing at my phone while waiting for Natalie to get home. She sent me some weird text about needing help with her pipes. I thought she had a landlord, but I guess he's not available. Whatever. I realized that I've missed her in the last two weeks, and I'll take any opportunity to check on her.

Fortunately, my family is keeping me entertained while I wait for Nat.

> Isabella: No one needs this many cookies.
>
> Luca: Those MC guys are growing boys, Belly.
>
> Dom: Yeah, I'm sure he's just being considerate for his club. There couldn't possibly be any other reason Sebastian keeps coming back to your bakery.
>
> Mom: Did I pass him this morning? You were glaring at him, sweetheart, and his face was red. What did you say to him?
>
> Isabella: Nothing.
>
> Luca: Liar, liar, pants on fire!
>
> Isabella: I didn't say anything.
>
> Luca: That's not what I heard.
>
> Isabella: LUCA I WILL HUNT YOU DOWN AND TAKE AWAY YOUR ABILITY TO HAVE ANY MORE CHILDREN
>
> Hannah: Hey!
>
> Isabella: No apologies. Tell your husband to shut up.
>
> Hannah: You threatened to take away MY prospective children, so you get no help from me.

Hannah: And since now I'm allll pissed off …

Me: Uh oh. The Georgia peach never gets super mad.

Luca: Batten down the hatches.

Arianna: (claps hands gleefully) God, I LOVE when Hannah gets unhinged.

Dad: Stop adding me to this nonsense.

DAD HAS LEFT THE GROUP

Kate: Somebody add him back in. He put me in a group text with a podiatrist last week, talking about a wart on the bottom of his foot. I couldn't figure out how to get out of it, so I can't figure out how to add him back in!

DOM ADDED DAD TO THE GROUP

Kate: How's your foot wart, Nick?

Dad: How did you know about that?

Hannah: FOCUS

Isabella: I'll babysit for a week if you don't tell them.

Hannah: Tempting, but too late.

Luca: Sebastian point-blank asked Isabella out to dinner, and she laughed at him, then tried to hook him up with one of her employees.

Me: Holy shit. That's harsh.

Mom: Isabella Marie!

Dom: Uh oh. Mom brought out the middle name.

Isabella: He laughed too! I don't know which one of you put him up to it, but I know he didn't mean it. He's been coming in for years and he's never even hinted at dinner.

Me: You're a ballbuster, so I'm not surprised.

Isabella: I am not.

Arianna: I love you, but you absolutely are a ballbuster. The fact that he's been coming in there for years and you never realized it was for YOU is what we should be focusing on.

Isabella: Please. No one wants to date the fat chick, especially a guy like Sebastian. He's just being nice since I'm one of you.

Me: Wow. Didn't realize you had such a poor opinion of yourself, sis.

Dom: Seriously.

Luca: Belly, you're gorgeous. I wish you could see what all of us see. Hell, I can count a handful of college buddies who asked about you or wanted your number.

Dom: I agree with Luca. You're curvaceous and beautiful.

Gia: I've always thought you were the best looking girl out of the three of us. Sorry, Ari.

Arianna: Oh, I completely agree. Belly's always had this sex kitten thing going on without even trying. It's just not fair.

Isabella: Okay, I get that you're trying to cheer me up, but you're laying it on pretty thick.

Mom: Reginetta, you are stunning, and any man would be lucky to have you by his side.

Dad: I agree.

Dad: But how the hell did Kate know about my foot wart?

Kate: Sometimes I hate this group chat. But I figured out how to leave, so …

> KATE HAS LEFT THE GROUP
> DOM ADDED KATE TO THE GROUP
>
> Kate: DOMINIC!
>
> Dom: For better or worse, Katharine. You signed on the dotted line knowing us. This is my worse.
>
> Kate: Wanna bet?
>
> Dom: If I say yes, how long am I forced to sleep on the couch?
>
> Kate: No comment.
>
> Dom: No, I don't want to bet.
>
> Me: Good call.

"What has you grinning like a fool?"

Looking up, I find Natalie watching me with an amused expression. "My family's group chat. We always have one that goes off the rails each week."

"Our girl chat does the same thing. I'd blame Arianna, but Hannah and Kate are in there too, so who knows," Natalie says with a shrug. I follow her inside, and up the stairs to her second-floor studio.

"This was mostly due to Isabella today. We think a friend of Dom and Luca's has a thing for her, but she vehemently disagrees, based on no one would want to date the fat chick. Her words, not mine."

Natalie's mouth drops open as she unlocks her apartment door. "She is not fat! God, I'd love to have her figure. I honestly don't know how she stays as skinny as she does, since she's around baked goods all the damn time. Totally unfair."

"I feel like this is a trap, but I'm diving in anyway. You know you aren't fat either, right?"

Natalie scoffs. "Please. I was considered obese before I got pregnant, and now I'm rivaling one of those manatees in Florida rivers. I think I heard the scale at the OB's office scream when I stepped on it for my last appointment."

"Dramatic much?" I remark dryly.

She laughs, a melodic sound that flitters over me like the wings of a butterfly. "I'm not trying to be dramatic. Before I got pregnant, I rocked my body. I knew I was overweight, but I loved my curves. But I also love food, and I have no intention of giving that up anytime soon. It's just seeing the changes on my body the closer I get to delivering, and it's hard to process sometimes. It's especially hard when it's difficult to put on shoes by myself, too."

"Should I start coming over every morning so I can make sure your shoes are on properly?" I tease.

"You laugh, but I just might make that a baby daddy responsibility."

Natalie shoots me a mischievous wink over her shoulder as she flips her hair down her back, and I'm stunned with how extraordinary she looks. She's as breathtaking as always, but I can't tell her that. Her hair cascades down her back in lustrous waves, the mahogany color the perfect dichotomy for her porcelain skin. The weight gain she speaks of is located almost completely in her abdomen and breasts, and God damn do I want to get those perfect mounds in my mouth. I find myself staring, and watch mesmerized as her nipples pucker under her shirt, as if they know what I'm thinking.

"Alex," she whispers, dropping her bag next to her. "I called."

"You did."

"You told me to call, when I — when I needed to be reminded about how good it is with you. Well, I mean, I texted." Her voice, breathy and uneven, gets higher as I slowly stalk toward her, like a predator toward his prey. Coming to a stop only inches from her, I slide one hand up her side, letting my fingers dance across her chest for a moment before continuing on to her neck. Natalie's pulse beats wildly against my thumb as my hand wraps around to grip her tightly, tilting her head slightly to the side. Her lips part with a gasp, one I desperately want to swallow.

"You asked me to help you with your pipes — oh," I say, realizing what she meant. "Your pipes."

"I didn't want someone else to read the text, and know what it meant."

"Need the words, Sunflower," I rasp, my own voice deeper than normal. Natalie hesitates, her gaze clearing as her eyes center on mine, and I fear she may second-guess her decision to contact me. I feel her hands grip my shirt at my hips, and she steps closer, lining our bodies up. I love how her baby bump pushes against me, and it gives me the perfect view down her shirt. Fuck do I need to taste her.

"I need you," she whispers.

"Louder."

"I need you, Alex," she states a little more clearly, and because it wouldn't be us if there wasn't a push-and-pull, I bait her again.

"What do you need?" I ask as I push her slightly until her back is against the wall.

"You should know what I need." A fire has taken over Natalie's eyes, and fucking hell is it sexy.

She impatiently growls, and I fight the urge to chuckle. "I've only been with you twice, baby girl. I highly doubt I know what you need."

"Jesus, that was hot," she mutters, her pupils blown out with need.

"What?"

"Baby girl."

"Really?"

"Yeah. Way hotter than it should be." Natalie drags her index finger up my abs, and I reflexively shudder. Her eyes lighten triumphantly, and I realize how quickly she can take control of this situation. That's not how tonight is gonna go. Natalie may think she wants to be in charge, but secretly, she wants me to make all the decisions.

Leaning down, I rest my mouth along the outer edge of her ear. "If you want to be my baby girl, you need to do as I tell you to. You want that, don't you? Want me to control you as only I can. I can get you there, Sunflower. But it only happens if we do it my way."

"This is a new Alex," she murmurs, but her pupils are so blown with lust I can barely see the green.

It is a new me. A different me, I guess. A version of myself I can be with Natalie that I never could with Sara. Or maybe I just never allowed myself to be like this. It could be that I curbed that need, the desire, to own someone. Possibly I thought Sara would be horrified at this kind of treatment. Our sex was always sweet and loving. Maybe this version of Alex was always there, right under the surface, and now I'm just tapping into him.

"Answer the question, Natalie," I command, gripping her hair and pulling it tight. Her eyes drift closed as a slight smile graces her face. I can't resist the temptation of her neck, dragging my tongue along her collarbone. "Tell me what you know I'll give you."

Her eyes flick open, and I grin wickedly. I can see the submission in her gaze, and I'm immediately hard as steel.

"I need to come, Alessio. I need you to fuck me," she whispers.

"My fucking pleasure," I respond before crashing my lips against hers. We moan simultaneously, the relief immediate. I've been craving her taste. Her scent. Her presence. And as much as I'd love to edge her again and again, I feel this innate need to bury myself so far inside her that no one will ever question whether Natalie is mine.

Natalie is fucking mine.

I don't know what that means. How she may feel. But I know in my soul that she's mine.

About time you got on board.

For fuck's sake. This is not the time to have an internal conversation with my dead wife.

She needs you.

Sara, stop.

But you need her more.

"Alex," Natalie whimpers against my lips, lifting a knee to wrap her leg around me, and bringing my mind back to the woman in my arms. "God, I should have called you sooner."

I'm glad she didn't. I've taken the past couple of weeks to dig deep. I needed that time more than I thought I did, but I still have a long way to go. I might say in my head that Natalie is mine, but I'm nowhere near ready to tell *her* that, because I don't think Natalie is ready to admit she wants more with me. Besides, I think I want to woo her.

Crouching slightly, I grab Natalie behind the thighs, hoisting her up. She screeches as I walk to her bed, sitting with her straddling me. Her stomach protrudes slightly more than it did the last time, and I resist the urge to bend down to kiss it. It's fucking feral how hot it is to me that she's having my baby.

I take her lips in another deep kiss as her hands find my hair, scraping her nails along my scalp. Her hips begin to gyrate in my lap, subconsciously seeking the friction she needs, and I don't stop it. I want to watch her make herself come. Natalie breaks off the kiss with a loud moan, laying her head down on my shoulder. Nope. That's not gonna work. I want to watch her come.

Grabbing her hair, I pull her head up. "You gonna come, baby girl? Gonna get yourself off on my thigh? Keep your eyes open. I need to see what color green they turn when you come all over me."

"Jesus, your mouth," she pants.

"You have no problems with my mouth, and you know it."

"Sometimes you could shut up a little," she says, shimmying her hips faster as her hands latch onto my shoulders.

"If my mouth is closed, I can't eat your pussy. I can't suck on your nipples. I can't lick your asshole like I know you love, but won't say. You fucking love my mouth, Sunflower. Now fucking come," I command, and my girl immediately acquiesces. Eyes remaining open, I witness the beauty of the emerald green color as she shudders through the aftershocks. I let her rest her head against mine, and I'm struck at how right it feels.

"I'll admit, you give a better orgasm with your tongue," Natalie confesses, and I throw back my head in raucous laughter.

"Noted," I chuckle. "Might as well give that one an immediate try."

"Actually, wait." Her head lifts, and she gives me a coy smile. "Can I try something?"

"Yeah?"

"Good. Help me up and then get naked." When I don't move, she giggles. "I thought that was pretty specific."

"I thought I said I run this show."

"I asked if I could try something, and you agreed. Therefore, I get to run this part of the Alex show."

A slow grin spreads across my face. "Are you taking control on a technicality?"

"It would appear so," she responds sweetly. I help Natalie stand from my lap, then do as she asked, removing my shirt and jeans. "What would it take for you to wear a suit?"

"A sibling getting married," I answer honestly. I'm nothing like Dom. He lives in suits, whereas I'm all for comfort and a relaxed fit. As Natalie drags her fingers along the hem of my boxers, she looks up at me through thick lashes.

"I was at Dominic and Kate's wedding renewal ceremony," she says quietly. "Did you know that?"

I think back to that night at Everlasting, when Dom's ex-wife crashed the wedding, and got Kate hurt in the process. Closing my eyes, I scan the imaginary picture from that night of the crowd. I remember telling Dom I was miserable, and how much I missed Sara. I remember Arianna gabbing with her friends, and I thought one of them was really pretty, but I didn't think much of it until now … "Holy shit. I saw you. I remember you."

"You're just saying that," she responds.

"No, I'm not," I answer adamantly. "You wore a red dress."

Natalie's face noticeably pales as she nods.

"You had your hair half up in some kind of twist. You smiled at me, I think."

"I did," she whispers as her hand dips below the waistband of my boxers. "And you smiled back."

"Did I?" I murmur absentmindedly.

"You did. Claire told me to talk to you after the ceremony. Then all hell broke loose, and I didn't see you again. Until that night at the bar." Natalie's hand slips closer and closer to my length, rigid between us, and I'm struggling to focus.

"I wasn't in a good place that night," I murmur. "I don't know if I would have talked to you, but I really can't concentrate on talking right now."

Natalie laughs lightly as she pulls her hand out. "Gotta admit, this control thing is kind of nice."

"I will take that away, you know — holy hell, Natalie!" Before I could realize her intentions, Natalie dropped to her knees, whipped down my boxers, and sucked my entire length into her mouth. She gags when I hit the back of her throat, and I expect her to let up, but in true stubborn Natalie fashion, she takes a deep breath through her nose and fights through the gag reflex. "Goddamn, baby girl. Your mouth is fucking sinful."

Natalie begins a pattern of sucking and licking that has black spots dotting the edges of my vision. Grabbing hold of her hair in a makeshift ponytail, I test pushing her head against me lightly, and her eyes light up. When she nods, I start fucking her mouth. "Tap my thigh if you need a break, okay?"

She nods, reaching in between my legs to fondle my balls. Tears drip from her eyes, but her gaze doesn't break from mine. I'm barreling into an orgasm that is bound to be one for the record books. "I'm close, Sunflower."

I expect her to release my cock so I don't come in her mouth. Maybe whip up her shirt so I can come on her breasts. What I don't expect, however, is the hand holding my balls to slip further back, her fingers pressing against my asshole. I'm so surprised that I don't tense up, allowing one digit to slip past the rigid muscle, pushing perfectly against my prostate. I come with a yell as my vision completely darkens. A wave of pleasure unlike anything I've ever experienced crashes over me, and I collapse backward onto the bed.

Natalie moves with me, patiently lapping up my release as I'm overcome. "Jesus Christ. What the hell was that?"

She finally releases my cock from her mouth with an audible pop. "I figured if I was going to call you, I wanted to make it memorable. And I know I should have asked you first, or told you what I was gonna do. Consent and all. But I figure you licked my asshole without telling me that was your plan, so turnabout is fair play."

"Yeah, I'm not gonna forget this anytime soon. And noted about the consent. I'll be sure to tell you my nefarious plans beforehand," I pant. My entire body hums as I wait for my heart rate to return to normal. "Think I'll need a minute for round two."

Natalie rises to her feet and sits next to me on the bed. "Take your time, old man."

"Thirty eight is not old," I murmur.

"It is when I'm only thirty two."

"I forgot you're younger than me. Dom is nine years older than Kate, and Stone is eleven years older than Ari. Age doesn't bother me."

"Not that it matters, anyway. We aren't together. While you rest, I'm going to take a quick shower." Natalie pats me on the knee as she stands. I open one eye to watch her walk to her bathroom, and a hand comes up to push against my heart.

Why does it hurt this much for her to say something I already know is true?

How can I convince her to give me a chance, when I've been so damn wishy-washy this entire time?

And will she say yes?

Chapter 25

Natalie — April

I'll admit, I'm using the shower as an escape. The look in Alex's eyes is … different somehow, and I don't know how to interpret it. Some of his looks are very easy to define. I can tell when he's thinking about Sara, or when he's thinking about his job. I'm starting to learn his expression for when he has his dad hat on, and I can even recognize the moment when he feels like he's getting too close to me and begins to pull away. Slam the shutters down and close up shop. Oops, Natalie almost saw the real me. Rein it in, boys! Can't have her getting the wrong idea.

But today, watching him laugh so openly at his phone, I was taken aback. I've seen a variety of Alex smiles over the past few months, but reading his family group text had a carefree smile I've never seen. I'm not even sure if I saw it before he got married. When I finally approached him, after watching him for a minute or two and ogling him unabashedly, I had the wind knocked out of me when he turned that smile onto me.

I've tried to keep my feelings in check because I knew where Alex stood. He's still firmly in Camp Sara, staying devoted to his dead wife, while doing the right thing by supporting me. I'll never be her. I get that. I'm not trying to be.

Today he's different, and I'm scared as hell to let any more of my heart get invested. If I let myself think he wanted more, and he had to tell me otherwise, I'd be so humiliated. Heartbroken. I have to be around this man potentially for the rest of my life, and I simply can't embarrass myself any more than I already have.

So I'm hiding in the shower.

Get it together, Nat.

The only thing that matters is having a good co-parenting relationship with Alex.

Taking a deep breath as I attempt to calm my nerves, I calculate how much time I can waste in here before Alex gets suspicious. Shampoo and conditioner take five minutes. Body wash another five. How much does he remember about pregnancy? I could say I shaved, but my bump is now large enough that it's blocking a good portion of my legs, and I'm just blindly hacking away at whatever is down there and hoping for the best. I look longingly at my bath salts and bubble bath. This little tub-shower combo is really tiny, and I've certainly had my shape change in the last few months, but there's nothing I like better than relaxing in a bath.

Another time.

Knowing my luck, if I tried it today, I'd get stuck and have to call Alex in here anyway to help me up.

I've only barely gotten my hair wet when the shower curtain is dramatically swished to the side as Alex steps into the shower.

"What are you —" I sputter, but he covers my mouth with his hand.

"I'm not done with you." He drops to his knees, and I shriek.

"No! No, no, no," I chant.

He looks up at me, droplets of water sticking to his thick, black lashes. "You're supposed to shout yes, yes, yes."

"It's just ... I haven't finished my shower, and I'd like to clean there first, please."

Alex raises a brow at me. "Pretty sure I've told you I don't care about that."

"Well, you should! I've been chasing around fourth graders all day. I don't want your mouth on me if I'm stinky and sweaty."

"I came in your mouth ten minutes ago. I hadn't showered all day either."

"It's different."

"Not even a little bit."

Alex rises to his full height, crowding me against the shower wall, putting his hands between my back and the wall. Because of course he's that thoughtful. His lips crash into mine with intensity, and I immediately moan. As I moan, Alex sweeps his tongue into my mouth, circling mine quickly. His fingers grip my back tensely as the kiss continues. I feel his cock harden against my upper thigh, and I rise on my tiptoes, trying to get it between my legs. He breaks off the kiss and steps a few inches away, and I whimper in disappointment and sheer need.

He chuckles as his eyes rake down and back up my body. "I came in your mouth."

"Yes?"

"After not showering."

"Okay?"

"And I just stuck my tongue in your mouth."

I don't answer.

Alex grabs my chin between his thumb and forefinger. "Because I don't fucking care, Sunflower. I want to make you come with my tongue. I want you to coat my face with your orgasm. Then I'm going to fuck you, harder than I ever have, because I'm so fucking turned on right now that I'm about to burst. Now, be a good girl and let me have you the way I want."

Holy shit.

I must nod, because he gives me a feral grin as he drops to his knees once again. Throwing my leg over his shoulder, Alex dives in, sucking hard on my clit as one finger plunges into my core. He's hinted about edging me before, but this is fast and to-the-point. He's not tentative as he brutally forces me closer and closer to the edge, nibbling on my clit at just the point of pain before pushing me over, the free fall so exhilarating and sensual that I forget to breathe. I barely register that Alex has removed my knee from his shoulder, and he stands before me as I slowly come back to my senses. When I open my eyes, he watches me as he slowly strokes his erection. I must lick my lips, because he chuckles darkly. "Not this time, baby. I'm coming in that pussy. I need to feel you grip me."

The mouth on this man!

"Turn around and put your hands on the edge of the tub," he commands. I do as he asks because I'm still reeling from my orgasm, but also because I can't wait to see what it's like when Alex really lets loose. He's fucked me before. It certainly wasn't slow and tender. Can he be even more unhinged than that?

I'm barely turned around before he slams his dick into me, and I let out a guttural moan. Alex begins pummeling me, grabbing my hair and pulling my head back. I can't help the loud cries that burst from my mouth. He's hitting my G-spot every damn time, and he's not just touching it. It's like he's trying to break right through to the outside. Grunting with each thrust, Alex slides his other hand around my body, briefly touching my stomach before continuing between my breasts. He shoves two fingers into my mouth, holding my head with a thumb under my chin, then he lets go of my hair. That hand quickly swipes around to cup my breast, the weight heavy in his palm. When he pinches the nipple between two fingers, I moan loudly. "Suck, baby girl. No one else gets to hear your sweet sounds but me."

I immediately do as he asked, sucking on his fingers, which taste of me. I'm still somewhat level-headed, and bite down on the digits, making Alex swear behind me. He lets go of my nipple and smacks my ass, but his thrusts never stop. I can feel another orgasm barreling toward me, but I want Alex to come with me. I know I'll probably fall over if I lift a hand from the tub edge, so my only option is to suck his fingers as far into my mouth as they'll go, letting his middle digit touch the back of my throat. He lets out a groan as the consistency of his pace falters just enough that I know he's close. His free hand finds my clit as he turns my head to one side, capturing my lips with his. As his tongue thrusts into my mouth, he pinches my clit, and I explode. I feel him swell inside me as he moans into my mouth, and his slowed movements push my aftershocks out further.

Alex breaks off the kiss, and as my head falls in exhaustion, I feel his hand let go of my hair. I didn't even realize he'd grabbed it again at some point, I was too far gone to care. My entire body zings with pleasure, and I know my legs won't work right if I attempt to step out. Holy moly. Three orgasms. I'd say Alex delivered on his promise.

"Was I too rough?" he whispers against my back.

"What?"

"Too rough. Was I too much? I don't know what happened. I'm not like that normally. At least I don't think I am."

"You weren't too rough."

"I wasn't?" he asks quietly.

"No. I — I liked it, Alex," I confess.

"You did?"

"Yeah. That was, well. That was something."

He chuckles awkwardly before slowly sliding out of me. I wince slightly, fully aware that I'll be feeling it tomorrow, but I regret nothing. "Stand up and let me wash your hair, Nat."

"You don't have to do that." My voice is barely above a whisper. I want him to wash my hair, but I don't want him to think he has to.

"I'd like to, if you'll let me." Alex's voice sounds tentative and raw. It's possible he's as unnerved with how intense the sex was, and he's also having difficulty processing it. I carefully straighten, my knee buckling instantly, but Alex catches me. "Turn around so you can lean your body against mine."

My movements halt, as I'm unsure if I can face him. I'm thrown by how I feel. He consumed me unlike anything I've ever experienced before. I feel his head drop to my shoulder as he applies a gentle kiss. Such a strange dichotomy to what we just did. "Please, Sunflower."

God dammit. That nickname is my kryptonite. I slowly turn, choosing to keep my eyes closed as my head dips back into the spray. I hear Alex grab the shampoo bottle, squirting a healthy amount into his hands, before he gently touches my hair.

"I hope he has your hair," he says quietly. "The color, I mean. I'm fine if he wants to have long hair. I don't care about that masculine shit. I'd love a little mini-Natalie running around with the same hair, and a fiery attitude."

I can't help the snort that comes out of my nose. "Then I'd like him to have your eyes."

"Fuck no. He needs your eyes. Brown is a dime a dozen. Green eyes like yours are unique and breathtaking. And he needs your lips. Your cupid's bow. Maybe even your cheekbones."

"Is there anything of yours you'd like him to have?" I tease.

"Yeah."

"I'm guessing you're gonna say your dick size."

"Well, not as a baby. That would be difficult to explain to other people, and I imagine he'd have trouble learning to crawl with a foot-long between his thighs."

"Clearly he needs to have your modesty and humble attitude."

"I can't help it if I'm an absolute blessing, baby girl." I can hear the smile in his voice, and it makes me giggle gleefully. "Turnabout is fair play. What do you want him to have?"

He dips my head back into the water as he washes the shampoo from my hair. "I haven't thought much about his physical attributes. I hope he has all ten fingers and toes. No birth defects. No birth trauma. I've thought more about his personality."

Alex squirts the conditioner into his hands, then drags his fingers through my tresses carefully. "What have you thought of?"

I sigh. "I want him to have your patience and drive. I don't think I've ever met a man as patient as you. I see how you interact with your kids, and you meet them exactly where they're at. That is such a commendable trait, Alex. I deal with parents every day, and no one is as thoughtful as you. I love how you support your kids so unconditionally."

He's quiet as he massages my scalp. "I feel guilty."

"About what?" I want him to say it. I need him to tell me.

"About not being here when Sara died," he whispers. "I didn't find out for a week, and then it took almost another week for me to get back here. By then, Sara's parents were in talks to try and take my kids. They'd lost their only child, and they wanted to latch onto the only part of her left. I was so angry with them, but I completely understood. I couldn't lose them either, because they're my daily reminders of her."

"Oh, Alex," I whisper.

"All this time, I thought if I had been here sooner, or if I hadn't deployed at all, I'd have taken away the pain. Or maybe Sara wouldn't have died. I've felt guilt every day over her not being here. Them not having their mom."

Tears stream down from beneath my eyelids, and I'm thankful for the water so Alex can't tell. This poor, broken man.

"It's been almost six years since she died, and I finally feel like I'm coming out of the fog. I can't change the past, but I can make up for what I missed when I was desolate. I can treat my children to a present father who respects and values them. I can spend time with my family, because who knows what tomorrow will bring. And I can find a job that I actually enjoy, because this police job ain't it."

"You're that unhappy?" I ask softly. I open my eyes to stare up at him, watching as he shrugs with a hint of a smile. This is the first time he's spoken so openly about Sara, and he doesn't look devastated. There's a peaceful aura that I haven't seen before.

"Maybe it's not that I'm unhappy. But this job doesn't bring me joy. I don't want to do something just because I'm good at it, or that it's available. I want to be happy. I want to show my kids — all three of them," I smile at that addition, "— how important it is to place happiness above all else."

"That's really great, Alex," I whisper. He opens his eyes, a beautiful smile gracing his face as he looks down at me. Leaning down, he kisses me softly, a far cry from the beating my vagina just took from the same man.

Alex looks down at his watch, grimacing. "Fuck. I forgot I told my mom I'd bring dinner over tonight."

"Oh, okay," I say hurriedly. "You should probably go." I quickly wash the conditioner from my hair, then turn off the water.

"You want to come?" he blurts out.

"What? To your parents for dinner? Uh, no, I don't think that's a good idea," I answer hastily. Why the hell is he even asking? I basically invited him over for a booty call.

Alex is quiet as I pull the shower curtain aside, handing him a spare towel to dry off. I realize I didn't wash anything important, but I can do that later when I'm alone. Wrapping the towel around me, I step out of the shower and open the bathroom door. I'm a step out of the bathroom when Alex's arm slides around me, pulling me back against him.

"I'd like you to come," he whispers.

"Why?" I blurt out.

I feel him inhale against my hair as his other arm comes around my shoulders. "I think I'd like all my children in one spot, and seeing as how you're baking one of them, you should be there, too. But I also know I want you there. With me."

"I texted you for sex," I stammer, and he chuckles against me, making goosebumps prickle along my neck and shoulder.

"I know. Will you come with me? Please?" His voice is quiet, a nervous tenor I haven't heard before.

"Okay," I find myself answering, and he lets out a relieved exhale.

"Okay. Good. Get dressed." Letting go of me, he quickly spanks my ass before crossing the room to get his clothes. Still standing by the bathroom, I stare at him incredulously. He turns around and smiles. "You need help, Sunflower? It's been a while since I've put clothes *on* an adult woman, but I'm pretty sure I can manage."

I shake my head in shock, making him let out a peal of laughter. "Who are you, and what have you done with my Alex?"

He cocks a brow at me. *"Your* Alex?"

Shit. "That's not what I meant. Typical broody and stoic Alex. You have to admit this sarcastic and scrappy Alex is unusual."

He shrugs. "Maybe it's new. Or maybe it's who I was meant to be all along. Now chop-chop. Get dressed, or I'll be forced to fuck you again, and my family will have questions when you walk into their house all bow-legged."

"When I said I was fine with you being in control in the bedroom, I didn't mean all the time," I say, slightly irritated.

"We're in your bedroom, baby girl. I'm still in control."
For fuck's sake.

Chapter 26

Alex — April

I'm not sure what came over me when I asked Natalie to come to dinner at my parents' house. I only know I didn't want to walk away from her. Couldn't walk away. I want more time with her. As I watch her dry her hair, one hand sitting comfortably on top of her bump, I have to resist the urge to rip off her clothes and take her again. I've never had this insatiable desire before. I want to mark every inch of her body so that everyone knows she's mine, even if she really isn't. I want her to be mine, though, and I'm struggling with that.

My therapist is going to have a field day with my roller coaster of emotions at our session this week, that's for sure.

"Are you sure this is okay?" Natalie asks quietly. Dressed in leggings and an oversized maternity shirt covered in blue and pink flowers, she's an absolute vision. Leopard print ballet flats adorn her feet, and the juxtaposition of patterns is so quintessentially Natalie that I struggle to withhold the smile that threatens to break out on my face. She's loud, unfiltered, sweet, and demure, all at the same time. Twiddling her fingers nervously, she waits for my reply.

Standing, I cross the room and take her in my arms. I can't not kiss her right now. She sighs into my mouth, allowing my tongue entry as her arms wrap around my waist tightly. God, she feels so good against me.

Breaking off the kiss, I rest my forehead against hers. Feeling her abdomen move against me, I chuckle. "Little man says it's fine, Sunflower."

"Is that what he says?" she asks with a breathy laugh.

I press my lips to her temple as I reluctantly let her go. "Yeah. He's excited about getting to know his Santo family."

As Natalie grabs her jacket and bag, I can see her mind working. I know what she wants to ask, but I'm not forcing it. I know she'll ask me in her own time: she wants to discuss his last name.

I really want it to be Santo, and I'm not sure if she'll fight me on it.

Make her last name Santo, too.

I sigh. These odd Sara thoughts are growing fewer and farther between, but she always pops up in the most random times. I'm not dating Natalie. We haven't discussed anything about the future, other than how we both want to have a good co-parenting relationship. I don't know what to expect. How often will I be able to see my son? Does Natalie want a fifty-fifty arrangement, or does she expect more time with him? I need to force these important conversations, but I don't want to. My stomach turns with the thought of them.

That's because you want her, you need her, and you know I'm right.

For fuck's sake, Sara. Get the hell out of my mind!

Fine. But you'll need to apologize when you finally realize you're in love with her, and that you're sorry you doubted me.

Sighing, I open the door for Natalie. After she locks the door, my hand automatically grabs hers, almost like a reflex. I feel her jolt against me, and I realize it's the first time I've held her hand. She's only a couple of months away from delivering my son, and I've never held her hand like this.

I can't stop myself from bringing our joined hands to my mouth, kissing the back of her hand. I notice a black smudge along one digit. "What's that?"

She snickers. "I was marking something with permanent marker, and I dropped it. Couldn't get to the bathroom until lunch, and by that time, the mark was pretty much set. The class found it hysterical."

"Why?"

"I think pregnancy has made me clumsy. I'm routinely dropping things, misjudging depth and running into corners. That kind of thing."

"Is that normal?" I ask as we reach my truck. Opening the passenger door, I wait until Natalie steps up before grabbing her seatbelt. As I put the belt on for her, she watches me.

"Um, I'd say it's about as normal as you putting my seatbelt on for me," she says, deadpan.

I chuckle. "Not sure what came over me. I think I want to take care of you, and I was deployed a good chunk of both of Sara's pregnancies. I'm kinda enjoying this, to be honest."

She gives me a cute, but nervous, smile as I close the door and jog around to the drivers' side. One stop to grab dinner, and we're headed to my childhood home. It's comfortably quiet on the short drive to my parents', but I resist the urge to reach over and take her hand. The connection calms me more than I ever thought it would.

As I pull into the driveway, Natalie sighs. "I love this house. I remember coming here a couple of times as a teenager and wanting to move in here. It's so idyllic."

Looking at the exterior, I realize she's right. A well-loved front porch. Shutters that Dom and I painted more than once. Two rocking chairs we gifted our parents a decade ago for Christmas, and a smattering of childhood toys that now belong to the growing list of grandchildren. The home I grew up in, the one that holds so many pivotal memories, now helps to grow the next generation of Santos.

"I love living here, but being this close to the mountains, I hate how the snow never melts," Natalie comments as we gingerly walk to the front door. "Denver snow melts a lot faster, unless the driveway faces north."

"We're in the mountains here, Sunflower," I respond, winking when I catch her eye. She giggles, rolls her eyes, and immediately hits a patch of ice right by the front door. She shrieks as her leg flies out in front of her, as I frantically try to catch her to ensure she doesn't land on her abdomen. Natalie winces as gravity takes over, landing with one leg outstretched, and one sandwiched underneath her. I manage to grab her arm at the last second, yanking her back up.

"Ow, my foot," she says, grabbing at her ankle. The front door opens at that moment.

"Oh no! Nick, I told you to salt the front sidewalk!" Mom says loudly. "Alex, bring her in to the living room so we can look at her ankle."

I swoop her into my arms, carefully walking through the doorway and into the house, gently setting Natalie on the closest couch. Crouching in front of her, I fuss over her foot, carefully taking off her shoe. Just another thing that is my fucking fault. "I'm sorry, Nat. I should have been paying better attention."

"Hey," she says softly, cupping my cheek in her hand, "look at me."

Remorsefully, my eyes meet hers. I expect some pain in her gaze, or at least some aggravation. Something.

I should know better, because this is Natalie, and there's nothing she likes more than proving me wrong. Her gaze is full of love. There's no other way to describe it.

Natalie Jackson is in love with me.

"This isn't your fault, Alex. Okay? This isn't your fault," she whispers. "I'm clumsy. Accidents happen. Ice is slippery. None of that falls on you."

I'm overcome with emotion as I stare at her. I can't respond. I don't know *how* to respond. I'm not ready. I can't be ready. I feel like crying, but also shouting from the rooftops that she loves me.

Not knowing how to compartmentalize the chaos in my mind, I lean forward and press my lips to hers. We sit like that, for a moment, our lips touching gently, and I feel worse. A throat clearing breaks our connection, and I look up to find my mother watching me, her eyebrows so high they're almost in her hairline. "Let me look at her ankle, *angiolo*."

I hastily rise to my feet, scratching my chin anxiously. "I'll leave you to it. Excuse me."

I don't look at Natalie as I race from the room. Taking the steps two at a time, I stride into my childhood bedroom, one that I shared with Dom until I got my own apartment shortly after I met Sara. Closing the door softly, I take a seat on my bed, looking across at my desk. Many of the rooms in my parents' house have been updated, but this room is like a time capsule. Posters from the Denver Wolves inaugural season in the mid-nineties, when they won the Stanley Cup. Me and Dom at the football game when I met Sara. Ticket stubs to various events throughout my late teens and early twenties. A box that sits to the side of my desk grabs my attention, and I know what it is. Something I haven't looked through since I packed it up, nearly six years ago.

A few months after Sara passed away, I finally had the strength to pack up Sara's desk. I couldn't look through most of it, choosing instead to shove it all in a box. Lots of mementos. While I only saved items from truly big events, things where our lives were altered forever, Sara seemed to save everything. Any letters I wrote to her while deployed. Art projects the kids made anytime I was gone. Tons of pictures while we were dating. I'd honestly forgotten I brought the box here.

My hands shake as I remove the lid, slowly sinking to the floor beside the box. All the times I've heard her voice over the past year, but right now, nothing. Here I am, sifting through a box of her most important memories, and she's quiet. What does that mean?

Rifling through all the memorabilia, I come across an envelope I've never noticed before. My name is written across the front in her familiar handwriting. She always wrote my name by adding a heart to the x at the end. Emotion clogging my throat, I slowly peel open the envelope.

My sweet Alex,
　It's your fourth deployment, and while it may seem that I'm used to this experience, I'm not. Each time seems to feel

worse, if I'm being honest. I know you hate it as much as I do, but I'm so proud of you for serving our country. You're showing our children how duty and bravery are two of your most valued attributes.

Each time you deploy, I know you write me a letter that will be given to me if you are killed in action. While I hate that you must do that, I know it's something I would cherish as one of my most prized possessions. Knowing those could be your last words to me would break me, but God, I'd be so thankful to have that. I decided to write this letter just in case something happens to me.

I love you.

There aren't enough words in the English language to describe how much I love you. How perfect our life is, and what an incredible husband you are to me.

My heart didn't know unconditional love until I met you. When I saw you that first day, I knew you were about to change my life. I wanted to marry you after our fifth date, and I was ready to have your babies within the first six months. You are the best person I know, and the best father to our children. I'm so incredibly thankful for our life together. I will never regret marrying you. When I'm in heaven, I'll be in your arms, because there's nowhere else as perfect as your embrace.

I know my death will be a struggle for you. You'll undoubtedly feel immense guilt, thinking you're at fault. You could never be responsible. Bad things happen, my love. I want — no, I _need_ you to promise me that you won't blame yourself. I know you. You'll let that guilt eat away at your happiness and livelihood. Promise you won't. Promise me you'll live each day with joy. Love our children for both of us.

Abbie will need you. She's emotional like me (don't roll your eyes at me) and she's going to need all the quality time with you. Ben is so young that he won't understand. Please keep my memory alive for him. Tell him often how much I loved him, and how my world was finally complete the day he came into it. I can already tell how smart he is, just like you. He'll probably internalize his feelings, just like you. And when he falls in love, he'll be so devoted to her that he won't know a time without her. Just like you.

Promise me, my love. Promise me you won't let someone pass you by. Promise me you'll allow another woman into your life. Not only will you need to be loved by someone, but there's a woman out there desperate to be loved by you. I've never known a man who cares so wholeheartedly the way you do. You show your love to me in a million little ways. Kissing my forehead before you leave for work, even if I'm mostly asleep. Bringing me my favorite soda when you know I've had a late night with the kids. Spraying my pillowcase with your cologne whenever you'll be gone for more than one night. It is such a privilege to be loved by you.

I know in my heart there's a woman out there who needs your love, and I beg you to be open to it. I know she'll be different. I imagine she'll be my opposite, bound and determined to barrel into your life whether you like it or not. I'm a fairly easygoing person, and I know I never locked horns with you. I just wanted you to be happy.

Promise me you'll let her in. Let her challenge you, argue with you, and be the support you need. A strong woman with *fire in her veins will fight with you, but she'll also be the best partner, wife, and mother to our babies that you'll ever need. Promise me, Alex. Don't live life letting grief rule for too long.*

Love our babies. Tell them how much I love them. How precious they are, and how my world was finally complete when I became their mom. I can barely write this, thinking about leaving them. Make them understand I'd do anything to be with them. How I'd never choose to leave them, because I'm nothing without them. Without you.

Thank you for loving me, my sweet husband. I'll spend forever waiting for you.

Love always,

Sara

P.S. Now hurry home so you can give me the most perfect Alex hug, because I miss you desperately!

Crumpling to the floor, I lay in a ball as I silently sob. I imagine Sara writing this, undoubtedly after I was already gone on that deployment, thinking of her alone and trying to find the words. My letters to her were nowhere near as eloquent and thoughtful. I couldn't verbalize my feelings. Denial was easier. My letters were more a paragraph or two, telling her that I loved her and the kids. Sara was always better with words than me, but it's almost as if she knew she needed to write this. That I'd need guidance.

I don't notice when the door opens, or closes. I stay on the floor, crying as I grieve the life I lost when Sara died. Maybe it's the first time I truly recognize that fact. Alex before, versus Alex after. Perhaps I've been living in limbo between the two, and I take a deep, cleansing breath as the tears subside.

Sara is dead.

My wife is gone.

I loved Sara. I still do. But I can't bring her back, and nothing I've done over the past six years can change that fact. I'm allowed to move on, to love again. It's okay to take a step forward, and I know Sara would want that. I have proof in my hands.

"Alex."

I jolt, quickly sitting up and wiping my face, to find my mom at the door.

"I just wanted to let you know that Natalie left."

"What?" I ask in disbelief.

Mom gives me a pitiful smile. "She came up here. I assume she saw you like this."

"Fuck," I mutter.

"Why are you crying?" Mom asks.

I exhale a loud sigh. "I've been struggling with how I feel about Natalie. I came up here to sit and think, but felt pulled to look through this box of Sara's things from her desk. I packed it up after she died, but never looked through it. She wrote me a letter, Mom. It was all the things I should have read back then. How she wants me to support the kids and help them remember her. But mostly, she talked about how I needed to find someone who needed my love, who challenged me, and had a fiery personality. She basically described Nat."

"Oh, *angiolo*. That must have been truly emotional to read," Mom says softly, walking into my room and sitting on the edge of my bed in front of me. "Sara mentioned Natalie to me once, in regard to you."

"What?"

"It sounds odd. But right before that deployment, Natalie and Arianna were here for dinner. I think you were in training, and Sara brought the kids over. She watched Natalie play with Abbie, and how she and Arianna gabbed back and forth. She said something like, 'she'd be perfect for Alex if I weren't here.'"

It's like my world tips on its axis.

I told you so.

Did you send her to me?

She'll love you exactly as you need.

What if I'm not enough for her?
There's no one more perfect for her than you.
Love her. Let her love you. Let her complete our family.
"Mom," I blurt out.
"Yes?"
"I think I'm in love with Natalie."
"I know, *angiolo*. Now you need to tell her."

Chapter 27

Natalie — April

One step forward, two steps back.

If I had to explain a relationship with Alex, any kind of relationship, that's what I'd say. As soon as I feel like we're connecting on a new level, either he closes himself off to me, or something happens that puts us much further back than we were.

Opening his bedroom door to find him sobbing on the floor is definitely two steps backward. Seeing him surrounded by pictures of his dead wife while he cries? Infinite steps.

I'm in love with him.

I knew it was a possibility. Hell, even a probability. Anytime I'd started thinking about it, I forced myself to focus on something else. I wasn't ready to deal with it all. But the moment he started apologizing, as if me slipping on ice was his fault, I knew I was head over heels.

Unfortunately, something in my eyes told him, because I saw it in his.

I saw the exact moment he pulled away emotionally, then again when I found him crying amidst memories of his wife.

As I hobble from the rideshare up to my apartment, I barely make it inside before the tears come. I have to stop this. It's no one's fault, really. I didn't choose to fall in love with Alex, but I can't live like this.

Locking my door, I quietly set my things on the table. Grabbing my phone, I get undressed silently before climbing into my bed. I text Arianna the one thing I need her to do.

> Me: I need you to go to your parents' and get my key back from Alex. Right now, please.

> Arianna: What happened?

> Me: It doesn't matter. I can't deal with him tonight, and I know he'll just barge in here regardless.

> Arianna: Do you want me to come over?

I think about it. Do I want to be alone? Yes and no. I feel like I need to sob a million tears. Get out this emotion that's been right underneath the surface for weeks, just threatening to burst through like a geyser. But having my best friend here would be nice. Even if she gets the key back from Alex, I bet he still shows up.

Actually, what the hell am I thinking? He's not going to show up. I left him alone. He got what he needed.

> Me: I don't want to interrupt family time for you.

> Arianna: I'm already halfway to your apartment.

A fresh wave of tears hits my cheeks. My life might be a complete dumpster fire, but I have an amazing group of friends. Only a few minutes later, when Ari lets herself into my dark apartment, I'm so thankful for her. I'm not surprised when she slides under the covers with me, wrapping her arms around me.

"Do you want to talk about it?" Arianna whispers.

"Not yet. Did you get the key back?"

"No, but my mom told him to leave you alone."

"Do you think he'll listen to her?" I've barely finished speaking before we hear a key in the lock.

"Sunflower, *please*." His voice is full of raw emotion, and I squeeze my eyes closed, my body sinking into the bed.

"God dammit, Alex, I said don't come here! What the fuck?" Arianna snaps.

"Ari?" he asks incredulously. "Is Natalie even here?"

"Yes, she's here, you jackass. When she's ready to talk to you, she'll let you know."

"I can't — I don't want to leave like this, Ari. Please just let me talk to her for five minutes."

Ari leans closer to me. "Do you want to listen to him? I can totally kick his ass out. Or kick him in the balls. He has enough kids already."

I snort tearfully. "It's okay. I'll listen to him."

"I'm staying in the room. Just shout at me if you want him to leave." Arianna leaves the bed, and I scrunch my eyes shut as I feel Alex move toward me. That's the only way to describe it: I feel him. It's a magnetic energy that's tethered me to him. Every atom in my body is reaching for him, and only my mind is trying to keep away.

The moment I feel him sink into the bed, I realize a key error in my judgment. Alex curls around my body, burying his head in my hair, and I shudder. I try to pull my arms in to protect myself, but he's faster, engulfing me in his embrace as he spoons me. I hate how right this feels.

Alex waits a few moments before he speaks, and I don't recognize his voice. It's deep, raspy, and so emotional I don't know how to react. "Loving Sara was easy. Light. Refreshing. It was a slow increase that happened from the first moment I met her. We rarely argued, never truly fought, and it was as easy as smiling."

"Why are you telling me things I already know?" I whisper, my own voice staccato and full of anguish. "I get it. I'm competing with a ghost, and I never wanted that. I never asked you for anything, yet you make me feel guilty for giving you everything."

His arms tighten around me. "I wanted to give you everything, but I didn't know how to when I thought my heart was already taken. I felt torn. Torn between what I promised my wife, and what I wanted with you."

"One minute left," Arianna calls out, making Alex swear against my hair.

"I thought I was a stickler for time. Fucking drill sergeant," he mutters. I smile slightly, thankful he can't see my face, but he knows me too well. "You can find joy in my sister busting my balls, baby girl."

"It hurts too much to find joy," I admit. I feel Alex tense behind me as he exhales a sigh.

"I know. I know all too well how grief can suck the life out of everything. I need to explain a lot of what happened tonight, as well as the last six years. Will you let me? Tomorrow I'd like to explain," he says gruffly.

"Thirty seconds!" Arianna shouts. I can't help the light giggle that bursts from my lips.

"There's my girl," Alex says softly. "Please say you'll meet me tomorrow. I owe you so much, Sunflower. Please."

I should say no. Try to separate myself from him as much as possible. Find another job in the next town, and use Arianna or my other friends as my liaisons when handing the baby over to Alex. I can't be around him and not hurt. Instead, I nod my head, feeling Alex's relief as he dips his head into my neck.

"Alright asshole, you need to go. Give the girl some fucking room," Arianna snaps. Alex moves, and I relax into the bed. My momentary relaxation is enough for Alex to pull my arm, rolling me onto my back, and his lips crash onto mine. His hand comes to rest at its familiar stance on my neck, a thumb pushing into my pulse point. The kiss isn't passionate. There's no tongue, but I'm still reeling from the intensity of it. It's almost as if Alex is staking a claim, reminding me who I belong to … as if I'd forgotten in the last hour.

I'm well aware of the power this man has over me, and that thought is the only thing that helps me to wrench my lips away from his. When I open my eyes, tears stinging my eyelashes, I find Alex only an inch away. His hand slides up to cup my face, almost exactly as

I did to him earlier tonight. He wipes away the wetness of my tears before leaning down and kissing me quickly. "Trust me, Sunflower. Please — Jesus Christ, Arianna, enough."

"I said five minutes, and I gave you ten. Now go." Alex abruptly rises from the bed, and Ari immediately pushes him toward the door. I hear them murmur for a moment before Alex kisses her on the forehead, gives me one last look of longing, then leaves. I sit up, resting my back against the wall.

"What did he say to you when he left?" I ask.

She gives me a sympathetic smile. "He told me to stay with you until you fell asleep, and he wanted me to ask about your ankle. Oh, and he brought you dinner."

I snicker, looking over at the bag of food he left on my tiny table. "He has a habit of leaving in the middle of the night, so I don't find it surprising that he told you to do the same. My ankle feels fine. I don't think it's sprained. I'll happily eat the food, though."

Arianna comes to sit beside me. "He wasn't telling me to leave like he does, and we'll get to that in a minute. He was saying he didn't want you to be alone while you're awake. He wants to make sure someone is here for you, Nat. He doesn't want you to be hurting alone."

"Oh." I watch as Ari grabs the bag, handing it to me on the bed. As I open the first container, I salivate as the delicious aroma of barbecue hits my senses. I hadn't told anyone, but my most recent craving has been meat. I blissfully grab a chunk of brisket and pop it in my mouth.

"Yeah, oh. And furthermore, Alex obviously hasn't handled his feelings well with you, but his sneaking out isn't really about you. He had some big feelings he had to work through. I don't exactly talk to my big brother about his sexual partners, but I know it's been few and far between since Sara died. According to Stone, Alex didn't repeat with anyone. That already tells me you're more important than he's willing to admit."

"Or I'm just convenient," I mutter.

"Don't give me that bullshit answer, Nat. You know it's more than that."

"I don't know anything," I say defiantly, crossing my arms and pouting.

Arianna rolls her eyes. "You used to come to Eternity Springs fairly often, but once I moved into my apartment in Denver, we almost always hung out at one of our places. So you didn't see firsthand the devastation that I did. Broken doesn't even begin to describe it, Nat. I'd say he was inconsolable, but that's not it. No one could talk to him about Sara. He closed everyone off. We were all so worried about him. Slowly he started to come back to us, but he wasn't the same. The Alex after Sara was a shell of his former self."

"That's awful," I whisper. "No wonder he doesn't want to let go of her."

"Okay, we need to get you over this mental block you have about Sara." Arianna looks at me bluntly, her eyebrows raised in aggravation.

"What? I don't have a mental block."

"Yes, you absolutely do. You're convinced that she's this mythical being, and you'll never measure up to her. Sara wasn't perfect. Frankly, she let Alex get away with too much because she was either too afraid to stand up for herself, or she was afraid he'd yell, or she just figured it was easier. But I'd watch her, knowing she wasn't completely happy with something, yet she wouldn't tell him."

"So? Sounds like she loved him so much she put his happiness above her own. There's nothing wrong with that. I'm sure you do that with Stone."

"On occasion, yes. But not over and over again. And you know what? Alex knew. He fucking knew, Nat, and he just went along with it. I'd watch as he'd get quiet, because he knew she wasn't happy, but she wouldn't tell him, and he didn't know how to get her to open up. So then he wasn't happy either. That's not how a marriage works."

I frown, trying to process what she's saying. "I don't get how this relates to me."

"Of course you don't," Arianna mutters, rubbing the bridge of her nose in the same way Alex does. I think I've even seen Luca do it, and I wonder if all the Santo kids have the same tic when they're frustrated. "I've only been around you with Alex a couple times, and I can already tell how different he is with you."

"I'm well aware of the differences between us," I snap angrily. God, why does it always come back to this?

"You are not listening! I never said how you and Sara are different. Don't get me wrong, because you totally are. I said that he is different with you. He. Alex. He doesn't hide behind anything, Nat. He tells you what he's thinking. He asks if you're okay. And you fucking tell him when you aren't. Don't you see that? You're his equal. Sara never truly was."

I stare at her incredulously. "That's a really shitty thing to say about her."

"I know," Arianna responds simply, shrugging. "I was devastated when she died. I treated her as another sister, much more than I ever did Dom's nasty first wife. But I never thought she was the best match for him. When you told me you were pregnant, that night Stone and I talked about how hopeful we were. No way would you let Alex get away with shit. You'd challenge him, and we knew you'd fight. But I also knew there's no one who would fight for him like you."

"What happens if I'm too much for him?" I ask, my voice breaking. "When he realizes I don't filter my thoughts, and I say something in front of your parents. Or when I hear about someone at his work who disrespected him, and I'm ready to go light the guy's house on fire. What about when I yell at Abbie for being a little shit because he doesn't call her out on it?"

"Can you please promise me to do that last one? We're all sick of Abbie's attitude, but Alex just lets it go. She looks so much like Sara that he can't discipline her, and then she turns around and has a sweet personality. It's driving me bonkers," Ari says with a laugh. "Just promise me you'll listen to what he has to say. I know you love him, Nat."

"Loving him isn't the problem," I murmur brokenly.

"Loving you isn't either."

I don't know when I fell asleep, but I know Ari stayed with me until well past midnight. I woke only to pee, get a drink of water, and text the school admin team that I wouldn't be in the following day before falling into a dreamless sleep for the remainder of the night. Taking the day off was needed, mostly because I'm just too emotionally drained to interact with my students. We're into the fourth quarter, and everyone is exhausted. I spend a lot more time each day keeping them focused than at the beginning of the year, and there isn't enough time built into the schedule to reteach concepts. State standardized tests don't allow for any leeway.

When someone knocks on my door a little after nine that morning, I tiptoe over to look out the peephole. Expecting Alex, and not sure if I'm ready to see him, I'm surprised to find Abbie.

I throw open the door. "What are you doing here? Shouldn't you be in school?"

"Told my dad I was sick," she hiccups. "But I couldn't go to school today. Couldn't be around those awful vipers."

"What happened? How did you get here?" I ask, noticing the puffy eyes and red nose, telltale signs of a crying fit. I'm sure I looked similar last night.

"I walked. It's only a mile or so. Can I come in?" she asks, and I nod. Stepping aside, Abbie walks in.

"Wow. This is small," she comments.

"I'm aware."

"Where are you gonna put a crib?"

"I don't really know. I'm probably going to have to move."

"Where?"

"Not sure yet, but I'm assuming closer to Denver. I can find a cheaper apartment there, I think."

"You can't move!" she shouts. "When will we see the baby?"

"Your dad and I will work out an arrangement for that, Abbie. You'll see the baby."

"You promise you aren't taking him away from us?" she asks sullenly.

"I promise. I wouldn't do that. I couldn't do that to you. I want him to know you and Ben."

Abbie walks toward my table, staring at it. "Did you and my dad have a fight last night?"

"Not exactly."

"Was it about my mom?" I hear the fear in her voice. The trepidation.

"Why would you think that?" I pry.

"Because," she whispers. I sit on the bed, pushing back to lean against the wall, and Abbie comes to sit beside me, mirroring my stance.

"What happened?" I ask quietly. I hear a sniffle, then Abbie rests her head against my shoulder.

"Someone texted me. Told me you left Nani and Papa's house crying, then Aunt Arianna and Dad showed up here. A little while later, it was on *The Eagle Has Landed*, and the same phone number texted me a link to it."

That fucking gossip website.

Whipping out my phone, I pull it up.

Trouble in Babymoon Paradise?

While it's never been confirmed, we all know newcomer Natalie Jackson is pregnant with Alex Santo's third child. What we never knew, however, was whether or not they were in a relationship, or if the baby was a by-product of an evening of love.

Sources now claim Ms. Jackson has been desperately trying to replace the much missed Mrs. Sara Santo, and she's been pulling out all the stops to get our favorite retired veteran to forget his first love. Earlier, Ms. Jackson and Mr. Santo arrived hand-in-hand at the stately home of Eternity Springs' own, Nick and Sofia Santo, but within the hour, Ms. Jackson was seen in tears, being picked up by Gregory Hamlin, eight years her junior.

Shortly thereafter, our Alex chased after her, but not before Arianna Santo Dixon was called to Ms. Jackson's apartment. Loud voices were heard throughout the building, but residents have not confirmed what transpired. While Alex left shortly after his arrival, as of publication, Mrs. Santo Dixon remains.

What happened?

Who was hurt?

And most importantly, noting Mr. Hamlin's presence, who exactly is the father?

"Oh, for fuck's sake," I mutter. "Your dad is the father. Is that why you're here? He's the father, Abbie. I promise. It had been quite some time since I'd been with another man, and there hasn't been anyone since. And that man who picked me up is just a ride share driver. I've never met the guy."

"I figured. But that part about my mom …" she trails off. Oh her poor heart.

"I hate that you read this crap. That someone out there writes these articles without thinking about how they impact actual lives. I would never try to replace your mom. Never. I truly hope you believe me. If anything were to happen between me and your dad, I'd never act like she didn't exist. My mom is so important to me, and I hate that you didn't get longer with yours. I can't imagine how awful it must have been for you, sweetheart. I would never sully any memory you have of her."

Another sniffle, and my heart breaks. Arianna joked about me burning down the world for Alex, but she has no fucking idea what I'd do for this innocent young woman beside me. And the moment I tell Arianna, I know she'll be right beside me, lighting the fucking match. *The Eagle Has Landed* fucked with the wrong person.

"Why are you growling?" Abbie whispers. "It's low-key freaking me out, but I'm kinda intrigued."

"Nothing to worry about. Rest assured, I'll be getting that article removed from that ridiculous website within the hour, though."

She waves a hand in front of her. "I don't care about that. It's just stupid gossip."

"Alright. Can I go after the little bitches that anonymously texted you?"

"What?" she says with a shocked laugh.

"Anonymous texts are bullshit. Their parents need to know what they're doing. It's bullying. I don't play when it comes to bullying, and I doubt your dad does either. Middle school is rough, and hormones definitely come into play, but these kids need to know there are ramifications to their actions."

"How do you know they won't make it worse for me?"

"I don't," I admit. "But I hate that you're hurting, and my first instinct is to go after them, consequences be damned."

Abbie sits quietly for a few moments. "I think that's how a mom would react. She'd want to protect her child."

She needs you.

Woah. Where the hell did that voice come from?

He needs you more. Take care of my loves.

A whisper of feeling slides across my forehead, and in my periphery, I see Abbie's hair move slightly. She sighs, a smile gracing her cherubic face. "My mom is here. I can feel her. I know that sounds weird, but I swear when I'm really upset, she's always with me. I think she likes you, Natalie. I think she sent you to my dad."

Emotion clogs my throat as my vision clouds with tears. "But I met your dad before she did."

"My grandma told me once that all my mom wanted to be in life was a mom. When she'd play make believe, it was always playing house, or getting married, and then having a baby. Grandma said Mom came home after meeting Dad, knowing she'd met the one. Grandma thinks that Mom's life was always meant to be short, but she had to meet Dad so that she could make Ben and me. With anyone else it wouldn't be the same."

"Your grandma sounds like an amazing woman," I say thickly.

Abbie nods against my shoulder. "She wants to meet you. Grandpa too. They're excited about the baby. It should be weird, right? They want to be involved with the baby, even though he won't actually be related to them."

"I don't think it's weird. I think it's amazing. It isn't about the baby not being a piece of your mom. It's about the baby being a piece of your dad, and therefore a piece of you and Ben. They're finding joy in that."

"I guess," she murmurs. "So your fight with my dad last night wasn't about my mom?"

"We didn't fight. There are a lot of things we've put off discussing, Abbie."

"I'm worried about him. He was getting happier. Then last night he was devastated."

"What do you mean?" I ask, my voice barely above a whisper.

"Which part?"

"Both."

"I thought it was you," she confesses. "The happy part. I thought he was falling for you, and I could see a side of him I'd never seen before. I heard Nani and Papa talking about how he was 'the old Alex,' but I don't remember much before my mom died. They said he was happier, and how thrilled they were that you brought it out of him. And then last night ..."

"Go on," I encourage.

"I heard him crying. It's been so long since I've heard it that I went to check on Ben first, thinking it was him. When I realized it was Dad, I went to find him. He was in the nursery, and —"

I interrupt her immediately. "The nursery?"

"Yeah, and —"

"Wait. What nursery?"

"For the baby?"

"He has a nursery?"

"Well, yeah."

"Since when?" I shout.

"A month or so, I think." Abbie eyes me warily, as if she's waiting for me to sprout horns on my forehead.

"And he didn't think to tell me about it?"

"Now I understand your comment about needing to discuss things, although I never thought a crib would be an adult thing to talk about," she says dryly.

"I haven't been to your house in quite some time. How the hell would I know he'd gotten a nursery together?"

"I don't know, maybe because you're having a baby together, and you ask big questions like that when you're weeks away from delivering a baby?" she retorts, irritation clear in her tone.

"Watch your tone, young lady," I snap. "Eight weeks away. You're acting like I'm gonna pop a kid out on the sidewalk any day. I may not be your mother, but you're in my apartment, I'm carrying your brother in my stomach, I'm in love with your father, and you will be respectful. Why is he more prepared than me? I'm the one baking this crotch goblin, and I don't have anything yet. Fuck, I don't have anything! What if I deliver early? Alex is all prepared and I'm going to be a horrible mother!" My voice has risen a full octave as I lose my composure. I don't even have *clothes* for the baby, for fuck's sake.

Abbie tips her head up to look at me, a wide grin on her face. "You're in love with my father?"

Shit.

I sigh. "Yeah."

"You don't seem thrilled about that fact."

"When you're an adult, you'll understand what unrequited love is."

"I read books, dummy. I know what it is. And you're wrong. My dad is totally in love with you. He's just having a hard time figuring out how to love you and my mom at the same time," she states.

"I don't think that's the case here, but I sure do hope you're right," I whisper, resting my head against hers.

"It'll all work out, Natalie. My mom will make sure of it," Abbie says quietly, reaching over and squeezing my hand, before resting it on my stomach. She gasps when the baby pushes against her palm, then giggles as she pushes back.

It's bad enough that I'm in love with Alex Santo. It's even worse to be in love with Abigail and Benjamin Santo. The thought of things not working out, and losing all three of them? One hell of a bad nightmare if that comes true.

Chapter 28

Alex — April

"It's about time you came to me for advice," Nonna says, a wicked gleam in her eye as she watches me triumphantly. I'm standing in my parents' kitchen, tapping my foot impatiently on the hard floor. My mother and grandmother watch me, neither saying anything else.

"Well?" I say irritably, gesturing toward them. "I'm waiting."

"You need to explain where we're at with Natalie, *angiolo*. Nonna needs an update," Mom says.

"Yes, Alessio. Tell me," Nonna commands.

"I don't know what to say."

"Then I can't help you." Nonna gives me a gleeful smile.

"Don't recall asking for help, actually," I say, crossing my arms defiantly.

Nonna rolls her eyes. "You wouldn't be here if you didn't need help."

Sighing, I absentmindedly rub my chin. "I've had difficulty coming to terms with my feelings for Natalie. I felt like I was cheating on Sara by feeling … well, basically anything for Natalie. It's really messed with my head."

"Do you think Sara would want you to be miserably alone for the rest of your life?" Nonna asks.

"No, I guess not. But it's not like I can ask her."

Mom sighs loudly, running a hand through her dark hair, which is the same shade as mine. "Clearly we all know that. But you knew

Sara. You knew her better than everyone. Would she think you were cheating, or that you should never end up with another woman?"

"No," I admit. "She'd want me to be happy."

"Does Natalie make you happy?" Nonna asks.

I nod slowly. "It's different with her. She's so different, Nonna. Nothing like Sara. Like night and day."

"So?" she challenges.

"I think it's throwing me. Maybe I thought if I found someone else, it would be a woman who reminded me of Sara. Instead, I've gone for the antithesis of Sara."

"It isn't about who is alike, or different from Sara," Mom says quietly. "It's about who meets your needs where you are right now, Alex. I don't think a woman like Sara would appeal to you now. Late thirties Alex is pretty different from early twenties Alex. Back then, you needed someone who quietly supported you, and graciously let you run the show."

"Natalie sure won't let that happen," I chuckle.

"No, she won't. But she also won't stand for anyone hurting you, or your family. She has the patience of a saint, but the backbone of a Rottweiler guarding her babies. Natalie is a force to be reckoned with, and I think the two of you will make an excellent team. What have your dad and I always said about love?"

"Love out loud," I answer.

She nods emphatically. "There is no one who will love you louder than Natalie. She'll want everyone to know that you're spoken for, but also that she's beside you, ready to take on anyone who thinks you're an easy fight."

"I've never been an easy fight," I say, frowning.

"I never said that, Alex. I said she'd stand beside you. Look at your father and me. We are incredibly different, but no one would ever say we fight each other's battles. We're a team, and everyone in this town knows it. They knew it about Nonna and Papi too."

"That's right, they sure did. Although I think they knew I'd take anyone on, but your grandfather was freakishly quiet with that RPF, so no one wanted to take him on." Nonna says proudly.

"RPF?" I ask, intrigued.

"Resting Papi Face."

I let out a loud bark of laughter.

"What? I thought that middle word could be switched out," she says with a shrug. "Regardless, we think Natalie makes an excellent counterpart to you. She'll challenge the hell out of you, but be your biggest supporter at the same time."

It still worries me how insanely attracted I am to Natalie, but I can't bring that up to my mother and grandmother. I'm not even sure I can ask my dad about it. Only person who might understand is Dom. Sex with Sara was great, but sex with Natalie is unlike anything I've ever experienced.

"Natalie's better in bed, isn't she?" Nonna asks.

"For fuck's sake," I groan. "I'm not talking about this with you."

"What? You knocked her up. Obviously we know it's not immaculate conception. And seeing as how you're both in your thirties, and you already have children, we can discuss sex, Alessio."

"Speak for yourself," Mom mutters.

"Never would have thought I'd be the most open-minded out of the three of us," Nonna muses. She turns toward Mom and gives her a leering grin. "Nick was conceived on a beach in Italy. Papi could barely keep it in his pants long enough to take me, and I got sand in places that still haunt me."

"That's the same story you told Angelina about where she was conceived," Mom points out about my dad's younger sister.

Nonna raises an eyebrow. "Who says it didn't happen twice?"

"Considering you've only talked about one visit to Italy at the beginning of your marriage, and Angie is two years younger than Nick, I'm pretty sure it didn't happen twice."

Nonna rolls her eyes. "You and that stupid memory of yours, ruining my fun."

"Wait," I call out. "The beach story has to be Dad, right? Unless you left him at home with your parents and took off to Italy when he was only a year old. I can't see that happening, since you've proudly admitted to being a helicopter mom from pretty early on. Although you did say you took Dad to Woodstock, so I guess anything could be true."

Nonna shrugs, and Mom scoffs. "Neither Italy story is true. She's trying to get a rise out of me. Years ago she said all of her children were conceived the old-fashioned way in the marital bed. But I think Woodstock did happen. I've heard that detail before."

"I had eight children, Sofia. I'm sure one of them was conceived on a beach somewhere," Nonna snaps. " Woodstock is probably where Angelina was conceived. Now go get your woman, Alex, so we can put her through the normal Santo traditions."

I shake my head with a chuckle, but as I stand up, a weird sense comes over me. The threshold. "Holy shit."

"I wondered when you'd realize what already happened," Mom comments.

I turn to her, my eyes wide. "Why didn't anyone say anything?"

"It wasn't the place, or time," she says simply.

"Could someone clue me in, please?" Nonna shouts.

My mind is whirling. Only Mom knows I tried crossing the threshold with Sara again after that first time. It was a running joke between us. I didn't consider it to be a big deal until every one of my siblings failed the challenge. And all this time, Natalie was the one? "I accidentally did the threshold thing yesterday. Natalie slipped on ice, and I carried her into the house before dinner. I carried her over the threshold, yet I tried three times with Sara, and —"

Mom interrupts me. "It doesn't matter, *angiolo*."

"It *does* matter," I argue.

"No, it doesn't. You loved Sara. She gave you ten amazing years with two beautiful children. We will not discredit that by a silly myth about my front door."

"So you don't believe in the threshold legend?" Nonna asks.

"I never said that," Mom answers. "However, I will not allow Alex to go down the slippery slope that his mind will send him, thinking that his true love was in the background the entire time. Sara was an integral part of your story, son, and I will stand by that fact until my dying breath."

I sit heavily as I try to wrap my head around everything. Mom sits next to me, placing her hand on top of mine. "This doesn't change anything. You made up your mind before remembering carrying her. You knew you loved her before. It's throwing you for a loop, but you knew it was her."

"I know. It's a lot to process," I admit, pulling out my phone when it vibrates. I see I have a notification on my doorbell camera, and — "what the fuck?"

"What?" Mom asks.

"Abbie just went in the house. She told me she was sick." As I'm about to call her, my phone buzzes with two simultaneous incoming texts. The first text is from Natalie.

> Natalie: Abbie was just here. She walked, but I drove her back home.

Then in a surprise move, my daughter admitted her crimes before I could call her out on them.

> Abbie: I'm not sick. I'm sorry I lied to you. I went to talk to Natalie. You can ground me when you get home.

> Me: Is this a new trend? Trying to get in front of the parent police in hopes of an easier sentence?

> Abbie: No. I figured you'd see me coming back home on the camera. No sense in delaying the inevitable.

> Me: Why did you go see Natalie?

> Abbie: Honestly? I wanted to make sure she wasn't trying to replace Mom.

> Me: She'd never do that, Abs.

Abbie: I know. I think I needed to talk to her about it, though. Maybe it's been harder for me to think about you loving her than I thought it would.

Me: Me loving her?

Abbie: Yeah, Dad. I know you love her. You're an idiot about it, but you love her.

Me: Are you going to be okay if I do love her?

Abbie: I think so.

Me: If you aren't, you can tell me.

Abbie: I'll be okay, Dad. It's nice to see you living again. Natalie brings out a side of you I haven't seen before, and it's nice. I just don't want her to replace Mom, or act like Mom never existed.

Me: I'd never allow that. I'd never have you and Ben without your Mom.

Abbie: I like that Mom has your first heart, and Natalie has your second.

Me: Science education has failed you, my sweet daughter. You only get one heart.

Abbie: I don't agree. When Mom died, a part of you broke. I think that piece grew again. You're getting a second chance with Natalie. Why not use a second heart? That way you get to love both of them the same amount.

Me: I don't even know how many hearts I have, then. Your aunts and uncles, Nani and Papa, plus you and your brother each get your own. No one will ever love you like I do, Abbiecakes.

Abbie: I love you too, Dad.

> Abbie: Just don't ever call me Abbiecakes in front of any of my friends.

> Me: You said I'd see you coming home on the camera. Why wouldn't I see you leaving?

> Abbie: I may have climbed out a window.

> Abbie: Hopefully my honesty here helps with a lesser sentence as well.

> Me: Not even a little bit.

> Abbie: Sigh. It was worth a shot.

I chuckle as I turn off the screen and shove my phone back into my pocket. Abbie could have gone in through the window when she returned, which makes me think she wanted to get caught. She needed to have this conversation with me. It's as if she felt she should give her blessing.

"Do you have a plan in mind for winning Natalie back?" Mom asks when I look up to find her watching me with a hint of a smile.

"Yeah, I think I do."

Six hours later, I'm nervously waiting for Natalie to arrive. I've second-guessed myself so many times this afternoon on my plan, but both Mom and Nonna agreed it'll be a wonderful way of introducing my past and present. It's slightly morbid, I guess, as I wait at Sara's grave. But I want Natalie to read Sara's letter, and I think Sara should somehow be involved in it. Weird, I know.

When I see Stone's car pull up, a wave of nerves overtakes me. Butterflies erupt in my stomach, and I'm brought back to a conversation I had with Sara once about butterflies.

"I hate that we don't get cardinals here," she'd commented.

"The dude in the Catholic church, or the bird?"

"The bird," she said with an emphatic roll of her eyes. "Cardinals are a sign from Heaven that a loved one is visiting you."

"Cool thought, but that's ridiculous for all the areas cardinals don't live."

"I know. That's why I've decided when I die, I'm coming back as a butterfly. Then I can be light, airy, and colorful."

"A butterfly."

"Yep. I'll skip the whole metamorphosis in the cocoon thing, though. That gives me the creeps," she'd said with an exaggerated shiver.

"Good to know," I'd laughed.

"So when I die, look for the butterflies. I'll be the one irritating you the most," she'd said with a twinkle in her eye.

Natalie has two butterfly tattoos: one on her ankle and one on her hip.

"Alright, Sara, I get it," I murmur as a light breeze whips around me, scattering the dead leaves sitting around her gravesite. I get it, sometimes I'm not too aware of details. But she's laying it on pretty thick.

As the car door opens and Natalie steps out, my phone buzzes twice.

> Arianna: We're staying in case something bad happens and she needs a ride home.
>
> Arianna: But we also have a shovel in the back, and we're already at a cemetery, so choose your words wisely.
>
> Me: Noted.

As Natalie approaches, I see the apprehension on her face. Hands gripped nervously in front of her, she chews on the inside of her cheek as she slowly approaches me. She takes a deep breath, and I hear the tremor of a sob fighting to breach the surface. She stops a few feet away from me, but I can't be that far away. I step forward, the tips of our shoes touching, and rest my head against hers. That familiar vanilla scent wraps around me, and my heart rate slows. Without touching her pulse, I know our heart beats synced up.

This.

This is who I've been waiting for. Who I'm meant to be with for the rest of my life. That immediate thought allows me to open my heart and confess what I'm feeling.

"I thought you'd only wear a suit for a sibling's wedding," she whispers. I chuckle against her hair as I look down at the only suit I own.

"I'd like to retract that statement and issue a correction."

"Oh?"

"I will only wear a suit when it's of utmost importance, and when I need to make a good impression."

Natalie sighs softly, dipping her head to rest against my chest for only a moment, before stepping back slightly. "I don't care about your clothes, Alex. You look nice, obviously. But why am I here?"

I take a deep breath, willing my pulse to slow. Here goes nothing. "I knew I'd end up marrying Sara within a few dates. Our relationship was easy from the beginning. No arguing, and rarely even a disagreement. I realize now that she appeased me quite a bit, choosing not to argue instead of being true to herself. I don't know if she thought I'd stop loving her if we argued, or if she felt it was easier to be submissive and easygoing. But I look back now and wonder. If she'd argued with me, how would our relationship have changed? Would it have made me doubt everything?"

Natalie's shoulders shake, and she grabs onto my shirt with both hands. "Why are you telling me this?"

"Because I need you to know what I'm thinking, Sunflower. I don't ever want you to second-guess if you can be honest with me, and I want to do the same with you. It's taken me a lot of time to come to terms with all the questions I'll never get answers to. That's why I want to get everything out in the open with you. If something were to happen to either of us, I want you to know exactly how I feel. But first, you need to know how Sara feels."

"What?" Natalie gasps. "How is that possible?"

"Last night, when you found me in my childhood bedroom? I found a letter from Sara that she wrote at some point during that last deployment. It rocked me to my core, Sunflower. I'd never known she'd written it, and certainly hadn't read it before yesterday. If it hadn't been in her handwriting, or written in her voice, I'd have thought someone staged it. Why didn't I find it yet? I guess I wasn't ready."

"What did she say?" Natalie whispers.

I pull the folded letter from my back pocket. "I think you should read it."

I hold it out to her, and she gingerly takes it from me. Unfolding it, I watch as she soaks in the words from my first love. Eventually, one hand covers her mouth as she openly cries. When her eyes close, I know she's reached the end. "My mom told me that you had dinner with my family while I was in training for that deployment. Do you remember?"

"A little," Natalie whispers. "Arianna and I played a lot with Abbie. Ben stayed with Sara and your mom. I didn't really talk to Sara at all."

"Mom said Sara watched you with Abbie, and said you'd be perfect for me if she wasn't around."

Natalie's head whips up, her glassy eyes latching on mine. "What?"

I nod.

"I barely spoke to her. How would she know?"

"No one knew me better than Sara. Maybe she recognized that I'd need a powerful woman who'd challenge me."

"So the exact opposite of her," Natalie says sullenly.

"I don't think that's what was going on. Yeah, you're different. But so was I when I met Sara. She's what I needed at that stage of my life. But right now, I want — no, I *need* a headstrong woman who will love my children like her own. A woman who has the patience of a saint, but will willingly commit a crime for someone she loves. A passionate woman who spits fire in and out of the bedroom, but one that also trusts me implicitly. One who will love me exactly as I am, broken and stubborn, and who lets me love her, because she knows I'll give her everything she needs."

My hand finds her cheek as I continue. "I have no doubt we'll argue. You won't give in just because you don't want to rock the boat. But we'll never find another who will love so fiercely, so perfectly, than us."

"But I saw you last night, sobbing on the floor. You were grieving her again. What if you regret me?" Natalie confesses.

"I wasn't grieving her. I was grieving the time lost. Had I known she had written that letter, I'd have gotten the closure years ago. All this time I'd felt like I was cheating on her by falling for you. I finally got what I needed, and all that pent up grief just exploded out of me." My hand slides down to bracket her neck, her pulse beating wildly against my thumb. "I'll never regret Sara and what we shared. She gave me two beautiful babies and a decade of one hell of a love story. And yeah, her death changed me. But there's no one in the world more perfect for me than you."

"Why do you call me Sunflower?" she blurts out, making me chuckle.

"For a multitude of reasons. Sunflowers are insanely happy plants. They face the sun no matter where they are planted. Did you know that? At first, I thought you were the sunflower. You are full of sunshine, and you see the best in every situation. Now I'm thinking I'm actually the sunflower, because I'm tracking you wherever you go. Following you like a sunflower follows the sun. You can't get rid of me now."

Natalie gifts me a half smile before her face dims. "Are you sure you know what you want?"

"You. I want you."

"Only a few days ago, you'd have argued that you didn't want me at all. It's whiplash, Alex. I can't handle the constant ups and downs of your feelings."

"I know. I can't imagine how hard that must have been for you. I've been fighting my feelings for quite some time. Yesterday reading

Sara's letter, and then knowing I'd unconsciously hurt you, made me realize I can't go one more day without you knowing how I feel."

"How do you feel?" she whispers.

Gathering her into my arms, I rest my forehead against hers, breathing her in. "I'm in love with you, Natalie. I don't think I can go one more day without saying those words. I love you. I'd do anything for you."

She sighs against me as her hands grip the back of my shirt. "I love you too, Alessio."

It's as if the weight of the world is finally lifted off my shoulders. I smile against her hair as I squeeze her against me, feeling her stomach move as little man kicks.

"Now what?" she murmurs.

"Now I'd like to take you on a proper date, if that's okay."

"What does a proper date entail?" she teases lightly, resting her chin on my chest and looking up at me. Her green eyes sparkle, and I'm proud to be the reason she looks so happy and content.

"Well, I'm hoping you'll come to my house for dinner with me and the kids," I tell her hesitantly. That's not exactly a date, but I want them to be on board with Natalie being a bigger part of our lives than I'd suggested before.

"Sounds like a perfect date to me," she says with a smile.

Thank fuck.

An hour later, we're sitting awkwardly at my kitchen table as Ben and Abbie whip question after question at us. Is Natalie moving in? Does she replace Sara? Can she yell at us? Are we allowed to ask her for things?

"Guys," I interrupt their barrage, "Natalie and I just decided to be together. Let's take it one day at a time."

"But once the baby comes, where will you both be? It's weird that you'd be in that tiny apartment when you could be here," Abbie says.

"You haven't even seen the nursery yet. I helped," Ben boasts, puffing his chest out proudly. Natalie cocks an eyebrow at me, and I nod.

"He really did. There's a mural on one wall, and they both helped with it."

"A mural?"

"Yeah. I kept having these dreams about the night sky, and Ben said he'd dreamed about stars above the mountains. Abbie suggested it initially, and it worked out well once we found out the gender. We've been working on it for quite a while," I explain sheepishly.

"Why didn't you tell me?" Natalie whispers. "I could have helped."

Abbie clears her throat. "It was something the three of us wanted to do together. We didn't want to exclude you, but it was really important to us."

"I understand," Natalie says, but I can hear the hint of pain in her voice.

"I needed it to be just the three of us, Nat. I'm not sure how to explain it any other way."

Natalie squeezes my hand reassuringly. "I know. I'm glad you had that time with them."

"Would you like to see it?" I ask.

"Yes, please. Absolutely."

Chairs are pushed impatiently from the table, the sound of the chair legs catching along the hard floor as four pairs of feet quickly flood down the hallway and up the stairs. I get in the room first, giving me an opportunity to turn around to watch Natalie's unfiltered reaction. Her loud gasp echoes against the walls as she covers her mouth with her hands, tears instantly filling her eyes.

Ben and I sketched out our vision more than once of a brilliant night sky over rocky mountains, with blue spruce pine trees beneath a full moon. Abbie helped sketch the trees onto the wall, then added shading to everything once I completed the painting. Ben happily added hundreds of stars in different shapes and sizes. Encompassing the entire wall behind a comfortable glider in pale white, the mural is both warm and dark simultaneously, while giving the room a peaceful glow.

"Oh my God, Alex, this is beautiful," Natalie breathes. I watch as her eyes scatter from place to place around the room as she takes in all the details. A solid cherry stained crib sits in the corner with cloud crib sheets. A small bookshelf stands under the large window, already full of books. I can't help but chuckle as Natalie makes a beeline for it, dropping to her knees as she grabs one of the books. "This looks old."

"It is. Those were all my books when I was a baby. Mom saved a box for each of us so we could have things to hand down to our kids. They've already been in nurseries for Abbie and Ben, and now they get to be in little man's nursery."

"I love that. I'll have to ask my mom if she saved anything for me," she says absentmindedly as her fingers skim across the book spines.

"Only a teacher would be more impressed by Dad's old books than the mural that took us tons of time to complete," Abbie comments.

"The mural is gorgeous. This whole room is beautiful. It's a lot to take in, and I —" her voice breaks off as a tear slides down her face.

"Give us a few minutes, kids," I tell Ben and Abbie, motioning for them to quietly leave the room. After closing the door, I sit in the glider. "Come here, baby."

I'm used to Natalie fighting everything, so I'm pleasantly surprised when she climbs into my lap and buries her head in my shoulder. "What's going on in that head of yours?"

Natalie's body shudders as more tears fall. "You're so prepared, and I have nothing. Seriously, I have nothing. How am I supposed to care for a tiny human when I'm barely caring for myself?"

I gently stroke up and down her spine. "I think you're supposed to let me take care of you now."

"What?" she says, sitting up abruptly. I wipe the wetness from her cheeks as she sniffs. "That's not what I meant. I wasn't trying to force you into anything."

"I didn't offer because I felt forced, Sunflower. I offered because I want to. I want to take care of you. I want to wake up with you here, and help with midnight feedings and blow-out diapers. Especially when you're recovering from the birth, I'd be a nervous wreck if you and the baby weren't here." The thought of something happening to either of them, even only a few blocks away, makes me feel sick.

"So it would just be for a little while?" she asks hesitantly. "For after the birth?"

I clear my throat, tempted to shout that once she moves in, she's not leaving again. "One day at a time. But if you want to stay over tonight, I wouldn't be opposed."

Natalie giggles. "Do you think that's wise? With the kids here?"

"You're having a baby together," Abbie shouts from the hallway. "We know you've had sex."

"Did you know that regular intercourse can improve the immune system?" Ben pipes up. "I learned that from a YouTube video."

"Woah," I shout. "Get in here and give me your iPad so I can adjust some settings."

The door opens, and Ben reluctantly steps in. "I don't know why you bother. You know I can figure out how to bypass whatever settings or walls you put up."

"You're ten. You shouldn't be watching videos about sex," I answer.

Ben shrugs. "There's a whole unit on sex in fifth grade, Dad. I'm just getting prepared."

"He's right, unfortunately. It's one main reason I don't want to teach fifth grade," Natalie whispers. "It's a rough month for those teachers because fifth graders can't learn about sex and not make a ton of jokes about it."

"Anything will be better than what is discussed at recess," Ben says, a noticeable wince as he frowns.

"What is discussed at recess?" I ask warily.

"Did you fart?" Ben blurts out.

"Uh, no?"

"Oh that must have been me. It was my butt blowing you a kiss."

Natalie groans. "Boys and toilet humor."

"And we're about to have another one," I say with a smile.

"Another one?" she asks quietly.

"Listen," I say softly. "This isn't a quick thing for me. I'm not having a kid and then dropping you. I told you I'm in love with you. I expect this to be forever, which means you'll be their step-mom. That makes you part of this family."

"Okay," Natalie whispers, leaning forward and applying a quick kiss to my lips.

"Gross," Ben says with a shudder. "Can you not do that in front of me? You're my teacher. And you're my *dad*. This is weird."

"It is not weird. And in all honesty, this baby was created before we knew she'd be your teacher," I stammer.

"How exactly does a baby get created, Dad?" Ben asks innocently.

"You just got played," Natalie whispers against my ear.

"I know."

And we're having another one ... but I couldn't be happier.

Chapter 29

Alex — Early June

"Why did you let me decide not to get the epidural? This fucking hurts!" Natalie wails. She's on her hands and knees, bits of hair plastered to her face and neck as she rocks back and forth. She's been in labor for twenty two hours, and the last four have been brutal. Nurses assure me everything is fine, but that the 'ring of fire' happens to every woman during childbirth. The baby is pushing through her cervix.

"You're doing great, baby girl," I whisper soothingly against her head. Honestly, she's a rock star. Sara got an epidural both times, and her labors were half the time. Natalie even admitted she'd been having contractions for a day or two before she finally told me about them.

Going about a week past her due date, Natalie was able to work the entire school year without missing any time with her kids. I'd told her she could take time off if she wanted, but she was determined to finish the year with her class. They'd had enough change this year, and she didn't want to throw anything else at them.

"Alex," she breathes, her eyes wide, "I think something is happening."

"What?"

"I think I have to poop," she says hurriedly, then lets out a pained growl as her entire body tenses. Her hand grabs mine, closing on it fiercely.

"Sunflower, I need to get the nurse," I tell her calmly. "I think the baby is coming now."

Either Natalie ignores me, or she's so caught up in the contraction that she doesn't hear, because she doesn't let go of my hand. I try to reach the intercom on the side of the bed, but it's too far away.

Natalie gasps, dropping her head to the hospital bed. "Oh God, here's another one ..."

"Nat, let me get the nurse, or you're gonna —" I break off as she lets out one incredibly long grunt before sitting up, and then reaches between her legs. Placing a wet and squirming baby on the bed, she finally addresses me.

"You can get the nurse now."

Holy fucking shit.

This woman is a goddess.

Running to the doorway, I shout, "My wife had the baby by herself!"

Is Natalie legally my wife? No. But that doesn't change how I feel about her.

To me, she is my wife.

As I gleefully jog back into her labor and delivery room, Natalie paws at her face with her wrists, moving stuck hair. "I'm not your wife, dummy."

"You will be though."

"Will I?" she asks as multiple nurses run into the room. A cry pierces the air as my son lets everyone know of his presence, and I let out a loud bark of laughter.

"Yes, Sunflower. You will be."

Aidan Nicholas Santo cried loudly for the first hour of his life, then quieted down as he took in his surroundings. A habit of screaming and then silence was quite the juxtaposition of sound, and it certainly seemed to be as if he was comparing our two personalities. Natalie as the boisterous and loud beauty, and me the quiet and watchful one.

"Do you think your dad will be happy with Aidan's middle name?" Natalie whispers, staring lovingly down at our milk-drunk newborn as he sleeps against her breast.

"Yeah. I'd never wanted a junior, and certainly wouldn't name this one Alessio when Ben was already born, but I like the idea of passing on a bit of family."

"What is Ben's middle name?" she asks.

"Nicholas." I'm pretty sure at least one of my brother's included Nicholas as a middle name for their sons too. What can I say? We like family traditions.

Natalie sputters out a laugh, then gasps when Aidan's arms fling up in surprise. Already a pro, Natalie shushes him and pats his diaper, lulling him back to sleep. "Can you give two kids the same middle name?"

"I don't see why not. It's not like the name police are patrolling the birth certificate applications. Certainly they'd find tons of people to cite before this. I'd bet half of the Santo grandchildren have Nicholas as a middle name."

"I can safely say Arianna did not use Nicholas as Bianca's middle name, Alex."

I shrug, before winking at Natalie. "She might have. Maybe she'll change it now, since our dad had it out with her neighbor." While Arianna and Stone were initially hesitant to press charges against their disgusting neighbor for videoing them, Dad had no qualms about having a man-to-man talk with Frank Green. Within twenty-four hours of their conversation, police were taking statements from every resident on the street, and a for sale sign was in Mr. Green's yard. Arianna and Stone never heard from him again.

"I read a romance book last year where the female lead was named Bunny. I couldn't read anything from the author after that."

"A guy I deployed with named all three of his sons after himself."

"Wow. I can't believe his wife let him do that."

"Three different baby mamas. They all have his last name, though. He was definitely overcompensating."

"Oh?"

"Yep. Community showers. I've seen what he's packing, and it ain't much."

My phone buzzes with an incoming text, and I read the screen to see my parents are here with Ben and Abbie. "You ready for some visitors?"

Natalie immediately pushes her hair away from her face, then repositions Aidan so her breasts are covered. "Do I look okay?"

I study her, a slow smile covering my face. "Absolutely spectacular."

"No, really. Is my hair sticking up in every direction?"

"Baby, you just gave birth. You're not supposed to look like you had a blowout and your makeup professionally applied. But honestly, I don't think you've ever looked more beautiful." The setting sun casts a glow around the room, giving Natalie an aura. Holding my son in her arms, I can't think of a time where I felt this complete. Natalie has become my home.

"Can we come in?" I hear hissed from the door. Mom has her head poked through, then ushers everyone in when I nod. All four are quiet as they approach the bed, and Aidan senses their nearness, letting out a squawk as he stretches his arms out of the receiving blanket.

"What's his name?" Ben whisper-yells.

"We named him Aidan. Aidan Nicholas," I tell him. Glancing at my dad, I see a proud smile on his face as he nods at me. Ben, however, looks confused.

"How can he have my middle name?" he asks.

"Well," I tell him, crouching so we're eye-to-eye, "middle names can really be anything. Your mom and I chose to name you Benjamin Nicholas because Benjamin is her dad's middle name, and Nicholas is my dad's first name. Now giving Aidan the middle name of Nicholas means he's connected to both you and Papa, which is pretty cool."

Ben beams at me. "That is pretty cool. How'd you come up with the first name?"

I turn to look at Natalie, and she gives me a loving smile. "I had a dream last week that we named him Aidan. Your dad liked the name, so we decided to go with it."

"That's how I named you," Mom says.

"Really?" I ask.

"It was going to be a family name of either Lorenzo or Francesco, but I never felt either would work. I had a dream a few weeks before you were born about naming you Alessio, but giving you the nickname of Alex, and when I told your father, he was relieved. He didn't like either of the first two names, but he felt I was the one carrying the baby, so I got to pick the name," she says with a laugh.

I look back at Natalie, running my hand down the side of her face. She leans into it adoringly, and says, "Alex said the same thing to me."

"After what I just witnessed, you can rename me if you'd like," I tell her.

"What happened?" Abbie asks.

"Tell us while I hold my grandson, please," Mom says, motioning for Natalie to hand him over. Once Aidan is safely in her arms and she's cooing away, I sit on the edge of Nat's bed, sliding my arm around her. "Or do you want to wait until your parents get here to tell all of us together?"

"Oh, they were waiting until he was here before heading down. I can tell them when they get here," Natalie tells her, before looking up at me expectantly. Evidently, I'm the one telling the story now.

"Well, this woman delivered her own baby by herself with no epidural, and no nurses were in the room. It was like nothing I'd ever experienced before. She's a fucking rock star," I tell my family proudly.

"Language," Natalie hisses.

"Eh. They know I cuss, and they know they aren't allowed to. It's fine," I answer with a shrug.

"How did you manage to deliver without anyone knowing? It seems like Alex would at least realize what was going on," Mom comments.

"I couldn't see because she was on her hands and knees —"

"You can give birth like that?" Ben asks, horrified.

"You can give birth anywhere. I've seen videos of women having babies in the front seat of a car, on a toilet, or standing up," Abbie tells him.

"I'm so glad I never have to have a baby," he says with a shiver.

"Anyway," I say, getting them focused, "Nat was amazing. She delivered him, then calmly told me to get a nurse. He's already taken to breastfeeding like a champ, and passed all of his APGAR tests."

"Oh, that's wonderful news," Mom gushes. "How much did he weigh? He feels heavier than any of my babies did. You baked him for a whole extra week, so I'm sure he weighs more."

"Nine pounds, nine ounces," Natalie grins. "And I felt every one of those ounces. Counting my blessings that I didn't have any tears though."

"Tears?" Abbie asks.

"Don't worry about that," I answer hastily, but Natalie shushes me.

"She's a woman. She needs to learn about these things. You can tear as you're giving birth, Abbie. Down there. If the baby comes too fast, or if he gets stuck, or if his head is just too big, you can tear."

Abbie's face drains of all color. "I'm never having children."

I laugh as I place a tender kiss on Natalie's forehead. "You say that now, but I bet you change your mind. Just don't change it for fifteen or so years."

Natalie and Aidan are discharged a day later, and on the way home, Natalie asks if we can make a stop.

"Sure. What do you need?" I ask.

"I don't need anything, exactly. I'd like to take Aidan to Sara's grave if that's okay."

Pulling the car over into the closest parking lot, I turn to her. "You do?"

She nods. "It might sound crazy, but I've felt her around me a lot the last couple of months. I want to introduce Aidan to her. Let her know I'll take care of you and her babies."

My throat thick with emotion, I lean over to kiss her gently. "We can wait and do it another time."

"No," she says assuredly. "It needs to be today."

"Okay," I say tentatively. The hospital we gave birth at resides closer to Sara's grave, but it's still out of the way. We stop once for Natalie to feed Aidan, arriving at the cemetery close to sunset. Natalie removes Aidan from his car seat, and we slowly walk toward Sara's final resting place.

I've made this walk hundreds of times. Every time before today involved grief. Sadness. An overwhelming wave of heartbreak. The last time I visited, I waited for Natalie to arrive, and my feelings were of anxiety and nervousness. Today, however, I finally feel at peace. I can't change the past. I can't bring Sara back. But I know she'd be happy with how I've moved on, and how I'm raising our children.

"Hi Sara," Natalie whispers as we reach the grave. "The last time I was here, I didn't introduce myself. I'm Natalie, but I think you already know that. I think you've been pushing us together for some time now, and I'm so incredibly thankful for that."

I rest my head against hers as she continues. "I was in a crappy relationship before Alex. I didn't know how to get out of it, and afterward, I didn't know who to trust. I felt alone and so unworthy. I'd put on a mask for everyone. No one will ever think the loud and mouthy girl is unhappy, right? But Alex saw through that so damn fast. He recognized what I didn't see in myself."

Natalie sniffs as she looks down at Aidan. "I wanted you to meet Aidan. And I want you to know that I will love and adore Ben and Abbie just as much as I do Aidan. They may not have come from my body, but they're in my heart just the same. I'm so sorry you can't be here to watch them grow up, but know that I'll love them enough for both of us."

A light breeze rustles through the cemetery, and a few leaves flit around us.

I watch, captivated, as a butterfly lands on my newborn son. A butterfly.

I told you I'd come back as a butterfly.

"Look," Natalie breathes, staring down at the butterfly.

She needs you.

I'll always love you, but she'll love you the way you need.

I squeeze my eyes closed as Sara's words cover me like a warm blanket, and I swear I feel her hand on my cheek.

"There won't be a day that goes by when I don't think of you," I say aloud, needing Natalie to hear the words. Tears fill my eyes as I continue. "You are my first love, but Natalie is my forever love."

Love her like only you can.

I can finally cross over.

Until we meet again, sweet Alessio.

I feel her the moment she's gone, a sweet caress against my face as the wind carries the butterfly, my Sara, away.

"She's gone," Natalie says wistfully. "She told me Aidan is beautiful, and to love you as you need in the way only I can."

"She said basically the same thing to me," I confess. "Is it weird we both think my dead wife is talking to us?"

Natalie shrugs, looking beyond Sara's headstone to the rays of sunlight bursting from behind the mountains. "It only matters what we feel. I think she gave us her blessing, and now we can go home and settle into life as a family of five."

Five.

One year ago, my family was three. I was barely surviving, and my kids paid the price for that. Now I have a new zest for life, a new son, and most importantly, a new love. Once a shell of myself, I'm ready to start the rest of my life.

Epilogue

Natalie — Four years later

"I don't see why this is a problem."

"Ben, I'm not allowing you to dig up the backyard to build a volcano." Alex's words are laced with exhaustion as he rubs the bridge of his nose. Now forty-three, my husband has quite the bit of gray in his beard, giving him a distinguished look. When his eyes meet mine, they sparkle with mirth as he deals with his firstborn son.

"I need to determine if my calculations are correct for the scope of my project, Dad. It needs to be larger than the normal science fair size."

"No."

"Fine." Ben's eyes light up as he comes up with another idea. "Would a space shuttle work? Abbie can drive me to the Wyoming border for some fireworks. Then I could really test the —"

"NO."

"You didn't even let me finish."

"No explosives. No chemical reactions the size of my house. Nothing that could permanently stain any part of the property, and nothing that puts any of us at risk for injury, death, or toxic exposure."

"Hmm. I can work with that." Ben gives me a wink as he struts out of the kitchen. I laugh loudly as Alex gives an exasperated scoff.

"Don't encourage him, Sunflower. You know that's you coming out of him right now, don't you?"

"I will neither confirm nor deny that I've spoken the phrase 'I can work with that' to your sister," I tell him.

Just then, Aidan bounces into the room. Our sweet four-year-old bounces everywhere. "I heard Ben talking about gas and a coffin."

"Jesus Christ," Alex swears, standing up to chase after Ben. "I knew taking the kids to those coffin races in Mountain Springs would end up biting me in the ass."

"What's a coffin?" Aidan asks after Alex disappears.

"Well, when a person passes away, or dies, they are buried in a box. That way the people who loved them can still visit them," I explain.

"Is that what happened to Sara?" he asks, and I nod. We've never sugar-coated things with Aidan. He understands that Abbie and Ben have a different mom, and that she died in a car accident. This is the first time he's connected a coffin and grave to Sara, though.

"Yes, that's what happened to Sara. That's why we visit the cemetery before we go see Grandma Nancy and Grandpa Jim." Sara's parents welcomed me with open arms, and gleefully accepted Aidan as a third grandchild. Never once have they made me feel like an outsider. Aidan loves them just as equally as his other grandparents.

Alex returns, shaking his head. "I think somehow I just agreed to build the gas-powered coffin with him."

"We need to sign him up for debate. He's just too good at turning things around," I comment as I stretch my arms above my head, making my shirt ride up dangerously.

"And how are two of my favorite girls feeling today?" Alex asks huskily as he places a hand on my very large baby bump.

"About as good as any forty week pregnant woman can feel," I say, deadpan. We didn't intend to have any more babies. Alex even got a vasectomy. But after two rechecks, somehow his vasectomy naturally reversed itself. Abbie, now seventeen, is beside herself that she'll be getting a little sister. Ben doesn't care, but Aidan is so excited. He can't wait to teach her all the things about being a Santo.

Alex and I were married in a small ceremony when Aidan was one. Even with only family in attendance, Alex's massive family meant it was a big party. Hannah and Luca hosted, and it was perfect. My brother and parents were able to attend, and they were welcomed into the Santo fold immediately. Our dads, including Sara's dad, enjoyed smoking cigars on Luca's patio, discussing 'the good old days' before technology took over. Nancy bonded immediately with my mom over a love of crafts, and soon they were discussing cross stitch and handmade cards over pieces of wedding cake. Everyone was having so much fun that they didn't even realize Alex and I snuck out.

Around the same time as our wedding, with Alex's brother Leo finally home, they decided to go into business together. While Alex has never said he truly hated his job with the police department, it's obvious how much he loves what he does now with Leo. I don't quite have a gauge on Leo, though, as he's even more closed-off than Alex ever was. I'm told he's always been introverted, but anytime I'm in his presence, it's rare he says more than a dozen words.

"You nervous about tomorrow?" Alex asks quietly, his eyes studying me. I know even if I attempted to lie to this man, he knows me too well. He can gauge my mannerisms and determine what even I sometimes can't decipher.

"Yeah," I admit. This baby is breech, and after using every trick under the sun in an attempt to move her into position, I'm having a scheduled c-section tomorrow. As I'll already be open, my tubes will be tied at the same time, since clearly Alex's body wants more kids. Mine most certainly does not.

"Have you finalized what name you want yet?" he inquires. True to his word, Alex has made suggestions on names, but says it's my final choice. I haven't had any dreams about names, and I've decided this girl is going to be as stubborn as both her mother and father, and I may have to see her face before I have a name.

"Not yet," I tell him.

"No rush," he teases, making me laugh. "Seriously though. Don't stress about anything. I've got you."

"I know you do," I tell him, slipping my arms around his neck. "As soon as Aidan is asleep, I'll let you have me one more time for the next six weeks."

"Fuck," he chuckles. "I forgot about that part."

A few hours later, I'm naked and straddling Alex. Sitting on the edge of the bed, he has me turned so we can watch through a floor-to-ceiling mirror we have next to the bathroom door. It's become one of our favorite positions. I do appreciate switching things up from time to time, including some outdoor sex like Arianna and Kate wax poetic about, but tonight is for us.

"God, you're so fucking hot like this," he mutters against my neck as he sucks on my pulse point. "I can feel you milking me."

I love his dirty talk. He knows just what to say to get me even hotter. A few years ago, I'd have never felt confident or comfortable in this position. I'd have focused on my rolls. Extra flab. Dimples in my thighs. But Alex has shown me how beautiful I am. I can see the love and desire in his gaze. Now I ride him as he slams me down on his cock.

His voice becomes gritty as he cups both of my breasts, pinching each nipple perfectly to send a zing right to my clit. I clench and hear Alex groan. He knows my nipples are so sensitive, and he doesn't have a problem using that knowledge for his benefit. "You like this, baby girl? You like watching me fuck you? Own you?"

"Fuck, yes," I pant.

"Which part?"

"All of it, dammit," I hiss with a laugh. "Now make me come, husband."

"Fuck, I love when you call me that," he moans, his speed picking up.

"Do you like me owning you?" I ask breathlessly.

"You know I do, Sunflower." Alex slides one hand down to push against my clit as he shifts ever so slightly backward, and the new position hits that perfect spot deep inside me, setting off an immediate climax that rattles my entire body. I let out a loud moan, and he covers my mouth with his hand. I hear him chuckle as I continue to moan while riding out the orgasm. His own climax happens only seconds later.

"That was a good one," I whisper, smiling as I lean my head back onto his shoulder.

"I'm glad, wife." He knows I also enjoy the ownership. "Let's get cleaned up so we can at least try to sleep a little."

"I don't think I can sleep," I tell him. "I'm too nervous about tomorrow."

"I know. We can cuddle then."

"Your version of cuddling and mine are very different," I mutter. It's like Netflix and chill, only it's Cuddling and Alex. Either way, someone's having an orgasm.

Alex playfully slaps my ass as I gingerly stand up, my legs somewhat shaky after that great bout of sex. "I swear this time will be actual cuddling."

It was not.

But that was more my fault than his.

I can't have sex for at least six weeks, so I need to enjoy him while I can.

Twelve hours later, I'm blissfully drugged out and staring at Alex and our newborn daughter.

"Brielle."

"Hmm?" Alex responds.

"Brielle. Her name."

He looks up at me with a smile. "What made you go with that one? You've never mentioned Brielle before."

"I like the name, and I want to call her Bree. But I also like that it's consistent with everyone else. Abbie and Aidan, and now Ben and Brielle."

"I like that," he hums. "Brielle. What middle name were you thinking?"

"I don't know," I murmur. Alex places Brielle in my arms, and I sigh happily.

"I have an idea, but I'm not sure how you might feel about it," Alex says quietly, leaning over so his face is next to mine. His gorgeous brown eyes twinkle with love as he rests a hand on my cheek. "I'd like to give her your middle name."

"Mine?"

"Yeah. All of our kids have family connections in their middle names," he says as he drags a finger down my cheek and onto the bundle in my arms.

"I thought it was just a Santo thing," I admit with a light laugh.

"It's an us thing, Sunflower. I want Brielle to have a piece of you with her always."

"I love that," I breathe. "And I love you."

"I love you, too. So we're going with Brielle Anne. Final?"

"Final."

"Okay. Little Miss Bree, welcome to the family," Alex says, giving her forehead a sweet kiss. "Brielle Anne Santo."

"Bree Santo."

"They both sound good, Sunflower. You did good," Alex says with a smile. Leaning down, he gives me a tender kiss. "I love you."

"Not nearly as much as I love you," I respond.

"Impossible," he jokes. As Brielle lets out a mewling cry, he laughs. "I think your daughter would like to be fed."

As I cuddle Bree up to my breast, I can't help but send up another round of thanks to Sara. With each passing day, I know she was instrumental in pushing me and Alex together. If it weren't for her, I might still be alone, living in that tiny studio apartment. Now I get to be a mom to two, bonus mom to two more, and the wife to a man I can't stop gushing about. If I knew my life would end up like this, I'd do everything the same. Every test. Every trial. Every moment. Alex Santo is worth everything.

Turn the page for the first chapter of Blue Lines and Lullabies (formerly Get Pucked) to refresh your memory on Gabe Dawson! Get ready for more Denver Wolves shenanigans, as well as other Denver sports professionals, starting in Spring 2025 with Forecasting the Forward. Get it here!

Isabella and Sebastian will get their happily ever after in summer 2025 in Worth the Heat. Can Sebastian handle the heat in Isabella's kitchen? Pre-order here!

. . .

Want to make sure you never miss an update from me?
Sign up for my newsletter!

Join my reader group here!

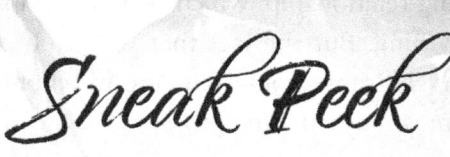

Cassie

My back slams unceremoniously against the wall right inside my hotel room door, but I don't even register any pain. Why? Because the man who pushed me into the wall just dropped to his knees in front of me, ready to devour my pussy.

I should back up a few hours, I think.

It's my first night in Denver, Colorado, where I moved to be closer to one of my older brothers. Grant plays for the NHL team here, the Wolves, and he's been pretty miserable since he was traded last season from our hometown of Portland, Oregon. Grant and I have always been close, and it was an easy decision to follow him to Colorado. Once I found a job, I excitedly packed up all my belongings and started the two-day drive across the Rockies.

Grant volunteered his bare-bones apartment for my first night, but I graciously declined. His mattress is on the floor for crying out loud, and he survives on takeout food and energy drinks. He has barstools, a couch, and the biggest television I've ever seen. If this is where he brings women home, I'd imagine this is also why I haven't heard a thing about any relationships. I bet he doesn't even keep cookable food in the place to make them breakfast after a night of debauchery.

I've read so many stories about athletes and their strict diets, how health-conscious they are, and how they never put processed foods into their bodies. Grant is the exception to that rule, since his diet rivals that of a fifteen-year-old boy going through puberty and eating a family-size bag of pizza rolls every afternoon. It's appalling, and I want no part of that. Don't get me wrong, I love my brother. We have a fantastic sibling relationship, which seems to improve as we age. I can tell Grant anything. But the fact that we barely survived the teenage years living in the same home tells me we shouldn't live together as adults. Plus, most boys are just gross.

I decided to treat myself to a nice hotel on the outskirts of town for a few nights, until I could find an apartment that meets my needs and budget. Is this realistic? No, not really. I'm thankful I have my brother here to fall back on if needed. But I knew I needed to get out of Portland. I just felt so stuck. Stifled. Twenty eight years old, and I'm starting over in a new state. While I have some savings to ease the pain of no current income, I knew the hotel and meal out would be my last hurrah for a while. And it's just my luck that the most attractive man I've ever seen sat next to me at the restaurant bar next door to my hotel. Devilishly handsome. Dark brown hair with a natural wave that kept falling across his forehead. The deepest brown eyes I'd ever seen. He's quite a bit taller than me, well over six feet, and I quickly had inappropriate visions of what it would be like to be with him.

He told me his name was Gabe, and we got to talking about Colorado. He's also not from here, but he gave me tons of advice on Colorado survival.

"It's crazy windy here. Way windier than you'd think," he said.

I shrugged and rolled my eyes. "It's windy everywhere."

"You'd think that, wouldn't you? But we routinely get hurricane-force winds here."

I'm sorry, what now?

"Oh, and don't rent an apartment, or house, where the parking is on the north side of the building."

"Why?"

"Because the snow won't melt. Ever."

I laughed, thinking he was joking, but his expression never changes. "You're kidding."

"Nope. Tons of memes about it. A tale of two Colorados. South facing buildings have the sun to melt all the snow, so you won't even need to shovel it. Well, most of the time."

"Most of the time?" I remember asking.

He scratched his head in thought. "If it's a blizzard, or we get two or three feet of snow, that changes things."

Holy shit. Feet of snow. *Feet*. Snow in Portland was rare, and hardly ever amounted to more than a couple inches.

"Are you a sports fan?" Gabe asked suddenly, jarring me from my hyper focus on snow.

"Why?" I asked warily. I'm always hesitant to tell anyone about my brother. Grant had already told me the sports fans in Denver were nuts.

"Fans here are pretty rabid for their teams. If you're a fan of another team, I'd suggest keeping quiet about it." I don't say a word about Grant, hockey, or my overall interest in sports. I'm thankful I didn't wear Grant's number twelve Wolves jersey, or any of the other hockey related paraphernalia I've accumulated over the years. I did always think it was cool to wear a jersey with our last name, McNally, on it. Back home, people even call me by Grant's hockey nickname, Nally. But, for all I know, Gabe could be a huge hockey fan, and then he'll try to get me to introduce him. No thank you.

Unfortunately, it wouldn't be the first time a man used me to get to Grant, or his teammates.

I'm the youngest in my family, with all three of my brothers playing professional sports. Honestly, it's a wonder my parents survived all of our childhoods. You'd think we must have some amazing genetics at play, right? Not even close. My father owns an HVAC company, and my mom is a nurse. And I'm quite possibly the least coordinated woman in the world. I can trip on air. Don't put a set of skates on me and expect it to be successful. Granted, I did play hockey growing up. Since the rest of my siblings were obsessed with sports, I figured I could try one. Hockey was the only sport that excited me. And if I'm stationary, I have excellent aim with the puck. Just don't ask me to move while controlling the stick *and* the puck.

And if you want me to throw, or kick, a ball, don't be mad when it somehow hits you in the face when you weren't even on the field.

I'm digressing.

The more Gabe and I talked as we ate, the more I could feel the sexual chemistry building between us. Our conversations got a little more intimate. We turned toward each other. I touched his hand. He pushed a piece of hair behind my ear. I dragged my fingertip down a line of script on the inside of his arm, and then he put his hand on my thigh.

He's lucky I didn't mount him right there.

When our bills came, and he grabbed mine, I thanked him by asking if he'd like a nightcap in my hotel room. His response of, "I'd fucking love one," will forever be embedded in my memory for how husky and seductive he sounded.

Gabe's lips are on mine before the elevator doors close, and my hands are carving a path along the spectacular back muscles under his shirt soon thereafter. When the doors ding, signaling the arrival at my floor, he unceremoniously throws me over his shoulder before taking off down the hallway.

"Room nine-fourteen," I giggle.

"Get the key ready, or I'm fucking you in the hallway, Firecracker," Gabe grunts as he sprints toward my room. He's called me Firecracker a few times tonight, and I love it more than I thought I would. Typically, I find pet names to be icky, but this seems endearing and cute.

"Why are you calling me Firecracker?" I ask as we arrive at my room, and he puts me back on my feet.

"Because your face lit up more than once when you were talking tonight, and I have a feeling it's going to be fucking spectacular to watch you come," he says against my hair. I stifle a moan as he pulls me back into his body, leaning down to kiss my neck and slide the tip of his tongue against my skin. I shiver and reach up to grab his hair, holding his head against me. My neck is incredibly sensitive, and I love it when men spend time kissing me there once they realize how much I like it. I don't miss the vibration of Gabe's chuckle as he slides a hand around my waist, covering my hand, before dragging it up to wave the keycard in front of the room lock.

Goodness. Gabe teased fucking me in the hallway, and I'm already so far gone that I'd probably have let him. Gabe pushes me gently into the room after I open the door, and once it's closed, I drop my things on the floor and turn into his arms. His lips are on mine immediately, his tongue flicking into my mouth as I wrap my arms around his neck. When his hands finally slide to my ass, he grabs and lifts me, my legs wrapping around his waist.

Moaning, I latch onto his hair as I suck his tongue into my mouth, and Gabe kneads my ass as he spins us to push me against the door. He breaks off the kiss and pants against my cheek. "You can't suck my tongue like that, Firecracker. Makes me want you on your knees right fucking now, with my cock down your throat."

"God, yes," I whimper. I'm not a big fan of blowjobs, but for some reason, I'm aching to taste him.

"Not yet. First time I'm coming, it'll be in this pussy," Gabe growls as he slides a hand between my legs from behind. Looking up at him, his lips are puffy. Eyes hooded, he's staring at me fervently as his breathing quickens. I'm only wearing a very thin pair of leggings, and my utterly saturated thong is doing little to conceal how hot and wet I am. "Jesus Christ, Cassie. You're soaked. This all for me, baby?"

For crying out loud. Why is a man calling me baby so damn hot?

Gabe reaches around to grab one ankle, pushing it down so my legs move from his waist. When my feet touch the ground, he drops to his knees. Shit. I've been driving all day. I haven't showered yet. There's no way I'm fresh and ready for oral. "Gabe, no, wait."

He looks up at me, and I can barely see his eyes in the dark room. "If you're about to tell me that you've been on the road all day and you don't want me to get your taste on my tongue, I've got half a mind to throw you over my leg and spank the hell out of you. I don't want to taste fucking soap, Firecracker. I want to taste *you*."

Good God. I may have just come. That is the hottest thing a man has ever said to me. Quite possibly the hottest thing any man has ever said.

I must moan incoherently because Gabe rests his head against my thigh and laughs. "May I continue?"

I'm fairly certain I reply in the affirmative, but it is complete gibberish. Gabe's hands grab the hem of my leggings, pulling them down to my ankles, before helping me to step out of them and my shoes. I'm a heartbeat away from grabbing my thong to remove it as well, but Gabe stops me when he leans forward and tongues my clit through the fabric. At that point, I forget how to breathe.

It's an odd juxtaposition between the wetness of his tongue and the coarseness of my lace thong against my clit, and it's making me crazy. I don't know what feeling to focus on, and then he slides one finger underneath the fabric to swirl against my opening. Pushing inside, my body clamps down on his digit as he quickly finds my G-spot and rubs against it. I'm two seconds from coming when he leans back slightly, and I cry out in frustration.

"Don't worry, baby. I'll get you there," he whispers as he grabs ahold of the side of my thong and snaps it in half. "Put one leg on my shoulder."

I dutifully follow his order as his thumb finds my engorged button of nerves. I cry out again, this time from pleasure, as Gabe slowly rubs his thumb around and around. Collecting my wetness, he swivels his hand before pushing his thumb against my untouched rosebud. I don't have time to think before Gabe latches his lips around my clit, adds a second finger inside my pussy, and pushes his thumb just beyond the ring of muscle. He moans against me as my hands grab his head, and I reflexively begin to move his head how I want him to lick me.

"That's it, baby, use me," he mutters against me, and I feel emboldened, so I push his face further into my pussy. I'm moaning loudly, gyrating against Gabe's face, and I vaguely hear voices outside the door. Stiffening, I move to push Gabe away, but he latches harder on my clit. "Ignore them, Firecracker. Come for me. Give me what's mine."

Sucking my clit again, he nibbles just hard enough to send me into one hell of an orgasm. The triple threat of his tongue, fingers in my pussy, and his thumb in my ass make me erupt in a way I've never experienced before. A wave of white-hot pleasure courses through my body, starting at my feet in a wave that overtakes me, and robs me of the ability to breathe. My knees buckle, and I begin to collapse, but Gabe catches me as he stands.

Three long strides later, we're catapulted onto the bed.

"I figured you would fuck me against the door," I say breathlessly.

"Thought about it. But I prefer having more room to move around. Since you're a good eight inches shorter than me, Firecracker, it could be a feat of physics and prayer for sex against a door. Also, who the hell knows when that door was last cleaned?" Gabe shudders against me dramatically.

"Germaphobe?"

"Sort of. I'm around gross guys a lot. I can't make them be cleaner, though."

I don't ask any further questions. We decided a while ago that we wouldn't share personal information, other than our first names. I think we both know this is a one-night thing. Scratching an itch. I'll never see him again in a city this big.

"How about you stop talking and fuck me?" I ask as I pull his head down to mine. Gabe chuckles against my mouth as he slides his tongue against mine, and I'm pleasantly surprised that I don't hate the taste of myself. Maybe it's a combination of his manly taste with mine, or perhaps I'm just so turned on that I don't care. But a few long kisses later, I'm shimmying against him like a nympho needing another hit of an orgasm.

"Slow down, Firecracker. We've got all night," Gabe says as he bites my nipple through my shirt and bra.

"I'm the most impatient woman you'll ever meet, dammit," I moan.

"I highly doubt that. You strike me as a woman with infinite patience."

He's not wrong. My degree is in early childhood education, and I usually have more patience with children than I do with adults. But right now, my body is taut with feral need, and if he doesn't make me come in the next minute, I'm taking it upon myself to finish the task at hand. Yeah, I had an orgasm against the door. But Gabe makes me want more. Need more. I have this nagging feeling that every orgasm with him will get better.

"I think the next time you come needs to be on my cock," he murmurs. I look at the door, somewhat disappointed that he didn't throw me against it. I read romance books. All the heroes seem to toss their women around. Sex against doors, walls, and even in the shower. When am I going to experience all that? "Fucking hell, Firecracker. You're still thinking about the door."

"I mean, I know I'm not skinny, but you're solid muscle, and I think you could easily hold me against the door," I comment. I have curves. Pockets of flab here and there. I'm not skin and bones, and I never intend to be. I like food too much.

Gabe's head pops up from my chest. "Did you seriously just say you aren't skinny? Jesus, Cassie. Your body is fucking perfect."

"I just meant I'm not tiny."

"What is your definition of tiny?" he asks.

I shrug. "Well, I guess thinner than me. Bony. Easy to pick up and throw around."

Gabe's eyes narrow as he studies me. "Guess you threw down the gauntlet, didn't you?"

"What? No, I didn't throw anything — woah!" I shout as Gabe instantly picks me up and holds me over his head.

"Want me to try it one-handed?" he asks with a devilish glint in his stare.

"Uh, no, I think I'll just give you the benefit of the doubt," I answer hastily. I'd prefer not to have to visit a hospital tonight.

Gabe slowly lowers me until our faces meet, kissing my lips softly. "You really want sex against the door?"

I ponder for a moment. Do I? Honestly, I've never been with someone so virile and strong. I like that Gabe can manhandle me, yet I feel safe and cocooned in this warmth at the same time. And since I'll never see him again, I finally nod. When in Rome. Or maybe it's bite the bullet. Whatever.

Gabe chuckles as he pivots and walks to the door. "You gonna be quiet, or you want to alert the entire floor to what we're doing?"

I hesitate before responding, "I'm not entirely sure."

The answering smile I get is full of fondness, with a cheekiness I didn't expect. I think Gabe wants me to be loud.

"Do you want me to alert the floor to our shenanigans?" I ask incredulously.

"Shenanigans?" he laughs. "Yeah, baby. I think I'd like you to be loud. Bet I can make you really sing."

He did.

Four times.

Grab Blue Lines and Lullabies Today!

Ready to pre-order your copy of the next Denver Wolves star to find his happily ever after? Get Forecasting the Forward!

Acknowledgements

I knew this book would be emotional well over a year ago when I decided to make Alex be a widower. Tapping into his guilt was a challenge, and that letter from Sara to Alex? Brutal. But Alex is my favorite male character to date, because he put in the work. He got past his grief, worked through the stages, and came out the other side a recharged man.

First, thank you to my wonderful PA, Morgan, who attempts to keep me in line and on task when I derail the conversation with randomness.

To my beta team of Morgan, Daisy, Valerie, Catie, and Anna: thank you for being honest with me, making me laugh, and giving your time to ensure Alex and Natalie had the best possible story.

To my permanent arc team and all the wonderful readers who decided to take a chance on me with this book: thank you. Thanks for taking time out of your never-ending TBR to read my story. I always thought writing, and publishing, were just a pipe dream, and I still find myself shocked that this is my life. Thank you for pushing me to continue writing these characters.

To Mr. Williams, who now proudly boasts to anyone who will listen that his wife writes spicy books, thank you for supporting me on this journey. At least now I make more money than every failed MLM I ever tried.

And lastly, thanks to my boys. You (mostly) respect my work-from-home space, and you understand the importance of this work. I hope that this "job" allows you to see that creativity is welcomed in this house. Imagination is a gift. Choose joy in what you want to do in life.

I'll always support you exactly as you are, and I love you more than you'll ever know.

Jen

PS: If you're wondering how I came up with coffin races, I didn't. Feel free to Google the term, along with the town of Manitou Springs, Colorado (which my OG fictional town of Mountain Springs, is based off). It is as completely nuts as you'd think it is to have coffins racing down a road. And yes, there's a live person in every coffin for the race.

Forever Series

Forever Sunshine

Forever Yours

Forever Ours

Forever Mine

Forever Us

Forever Together

Eternity Series

Worth the Risk

Worth the Trouble

Worth the Vow

Worth the Test

Worth the Heat (Summer 2025)

Mile High Series

Blue Lines and Lullabies

Forecasting the Forward (Spring 2025)

About the Author

Jennifer was born and raised in Ohio, but currently calls Colorado home. A lifelong lover of romance books, Jen felt pulled to write stories with older characters, because "old farts" deserve love too. Jen prides herself on delivering realistic characters that struggle with normal problems. She spends most of her free time within her zoo: two kids, two dogs, and two cats! When not containing the chaos, Jen can be found lounging on her covered porch devouring books on her Kindle.

Made in the USA
Monee, IL
04 May 2025

16826733R00207